A TALL, IMPERIOUS BLOOM

Also by Agata Stanford

A TALL, IMPERIOUS BLOOM

Agata Stanford

A JENEVACRIS PRESS PUBLICATION

A Tall, Imperious Bloom
September 2014

Published by
Jenevacris Press
New York

This is a work of fiction. Names, characters, places, and incidents either are the product of the author's imagination or are used fictitiously. Any resemblance to actual persons, living or dead, events, or locales is entirely coincidental.

ISBN 978-0-9857803-5-7

Printed in the United States of America

DorothyParkerMysteries.com
Visit 'Dorothy Parker Mysteries' on Facebook

For Richard, who now resides
in a constant home in my heart.

Acknowledgments

Many thanks to Larry Lockridge and the estate of Ross Lockridge, Jr. for graciously granting me permission to quote from his father's masterpiece, *Raintree County.*

A Tall, Imperious Bloom

"What difference now does it make that love was a tall, imperious bloom beside the river . . . ? There was only love that is the desire for beauty. We were like flowers that seduce each other without memory and without guilt."

Raintree County

"And naked with uncut hair, he would follow her, riding a winged horse, until he reached the ledge of the great pediment. . . ."

Raintree County

ONE

Winston William Davidson

More and more of late he wondered why he did what he did. And because of the wondering—that self-searching that seemed to creep into his thoughts more and more, making him turn back to look over his past thirty-eight years—he suspected that it was a sure sign of impending middle age. With that sense of urgency that had been creeping into his mind, it dawned on Bill that these thoughts had less to do with what he did and more to do with what he *should* be doing.

After a long day of working on a brochure for the proposed and controversial new trash plant that his public relations firm represented, Bill was tired. Everyone else had left the office early to prepare for an evening of parties, but Bill had remained at his desk. At eight o'clock he left to dine on steak, pasta, and a couple of Jacks on the rocks at the Grist Mill Restaurant. By ten o'clock the food, drink, and day weighed heavily on him and he wanted nothing more than to roll into bed. His girlfriend, Margie, was still in California visiting her parents for the holidays, and it was an opportunity to do nothing but flop, maybe watch Dick Clark and the insane crowd in Times Square at midnight.

Arriving home to the rented bungalow, he showered and then, as was his habit, poured a Jack Daniels before settling into the leather recliner he was awarded in the divorce settlement from Cassie almost two years ago. He stretched his arms and legs, causing the chair to creak loudly. Then, with a gulp of the liquor hot along his throat, first steps toward affecting to crack the crust of tension that had lodged along his back and shoulder blades, he appraised the grim room.

None of the furniture suited the house. The small, two-bedroom bungalow had a rural-rustic interior, from the dark wood paneling and stone fireplace in the living room to the old-fashioned blue floral wall paper in the bedroom. The chrome-and-glass coffee-table and lamps and butter-colored Italian leather contemporary living-room set were more suited to the sky-lighted condominium he had once shared with his ex-wife, Cassie. Closing his eyes against the mishmash, he thought that building a fire in the grate might make the place cozy, the flames making the sad walls recede in the night-darkened space, bringing light and warmth. He was too tired to bother. Too lazy even to exert an effort to dig out the TV remote, which was undoubtedly stuck between the seat cushion and the arm of the chair. With that he drifted off.

The Davidson family joke was that a Viking ship dropped Baby Winston off at the port of Manila where he was found by Air Force Captain Robert Davidson and his wife, Sarah, as they strolled along the harbor one evening in June 1961. The tale was a light-hearted response to those commenting with wonder, upon seeing the brunette couple and their raven-haired children, at the sight of the platinum-locked baby boy.

By the time Winston was five years old and could understand that he was different from his parents and siblings in coloring, he believed the story as fact. Despite his parent's reassurances that the Viking tale was nothing more than a silly story, the romantic fantasy had taken root. During adolescence, when his family moved back to the States, his father assigned at Kirkland Air Force Base in New Mexico, his imagination expounded on the first of many adventures of the Viking boy, Leif, who was adopted by the Pueblo Indians, riding on the back of his white buffalo, Vittorio, along the vast open plains. The image of the tall, tan, sinewy youth with long, flowing butter-blond mane astride the buffalo companion, poised on the edge of a cliff overlooking a vast open valley, was an image of power and freedom and infinite possibilities that Winston could cling to when life made him feel ordinary and unimportant.

Now, at nearly forty years of age, "Bill," as he had come to be called, after adopting his baptismal name, William (which was far preferable to Winston), stood without his companion Vittorio at a different sort of precipice. Still he was tall and firm-muscled, and if his hair had been cut short and tamed as middle-age approached, he was of sound health on the Eve of the Millennium when people were all hyped-up, wondering if the world was Y2K-ready, if systems would fail, if the world would blow up by means of its own technology. The niggling fears harbored by even the most optimistic of natures had been addressed by the "experts" of various fields of concern over the months preceding the New Year celebrations planned around the globe: The world was not at risk.

But, Bill Davidson was at risk and didn't know it. Having fallen into complacency through an exercise of routine, he had yielded to feelings of obliviousness, all dreams on hold, if not lost, to a place where he lived cocooned with the odds-and-ends of his passing youth. And if, as he dozed, the imaginings of his childhood has resurfaced from deep within his stores of memory as prescience of future events, Bill Davidson unknowingly stood at the brink of change, a precipice where from one aspect he could recognize the man he believed himself to be, while below, should he venture a valiant leap, stood the stranger he was to become. The remembrance, the sense of warning, of alarm, whatever it was that swept through him, startled him awake.

The telephone was ringing. He decided to let the answering machine screen the call, even if it was Margie calling to wish him a Happy New Year from three thousand miles away. It was John Powel, calling from his car, saying that he'd passed Bill's house earlier and "saw your car in the drive, so pick up the phone, damn it! I've got a flat and no jack!"

Bill reluctantly picked up, and after suggesting that John call Triple-A, John said he'd "wind up waiting for a truck all night. Shit! It's New Year's Eve! Have mercy on me!"

—Give me ten minutes.

John said Bill was the best son-of-a-bitch in the world. Thanking him for the sentiment, Bill hung up.

Bill went to Jerry Raymond's party with John as his date, and wouldn't you know, thought Bill, Cassie was there. He should have guessed she'd be there. Why shouldn't she be? The friends he and Cassie had collected before and during their marriage hadn't taken sides when they split, and it wasn't the first time they'd collided at a public or private function since the divorce. After exchanging polite greetings, complete with fixed smiles, each would spend the rest of the evening avoiding the other. They had tried to behave like grownups, but that night the children within each sprang out with a petulance that Bill feared might provide the party's sideshow. What started the tiff didn't matter. Perhaps exhaustion had loosened Bill's tongue or the whiskey had lessened his ability to edit his thoughts, but he had said something that caused Cassie to bristle.

He had married a woman he didn't particularly like, even though he thought at the time that he loved her. But he loved her for all the wrong reasons, he realized after the divorce: for what she represented and for how he would be viewed for having her as his wife. They were right for each other by standards that were bloodless and passionless.

After nursing a drink for twenty minutes, all the while feeling more and more isolated and disturbed by the deliberate party atmosphere, Bill escaped the over-decorated and overheated party undetected. He was glad to leave behind the wounded ex-wife and John's callous and drunken take on the sharp exchange prompted by Bill's subdued demeanor: "Forget it, forget her! People fuck and move on! Remember that, Buddy! Move on!"

It was snowing lightly when Bill left Jerry Raymond's house and started off the porch steps: the first snowfall of the season. His loafers flicked the powdery stuff into his socks as he slid to the car, grabbed gloves and an old ski cap from the passenger seat, and once donned, brushed the accumulation off the windshield. All he wanted was a drink and a warm bed without Margie in it, without argument, or compromise, or effort. Just solitude, uncluttered by artifice or forced conversation.

He rolled down the window as he drove away from the curb. The cold air felt good on his face, refreshing, and his spirits lifted with each clean breath. The silence of the streets was broken only by the swish of the intermittent wipers. Year-two-thousand. He relished being alone and felt protected from the frenzy of too much celebration and the dangers of human encounters. The night lent an odd sense of comfort: to experience this historic juncture of passing time with gentle and quiet observation.

Bill pulled to the side of the road, turned off the ignition, and got out of the car. The village side street was dark, the streetlamp barely aglow. With face raised toward the sky, he watched the pattern of the snow's descent, interweaving tumbling threads shed from the fathomless heavens. A barely audible tinkling, like thousands of toasting glasses, as the flakes pinged the windshield filled him with a sense of wonder. He'd forgotten "wonder," and saw that it was beautiful, and was content not to dwell on the incongruity of the simplicity of the complex nature of the earth.

He checked his watch: 12:03. The second that marked the new millennium had arrived and passed, just as any other moment measured by our time schemes surely would have, with silent inevitability.

The thought that next year would be the start of the new century, the New Millennium, made him smile. Were people in such a hurry to find something to celebrate that they needed to rush ahead of schedule? Are their lives so empty they must find reasons to have fun through manufactured joy? Is my life any better? he asked himself brutally. Perhaps, he thought, getting back into the car, he might spend the passing as he had tonight, in reverent solitude. Nice. At peace and at one with the universe.

As he drove off, the brightness of the last few minutes was shrouded by darker thoughts. Turning onto the main route for the mile-long trip home, he tried to restore that midnight feeling, the pleasure he'd felt in the stillness. How good it had been. Being alone didn't mean being lonely. . . .

But, the truth was he was alone, had always felt alone, had always *been* alone, and moments of peaceful solitude were few and overshadowed by loneliness.

As he turned off the main route and onto the street where he lived, there was a sudden break in the short stream of the headlights as something shadowy moved in the car's path.

Steering to avoid the dark bulk, and then punching on the brakes, the tires skidded on the icy pavement.

Suddenly, the shadowy figure was again in his headlights.

An impact on the fender, a dull thump, signaled the hit. The car lurched and rocked. Bill lost his bearings, not knowing if the car was still on pavement or heading into the woods that lined the road.

He fought for control of the wheel, but as soon as he secured it, the thrust of the car over uneven terrain broke his tenuous hold on it. A wall of snowy branches battered the windshield as the car rushed forward at an incline.

Now Bill realized which side of the road he was traveling, and he prepared himself for the worst. If he could only slow the car by allowing the brush and trees to tighten their limbs against the vehicle, he might have a chance. The car slid down a flat course, like a sled, and when the car's thrashing had settled into a more even slide, Bill caught onto the wheel.

The path ahead was black and unobstructed, and no brush or saplings plummeted to strike at the windshield now. He could actually see out, in time for the approach toward the final ledge of boulders: a thirty-foot drop into the Kresskill River.

Peripherally, he glimpsed the trunk of a big tree, and abruptly steered toward it, aiming for a direct hit, hoping the tires would respond by gripping onto something so that he might make a last-ditch effort to swerve again just at the right moment to graze the side of the car to a stop.

I'm going to die, he thought, and felt the strange calm acceptance of the fact, the final moment when survival is no longer a consideration.

The car lurched upward off the ground like the lift of a carnival ride, and although prepared for impact, Bill instinctively turned the useless steering wheel toward the tree. Once again he lost hold on the wheel and it swung out of his grip and veered to the left.

The car landed hard, crushing the brush beneath it, branches scraping glass and steel like chalk on a blackboard, as it grazed the big oak and finally came to a stop. The airbag deployed, and for a couple of mindless seconds Bill sat motionless, feeling the prickle of adrenaline rushing down into his feet. When he tried to open the door the tree was obstructing it.

His brain wasn't working. The obvious was hard to come by, but when it did, Bill got out through the passenger door. Standing proved difficult and he had to concentrate to keep his knees from buckling under him. He began to shiver, not from the cold, but from shock.

A dog yelped in the distance.

Had he hit a dog?

There had been a figure at the windshield, too tall for a dog. A deer?

What if it was a person? *Oh, God!*

He struggled and slid up through a maze of branches, knotted brush tripping his frantic advance up the embankment. It was dark, and the car's headlights facing away from the road lent little light for the progress upward through the woods. Finally, seeing a clearing, the road above, he risked the support of several downed saplings to pull himself up the final few feet toward level ground.

Something lay on the road, a shadowy figure fifty feet away. A dog was circling, pawing and crying at a shapeless heap.

Bill felt detached, as if floating above his body. His mind told him to move, but he just stood there waiting for something to break through the paralysis that confined him.

When suddenly the dog settled in motionless guard beside the figure, Bill broke out of shock, and suddenly free, set into motion.

As he hurriedly approached, the dog met him, then turned back to lead the way.

Oh, my God, I've killed someone. Oh, my God!

He was beginning to function again in fits and starts.

His cell phone was back in the car. Why hadn't I thought to call 911? I should go back and get it!

No!

I should get the person off the road before another car—

Then, the cell phone—

No . . . check to see if he's alive.

The dog paced and circled as Bill stared down at the figure, and the sight transfixed him with a panic he had not known since he was nine years old.

I'm not nine years old, for God's sake, he told himself, stifling a childlike scream that was forming in his throat. The person was face-down in the road, and if alive, moving might cause more harm.

The decision was prompted by common sense, when he saw the dual pinpoints of headlights turning off the main route and moving over the first rise in the road before disappearing in the dip that led to the next.

The dog circled nervously as Bill lifted the body, and as he carried the weight to the side of the road, headlights flashed over the last rise illuminating long hair and a woman's face. The dog whined as Bill placed the woman down. He took hold of its dragging leash and stepped out into the road in time to wave down the car.

A man in a red sports car yelled through the window —What the hell?

After a quick appraisal of the situation, the driver got out of the car, saying, —Cover her up, she's going into shock if she hasn't already.

—I live about a hundred yards down this road.

Both men considered the two-seater and discarded the obvious solution.

—If you can carry her to your house, directed the man, I'll call 911 from my car. Start walking. Give me the leash. I'll take the dog.

Bill lifted the woman into his arms. Her warm breath on his collar told him she was alive.

Arrived at the house, the man preceded Bill in, asking where the blankets were kept. He found them, and covered the woman on the sofa.

She moaned, opened her eyes and stared blankly at Bill.

A rush of relief flooded through him as he gazed down at her. But the sense of relief was followed by a crushing sorrow. She had an identity he had failed to see on the dark road. There, she was an unidentifiable mass, could have been a dark-plastic garbage bag fallen from a truck. Here she was flesh, blood, color, and texture: green eyes, auburn hair, pale skin, and perhaps quite pretty.

As he pulled off his ski-cap, snow fell onto the blanket and a couple of flakes onto her face. She blinked, and he cursed his carelessness.

He was about to ask if she was in pain, but never got a chance to utter a word, for her face transformed into a look he would later remember as luminescent.

—William!

Tears welled up in her eyes; tears of joyous recognition.

—Oh, my Will!

Everyone called him Bill. He had gotten stuck with Winston at birth, but once off to college it was W. William Davidson. He'd answer to William, but his friends called him Bill. She knows me, though, but how? From where?

—Find out if she's bleeding, the man said, as he went out the door to look for the ambulance.

—Oh, my William, my heartbeat!

Eyes dilated and bore into his eyes, and for a moment Bill felt heady, dizzy, disoriented, yet captured.

A siren whined and then a light strobed through the living-room windows. Paramedics tramped in followed by two policemen. One of the officers asked

Bill to come into the kitchen to answer a few questions. Sweat trickled down his back and his palms itched.

The woman called out again and reached for Bill. The paramedics were cutting away the turtleneck sweater and in doing so cut a gold chain that was around her neck. She grabbed frantically as the chain and locket slid to the floor. Bill picked up the necklace, displayed it for her benefit, then slipped the jewelry into his pants pocket, promising its safe return later at the hospital.

As paramedics began to assess her injuries, the policemen beckoned. Again, as Bill started out of the room, the woman called out to him.

—William! she cried out, with enough despair in her voice that he turned to the officer and asked if he might stay with her for a few more minutes. The officer acquiesced, so Bill remained, reassuring the woman of his presence by holding her gaze as the paramedics worked to ready her for the trip to the hospital

—Don't go away again!

—It's going to be all right. They know how to help you.

—You'll take me with you!

He didn't know what to say. Hers wasn't a command, it was a plea, strained with poignant desperation, and the sound of her voice touched something in him that was tender and new. He shut it away behind a door, thinking, this delirium is a result of shock.

—Promise! I've waited for you! I've waited for you to come for me!

An oxygen mask was placed over her mouth and Bill was told to move aside. As they lifted her onto a stretcher and wheeled her out of the house, Bill offered sincere, if empty reassurances.

It took about twenty minutes to explain to the police officer the course of events leading up to the arrival at his house. The Good Samaritan, Wayne Morgan, corroborated the account from the point of his arrival at the scene. Wayne was on his way to a party.

How much had Bill had to drink that evening? Three drinks since about eight-thirty. It was about twelve-fifteen when the accident occurred.

The officer said that the woman's name was Ariel Trent.

—That's the name on the dog's tag. She lives at number three Harvard Road. She's your neighbor.

—Number three . . . ? That might be . . . that's the old Quaker Meeting Hall, isn't it, near the turnoff from Route 22?

—That's it.

—Yes! I know that place. It's a residence, now. I wondered who . . .

—Then you do know the woman?

—No.

—She knew you. Called you by your name.

—What I mean is, I know the house and I've seen a woman working in the front garden. We've never met before, at least not to my recollection; and I've never been close enough to her when driving by to see her face clearly.

—Strange that she would know your name.

—I don't have an answer to that, officer.

Wayne shifted several times in the chair with obvious impatience.

—Well, did somebody contact her family, or anything? he asked, stretching his legs out and leaning back so far in the chair Bill thought the wood might snap.

—Everything will be taken care of, Mr. Morgan.

—Oh, yeah? Well, somebody's got to come and deal with that dog. It's still in my car.

—Well, if one of you doesn't take it until we reach her family, then it goes to the pound tonight.

For some reason, guilt, perhaps, Bill volunteered.

That settled, and passing a blood alcohol test, the officer suggested Bill call his insurance agent later in the morning, "as I'm sure he would appreciate not being hauled out of bed at this time of night."

The car and the scene of the accident had been gone over, so a tow truck could be called in the morning, too.

Bill followed Wayne and the officer outside and got the dog from the car. Wayne said, —It's been great! and squeezed his bulk into the seat of his sports car. The officer said he'd be in touch, and joined his partner in the police vehicle.

The snow had stopped, and it had gotten colder. Every surface had a stiff, stark edge under the gray night sky. Wind whipping through the bare branches of the tallest pines wailed with the plaintive whistle of a reed instrument. Bill shivered. The dog, poised, watching the cars' tail lights in the distance, turned to look up at him as if asking, what next?

—Hello, I'm Bill Davidson.

The dog responded by tugging at the leash and stooping to pee.

Bill led her toward the front door and into the house, where she went directly to the sofa and sniffed around for her mistress. When her lady didn't appear, she sat on her hind legs facing the sofa. It was an opportunity to look at her collar tags. "Little Eva." Bill called her name aloud, and sat on the sofa and scratched behind her ears. With her mouth hung open she appeared to smile. She was a sleek mixed breed, probably black lab and Dalmatian. A reasonable assumption, as Bill noted a lacy-looking triangle of white sprinkled with black fur running from neck to chest. In the lamplight her short black coat shined a velvety texture: A very-well-cared-for animal.

Bill missed Coco, his exiled shepherd puppy, and as if Little Eva sensed his regret, she licked his face with her fuzzy tongue. He laughed, which encouraged her to leap up on him. He fell back against the cushions as she nuzzled his face and neck.

When she let Bill sit up again, she followed him to the kitchen, fascinated by the various smells of a new environment. Her nose led her around the room.

Bill took out a bag of cookies. The crackling sound of its paper packaging brought the dog to attention, and she sat, waiting expectantly. Bill ate a cookie. Only her eyes moved, following the path of his hand from bag to mouth and back. He offered her a cookie. She rose and walked nonchalantly to sit at his feet, taking the offering carefully from Bill's fingers. He ate a cookie; she had another.

Bill filled a mixing bowl with water and placed it on the floor. She lapped up a bit before following him back into the living-room, where she jumped up on the sofa, circled a couple times on the blanket, and after a great sigh, nestled down to sleep. Bill wished he could sleep as easily. If life could be as simple as a dog's. . . .

He was tired, but knew he would not sleep. But, what should he do next?

The evening had ended abruptly, and now Bill stood rooted in the middle of the living-room as if waiting for Divine direction. He felt frustrated, fearful:

not only for the woman's life, but for his own. What if she dies?

He went over to the liquor cabinet and poured a drink for something to do and to calm his nerves. His mind was racing. He fell into unconscious activity, aware that *doing* filled time that might otherwise be spent in contemplation. Thinking had often gotten him into trouble or resulted in depression. He was trying to view life without judgment, as it was easy for him to evaluate the facts and come to an opinion on just about any issue political, social, or philosophical. When he felt passionate, he had never feared voicing those opinions, though in recent times he had learned to compromise.

Sometimes, outspokenness can be good in public relations. It can also make one a hypocrite when espousing the virtues of some plan, some project, or some lie the company he was representing wants to perpetrate on the community: a stock-car racetrack; a new trash plant; a PCB problem in the river. . . .

When he was hired to work for Harris & Reynolds Public Relations, located in the small city of Linden Falls, the company's biggest client was the Coalition for Parkland Conservation, a group that held firm the belief that it was not right for the state to sell parcels of one of the biggest and most beautiful reserves to private individuals. Bill happened to agree wholeheartedly with the CPC; He had two friends on their board of directors, and after working fifteen months on the project, felt accomplished and happy when the Coalition won. To Tom Reynolds, Bill's boss, Bill was a prince.

But then there came the real test. The test in the name of the County Waste Facility, a euphemism for *dump*.

The county of Dunham is composed of Linden Falls, a small city of about twenty thousand people. The city is landlocked by a surrounding township that contains three villages and further out is ringed by farmland, miles and miles of grazing, dairy and corn, ending on the east and west at mountain ranges, and at the north, Paradise Lake, which brings in lots of tourist cash from New York City every summer. Bill jokingly calls Linden Falls "the final circle of hell" because of its geographic position on the county map, at smack-center to its satellite villages and hamlets.

Farmers don't like garbage unless it is of the organic variety. Never mind the smell of a dump; you can't argue that. The smell of treated manure they spray in great gushes into the air to fertilize their crops twice a year can make some summer days unbearable. It wasn't the smell so much as the taking of land, albeit at a premium price, that got the activists going. The argument had to do with spoiling the beauty of the land farmers had a right to farm. Bill had to learn to swallow hard.

So Bill would do his work and get through the nights without determining right or wrong, good or bad about practically anything.

I've got to find another line of work, he'd think. But, where? Doing what?

The drink didn't mellow him, just made him more weary. He called the hospital to inquire of Ariel Trent's condition. They told him nothing.

Triple-A promised to tow his car from the ditch as soon as possible. Then, he called and left a message for the insurance agent.

By four A.M. Bill was revved up and wide awake. He had to get his car. If there was too much damage, he had to rent or borrow one, and damn it if it *was* New Year's Day, he had to get to the hospital. His anxiety was building. He felt that time was of the essence. He just couldn't sit idly by when a woman he had injured was in pain or dying and alone in some hospital emergency room.

He went into the bedroom for a change of clothes, taking out jeans and a sweater.

An unfamiliar weight in his pants pocket, and he pulled out the necklace he had pocketed earlier. It was a seashell, a small clamshell, polished to a soft pink, edged in gold metal and fastened like a locket. Given the force of the car when it hit her, he was amazed that the delicate shell had not been crushed.

He pressed the clip that held it closed and onto the dresser-top fell a piece of folded paper and a tiny photo. The face of a man, blond and smiling, ageless. Maybe forty, maybe fifty.

He picked up the paper. It was folded many times over. It was a letter. The handwriting was small, and whoever had written it had little paper available to write it.

He was about to read the letter but stopped. It was like entering a stranger's home to find a person naked, unaware of his presence. He had no right to be there, to view the imperfections one shields from the world, no right to read something that was intensely personal, if the salutation was any indication of the letter's content and she wore it close to her heart.

Bill refolded the paper and, together with the photo, returned them to the seashell.

By five A.M. the car had been pulled out of the ditch and the tow truck driver managed to get it started. The only damage visible was a long scrape on the driver's side of the car and a mangled side-view mirror. Nothing a few thousand dollars' worth of body work couldn't fix.

Little Eva slept on the sofa as he made his way to the frigid car.

Upon arrival at the hospital, he was told that Mrs. Trent was in the recovery room, her condition was stable and she would remain there for several hours before going into ICU. He should check back in the afternoon.

Once home, Bill made bacon-and-eggs and toast for breakfast. He rarely cooked since the divorce, but there was a dog to feed and no dog food, so he cooked for the dog as well as himself. He brewed coffee, drank a couple of cups, walked Little Eva, and then fell asleep next to her on the sofa.

The phone rang at ten-thirty. He had slept for three hours, felt groggy, but was alert enough to listen as the insurance agent went over a list of things for the claim. Not to worry, he was amply covered.

So my ass is covered, he thought.

At noon he called the hospital. Mrs. Trent was now in ICU. She couldn't have visitors until seven o'clock. He opened a can of Dinty Moore Beef Stew for Little Eve's lunch, then walked her.

On the way to the hospital he passed the Old Quaker Meeting Hall that was now Mrs. Trent's home. The day had not brightened much since dawn. The sky and earth looked gray in spite of any attempt by nature to brighten the winter landscape with snow. And yet, the residence had a charm about it, a warm spot on a drab barren plane, a square structure with a clapboard exterior. The windows were tall, and a cupola rested daintily on its peaked roof. It was tri-color painted, red on its board, with cream-and-black trim accenting the windows and portico. A picket fence ran the length of the road frontage and an arbored gate led to the front entrance. Bill imagined how it might look in late spring and summer with flowers in the front garden and canopying the arbor. He had moved into the rented house in October, and had seen Mrs. Trent raking leaves off the lawn. He had been more than a little curious to see the inside of the house.

Now he was curious to know more about the woman. Was it guilt? He felt a responsibility to her even though her injury was something he could not have prevented. There were no excuses. Reliving the moments before the accident, he knew he was driving more slowly than the speed limit because of the snowfall. He was not intoxicated, and had tried to avoid hitting her at risk to his own life. There was nothing he could have done differently. He was at the wrong place at the wrong time. So was Mrs. Trent.

After calling into the ICU, as commanded by the sign on the entry doors, Bill was told to check in with a nurse. The ICU was one huge room with a nurses' station at center and curtained cubicles circling the outer walls. The station was equipped with video monitors. He could visit for five minutes, and was directed to cubicle 8.

A nurse was coming out as Bill was about to enter. She was a slim woman in her late twenties, with long, dark-brown hair tied back in a ponytail. Her name, as indicated on her pin, was Matilda Chanson. When she smiled, the world became a better place.

—Are you William?

—I'm William, he replied.

—She's been asking for you.

—Oh?

—She's dozing, go on in.

Bill turned to enter, then stopped.

—Has her—I mean, have family members been called?

—I don't know. I just came on my shift. I'll try to find out.

Along with a deep, strengthening breath, a final intuitive thought resounded loudly in his head as he moved the curtain aside to enter.

My life will never be the same.

"He had a way of joyfully crossing the thresholds at which Mr. Shawnessy lingered."

Raintree County

TWO

William Arnold Trent

When William Arnold Trent was six months old, his father, Arthur, a private in the United States Army, knocked him out of his high-chair with a swing from his arm.

As William, called "Willy" by his nineteen-year-old mother, Violet, sprawled motionless on the floor, his eyes transfixed on a pea as it rolled along the linoleum and disappeared under the ice box in the kitchenette of the trailer his parents rented at the Green Meadows Trailer Park outside Albuquerque, New Mexico.

More maddening to Arthur, or "Ace" to his drinking buddies on base, was the mess the kid had made on the floor that Violet had washed before going off to her waitressing job at the Clearview Diner. This was not how he wanted to spend the morning, picking up after "Little Shit," as he affectionately called the boy.

Ace picked up the stunned infant, whose face transformed from a look of complacency to one of absolute terror, contorting into a wrinkled red mass, its jaw dropping to expose two baby teeth that had been pushed halfway up from slippery gums, the drool oozing out from the pink, cavernous mouth to dribble like a coat of wax all over the food-splattered pajamas. Ace knew a moment of trepidation when he held his son out in front of him and no sound accompanied the tears.

In frustration, he shook the boy, as he might an old clock that wouldn't tick. It seemed to work, since the air that had been stuck inside the boy pushed out with an ear-busting howl.

Over the screeching cries, Ace did not hear the car drive up, nor did he hear the screen-door slam. He decided that if a shake could save his son from swallowed air, then a shake might work to stop the screaming.

After his mother-in-law, Fatima Mae Arnold, yanked her grandchild out of the man's grasp and took in the situation, noting the lump that was forming on the baby's head, she placed the hysterical child in his crib, grabbed a broom, and headed back to the kitchenette. Ace, pulling a beer out of the icebox, thought she was about to sweep up the mess and was taken by surprise when Fatima Mae smacked him across the back, exerting the full power of her plump body to chase the small, but tightly muscled little soldier out of the trailer, yelling things she had never dared to say in all her forty-two years. Such awful filth coming from the mouth of a refined southern lady brought people from the neighboring trailers, pushing through lines of laundry and barking dogs to help the woman in distress. Upon seeing a boy half her size chased down the road, several men who had gathered ready for a good fight broke out in laughter, encouraging the young soldier to "run faster" because Mama was gaining!

On and off over the next five years, William would live at his grandmother's house with his mother. He was never to see his natural father again.

His first memory was at age three, when his mother, Violet, took him to her job at the army post. She brought him into an unnaturally dark room to see monkeys and chimpanzees inside cages. When William was older he asked his mother about it. She explained that she worked for the Atomic Energy Commission at Sandia, where she kept records of the experimentation they did. The room was dark, she said, because it had been carved out of a cave in the side of a mountain, and the monkeys weren't in cages, but behind walls of iron bars, taken out singly for exposure to radiation: They were test animals, but she thought Willy would like to see them.

When his mother married Airman Henry Dobson, they moved to Brooklyn for a while. Hank Dobson was transferred to Hickam Air Field in Hawaii, and after he was settled there, Violet and William took the train from New York City to San Francisco, where they boarded a Cunard Liner to Honolulu. Willy spent most of the trip puking, but on the off-time he watched for whales from the deck, which he never did see, only porpoises and flying fish.

Hawaii was a land as vibrant with color as a Disney cartoon, a landscape of sun, huge flowers, and discovery: Thanks to his new dad, he got to sit in a jet fighter, and another time in a small one-man Japanese submarine. His first performance was as Ring Master of the neighborhood circus. He got his first bee-sting there, having sat on the bee, and resulting in an ongoing family recollection. He got his first dog there, a yellow mongrel named Buster, whom his mother gave away because he snarled and barked at everyone except Willy. Violet got him a blue budgie, the first in a series, called Tweety Bird, who'd fly to sit on Willy's head when he walked in through the bungalow door. He cried for days after Henry entered through the kitchen door and Tweety took flight into the koha trees. He kissed a girl for the first time. Her name was Sally. They would go

out behind the Hibiscus bushes on the side of the house
and smooch. Kissing wasn't what it would become later
in life, but it brought the first stirrings of pleasure. They
hugged a lot, and that felt good, too.

Violet, Hank, and Willy went on a daytrip by boat
from Oahu to the big island, Hawaii. For the entire day
Willy watched in fascination as Kilanca erupted. They
were coming home from the beach that afternoon when
Hank's car stalled out on the road that ran along the edge
of a mountain. To the right, a cliff to the ocean, to the
left was mountain. Suddenly everything began to shake
and a chunk of the road disappeared ahead of them.

Hank got the car started and turned the vehicle
back in the direction from which they had traveled. They
were roaring down the road, speeding around a curve,
Willy on the floor behind the front seats, frightened that
they would skid off into the ocean. Violet screamed,
"Jesus Christ!," and then there was a thump and the car
lurched to a stop.

While Hank cursed a blue streak, Violet was
screaming and crying for Willy, to see if he was all
right. Willy peeked up at his mother from the backseat
floor, and then beyond to the expanse of sky outside the
windshield. Shaking sobs rumbled in his throat, as he
waited for the drop into the water below. Hank evaluated
the situation by cracking open his door, and told his
hysterical wife that the front of the car was sitting on
one side of the road, facing the ocean, while the rear was
on another. The middle of the car was topping a chasm
that looked down into the Pacific. The news was not
calming: Violet, easily hysterical, screamed louder. It
was a long way straight down into a jumble of boulders
and crashing water.

Hank cursed about the damage to the car and Violet yelled, "Who cares about this heap? What about us?" But, Willy was not distracted by their argument, for he was listening to something beyond their frantic voices, his ear intently tuned for the guttural rumbling that would precede the tremor that would surely send them tumbling into the sea.

A car drove up, and a rope flew in through the driver's window. Hank tried to catch the rope, and in doing, the car lurched, and everybody screamed. Then all was still.

Hank tied the rope around his own waist, gingerly opened the door, and timidly crawled out onto the hood and to the other side of the remaining road. When the rope was thrown in again, Violet tied it around Willy's waist, and slowly, he crawled out of the car, his mother's high-pitched voice telling him not to look down. Safe, now, in the arms of the man, his rescuer, who held him tight, he began to sob until Hank pulled him away. His mother came last, and the terror he felt, watching her try to get out of the car and onto the hood kept him breathless with the fear of losing her. When she got to him, the rope still tied to her, she swooped Willy into her arms and they stood shivering and crying and rocking for a long time.

From that day on, William noticed a change in his parents' attitudes toward each other. The ongoing chatter he'd become used to was replaced with clipped utterances and there were no more day-trips. It was always just him and his mother.

Hawaii's contrasts touched Willy's vulnerability by example of Nature's random threats and acts of violence on his environment. One such threat was when they were evacuated up to Schonfield Barracks, because a tidal wave was headed for the island. The very thought of the devastation they would find when they returned home and the memory of peering down from the window of the car into the hole in the road was enough to bring a lifelong series of nightmares where he was drowned in the ocean by a great wave. And if a young child coming to terms with the perils of nature were still not enough, human invention could prove foreboding: For he was plagued, too, by a dream, a variation of which was repeated from an incident that left him frightened, not for his own life but for the lives of strangers. A sense of helplessness to effect change settled somewhere deep inside William, which he carried through adulthood. But it was another incident that made him wonder if his attention could cause tragedy.

It happened on a cloudless day, a wind-and-sea-swept blue day. The heat was building with the bleached noon sun. A boy whom Willy knew down the hill from his home had an inflatable wading pool and invited William to come and play. With Violet's permission, William started walking on down the road to the boy's house when he heard a plane fly over. He stopped and watched it. While he did, he heard the engine sputter. By then, the little Piper Cub was still high up in the sky and had passed the mountain and was over the flats by the ocean.

William had heard lots of planes sputter and cough, but the silence that followed this one kept him riveted with his face to the sky, anticipating the return of the hum of an engine. It seemed to happen in slow motion: The nose of the plane dropped down and it spiraled dizzily, like a falling sycamore leaf, until it hit the ground. There was a big explosion, and over the line of trees flames shot up into the sky. William stood there and peed in his swimsuit.

He didn't tell anybody about it until he got home later that afternoon. Violet didn't believe he had seen a plane-crash until after she saw it on the front page of the newspaper the following morning, and it disturbed him that she just wouldn't believe his account of it. That she needed proof from strangers.

William was to fly in all sorts of planes throughout his teenage years, and had no fear of flying. But, until he was in his early thirties, the plane-crash nightmare continued with regularity. He would find himself standing helplessly as he watched jetliners, B52s, or dirigibles take off, noses pointed almost straight up, slow to a stop, hover, and then fall to the ground and explode with eerie silence. When his son, Timothy, was a baby, William dreamed that his son was with him, about to view the crash. He held Timothy in his arms and turned him away from the scene. As there was no noise, Timothy, in the dream, never knew of the devastation.

During that same year in Hawaii, there lived a boy on the street named Robby. He had polio and walked with heavy braces and a pair of crutches. He, too, was six years old.

One day, when Robby didn't think William could see, he deliberately smashed the wooden Ace Flyer that William had let him play with in the backyard while their mothers visited over coffee in the kitchen. William smacked Robby's face with an open hand. When the women heard the ruckus made by Robby and saw the crimson circle on his pale face, Violet laid into her son. He was never to forget, under any circumstances, that it was wrong to verbally or physically oppose those weaker or less fortunate than himself, she told him. Violet would hear no objections or explanations, and so William just stood there, humiliated from the spanking witnessed by the nasty Robby, and for the first time hated his mother.

Sometime during the months that followed, on a hot and sultry day, the ice cream truck jingled along the neighborhood. William ran outside with his nickel as Robby hobbled toward the truck. Having bought the last of the chocolate-crunch pops, Willy started to unwrap the ice cream pop. Robby stared as he bit into the bar.

The ice cream man asked what Robby wanted, and he pointed at Willy. The man told him Willy bought the last one. Robby didn't want anything else, just the chocolate-crunch bar. He got off the line of waiting children and moved closer to Willy, who stood licking the pop.

William remembered his mother's words, and the pain of the spanking he received, so he offered Robby a bite from the pop. But, the boy was not satisfied with a bite, he wanted the whole thing. When Willy said, "No," Robby started to beat him with one of his crutches. The ice cream fell into the gutter, and Willy returned home with several goose-eggs on his head and bruises all over his body. He assured Violet that he had not hit back. Wanda Martin's mother saw the beating and had come to William's rescue. She picked Robby up and carried him home and yelled at his mother, who disposed of him and came marching down to Violet's house for a confrontation. Willy sat on the sidewalk crying until Mrs. Martin and five-year-old Wanda sat down next to him with an offering of a fresh cherry-vanilla pop. When Robby's birthday came along, Willy received the biggest piece of the birthday cake. Robby and Willy hated each other. The cake was meager consolation for attending the party.

The next school term, Miss Abata, William's Japanese-American teacher, made William Robby's official helper. He had to see that the crippled boy got on and off the school bus safely, to carry his books, and to see that he got through recess without serious injury. Their contempt for each other grew, and every moment Willy was forced to spend with him was prickling. He could not forget the ice cream incident. He was grateful when three months into the school term his stepfather was rotated back to the States, for the burden of his secret plan to kill the boy could now be abandoned.

As a child trying to understand contradictions, William learned that there were no real rules in life, no guarantees. Life was not fair. Sometimes, people took advantage of their weaknesses and got away with things he would have been punished for. Later in life, when he remembered these days, he didn't believe he became a better person for not hitting the boy back. William was rewarded for the bruises and contusions he received with an ice cream pop, a big piece of birthday cake, but was then punished by being forced to assist a child he hated, and only because by following adult dictates he was trusted not to clobber the boy. William became aware that sometimes there were riddles imposed by adults for a child to figure out alone. Some he never deciphered. The answers had to be found by himself, and if the grownups knew the truth, they weren't sharing it with him. He could only hope to trust his own intelligence as the adults around him didn't make sense. The family moved back to Albuquerque and then to Roswell where Hank was stationed.

Then, without warning, Violet took William to live at her mother's house in an Albuquerque suburb.

One morning, soon after the move, Violet and his grandmother raised their voices as he sat between them having breakfast. This was not unusual. The two women were always yelling at each other about almost everything. William learned not to pay them too much attention when the yelling started. Grandma said he wasn't the reason why they had their "discussions." It was just "our way," she said. So, William continued to eat his Rice Krispies, even though the snap-crackle-pop was overpowered by the braying women.

When Hank's name was mentioned, though, his ears perked up. He hadn't seen him for a long time, and said as much to Violet.

—When's Daddy coming to get us, Mommy?

Fatima Mae raised an eyebrow, got up from the table, and went to the stove to refill her coffee cup from the percolator.

Violet took a breath, and then asked William, — What would you say if I told you Daddy was not your father?

William thought for a second, and seeing the scary look on his mother's face, replied, —I don't know, why don't you tell me and we'll both find out!

He turned to look at his grandmother, who dropped her stirring spoon and chuckled as she picked it up off the floor. Violet's eyes bulged with a look of surprise.

William thought his remark quite clever since it made his grandmother giggle, but the joke was lost on his mother. With great seriousness, Violet told him that Hank was not his father, and that she and Hank were divorcing.

Learning that Daddy was not his daddy, and that the man who fathered him was somebody he didn't remember, seemed less upsetting than the fact that his mother did not acknowledge his clever remark.

Everybody left. Dogs, Tweety . . . fathers.

Secretly, William was glad about the divorce; Hank always seemed more interested in his cars than in him and his mother. And, the guy was such a "wimp" a new word he'd learned: When they would occasionally have wrestling matches, Hank would always let him win. Willy knew that a kid couldn't beat a great big man in wrestling. Anyway, he was content to remain at his grandmother's as she was much more fun to be with than Hank.

To say that Violet "had a thing for a man in uniform" would be correct. Although she would have preferred a soldier in officer's garb rather than an enlisted man, she did not possess the necessary qualifications to snag a man with multiple stripes: twice divorced with a precocious child, a woman with little education and even less refinement. She was certainly pretty enough, a petite and blue-eyed dark blonde, and would easily attract an officer's attention, but there was also a coarseness that was immediately apparent on first meeting that negated her more positive physical attributes.

She liked to do the bars, staying out until the wee hours of the morning. Her mother was not pleased. They battled about what Fatima Mae called Violet's "sluttish behavior." Violet would counter with her own illegitimacy and a fatherless upbringing. The name Benedict Arnold was shouted out one time, and when he asked who that was, he was told to go out and play. But William would not forget the name and, pressed, his grandmother finally admitted that they were direct descendants of the British hero. This fact was soon challenged when he studied the history of the United

States of America in sixth grade, and he set out to prove what was not in the textbook: that Arnold was not a traitor and that a statue of the British hero had been erected in England. There were two sides to every story.

William heard, repeated daily, the typical statements that are exchanged between mothers and daughters: "This is not a hotel!," and "Believe me, I can't wait to get out of this house as soon as I can!" But if the verbal violence between the women was not frightening enough, once, William saw the flash of hatred spark between them when an outraged Fatima Mae slapped her daughter across the face. The women parted to their respective corners to glower at each other with tears of recrimination and regret. William retreated quietly outdoors to sit under the protective fronds of the low palm where he wouldn't be seen.

Violet was not particular in her next soldier, as long as he was pleasant and let her run things her way. Most important, he had to believe that she came first in his life, and would never hurt her son. That same year, she found the very enlisted man who met those terms. But, she wouldn't realize until years later that the phrase, "Be careful what you wish for," applied to her. By the time she understood that wishes are often granted whether or not they make you happy, she had grown into a frustrated, resentful, and domineering woman who would complain that her husband would never take the initiative, didn't listen to her, and had the spine of a jellyfish. By that time, she had driven *him* to drink in an effort to achieve a more manageable state of lethargic indifference. But, for a time, for a number of years, she had the man she needed. Ron Isele was in the Air Force.

William and his mother were to remain with Fatima Mae for a little more than a year. He was happy to settle into school off-post and began to make friends. Violet and Fatima Mae were concerned, however, about his weight. William was a sprig of a boy, a tow-headed little sprite, taller than the other boys at school, but frighteningly skinny. He was offered huge quantities of food and he ate everything on his plate and would ask for more. Fatima Mae considered tapeworm, but the doctor they brought him to said it wasn't a parasite at all. William was just a very active and healthy boy who would fill out by the time he reached adulthood. The women were relieved, and William was, too, as he would not have to hear about how misshapen and unpleasant-looking his body was. He knew he was different in the way he looked, and in other ways, too. All the kids tried so hard in school to learn how to read and write. For William it was all so easy. He had overheard his teacher, Mrs. Lewis, talking with his mother one morning and his name was mentioned. He worried about what they spoke about for the rest of the day. He had all but forgotten their hushed tones as they spoke outside the classroom, until Violet discussed it with her mother during dinner that evening: Mrs. Lewis suggested that William be advanced a grade. His mother stated she didn't think it was such a good idea to put him with the older children. His grandmother thought that if he was smart enough to do it, he should get to move up a grade. As the women spoke over his head and across the table, William was becoming angry. With petulance he interrupted, "Isn't anybody going to ask me what I want to do?"

—See! his mother shrieked, —Listen to him! He's already too smart for his own good!

The next week, William moved up to Miss Russell's fourth-grade classroom.

One evening William was left at home with a babysitter, Mary Donovan, a twelve-year-old girl who lived across the street. His mother was on a date with Ron and Fatima Mae was taking a night-school bookkeeping course. William liked Mary. She used to play catch and hopscotch with him sometimes after school.

When the women had left for the evening, William settled on the sofa to watch *I Love Lucy* with Mary. During the commercial, she went to the windows and closed the curtains. William didn't think anything of it until she walked to the television set and turned it off. He began to protest that he was allowed to stay up until the show was over. She then told him to take off his pajamas. William did as she asked, and then she proceeded to examine every part of his skinny body with a petting touch that made him giggle.

Mary took off her clothes and asked William what he thought. William said she was different than he was. She took his hand and placed it on a budding breast and told him to gently pinch her nipple. It wasn't long before she attempted to insert his flaccid penis into her. This was very funny to William. He thought she wanted him to pee on her, but she said, "No, I don't want you to pee on me, I want you to fuck me."

It was a familiar word he had often heard people say, especially Hank when he was angry, and sometimes, even, his mother when she was really mad. William wondered why Mary would want him to be angry.

Eventually, Mary gave up on the idea as things were not working as she had expected. She told William to put on his pajamas and get into bed. She put on her bra and panties and crawled into bed with her charge, where she, too, fell asleep. Mary was never invited back to sit with William.

William didn't tell anyone what had happened. Violet and Fatima Mae didn't ask and the story would not be told for another forty years. It wasn't because of shame or guilt, but because when he later remembered it he thought the story would shock people, even though he could intellectualize Mary's behavior as quite natural and not in any way perverse. She wanted to know how boys worked, and who better to find out with than a little boy who trusted her?

By the time he was twelve, he was more than able to fulfill a young girl's request. By that time, Violet had married Ron, had the first baby of their union, and they were living in West Germany where Ron was stationed. She who assisted in the loss of William's virginity, as well as her own, was a girl named Suzanne Davidson.

This was a time of great awakening for William as it is for all boys who are on the brink of manhood. When William pushed eagerly into that place he had heard so much about from older boys, he was not aware that there was more than just a tearing away of a young girl's virginity. More profound and lasting tears to the heart could occur because bonding flesh could become bonding spirit.

And so it would happen that the very act of intercourse would cause the terrible tearing asunder, when Suzanne's family was suddenly rotated back to the States.

It wasn't until several years later when William's family lived in Denver that he heard mention of Suzanne in casual conversation between a girl and boy who had been stationed at the same base as she. After many aborted conversations with the girl, William was finally able to get some of the details of Suzanne's life up to that time: Suzanne was graduating high school in the spring, and she had a baby brother who was about three years old.

—Everybody thinks it's actually hers, said the girl, somewhat meanly. Her tone made the implication clear.

Over the next year, William managed to get snips and snatches of the story: Suzanne was dark-haired and brown-eyed, as were her parents and other siblings, but her kid brother had golden-blond hair and blue eyes.

When William first discovered these things they raised his suspicions, suspicions he'd harbored deep within. He felt terribly alone. Who could he tell? And if he did tell someone, what was he prepared to do about it? He may have been a biological part of the child's life, but certainly no more than that. William had been left behind three years before. He didn't count in the lives of Suzanne and the child. There was no place for him there. Wanting a brother so badly, and knowing he would never have that kind of companionship from the two toddler girls his mother had borne, he mourned the loss of inclusion in the lives of Suzanne and the child with great sorrow.

He had been a lonely child and was now a lonely teenager. His mother and stepfather seemed to have a life with their two little girls that often made him feel like unwanted baggage. His stepfather never mentioned adopting him, so even his name was different from the others in the family. William refused to acknowledge his disappointment even to himself, but resentment was buried under a thin layer of affection for Ron, and a deep sense of isolation permeated his life.

And, it was in the twelfth year of his life that William would once again be confused by the actions of the adults around him. Late in the autumn of the same year that William found that heartbreak accompanied bliss, he learned that shame accompanied sex.

The men in Ron's squadron in West Germany were mostly single and lived in the barracks. Violet and Ron would have all the squadron drinking parties at their house.

Randy Latham, a mechanic in the squadron who had built a stock-car to race at a nearby track, was always a happy addition to the gatherings. He was twenty-four and had the youthful looks and cocky stance of James Dean. This made him very attractive to the wives of the men of the squadron, if not more so to their sons, who would watch in fascination as Randy worked on his racecar while they dreamed of driving it around the track. William was the only boy he allowed to drive the car, and William found his mentor in Randy, for more than anything William dreamed of racing at Indy.

Late one night, after William cleaned the drunks out of their money at Black Jack and had gone to bed, Randy entered William's room on the drunken pretext of tucking him into bed. William thought that very funny. He was too old to be tucked in. Even his mother hadn't done that since he was a kid. Randy nodded, and then pulled the covers off William, saying he would then "Un-tuck him out." William threw his pillow at him, laughing as he pummeled Randy, enjoying, as always, the serviceman's attention. Randy was the only adult he had real fun with.

William became very still when suddenly Randy's hand pushed into his pajama pants, wondering, what game was this? William did not respond, only lay there trying to understand why a man would touch a boy that way. But, soon Randy began to suckle William's penis, and William, embarrassed and surprised that he had grown hard, responded with a giggle, which ended abruptly when he ejaculated in Randy's mouth.

Randy indicated to William that he wanted him to reciprocate the favor, and pulled the boy's head to his lap. He objected on the grounds that it was unsanitary, and revolted by the idea, leaped out of the bed and made for the door. Randy was very matter of fact about the whole thing, and he didn't appear upset at William's refusal. His calm reaction eased William's sudden fear that everything was not as it should be. Randy got up from the bed, rustled William's hair, and left the room to rejoin the party downstairs.

In 1962, relations between people of the same sex was not a topic of discussion, so William had no prejudices, nor basis for deciding what was right or wrong in human relations. He sensed there was something unusual, though, that men would touch each other in this way. The boys he knew only wanted to get inside women. William didn't mention what happened with anybody; people didn't talk about sex, unless one of the older boys was bragging of his conquests in the locker-room. Even then, not all the kids were gullible enough to believe that kids like Andy Newman or Eddie Shoemaker could have fucked all the girls they had boasted about, if any at all. So he wasn't so sure that what had happened was really wrong. He only sensed it was. He had many questions, but intuitively guarded the incident.

At Thanksgiving, a couple of weeks later, Violet and Ron hosted the dinner for the squadron. Randy was there.

As usual during these gatherings, everybody got drunk, and William would take advantage of the situation to beat the adults at the card table. By midnight he was tired and went off to bed. Violet and Ron were drunk and playing cards, so he didn't bother to say "good night."

He was asleep when he awoke to movement in his bed, and when he turned, thinking his mother had come in, he saw Randy in the darkness, standing near the window, the dim light of a street lamp tracing his figure in silhouette. This time, Randy had other plans.

He threw aside the bed cover and then flipped William forcibly onto his stomach. William was frightened by the violent movement, the tearing at his pajama bottoms, the spreading of his buttocks by the burning palms that held his weight down. Randy's hot, reeking alcohol breath made a wave of nausea rise in William's compressed chest as Randy forced his stiff penis into the boy's small rectum. William let out a cry as he felt a tearing heat rip up through to his spine. He wanted it to stop, but knew there was nothing he could do to stop it. After the initial muffled scream, he hadn't the breath to call out again. No one downstairs would hear him anyway; they were playing the phonograph and laughing.

Randy kept pumping, harder, brutally, more forceful with each thrust, and all that William could do was lie there as tears soaked his pillow, hoping not to die from the impaling, or suffocate because he could not lift his head off the pillow.

And then, a rectangle of light poured onto the bed, and with one eye he saw his mother's silhouette at the door.

She will end it, now, he thought; she will make it stop.

But the shadow of his mother kept vigil in the doorframe. She did not move. She did not rush in. She did nothing. She stood there as Randy moaned out in ejaculation, and before Randy was ever aware of her presence she backed out and closed the door.

Randy withdrew very quickly and pulled up his trousers and bolted from the room. William did not move for a long time. He was soaked and sticky from Randy and the blood from ruptured tissues. When he did move, it was to sneak out of his room and to the bathroom down the hall to wash away the throbbing sting with cold water; the washcloth rough against his tender skin, and then returning to his room, to pull off the bottom sheet soaked with his own urine and soiled with blood. He lay down on top of the blankets that had been thrown off the bed, and finally, when the throbbing ache subsided into a dull discomfort, he drifted off into a troubled sleep of jumbled dreams.

It was dawn when he woke up, before his stepfather's alarm clock sounded. He gathered the soiled sheets and pajamas, and barefoot in clean pajamas, walked gingerly to the shed where the washing machine stood.

His mother said nothing that morning at breakfast, and after the girls had gone off to play, she made herself busy with dishes and then dressed to go off to the market. It might all have been a dream, thought William. His distress was so acute; he so desperately wanted her to take him in her arms, to rock him and to tell him she would take care of him. As the next two weeks wore on with an almost deliberate avoidance of any conversation between them, William became withdrawn as a new kind of isolation overwhelmed him.

One afternoon, Violet caught William unaware, and she finally asked what had happened that night. Just as William was about to tell her, she turned away from him in a posture he read as shame, taking him by surprise and making him hesitate in his reply. It was as if she didn't really want to hear what he would tell her, as if she feared him at some level, feared the truth of what he had to say, and this was unnerving as she had never appeared afraid of him before.

He considered the implications of this strange reversal. He held a certain power over her, he realized, and knew that whatever he would say would either cut her or renew her. Before he could reply, Violet spurted out, "There are some men who like to treat boys and other men like their girlfriends." That said she walked out into the yard.

That was it. Discussion ended. She was angry at him for what she saw and she blamed him for what Randy did, thought William. She really didn't want to know how it all happened, about any of it; she didn't want to, and yet, she didn't want to punish him, either.

She thinks I wanted him there to do what he did.

As she stood in the yard, shaking a cigarette out of the pack pulled from out of her apron pocket, William watched her through the café curtains. *She's afraid*, he thought. *Of me!*

He felt the frigid blast of rejection, and for the first time in his life, despair. For Violet was never a subtle woman and lent no care to how others perceived her, nor understood the consequences of her behavior. She had left him alone in the kitchen, with the smell of Clorox in the sink, stale beer bottles neatly arranged in their cardboard carriers beside the back door, and the acrid stench of her shame.

He felt cut down, cut off from his mother. She had done the cutting. A complete severing, severe and final.

Mom! Mama! Please, Mommy!, he choked out, the words stuck in his throat, with a harsh and bitter taste of bile. This feeling of desolation was piercing and far more violating than Randy's pitiless thrusts. Defying hot tears, he viciously wiped them away.

A few days later, after the unanswered question was posed, Violet called William indoors, saying she wanted to talk to him. She brought him into the small living-room, telling him to sit down on the sofa. She sat next to him. William knew it was something serious, not only because of the look of dread on Violet's face, but because they were seated in the parlor, not the kitchen where family issues were usually discussed. There was a cold formality in the room and in the guarded way she sat rigidly on the edge of the cushion, and he suddenly thought that something bad had befallen his grandmother back in the States.

Violet told him that Ron had been taken to the Air Police Station for questioning. Randy had been murdered the night before. As Ron had been miles away at the missile site when the murder had taken place at the barracks, Violet assured her son that his father would be cleared of suspicion, and as all the men of the squadron were being questioned, he had only to account for his whereabouts like the rest of them.

His stepfather's indifference toward William over the years had hardened into a firm dismissal these past days. And he *knew* without being told that the man and his cronies had avenged themselves in murder. And he knew, too, that it had nothing to do with avenging a crime against William. It was sex and the honor of men and the betrayal of trust that made them do it. Pride was at stake here. After all, Randy had fooled them; he was an abomination, and they rendered vengeance as God-fearing men should do. But certainly not to avenge William.

Over the next few days, William was to learn of the gory details of Randy's murder. His penis had been shot off at close range, whereupon he bled to death. Violet would cry and say to William over and over again what a terrible person Randy had been, and how he had ruined William's life. Why hadn't she seen him for the bad person he was? William viewed her self-deprecation as out of character, an attempt to assuage her own guilt. He thought that she actually appeared thrilled, displaying a nervous excitement he could not fail to recognize, when she spoke of it. Her color was high, and there was a trembling in her fingers, a quaver in her voice, like the time they went to see President Kennedy arrive at the air field on Air Force One. She was titillated by the details of the young man's murder, and William's recognition of it sowed the seed of contempt he held for her for the rest of his life, and a horror at the violence of men.

How could he make her understand that his life had not been ruined, that he had suffered no lasting trauma from Randy that night? It was her failure to act, to confront, to stop Randy that traumatized him. It dawned on William that she wanted him to take some blame for the assault, that she couldn't face assuming all of the burden herself. Since his mother hadn't, after all, pulled Randy off of him when she had peeked into his room, she had no right to pretend outrage after the fact with her high-pitched trilled protestations. As desperately as he wanted to believe that his mother's displays of affection toward him and her sorrow and anger over the incident were heart-thumping expressions of grief for her precious son, he could see the underlying dishonesty; by not intervening she had been nothing less than Randy's conspirator.

He was expected to show a modicum of shame. He refused to. He was saddened by Randy's death, not glad like some of the adults. With Randy gone there was no longer a threat to the young boys at the base. But there was no car racing, no laughter, no fun, either.

After some time, when he was older and about to go off to the university, and he'd grown more critical of his parents, as is often the case during those years, and because he had had those years to look back upon that day, he came to believe that his mother saw him as a burden from her past, haunting this new life of hers with the better husband and baby daughters. He hadn't felt like he was a part of a family since he'd left his grandmother's, since Violet married Ron. That was five years ago, and although it was as if his real father, Arthur, had dropped off the face of the earth since William's infancy, there was never any talk about Ron adopting him. He always felt that the man didn't like him much; it got worse after what Randy did, because now Ron avoided looking at William when he spoke to the family at the dinner table. Oh, he addressed his stepson pleasantly enough, a little too pleasantly, too softly, and William caught the disquiet lurking below the surface of his words, and William, growing wise, glimpsed fear, the same unsettling kind he had seen in his mother, at the bottom of it all. To the people in the house he felt connected by only a thin thread, a thread loosely tied to his mother, a thread that was fraying fast and would inevitably break, sending him off into some vast unknown all by himself. These weeks after the murder brought him back to a memory of a day when he was ten. It was the first time he realized that he didn't quite fit in. It was the day that they had moved into the new house, and he had been left outside the front gate as his mother and Ron and the baby girls paraded through and down the path toward the front door. The gate had slammed shut before he could get through with his bicycle, and he stood there for a time, watching how happy they looked, the four of them, they never noticing he'd been left behind. Like a stranger, a passerby looking in through the bowed bay window at the happy little family, he was left separate and apart from the scene. They looked complete without him in the picture, framed by the window. Like a Sears magazine ad. The perfect little family. He wanted to run away, sometimes, but there was nowhere he could go. He just knew they'd had enough of him.

Now, affronted by rejection, William became determined not to linger at any gate anymore, and he began to lay plans for when he might leave them all behind. A rage was simmering inside him and it manifested itself in a defiant attitude, a self-protecting arrogance that he wore like an impenetrable shield. The teenage anger fueled him and toughened him and rendered him independent. William made a mental list of his attributes and found he was far superior in intelligence and wit to most of the adults he'd encountered. In an exercise, not unlike learning the skills of self-defense, he was to feed his newfound arrogance with a constant stream of acquired knowledge. He closed himself off in his bedroom, found solace reading everything he could get his hands on, the classics, the histories, the philosophers; all were absorbed and digested and served to shape a cynical view of the world. And in his rebellion he became sharp and cold in his observation of the adults around him. They could only offer emotional responses, not genuine answers for the way they behaved, *why* they professed to believe what they did, expressing everything in terms of feelings, not *truths* based in fact. Their self-indulgence disgusted him, and he would constantly challenge their motives. He was considered by his teachers, and later, professors, as the golden boy: the shining, brilliant student who would undoubtedly make much of himself, if he could only rein-in that rapier tongue that put people on guard if not in their place.

And so William deliberately and forcibly cast off the rank heritage of white-trash ignorance he now saw he had been born from. But, that was all to come, and when he was a man standing in the middle years of his life, alone, apart, among the membership of a family of his own making, he wondered if he might have turned out differently had one brief moment in his past played out differently, had three people not convened in his bedroom at the exact same time.

Possessing a stubborn nature, William refused to allow others to determine how he should feel about anything. Within a year he had lost from his life the only two people he had ever been really fond of as a result of having sex with them, be it for affection or by force. He had not loved Suzanne or Randy, but they were in his life, and they would be missed for their good qualities. He could feel loss, but not shame. In his twelfth year he learned that sex combined with affection could have very serious consequences. He would try to keep these two aspects of human relations separate throughout his life, all the while longing for something more, something that he could not identify. Then, when he turned forty-three, unaware of how very lonely and isolated his world had become, he saw reflected in the eyes of Ariella Rodgers that life could be better if he followed his heart, not simply his intellect, to a place that encompassed both passion and love.

"Over the main entrance a draperied woman stood in a niche, blindfolded, leaning on a sheathed sword, holding bronze scales."
Raintree County

THREE

Ariella Østerberg Rodgers

Both of her parents had been musicians: Her mother, a first-generation Italian-American, was trained as a violinist but did not pursue a career after meeting and marrying Ariel's father, Stephen, a Norwegian cellist with the Berlin Philharmonic under Von Karajan, who later struck out on a soloist's career. They met in New York.

Ariel's was a lonely childhood with many people wandering in and out of the rambling prewar apartment on West End Avenue in Manhattan. *Ariella*, as she was named at birth, loved her parents, was in awe of her father, who was a large figure and jocular, when at his best, which was generally when he stood at the center of attention of his admirers and peers. Ariella keenly felt her parents' indifference toward her. Stephen was often distracted. She heard it said that Papa was an important man. Her mother, even though she had given up a career in music, was distracted by her husband's needs. Life in the apartment revolved around Stephen. She would *shush* Ariel; that's what her mother would do all the times she tried to speak when the grownups were around. And Ariel was a precocious child, lively and vastly curious. Her loquaciousness prompted the saying, *Children should be seen and not heard*, and it was the order of her days, most days. For the rest of her life when she heard a mother tell a child to "*shush!*" she'd be reminded that what she had to say would be considered of no account, and that would make her seethe inside.

She was small for her age, a delicate little figure, and the people who gathered around her father were big; they were adults of prominence, some, and better able to catch her father's attention. Her voice could never be heard over the music.

As she grew older, seven, eight years old, some in the crowd were kind to her, and she might engage in conversation with the likes of Mr. Bernstein or Signor Casals, and Mr. Heifetz was particularly jovial (she had no idea where they ranked in the order of the musical lexicon), and if they were simply humoring the daughter of their friend—for she was an amusing child, had a fast smile and a bell-like laugh, and was obviously of superior intelligence—she never felt patronized. She could easily impress these men and women who gathered around the house, not so much for her disarming manner, but for the magnificent head of flame-red hair that tumbled like a waterfall down her back, the whiteness of her complexion, and the startling color of her eyes, so like moss in sunlight, that arrested one's attention, making it difficult for one caught in that gaze to cast one's eyes away. And by the time she was eleven or twelve and hovering at the brink of adolescence, a bud trembling at the imminent burst of bloom, her nubile charms were compelling. Of this, Ariella was unaware. She believed the attention she received was due to her proficiency at the piano, which she learned to play quite well, thanks to her mother's instruction, and, having picked up her mother's instrument before her seventh birthday, she was proficient at the violin as well. This innate talent caught her father's attention at last, and she was pleased. She was now a child prodigy, who was never *shushed* by her mother when at the keyboard. Once, she told Teddy with a laugh in her voice, and a bit of defiance, too, that if she couldn't be heard over her parents "music," she'd make her own loud noise in the world.

Her father became another person, when the door was shut on the heels of the last departing visitor, from the man his colleagues and his admirers had come to know. When the house was empty he became sullen, with a frown that furrowed his winged brows, an expression he slipped on like the old silk dressing gown he'd wear in the evening when he was home from tour. These dark moods prefigured the next shift of disposition. His rich baritone voice would rise up a pitch, his speech slowed, and when he spoke it was as if he weighed each word for meaning, and there was a lilting, melancholy quality that suggested he was about to tell a sad story. Preparing to depart for, or newly returned from, a concert tour, he was often unapproachable, Ariel's mother closing pocket doors against Ariel so as not to disturb the artist's much-needed tranquility.

Occasionally, he would become agitated, which ended in flashes of a violent temper, which was just an expression of frustration, her mother would say. The special-delivery package from Munich hadn't arrived; the flight to Zurich would be delayed due to a snowstorm....

Shush! As if he could hear anything on the other side of the tall walnut doors.

As Ariella moved into her teenage years, she began introducing herself as Ariel. It was a time of questioning, of challenging authority, and she became critical of her parents. She wondered if her mother's tentativeness was part of her innate nature or the consequence of living so many years with an overbearing and temperamental husband. Ariel began to loath her mother's timidity in the face of her demanding father. It was the 1960s, and Betty Friedan was shouting to the women of America not to be subservient, but to strike out as equal partners with their men, that a woman could be a good wife and mother *and* have a fulfilling career, a life outside the home. Her mother demanded nothing of her husband, yet answered all of his demands. All he gave her was a nervous stomach that plagued her, gnawed at her, especially those last couple of years. —*How much can you stomach, Mother?*, a fresh-mouthed Ariel would taunt, contempt thick in her voice in response to her mother's obsequiousness when her father would start raving, and the reply would be, *Shush!* as a wounded look settled into her mother's eyes. That terrible wounded-animal look. . . .

This was not what Ariel wanted when she grew up! She would not become her mother! She resented and lost respect for her. She was weak, dependent, and had given up her career, for what?

—What has he ever done for you, Mother?, she asked one day, as if Ariel didn't already know the answer, the big answer that seemed to be taken out of a dresser drawer, starched and pressed and ready to present as testament of her husband's love:

—He converted for me!

He had to. He had to convert to Catholicism to marry her. Ariel's grandparents wouldn't allow the marriage, and her mother would never go against her parents. So he converted; it was his only recourse, and he was determined to have her—she was quite lovely back then—and he would have done anything, he was so crazed with desire for her. But he got off cheap; it cost him nothing, really; he had no faith, and it settled things. It was the last concession he ever made for his wife.

When her mother became ill, years later, while Ariel was attending Juilliard, Ariel moved back into the apartment to take care of her. It was stomach cancer, and who would be surprised after the years of stress, churning acid, and acquiescence? After her mother died, her father suddenly discovered his wife's value—to *his* life. She had been everything to him, he lied, and he believed the lie. It was a lie, wasn't it? Because Ariel had never witnessed much affection from him toward the woman while she lived, as her mother cow-towed to his needs to make his life comfortable, and if that's what love was—a slow freezing out *until death do us part*—well, the idea of living a lifetime within such a prison was out of the question! But she kept her harsh thoughts to herself. She could hear from some far distance the echo of her mother's warning, *Shush!* And it made her think that if he wasn't lying, if there was tenderness between them when she wasn't looking, when her back was turned, well, then there might be truth to his grief. Later in life she understood that no one outside a marriage ever really knows all that goes on between two people, especially the children.

When she returned from her studies in Europe, she found her father in a sorry state. He'd been retired for several years since the arthritis in his hands made it impossible to continue with the rigors of performing. The large, florid man from her childhood had become a gaunt figure, his features slack and pasty, shuffling from room to room of the big apartment on West End Avenue as if in search of some forgotten object, an ancient dinosaur in a silk dressing gown that had seen better days, trailing its sash behind him like a tail. His friends, his colleagues, were mostly dead or failing, many living confined existences in their homes or, those dead, in their coffins. Four years had passed since the death of his wife, and with her gone from his life he only now understood her true devotion and worth. He would talk about her with joy in his voice, his eyes would light up as he reminisced about their early days together, stories about a woman Ariel had never really known. For her father, it was as if one day he had looked up from his work, from his music, from his distractions, and she was gone, just gone. Oh, there was evidence that she had been there, constant reminders, but pathetically, he could not find the woman in any of the rooms he roamed about within that vast apartment. And, so, Ariel's resentment of her father and her frustration with her mother dissipated slowly after a time.

Ariel moved back into the rambling place, fired the housekeeper, hired a new one on condition that the woman cook healthy meals, and ordered her father a new silk dressing gown.

When she was not playing with the Philharmonic, or performing with a quintet, or as a soloist on rare occasions, Ariel would watch television with her father—he liked *The Andy Griffith Show*—play chess with him—he always beat her—or they'd go to the Metropolitan Opera in Lincoln Center to hear Domingo or that new Italian star, the tenor, Luciano Pavarotti, who had caused a sensation in the role of Rodolfo in *La bohème* that season. Ariel arranged for her father's more-mobile friends to come to dinner, and accepted invitations for her father's evenings out. It was at a dinner party that she first met Teddy.

She would play on the Steinway every morning, and when her father was in the mood, she'd play her mother's violin while he took up his cello. He would handle his old instrument as if greeting an old friend who was sick and frail in the hospital, with affection but with tentative care. Soon, he would take command of the cello and wield its bow in the old familiar way. Ariel believed the music was food for his ragged spirit.

She was pleased when he'd rail at her, a bit of his old temperament making a show, and she'd smile. The mail was late! Only one biscuit left in an otherwise empty box! *Where's the new box!* When he died two years later, Ariel wasn't sad, wasn't beset with grief, although she knew now that she would miss him, but she was grateful that there had been a settling between them, a letting go of resentments: Because during the last years, her father had finally heard her voice over the noise of the crowds. She had reached him. Over the music. They had come to know each other and that was all that mattered: a coming together through love.

Ariel's best friends had always been men. Not to say that she didn't have close relationships with women; the women she felt closest to and most free around were those substantially older than she. She saw the pattern of her attractions to people. By the time she was thirty, those closest were in their fifties.

Her closest friend at twenty-two was fifty years her senior. Naomi Garland, the very wealthy widow of a television producer who had fallen dead while playing doubles with his very glamorous Hollywood friends, returned to her home, New York, to live high above Central Park South at the Navarro. Sophisticated, opinionated, gloriously glamorous in stature, it was hard to believe that she had been the child of a poverty-stricken Rochester couple and had grown up skinny and raggedy alongside her five siblings. Naomi had married for love, and was surprised and humbly grateful that her husband's ambitions brought them so many rewards.

She loved Ariel, and Ariel, her. As Naomi's two daughters thought their ancient mother foolish to move to New York in pursuit of a career in the theatre, Ariel delighted in her daring and zest for living out her dreams. The age difference didn't matter to either; they had great pleasure in each other's company, although the generation gap often revealed just how wide the distance was, like the way Naomi used to address Ariel as *Pussy*. *Puss* mightn't've been so bad, but *Pussy*?

One evening Ariel broached the problem:

—Naomi?

—Yes, Pussy?

—I hope you won't take offense . . .

—Is my powder caking?

—No, *uhhh*, you look beautiful . . .

—Pussy! What is it?

—It's . . . *that*. That word. That name.

—What word? Darling girl, just come right out and tell me what's disturbing you!

—All right. It's the pet name you have for me: Pussy.

—What's wrong with it?

—Well, it might have been an affectionate way to address a girlfriend way back—I mean—but today it's just too . . . what you'd see inside a men's newsstand publication!

—Nonsense!

—I would be shy of calling my cat that name, that is, if I had a cat.

—I see, said the older woman with a sly smile spreading over her face.

—May I call you "darling"?

—Of course!

—Or is "cookie" better?

—I'd rather not. My mother called me that.

—All right, *darling* it is, Pussy.

The outrageous *Pussy* moniker prevailed, but from that time forward, she never said it in public.

When Naomi suddenly died while practicing a dance routine in tap class, the only consolation Ariel found was that she had died, as had her husband, doing what she enjoyed the most.

Teddy. He was gone now, too. Died in a plane crash on his way to London to visit friends at Christmas.

When Ariel met him she was struck by the innate wisdom underlying an acerbic wit. Teddy Christopher, the fifty-year-old gay musical theatre conductor who had arranged the scores of many musicals composed by other people, was himself the composer of numerous scores, including one success among many that never made it on the boards. By the time Ariel met Teddy, he was resigned to do what made him a living: conducting an orchestra.

This sophisticated Texan had his own table at Sardi's and enjoyed being among the privileged few who spent weekends in Connecticut with the Leonard Bernsteins, the Oscar Hammersteins, and the Neil Simons. He would humbly remind himself, and Ariel, with hubris peeking out from under a mask of humility, that he was nothing better than the guitar-playing white trash son of an ignorant dirt farmer, born in a ramshackle shack outside Austin and currently residing in a penthouse on Fifth Avenue. Ariel adored Teddy, his style, his fast wit, his intelligence, and his affection for her.

He was a proud man who shouldered life's disappointments with grace. He wanted Ariel to succeed, but he knew success would take her away from him, and he inwardly feared she would leave him to his mediocre existence. He was aware of his selfishness, for he lived in a selfish world. But she had opened his heart in a way no other person had since his first love, Jim, who had left him for a Hollywood glamour-boy thirty years before. So Teddy lavished his generosity on her, instead, with gifts not only material, but educational.

She once asked him why he sought out her company, and after he said he thought her "just grand!" he told her why he was so attracted to her: She reminded him of someone he had once known.

One mellow evening as they sat drinking many martinis at Teddy's apartment, she asked if he had ever loved a woman. Teddy said he had, indeed, when he was young, and she looked very much like Ariel. She was the woman Ariel reminded him of. The young woman committed suicide after he told her why he couldn't marry her in spite of the fact that he loved her. "It would have been a sin for a gay man to marry her."

It was on that same night that Teddy asked Ariel to marry him, assuring her with characteristic élan, that he would not mind if there were other men in her life, as there would, undoubtedly, be other men in his.

She loved Teddy for so many reasons, especially for his touching vulnerability that would reveal itself in honest exchange. At these times there were no pretentions between them, just the simple meeting of two minds, open and true. But, now, she simply smiled at his proposal and changed the subject in order to allow that other, more predominant quality in him, his arrogance, to resurface.

When she told him that she and John Rodgers were going to be married, and she asked Teddy to walk her down the aisle and to give her away, he became quietly resigned that his relationship with Ariel was about to change. And although he disapproved of the whole idea of marriage to this singer, whom he had come to refer to as "the stud," and whom he sized up on first meeting as a talentless amateur with a big voice and an even bigger appetite for fame and fortune, and that the marriage might put an end to Ariel's career, Teddy offered to pay for the wedding reception. When the babies started arriving, and he watched from his perch in his penthouse apartment his golden girl becoming the house-frau of his nightmares, doomed to a suburban existence, he began his retreat from her life. It was too painful to watch as the gifted young woman he cared about seemed to gladly forfeit her once-promising career for a no-account husband and a bunch of difficult rug-rats. He never forgot her birthday, was never delinquent with sending the cards and gifts at Christmas, but their days of companionship were now in the past.

Ariel was unaware of his disapproval until she took the train into the city on one of those rare days when she was free of the children, with the expectation that she and Teddy would have dinner together and see a show. After an hour of observing her decline into frumpy domesticity—the lingering baby weight, the new easy wash-and-go hair-bob that chopped off her lovely hair—and enduring the excruciatingly mundane details of the goings-on at the kids' playgroup, he could take no more, He apologized about dinner, but something came up and they would have to cut the visit short. During the train ride home, Ariel's mood turned dark, for she knew Teddy and she had glimpsed his impatience and distress although he had tried to disguise it. As gentle as he was with her, it was that gentleness that struck her hard. And she saw herself for the first time in a long time. And she didn't like what she was becoming.

Ten years after that day in the city Teddy died. Ariel was forty-four years old, twenty-four years after they had first met. She could not focus on the wonderful gifts of friendship he had bestowed on her life; she could only feel disappointment.

Women of her own age who entered her life often proved sycophantic: Ariel was a touch eccentric, her looks were unusual, she dressed with a certain flare, like a rich hippie, extravagant and with an edge of careless abandon that only she could carry off with her tall, full figure. Ariel sensed the attraction of these women to her was mere small-town curiosity. A source of new material, fodder for gossip. Sensing this, she revealed very little of herself, which often incited more intense scrutiny.

She became aware, too, that she attracted women with very low self-esteem. These women were more difficult to extricate from her life. They would show their adoration by mimicking her, by cutting or coloring their hair as she had, adopting fashion styles only Ariel could pull off, and arriving without warning on her doorstep to air their current traumas. They didn't care to know more about Ariel than what they saw on the surface, she deduced. But, she was too kind to be abrupt with these women. She endured their foolish infatuations, hoping that there was more to them than revealed and all the while frightened that there was little of substance within herself. For Ariel did not flatter herself. She was not beautiful in any conventional way, and whatever *they* saw in her was a reflection of their own desires. To protect herself from discovery that she was just as ordinary as everybody else, she maintained a distance and would eventually, with gentleness, ease these women out of her life.

And, so, Ariel filled her life with books and music and children, and poured her most intimate thoughts into her journal in an effort at distraction from the belief that in spite of her efforts, contact with other human beings was fleeting and ultimately failed.

She met John, a good-looking young man with an impressive baritone who was a chorus member in the Broadway musical in which Teddy was the musical director. He had a magnificent lyric baritone voice, and might have had the lead but for the fact that the actor who was cast was box-office, a movie star. After a long, miserable affair while she studied in Paris with a man who proved to be a sadistic monster, Ariel took Naomi's advice about marriage:

—The woman sets the social calendar, Pussy; she sets the tone. It is unacceptable for a man to be disrespectful if the woman sets the standard of civilized intercourse at the very first meeting.

She set the tone (and the social calendar) for John to follow. It was good to find a man who was agreeable, a man who was amiable. . . . Naomi's advice was sound. Ariel married John and they had two children—Peter, now sixteen, and Jillian, now fourteen. They lived in a nice neighborhood in Linden Falls, a bit above their means. John was often unemployed, as Ariel noted, "not fired, but laid-off." Ariel had worked at many jobs throughout their marriage. She was a musician, trained as a classical pianist, and there was not much work for her in the small community that preferred country western and rock over Rachmaninoff. For whatever tricks of fate had brought them to where they stood in 1994, after eighteen years of marriage, neither she nor John were fulfilling the range of their talents. John sold insurance, and Ariel had been working for the last year as an activities director at a senior residence. And regrettably, Ariel was stuck in a small town with a small-town mentality in which she would be forever viewed as an outsider. She was, after all, from New York City, that terrible place of crime and vice. The provincial attitude and prejudices of native-born "Lindeners" made her laugh, and frustrated her.

Linden Falls fancied itself the idyllic American town, since it was featured back in 1947 in *Look* magazine, which labeled it "Hometown, U.S.A." Town officials had since been struggling to maintain that image of Norman Rockwell perfection, and after Urban Renewal swept through its streets in the 1960s and did its dirty business by obliterating many of the city's most beloved treasures—the Rialto Theater gave way to the new Burger King plaza—it suffered further humiliations as many of its stalwart companies of industry left town for cheaper tax pastures outside of New York State. Settled in the early seventeen-hundreds by trappers and farmers, the city later thrived during the nineteenth century as a milltown on the Hudson River, the paper plants and sawmills fed by the millions of acres of pine forest of the Adirondack Mountains. Ariel equated the arrogance of the political machine that had run the city of Linden Falls for the past thirty years to that of "old money after bad," the robber barons of the past century evolving into the "old money" of the twentieth century. In 1947, the population's per-capita income was greater than anywhere else in the United States. As often is the case in small enclaves of industrial regions across the country, the well-to-do citizens of Linden Falls believed themselves exclusive when in fact their little city is today no more than a bedroom community of the great capital of New York State, the city of Albany. Still, "Lindeners" as they call themselves have their pride. Ariel once said to John, "After all, fifty years ago they had been honored as special by a national journal. That they followed misguided ideas at every turn was not the point. That many of its citizens suffer unemployment, the indignity of poverty and hunger, and substandard housing was not the point. That petty crime, child molestation, and drug abuse is on the rise was not the point. A copy of the *Look* article had been framed and hung in the lobby of City Hall for all to see as proof that the city of Linden Falls is doing just fine."

Had they not moved there for their excellent schools, Ariel would have left long ago. But her life was now all about the kids. And they were normal kids in most respects: loud, boisterous, determined, and each displaying their adolescent anger with frequent outbursts of violent sibling rivalry. There were several trips to the hospital emergency room: one, the result of a cut to Peter's forearm, occurring when he tried to punch Jillian. She ducked, and his swinging arm crashed through one of the panes of glass in the French doors. Jillian was so upset that Peter had been injured that she went to the hospital along with Ariel to comfort her brother. She then watched in fascination as the doctor cleaned out the wound and put five stitches into Peter's arm. Ariel told John later, "Jillian didn't so much as cringe. She just leaned over and watched the doctor wield the needle, asking him questions. Jillian would make a good doctor."

Another emergency room visit came after Jillian miscalculated the opening of her bedroom door and hit her forehead with tremendous force on the doorframe. Jillian eyes rolled back as she dropped to the floor while

Peter watched in horror. A welt the size of a golf-ball had risen within a minute, and Peter, hysterical, carried her unconscious to their mother's car and drove to the hospital. His erratic driving attracted the police, who followed him in hot pursuit until they arrived at the emergency room entrance, where they were able to see that the bat out of hell was a scared teenage boy. They returned their weapons to their holsters.

When Ariel arrived at the hospital, she saw her man-boy-child weeping quietly as he sat on the floor beside a potted fern in the waiting room. Jillian had stolen one of Peter's CDs. When he caught her in the act, he had chased her as she ran from his room to her own, but she never made it through the door.

Jillian regained consciousness, and when Peter was allowed in to see her, he laid his head on her shoulder and wailed great cries of relief. Jillian petted his head and cried, too, "not because I'm sorry I took the CD, but because that doctor wants to put a stitch in my head!"

Lately, Ariel had become sick of the sound of her own voice competing with the din of the noisy household. She said to John, —I hate the sound of my voice. I bray. I'm exhausted from the vocal sparring, one child always trying to outdo the other."

She would speak in softer tones, when she could get a word in at all. It worked for a while, until the kids got frustrated with her and their pitch got louder. She had to slow down, quiet down.

Add John to the mix, his "evil" voice when he'd get angry at the kids, and if it scared them, it frightened her even more. Even her father, when he ranted, had not had *that* particular edge to his voice. What could offer more comfort than to escape to a far-off zone of silence?

Ariel was a child of the Fifties: She grew up on *Howdy Doody* and *The Mickey Mouse Club.* The innocent Annette Funicello was the prepubescent model to emulate. The Everly Brothers crooned "Wake Up, Little Suzie," a tune alerting teens that the presumption of a girl's chastity could be in danger no matter how innocently she behaved; Peter and Jillian watched MTV and the blatant sexual writhings of Madonna, slinking about not so much "Like a Virgin." During Ariel's adolescence, the Beatles ushered in the Sixties, their music about love and joy and youthful possibilities. Then, the social climate had turned seriously stormy as America's young people rose up to demand Peace and Love in a world brought to war by their parents. Theirs was a call for justice, civil rights, and civility. Ariel's parents were financially comfortable, but her mother shopped at Macy's, and Ariel's wardrobe consisted of three pairs of shoes—Sunday-best patent-leather Mary-Janes, sneakers, and red Buster Browns. In her closet hung three skirts, three blouses, and two sweaters. She longed to dress like a woman, like her mother, wear stockings and garters, high-heels, and shirtwaist dresses. It was a time when children had time to be children, to play, to daydream, and the rush toward adulthood was the youthful striving for identity and independence—to claim one's place in the world. Her parents ruled the roost.

As children of the Eighties, Peter and Jillian were bombarded with advertising targeted at kids as the new consumers, as the stock market and interest rates soared and the real estate market boomed, making it nearly impossible for the middle-class family to afford purchasing a house. Parents like Ariel and John, children of the postwar era, the Boomers of the complacent 1950s, were determined to fill their children's lives with more, so they were miserable with the glut of their big, fat mortgages. The kids had their Transformers and dirt bikes and Cabbage Patch dolls and all the paraphernalia that was demanded and that assured them they were loved. Ariel found the shift of values and disregard for authority disconcerting; she was waging a losing battle at home, trying to reassert her own authority over Peter and Jillian, with little help from John. She was the common enemy of her children, the bad guy, and she longed for a recovery of the sweet affection of their early years. That rift, that tearing away was brutal.

Music had been missing from her life, and with a sudden burst of energy fueled by a need to escape the rut of her daily struggles, she organized a string quartet of musicians who lived in and around the area of Linden Falls. They would perform concerts twice a year in the Methodist Church. It was after one such concert that she met William Trent.

—I was fortunate enough to see your father perform when I was a child in Germany, he said, in reference to Ariel's bio in the concert's program

That this man saw her father perform thirty-something years ago during his last European tour immediately made this tall, blond man with the soft smile simpatico. He nodded with a just the hint of a respectful bow when they met, towering over her. First impression was that the color of his eyes brought to mind sunlight dancing on the blue Sargasso Sea. Such fancy made her chuckle. But fancy or not, William Trent's eyes were compelling, and had it not been for the creases set along his full, wide smile and the soft line of his chin, which offset the intensity of his gaze, she might have found the man a little bit frightening.

His handshake was firm, but Ariel felt his fingers tremble as they touched. A strike of preternatural knowledge wracked her. She tossed it off when William made mention of an old Deutsche Gramophone recording, on which his favorite selection, Brahms' *Sonata for Cello and Piano in E minor, Op. 38*, had been performed by her father. A bond was sealed, for rarely had she met anyone over the past decade who knew about her father's place in midcentury music, let alone possessed one of his recordings.

—I was hoping it would be released on CD, he said.

—My copy is quite worn. I've had it since nineteen-sixty-six, I think. Yes, sixty-six.

Ariel figured her jaw must have dropped, because William asked if there was something wrong.

—Nothing at all, she said, closing her mouth. — Surprised is all: You were a kid with a sophisticated taste in music. . . .

—I also like Tex Ritter, and one of my favorite songs is "Blue Hawaii."

—You seem an interesting character, she said, loosening up.

—Quite dull, actually. Some might say, boring. When are you going to perform Schubert's *Death and the Maiden?*

—We take requests, so . . . soon, I would say.

Ariel returned home that evening with a light heart and a new confidence in her work, enthused about performing the formidable Schubert, with plans to ready it for the next concert season.

Ariel wrote of William's letters in her journal: "Long letters in smallish handwriting, chock-full of wonderful ideas. I have fun with William. He is unadulterated, unedited, and a little bit unhinged. I've never known such enthusiasm. John and I like to be around him because he is clever and always makes us laugh. John hasn't any men friends, and I'm glad William and John are so comfortable together. I think I will work with William, as he has asked me to conduct for a musical he is directing for the Community Players. He's the only person I've met up here who reads, writes, knows music and art, and with whom I can argue politics and discuss philosophy. It's nice to have a friend at last!"

With the constant financial problems, little was left after paying their bills. A month out of work would set them back, and then Ariel, who was in charge of the checkbook, would try to juggle monies in an effort to get back on track. Twice, they nearly lost their home to foreclosure. One house, on the brink of mortgage default, sold just in time to save them from disaster. They bought another, bigger house, paying for it in cash so they would have freedom from the burden of house payments. In 1994, they were forced to mortgage it after John had been out of work for nearly a year. John took a job selling cars, and after a couple of months he was making decent commissions. Ariel found work as an activities director at a senior citizens' residence, where she included music therapy as part of the activity schedule.

John did not like his job, and he found the owner of the dealership contemptible. Ariel was used to hearing about the problems at work, the idiocy of management, the dog-eat-dog competition between the salesmen, not only in the car business, but in insurance, and in other commissioned sales jobs that John had held over the years of their marriage.

How could she not be sympathetic to John's career problems? He was always in the right, of course. It was a rat-race out there, and people in business were not to be trusted, she gathered from John's experiences. She listened to his troubles and comforted him when he got home from a long day of work. He was high-strung by nature and preferred a quiet home. She never did housework when he was home, because the hum of the vacuum cleaner irritated him, She'd keep the children at bay; they could be like spinning tops when Dad arrived home from work. Until he had a couple of drinks, a shower, and appeared relaxed enough, she'd hold dinner. It had to be done that way, Ariel knew, but why, she never questioned. She simply did as her mother might have. But, of course, her father had been successful and respected in his chosen profession where John was frustrated at every turn, and the only thing she could do to help was to make his home a place of comfort. She tried her best to make things right, to accommodate everyone, and to encourage a peaceful home life. By eight o'clock in the evening she had little energy left, and her efforts to keep the peace, ineffectual. The next day she would attempt again to bring harmony to a frazzled household of conflicting personalities and demands, never laying blame on John or the children but simply dealing with it all.

There wasn't a child-rearing book Ariel hadn't read and passed on to John. He would accept the books and leave them untouched on his night-table for months before Arial would shelve them again. It was up to her to deal with the kids, as John was disinterested. And sometimes, when he was out of work, or she sensed trouble brewing on his job, fears would rise and a feeling of powerlessness overcame her, for she'd see their future threatened and bleak.

There were so many homeless families. It was all over the news these days, and weren't they living paycheck to paycheck, when there was a paycheck? But the greater prevailing concern was for the children's survival to adulthood. Her prayers at their births were that they be survivors in life. Drugs, fast cars, and abduction was always in her mind. Sixteen years later she wrote in a journal, "Nobody survives life; it's a marathon race that you just try to get over the finish line."

By September 1994, Ariel was becoming a fragmented, overworked woman, steadfast in her goal to make her children's and her husband's lives better.

One day, while dusting a photograph of her parents taken when Ariel was a teenager, she stood a long time studying her mother's face, and although Ariel took after her father's side of the family, she recognized in her mother's eyes that old familiar look of weary subjugation. When she looked up from the photo and glanced at own her reflection in the bureau mirror she was shocked to see that same frantic, edgy undercurrent lurking under an outwardly calm exterior. And she said to herself, —*Oh, my God! I've become my mother!*

Her days had darkened by the end of November when John was laid off from the dealership. Car sales were down.

And then, Ariel discovered that John was secretly drinking. She found, by accident, five paper-bagged pint bottles, all empty, hidden behind the bathroom's plumbing access door. A search of the house rendered eight empty bottles of vodka in the basement behind the furnace, three discovered in the trunk of John's car, one of them half full when he left in the morning; checking the trunk on his return, two were empty. —I don't want to live this nightmare again, she wearily said to herself. It was not the first time she'd found hidden stashes of liquor and spent bottles. Several years earlier she had discovered dozens hidden under the crawlspace of their first house. The children were very young, and she'd confronted John about his drinking, threatening to leave if he continued She had no problem with social drinking, wine was often served at dinner, but the discovery, that first time, indicated that he was imbibing more than a cocktail or two before dinner. Now, again she was faced with his alcoholism, realizing that addiction had taken hold long ago and it could account for the many failures John had suffered.

During the weeks before Christmas it was difficult for her to hold onto the belief that John had lost his job by no fault of his own.

"Life's a restlessness of unstable compounds that long for the stability of death."

Raintree County

FOUR

Bill

Mrs. Trent looked small, doll-like, as she slept in the big hospital bed, pale in her shroud of neatly tucked white linens. Her auburn hair, combed back from her forehead, lent the only color to the stark whiteness of the room. Modern technology monitored the rushing movements taking place within her deceptively motionless figure.

Bill pulled a chair from near the window to sit beside her bed. He sat there, watching the rise and fall of her breathing, studying the peaks and valleys of the cardiac monitor, noting the fluctuation of her blood pressure as the numbers challenged the ones indicating her heart rate.

He studied the pale face on the pillow, so different from the fiery flush, and the green-eyed wonderment when she first looked upon him and called out his name the night before. There was something so ageless and fragile and soft about her in this sedated state: pearled eyelids against a sweep of dark brown lashes and brows. Her lips, although lacking color, had a fullness, a definition of youth in the way they curved and billowed. The back-lighting made visible the downy spiraling fuzz at her hairline.

He wanted to trace his fingers along that barely visible surface to know if the delicate pattern could even be felt with fingertips. Yet, he was afraid to touch her, although the compulsion to do so intensified. A bruise had formed beneath the abrasion on her cheek. And when he realized he had lifted a hand toward her face, he quickly pulled away. To touch her in that way would have been more intimate than a kiss: a violation.

Nurse Chanson entered to rescue Bill from those thoughts, and after she looked at the monitors and jotted on the chart, she looked at him in such a way that he thought she had read his thoughts. He felt the warmth spreading along his face and knew he was blushing.

—It's all right to speak to her, she said. —You have a visitor, Mrs. Trent. She might fall asleep in the middle of your conversation. Don't be alarmed: It's just the anesthesia from the surgery. She'll be more alert tomorrow.

—You mean, she'll be all right?

—Right now she's doing fine, considering what she's been through.

Happiness pulsed through him. His exhaustion and anxiety suddenly vanished.

—Oh, and, by the way, a neighbor's been contacted. Mrs. Wilkens. Mrs. Trent! Ariel! You have a visitor, dear!

It took a couple more attempts to wake her, and then Ariel Trent's eyes fluttered open. Slowly they moved toward Bill.

—Hi, he said.

—Doctor?

—No, *uhhh* . . .

An instant flash of recognition.

—I know you.

—Yes. I'm the man who—

—I hit.

—No. I think you mean . . .

Bill's baffled and troubled expression gave rise to a smile, and he noticed a dimple—no, not exactly a dimple, but a "comma" crease on her left cheek.

—No, I didn't jump purposely at your car; I wasn't committing deliberate injury to myself.

Then, as if suddenly losing strength, she added:

—Not if it put Little Eva in danger.

—Oh, no, of course not.

—I was making a silly joke. . . . Must the recently surgerized be humorless? I suppose I'm not very funny, today.

He understood that she didn't want to lay the fault on him for the accident.

—You are . . . ?

—I'm Bill Davidson . . . Are you feeling okay?

—I won't do the town tonight, she sighed and closed her eyes. They opened wide in a fast transition.

—Little Eva!

—She's all right. She's staying with me.

Bill looked up at the monitors. Her heart rate had skyrocketed.

—You don't mind keeping her?

—She's a nice dog. No trouble at all.

—Her dog food—she has chewy bones, you know, the rawhide ones. In the cat.

—The cat?

—The cat. The cat-shaped cookie jar on my kitchen counter.

—I'll walk down to get them.

—Walk?

—I live on Harvard Road, the blue bungalow across from Haley's farm?

—Yes.

—I was on my way home last night when—

—I hit you. William? Your name is William?

Bill nodded.

—I'm not sure where we've met before.

—We have?

—Before last night, I mean.

—I don't believe we have met before.

—It's just that you called me by name.

—I did?

She stared at him curiously.

—Last night.

There was a dreamy, otherworldly expression as she met his eyes.

—Oh, yes, I see. Eyes . . . Blue Sargasso Sea. . . .

—Excuse me?

She didn't explain the odd comment; she just drifted off to sleep.

Bill found Mrs. Wilkens' phone number in the directory. She was at number 6 Harvard Road.

She picked up after the third ring and he could hear the expectancy in her voice. It took a minute to explain who he was and why he was calling. He heard hesitation in her voice when he said he was the man who had driven the car, and no response when Bill added that Ariel Trent's dog was in his care. He went on to say he had returned from the hospital and that Mrs. Trent was doing well after surgery. At that news, her tone became cordial. When he asked about fetching dog food from Mrs. Trent's home, she told him to stop by for the key.

Number 6 was an old farmhouse across the road and a couple of acres down from Mrs. Trent's. Bill parked on the road and walked up the drive past four parked cars. There was the chatter of people within the house when she opened the front door.

—I have relatives visiting for the holidays, she said.

Mrs. Wilkens was an attractive blonde in her late thirties.

—Would you like to come in?

—Well, I didn't want to disturb you. Mrs. Trent asked me to get a few things for the dog. Her wide-eyed expression prompted Bill to explain. —I'm to fetch the cat chews. I mean, the dog chews that she keeps in the cat. The cat holder? And the dog food?

A smile crossed her lips and she said, —I'll get my coat.

Bill intended to borrow Mrs. Trent's house key, but from the tone of suspicion in her voice, he decided it best that she escort him there. It was bad enough the man who injured her friend was standing on her doorstep. She certainly wasn't about to let him run free among her private things. Bill sensed her need to place blame on him for the accident.

She came out the front door wearing a big, woolen fringed shawl against the cold, and as they walked along the road toward the Quaker Meeting House, Mrs. Wilkens wrapped it more snugly around herself.

—I'm Bill, by the way.

—Amy.

The sun was trying to break through the cloud cover, but the smell of another snowfall was in the air. Bill put up his collar, but it did little to protect him from the wind.

—This does seem rather odd, doesn't it? I mean, you knock Ariel off the road and then you take care of her dog.

She was right, of course, but the way she had put it, "knock her off the road," stung more harshly than the Arctic wind.

Bill didn't know how to reply. He was the culprit, of course, and what she said was the truth. His first inclination, to defend himself, would only alienate her. And right now he needed her help to do what he could for Mrs. Trent. He spit out a lame reply.

—Well, circumstances were such that—

—It's just unusual, that's all. Why aren't you in jail?

—Should I be?

—Well, you did run her down.

She was getting mean, now.

—It was an accident.

—Yes, yes, she said with an impatient frown. Then she stopped walking and looked at him.

When Bill realized she wasn't keeping step, he turned to face her.

—I'm sorry. I'm sorry to be so rude. I guess I just want to blame you. It's easier when you can be angry at someone.

To say he was heartsick to have hurt her friend was pointless. He didn't want her forgiveness. It wasn't due him, and anyway, if there was forgiveness to be had, it wasn't from Amy Wilkens. So Bill just stood there, waiting for her to do or say whatever she needed to say.

She tugged the shawl closer and began to walk alongside him once again.

—She'll be all right? Is that what the doctor said?

The concern was deep and obvious in her voice.

—That's what the nurse said—implied. I didn't see a doctor.

Bill felt so ineffectual.

—I'll go see her as soon as I can free myself from my sister and her family.

—You've been friends for a long time?

—Since I moved here, two years ago.

When they arrived at the front gate, Amy Wilkens led the way through the arbor and along the walk to the front doors. Slipping the key in the door, she turned to say:

—It's not locked. She doesn't lock it when she walks the dog. Anyone could have walked in!

They entered a foyer and then through double doors leading into the sanctuary. Light poured in through the ten-foot windows. A balcony above the entry doors ran the width of the front of the building.

The space was airy. The patterns and textures of the furnishings grounded the whiteness of the walls. It was clean and ordered and yet drawn with the detail of one's accumulated interests.

Amy walked through the hall, converted now into a living space, toward a door at back. Bill, who would have liked to have lingered in the room to look over objects that made it a home for Ariel Trent—the Persian rugs scattered about, the jam-packed bookcases, paintings, photos, and furnishings, thought it best to follow the woman through an archway to the kitchen.

A large oak refectory table and chairs dominated the old church kitchen. It reminded Bill of the sunlit rooms in Vermeer's paintings.

At the pantry Amy took out a bag of dog food and a box of biscuits. She gathered the dog's water bowl and food dish and placed them into a plastic supermarket bag. The cat cookie jar was perched on the counter, its big green eyes watching every move Bill made as he wandered around the room. Amy pulled out handfuls of dog chews.

She worked quickly, and when she was finished, Amy led Bill back out into the big room and toward the front doors.

—Is there anything else she might need at the hospital? A night robe, or something?

Amy turned to look at him, hesitation in her voice and impatience on her face as she considered the idea.

—I suppose . . . *uhhh*, wait here. I'll see if there's a robe and slippers in her bedroom. I can take them to her when I go over later.

She put down the dog's supplies, looked up at the loft, and then, stiffening her spine, walked up a spiral staircase.

Bill now had a couple of minutes to look around the room. What first? The books? The paintings? Sit on one of the sofas or chairs and take it all in? What's on her desk? Not much time before Amy returned, and he felt like a kid running amuck in a candy store, told he could keep all the goodies he could stuff in his pockets in three minutes. There was an elegance here, although the seemingly random positioning of the furnishings gave the room a warm, cozy feel.

He walked over to the baby grand piano covered with a silk shawl on top of which were silver-framed photographs of people from long ago and of children at various stages of growth. Several were signed by famous musicians—Casals, Segovia, Rubinstein, and Stern. Then, the image of a man of about forty years caught Bill's attention. The face was an interesting one, the eyes, especially. His features strong, and distinctive, if not traditionally handsome. There was no doubt in Bill's mind that the smile emanating through those arresting eyes captured a very intimate connection with the photographer. It unnerved Bill, who recognized something, some quality that sparked a remembrance of someone else. And then it dawned on him that the man in the photograph and he were of a type. Blond, blue-eyed, similar hairline, and the cut of their jaws was strikingly similar. . . . He realized that the face in the picture frame was that of the man in the tiny photo in Ariel Trent's clamshell locket..

He felt a little like a voyeur, an outsider looking in, and there was a rising sense of urgency as if he was missing something important and the loss of it made his life all the poorer. He threw off the ghost of shame when he saw Amy across the room, a small suitcase in her hand, watching him, a wary expression on her face. She had the uncanny ability to make him feel like a criminal, at best, an intruder. She shut him down. He decided it best not to ask who the man was in the photograph.

She gathered herself together, asking pointedly, —Are you ready to leave?

Bill nodded, walked passed her toward the front door, not looking back even after she had turned to lock the doors.

And so it continued as they walked down the path toward the gate. By the time they returned to Amy's house, Bill had recovered enough to thank her for her help. She nodded curtly and they parted, she to her house and Bill to his rented bungalow.

The man who does not review his life drifts; the man who does is at risk. Bill sat in the darkened ICU cubicle, a sentinel in the night, watching as Ariel slept, when he began the review.

There are moments in life that herald change: moments that can become lost in memory, disguised as the ordinary motions of day-to-day living, entangled in the threads of subsequent events that weave the fabric of our lives.

Looking back, Bill could identify the exact times his world shifted axis, silently, without dramatic fanfare. He made a study of those times, those often deceptively innocuous nanoseconds that influence the course of one's life, and found that it might take years before one could see the change effected by a thought, an idea, an inclination, a simple movement, a gesture that opens a door and leads one astray through a guise of opportunity. Simple, everyday occurrences. . . .

He traced one such life-altering moment back five years, two months and thirteen days ago, a Monday morning in October. On the john, with nothing to read but Sunday's newspaper, put down on the floor to train the puppy, who had missed the mark again. He grabbed the clean page, the classifieds. Maybe a good deal on an old MG, something to fix up on weekends for something to do? Nothing. Flipped the page over, and there in the Help Wanted was the job of his dreams.

Pulled up pants, patted the naughty puppy, called the number listed, got through the interviews, and by the end of the week Bill was fifty thousand dollars a year richer, with a full benefits package, expense account, and company Acura. Then came the new condo, the calfskin living-room suite, and the Caribbean vacations where he met the object of those other dreams, Cassandra, taut and tan alongside an aqua lagoon.

Life changed for the better. . . . for the better . . .

Chance? Luck? Serendipity? Kismet? Or Karma?

But then there was the divorce from Cassie, with all the ensuing complications: community property division; therapy sessions resulting from a not-so-amicable parting of ways; the stress of a job he was holding onto for dear life, even though he detested the work . . . he held on because a smart-ass upstart would take it all away from him by brown-nosing his way to the top. Add some Prozac, which wiped out any chance of sexual satisfaction, and a bit of booze and there was the cocktail for disaster.

Bill wanted to drown out Margie's braying demands and wash out of consciousness his cowardice for not telling her he was turned off by her constant obsession with her weight, and didn't like being called "Bumpy Buns" in public or *anywhere*; for not telling his boss he was the biggest asshole living in North America, and to shove the job and the company car up that most predominant feature of the man's anatomy. To drown himself and everyone around him away to oblivion, Bill found a drinking companion in Jack Daniels.

He tried to think back, to remember through the haze of days, when life became so complicated. When did that pivotal moment occur that infected each ensuing day to bring him to where he now was? When was the last time he could envision the golden Viking boy atop his buffalo companion with the incongruously Italian name, Vittorio? He suddenly realized that he was always alone with his buffalo while journeying the Western Plains for adventure. The Viking boy would encounter people along the way, but he belonged to no one, really, and to no place. And now he saw that in his real life his relationships with people had been limited and guarded, and if he hadn't loved and couldn't share his inner life with any real human intimacy, he preferred to be alone. There was the quiet comfort and security of his own company. He didn't need anybody because he found that trust in oneself was all that was necessary in life. All that he really missed was that cute little puppy, given away because Cassie said dogs were dirty creatures—"I'm not picking up a hundred-thousand pieces of shit," and anyway, she was allergic—feigned or real, he'd had his suspicions. He wanted that happy little puppy back, yearned for its unconditional affection, and maybe an old used MG to fix up on weekends. Then, to escape someplace, anyplace, just him and the dog, someplace where things would be simple and uncluttered.

Ah, yes! If only the dog had shit on the paper. . . .

A moment can spin change loudly and violently. You turn a corner and quite literally crash into a person and instantly every dream or carefully planned intention for a future is spontaneously aborted. Obvious and unmistakable, like the cock of a gun before the bullet rips through your flesh, or watching your brother fall through the ice when you're nine years old. Accidents of fate. We all know it can happen, but we don't, like death, anticipate the tragedy. It's the simple misfortune of being at the wrong place at the wrong time. You are innocent, of course, you did nothing wrong, nothing to contribute to the calamity, and there was no way you could prevent what happened. You were just there, and it did happen and now it is all going to be different from before.

Fate happens to you by no obvious fault of your own. Not driven by desire, and unanticipated by fear.

Like the night of the whispers. Whispers that tore up through the living-room to the landing where he huddled in his flannel pajamas, trying to make sense of the violent, sibilant voices. An ominous whispering that had arrested his progress down the stairs and had caught his breath. The hiss that had ricocheted in his memory from time to time ever since.

His father's distorted voice: —he can't ever . . .

His mother's insistent: —it's his right!

—Suzanne's dying, what's the point?

—He should . . .

—Let things be, for Chrissake!

—the truth . . . he must know. . . .

He'd heard his parents argue many times: the harsh, hoarse rush of over-articulation that was his father's style, overlapped by his mother's deliberately low-pitched tones. But there was something different striking Bill's ten-year-old ears that made his pulse pound, further deafening the sounds rising from the main level of the house.

—You're his mother.

—I am, but I'm not Suzanne!

—There's no point. He has enough to deal with.

The boy felt a sickly sensation as cold shivers coursed through his body. His older sister, Suzanne, was ill, he knew; she had Leukemia, but he never was told she would die! He was suddenly miserable. They were so close to each other. A gasping cry caught in his throat. And now, hearing of her imminent death, he was determined to pretend he knew nothing of the kind when he was around her. Suzanne was leaving him and he didn't want her to go. His younger brother, Tommy, had died the year before, fallen through the ice of the thawing lake while Bill had stood there helpless to save him. And now, again, he was helpless. Helpless to save his big sister.

Three days after the night of whispers, Suzanne died. But the whispers he heard that night were about other things he didn't understand. Words that would knock around in his head, words he could not forget.

" *I am, but I'm not Suzanne.*"

Now what? he wondered, wanting change, yet fearful of it.

January 2nd fell on a Sunday, so Bill did not have to go to the office. He was grateful to be free of the demands of his job for another day. There were things to do and things to think about without distractions.

Margie was due to fly in at three o'clock. She assumed that Bill would be there waiting to meet her when she got off the plane. He hadn't planned to, but when they'd spoken on the phone earlier in the week she said she'd like to stop on the way home for dinner at the Chateau. Bill said it sounded like a good idea.

Bill didn't want to go out for dinner that evening. The truth was he didn't want to go out to dinner with Margie. He didn't want to have to explain the last thirty-six hours to her. He was tired, and being around Margie could be stressful at times. He decided to call her at her parents' house before she left for her flight. When he told her that he'd had a difficult weekend and that it would be a problem getting to the airport, she wanted to know why.

—I'll explain it all when I see you.

—Oh . . . well, won't you even stop in to see me tonight? I can call out for Chinese food and you can pick it up and come over to my apartment. You'll tell me everything. Okay?

Her suggestion was logical. Bill supposed he was being petty, but the directness of what he *would* do prickled at his sense of independence.

His silence triggered a warning bell in her head, because she said in a softer tone, —I just thought . . . I hoped that you missed me. I missed you so much, Billy. I really had hoped . . .

Her words were gentle and whispering, no longer the strident tones but a sweet honest yearning, a declaration from her heart. It was what confused him most about Margie: The sudden changes that would catch him unaware. Just when he'd think they should part ways, she'd say something that would melt his resistance. Perhaps he had sounded cranky. He was. But, he cared for Margie and didn't want to hurt her.

—I missed you, too, babe. I'm just kind of . . . Listen, Margie. I'll stop in later tonight, all right?

—What time?

The previous tone had returned. He felt a little bit abused and a lot more tired.

—I don't know, yet. Eight-o'clock-ish?

—See you then, Billy.

It was a relief getting off the phone, and he thought, *How do I tell her I think we'd better slow down for a while?*

He was short-tempered because of work and the accident. He hadn't verbalized any of these feeling before she left, not to himself, anyway. But, during the ten days that she'd been away, he'd felt a lifting of pressure. And were the truth to be told, he'd stopped thinking about Margie a couple of days after she had left. It was only on New Year's Eve when he ran into Cassie at the party, that he'd felt a return of that "pressure." Maybe Cassie was a part of what was happening in his response to Margie. He couldn't figure it out, and at that moment, didn't want to. He'd visit Marge in the evening.

Sunday morning dawned bright and sunny, but with the wind-chill factor added in it was twenty-six degrees below zero. The snow's surface had remained powdery, and when Bill took Little Eva out for a walk she wanted to play. They walked through the wooded acres and Bill let her free to romp through the deep snow of the cornfields. She was not a small dog, but it was an effort, one she seemed to enjoy, just to get around. Letting loose the dog sprinted like a racehorse in great circles. When she fell into a deep drift, she'd roll on her back, struggling to aright herself, shake off the powder, and then, with head low, and her body stalking, take off again at a rapid speed. The sight of her frenzy made him laugh, black velvet against the clean white background. If any creature could express a joy for living, it was Little Eva.

Childhood days playing in the snow, not going home until the packed snow had penetrated his snowsuit, he remembered, when his father was stationed in Kalispell, Montana. When he did go inside it would be to change into dry leggings and mittens before returning to his sled. He'd pretend, as all children do, that he didn't hear his mother calling, screaming, that it was time for dinner, or he'd get frostbite or tonsillitis if he didn't get inside right away! Fun was of a different sort for a kid. The snow had been an all-encompassing delight, a substance full of creative possibilities. But it was in the snowy landscape of an iced-over lake that he watched his brother drown. And that put an end to his carefree days. With his brother's death he had left his childhood behind.

Now snow was simply a thing to be dealt with, to shovel away, to force the car through to get to the really important things that had to get done. Little Eva had only one important thing to do and she was doing it as she flipped and dove into the powder.

Once again that morning he knew he had to take the time to rethink his life. He wasn't a dog; he was supposed to have a higher and greater purpose in life. Something was wrong here. Life as a dog seemed far better and more fulfilling. When had he last felt joy relating to another human being, the way he had that morning with this dog? As Oscar Wilde was quoted, "Life is too serious to take seriously."

Once again home, Little Eva was so exhausted from her romp that she curled up on the sofa limp, as if she'd abandoned her skeleton in the snow-covered meadow.

Where an hour ago he was exhausted just speaking with Marge, he now felt invigorated, and filled with energy. He poured a second cup of coffee, and took it into the bathroom. After showering and shaving, he put on a sweater and favorite tan corduroy slacks, and then set off for the hospital. Halfway there, he remembered the seashell. It was odd: The one pressing thought he had last night was to go to the hospital, if for no other reason than to return the seashell to Ariel Trent. It was precious to her and would be the first thing she'd look for when she had awoken fully. He had forgotten it yesterday and again today, left on the bureau with a ribbon drawn through the ring until a jeweler could repair the chain.

Returning home, he left the car running in the driveway and fetched the seashell from the bedroom.

The desk nurse in ICU said that Mrs. Trent had been sent to a room on the third floor: 3 Central, Room 22.

Upon entering the elevator, Bill faced a man holding a large bouquet of flowers, and turning to face the doors, thought, *I should have brought flowers.* He'd send pink roses as soon as possible.

Bill stopped at the nurse's station to ask how Mrs. Trent was doing and was told she was doing well and that it was all right to visit.

As Bill approached the door, out came a familiar, though not so endearing face. It was Roy Carver's, the attorney who had represented Cassie in their divorce. His presence made Bill nervous. Ambulance chaser! He knew Roy could be very shrewd, and even the most gentle and forgiving of victims could turn rabidly litigious after a little coaxing from this attorney.

—Why, you're a lucky son-of-a-bitch!, said Carver, stopped in his tracks at the sight of Bill in his path, rocking on his heels like a puffed-up cock.

Bill stared, unblinking, waiting for him to continue while Roy looked Bill over with an "I-know-something-you-don't-know" smile, nodding like an imbecile.

—Carver . . .

There was animus in his tone as Roy Carver muttered, —Some people just don't see the opportunities.

—What the fuck—?

—Yeah, that's what I said, too.

—What the—?

—You repeat yourself.

—You got something to say to me, Carver, spit it out.

—Yeah, I got lots to say, but this ain't the time or place for me to—

—Want to bring it outside, huh? That what you want?

—Nothin' I'd like better right now, Billy-goat. Get a hold on! After what you did.

—You think I wanted to run her down?

—I didn't say that—

—And I wasn't drunk, if that's what you're thinking.

—Nah, I don't think you intentionally—

—I wasn't drunk.

—I know. I read the police reports. Just under the limit.

—Get the fuck out of my way.

Roy shook his head mockingly as he walked away. Then, as he turned toward the elevators he said, —It really is funny . . . hard to believe. Don't know why I'm not laughing.

Bill, angry from the confrontation, perplexed by the dubious insinuations and standing ready for a fight from the adrenaline rush that stiffened his stance and tightened his hands into fists, unraveled and flexed his tingling fingers. He needed a few moments to compose himself before he entered the hospital room.

Ariel Trent was sitting up in the hospital bed, her eyes closed, a book open and face-down on the pillow that was propped on her lap. The sunlight illuminated her pale face and gave meaning to the expression, "fiery red hair." The woman seemed to transform each time he saw her in a new light. Now, in spite of the relative stillness of her form, there was an element of patrician beauty about her where yesterday there was only fragility. Bill wondered who lived within that chameleon exterior.

She opened her eyes and turned to Bill. Her eyes were large and the color of moss. A smile washed over her lips and color rushed to her cheeks. Whatever trepidation he may have harbored after seeing Roy Carver vanished at the sight of her smile. It had been a long time since anyone had greeted him with the kind of welcome that can be had from a thing as simple as a radiant smile.

What quality did this woman possess that could dispel his fear with just the gesture of a smile? He felt a little foolish, considering that he might be reading greater meaning into his impressions of the woman, sensing things that did not exist anywhere but in his own imagination, things he *wanted* to believe existed in her. Was his subconscious building a fantasy to further bind him to her because of the guilt he felt in causing her present condition?

He spent a good part of the day, after leaving the hospital, thinking about it. There was no time to ponder anything that was not in immediate response to her questions.

—You're here. How lovely to see you!

—How are you feeling this morning?

—Like I got hit by a car.

Prompted by Bill's expression of distress, she let out a bark of a laugh. Then she clutched at the bed guard and said, —You should see the look on your face. *Owww!* that hurts, but the laugh was worth the pain.

—I aim to please, was all he could think to say.

—Forgive me! I'm getting restless just lying around here. The book Amy was kind enough to bring me was the one on my bedstand. It's only good to bore you to sleep.

—What is it you're reading?

—*Lucy.* They found the bones, and she's quite old. What more can be said?

—Oh, the primate. . . .

—I suppose you could call her that. She made a little smirk, and then said. —You see, I am restless. It should be a fascinating read, but not today or at night, for that matter. You know, Little Eva is a lot smarter than Lucy probably was. How is my girl?

—She romped in the snow this morning at the Haley Farm.

—You let her loose?

Her eyes were big, and Bill thought she disapproved. —I hope you don't mind? She came back when I—

—It's fine! I'm glad you did. She hadn't had a good run in a couple of days before you and I, uh, met. Did she do her "crazy run"? You know, where she—

—Runs around in wide circles laying low to the ground like a racehorse? Yes! She loves the snow.

—Thank you.

—What for?

—For taking care of her, for letting her play in the snow.

—I like dogs. I like her.

Bill felt secure again, and decided to "screw his courage to that sticking place."

—I just saw Roy Carver.

—Yes. He was just here.

She had only offered the obvious, so Bill probed further for the reason for his visit.

—I didn't know you knew him.

—I didn't know you knew him, either.

—Yes . . . professionally.

—Oh, uh-huh.

Then, before he could think of another approach, she said, —Sit down, Bill, and in the famous words of

Rick's in *Casablanca*, "Who are you really and what were you before? What did you do and what did you think?"

The lightness of tone, the slight knitting of brows and the direct look into his eyes were enough to say that Roy was now out of the conversation.

He took the armchair next to her bed, and asked where to begin.

—All right. Well, go backwards, from the moment we "ran into each other."

Bill said he had never thought of looking at life in reverse, and she said, —It gives one a new perspective.

—I'm thirty-eight years old. I work as a publicist for the firm of Harris & Reynolds, here in Linden Falls. I have been divorced for about a year and a half, before which I was married for five years, before which I worked as a reporter for the *Gazette*, after getting a degree in journalism at Columbia, after graduating from High School, Junior High, and elementary schools. I was an Air Force brat—

—Now tell me *who* traveled that path? she asked, her eyes intent on his.

—I'm not sure what—?

Bill looked at the space above her head as if to pull an answer out of the air. She waited for him to find meaning in her words.

He looked at her and laughed.

—I wonder sometimes myself.

She let him off the hook.

—Family?

—My parents dead, a couple of years.

—Siblings?

—Brother Samuel, sister Suzanne. Both dead.

He was relieved she didn't say she was sorry or ask for particulars. He remembered and shifted the conversation in another direction.

—I have your—

He removed the pendant out of his coat pocket and handed it to her. She regarded it with a gentle smile, and Bill was about to help her place it over her head when the ribbon looped over the IV line in her arm.

—It's not very practical for me to wear here. Would you keep it for me?

—Are you sure?

—Yes. Then, after a moment of shyness, she asked, —Did you happen to look inside the shell?

Bill couldn't lie; she'd see it in his face.

—I did open it. A photo fell out, and a folded-up piece of paper that looked like a letter. I didn't read it. I thought it might be personal.

—It is.

She fell deep into thought, and Bill could see flashes of emotion, a melancholy nipping her mouth, her brow. Then she turned and said, —It's all right if you did. I am no longer shy about these things.

Bill nodded, but said nothing, returning the necklace to his coat, and as he was doing so she sank on the pillow and lowered the head of the bed by pushing the control button at her side.

—I'm very tired, she said, closing her eyes with a little frown. —I'm sorry. Forgive me if I go to sleep.

He took the cue and said, "Good-bye." She thanked him, and then, as he started to leave her bedside, she reached out to him and called his name.

Bill took her hand, and asked if there was anything she needed: a good book, perhaps, some crossword puzzles, magazines? She stopped him with a shake of her head.

—I don't want you to let what has happened, the accident, my being here, make you feel you have to do anything. I don't want to be the cause of pain in your life. Do you understand what I'm saying? There is nothing to do to make up for anything. What happened just happened. I do not hold you responsible. She squeezed his hand and continued: —Neither of us need bear that burden.

Bill smiled and then started to lean over to kiss her brow. He patted her hand instead.

—Sleep well, and get better. I'll see you tomorrow. And then he left.

"... the river was an ancient valley of his being, and everything that came from its waters was intolerably beautiful."

Raintree County

FIVE

Ariella and William

It was not surprising that there would be a mutual attraction between Ariel and William. Men never would think to compete with her, and, for the first time since Teddy's death, she found another intellect that would challenge her own.

Ariel saw much of herself in William. Where she had repressed her Round Table Wit for fear of unintentionally hurting the witless, he had exercised his ability and didn't care if he was thought a smart-ass.

—I am a smart-ass! What's the problem with finding humor in the mundane? If Roger Harris is too stupid to realize I just insulted him, all the better. The people who got the joke were the ones I was hoping to please! And you did giggle, I saw you!

There were times that he'd miscalculate the wielding of that rapier wit and he'd become penitent and humble. Most of the time, he instinctively knew when and with whom not to flex his talent for juxtaposing the language. And that was what Ariel found so endearing about William: that sensitivity and kindness and fair-play toward others.

She once told him he was a compassionate human being, and he objected fiercely.

—What's compassion? People wallow in "their compassion." The real test in determining who is a compassionate human being is to ask, do they *do* anything about the injustices they rattle on about? If it's all *tsk-tsk*, then what they *feel* is an exercise in self-indulgence, nothing more. I can't say that I'm compassionate. Only when you take *action*, apply an effective *solution* can empathy become compassion; and only a few times in my life have I done that. If people would intelligently choose what is worth becoming compassionate about, from what is just plain silly, and *think* about the consequences their "outrage" might cause, the truly important problems of the world *might* be solved.

—Put your money where your mouth is?

William looked daggers at her, and then suppressing a smile, said, —I do go on, don't I?

—What's a friend for, but to *endure* the rantings of a friend?

—Nobody listens to me when I tell them the real problems of the world are most of the short-sighted people who live in it!

—Are you quite done?

—Quite.

The great joy of their friendship was that each had found in the other a kindred spirit. They may have disagreed on almost everything, but they each possessed a thirst for knowledge of the world around them and an insatiable curiosity for understanding why people did what they did. Their friendship blossomed as each began to unravel the other's tangled life, drawing each other out, in a climate that was temperate and accepting, and without the need to protect themselves, or the other, for fear of censure. Sharing their thoughts and observations about anything and everything was easy because of the security each felt in being accepted without condition. As each viewed the other as having radical and conflicting political and social philosophies, they locked horns more often than not. But that only worked to force each other to consider the strength of their beliefs, and their heated arguments always ended with a laugh and a teasing jab. Each found no fault in the other, except that one was a Conservative Republican and the other a Liberal Democrat. It was the stuff of many jokes between them.

They thrived on the battles, and each learned from, as much as they taught, the other. They'd feel a drug-like euphoria that began with, and continued long after, the verbal sparring had ended. They sought out each other's company as often as they could, unconsciously returning to the warm cocoon of their friendship.

Ariel's husband, John, and Susan, William's wife and the mother of his two children, Timothy and Elizabeth, did not appear threatened by their closeness. On the contrary, each was relieved that they no longer carried the burden of trying to keep up with their often insufferable spouses. Ariel and William were much more pleasant and upbeat to be around when, after an hour in each other's company, they would tackle the duties of their own households with renewed energy.

Their friendship fostered in each self-confidence. Ariel was composing, again, for the first time in fifteen years. For the first time since college, William's creative intellect was challenged, and he'd revel in new ideas and in finding the most effective ways to express them through his playwriting. For the first time ever, he completed a work for the stage that he felt was worthy of production, and that, along with Ariel's encouragement and unbridled happiness for him, inspired the enthusiasm he needed to see it produced. He would have liked to have dedicated the work to Ariel, but thought it was appropriate to dedicate it "to Susan, who has endured the years preparing for the time I was ready to write this play." When Susan said she had nothing to do with his writing of it, it was Ariel who had been his editor and sounding-board, he said, very quietly. —But, you are my wife. . . .

He had spoken too quietly, and Susan intuited a sense of resignation in his words. It was a feeling that troubled her briefly, and she didn't understand why it had hit a nerve, but it had.

William, Ariel, and John were working together on a musical for the Linden Falls Community Players. William was hired as the director of the production, which had been plagued with problems from its inception. The opening was in three days. The stage crew had failed to complete the sets and was still painting the flats behind the actors. The leading lady had laryngitis and the leading man still hadn't learned his lines. One of the supporting actors continually missed his entrance cue. The actor, a retired professor of literature named Henry Wallingford, was a difficult person to deal with, if a competent amateur. He had given various excuses for the physical inability to enter the stage from the wings in a timely manner, which William tried to solve. William knew he was working with amateurs and he did not want to undermine what little confidence this man had.

Just at the moment when William knew how to make it all work, John yelled out with a suggestion that had already been attempted several evenings earlier, when he had not been called to rehearsal. Frustrated with all the interruptions, and trying to retain a level of professionalism with his mostly amateur cast, William dismissed John's comment with a sharp retort.

—They wouldn't have hired me to direct if that was my solution.

Ariel touched John's sleeve before he could respond churlishly to William's retort, whispering at his ear that the idea had not worked when they tried it earlier.

Two hours later, on the drive home, John began a review of all the qualities he disliked in William. Ariel agreed that William often sounded officious and could be curt in his responses. But she saw humor in her friend's apparent arrogance, which shone through only when he was seriously focused at accomplishing a task at hand.

—He just tells it as it is, she said.

—Who does he think he is? yelled John, shifting from acrimonious to a mean-spirited tirade that continued on for a mile.

—You should never have interfered with William's direction of the show. You should have called him aside to offer your solution. Anyway, Henry Wallingsford is a stubborn old coot, tripping over everybody on stage, you know the man. Who wouldn't be at wit's end directing the moron?

—I don't want to work with William anymore.

—That's not for you to—is this all about your hurt feelings, John? William told you to mind your own business in so many words and you—

—He thinks he knows everything!

—Maybe he does! Maybe he knows better than you!

—Who the fuck does he think he is?

—You've said that already, and I'm getting tired of your rant.

She failed to see John's fear, for her own.

In the light of a streetlamp when they stopped at a traffic signal, John turned to look at his wife and was met by her stony countenance. If he hadn't seen the tear that plummeted and splashed on her skirt, he would have thought their argument was just another in a series wrought over the years in any typical marriage.

In that moment John became afraid, profoundly afraid for the first time in the last ten years of their marriage. Not since the episode ten years prior, when Ariel discovered his stash of empty bottles, did he fear losing her. Even back then, when the children were babies, he hadn't known the dread he was suddenly experiencing on that dark drive home.

"The noblest love is the intense awareness of another being."
Raintree County

SIX

Bill

Amy said that Ariel's favorite flowers were tulips, and she thought she liked roses, too, not the long-stemmed variety, but the pale-pink-and-cream ones (she didn't know their name) that grew over the arbor in the summer. Bill sent tulips.

She loved classical music. Ariel Trent had studied to be a concert pianist. Her favorite composers? Amy didn't know; she was into Pop. Bill grabbed a couple of CDs from his collection: Brendel's Beethoven sonatas, the Ravel, and Debussy. She might enjoy the Schubert chamber quartets, and the Brahms violin concerto, too, so those were added to the portable CD pouch. With the portable CD player he added the January copy of *The Smithsonian* and a Sue Grafton Alphabet Mystery novel.

Amy said she was pretty sure Ariel loved dark chocolate and fresh fruit, and would probably give anything for a decent cup of coffee. So after Bill spent part of the afternoon doing laundry he stopped at the supermarket and bought pears, oranges, seedless grapes, apples, and a box of Pepperidge Farm cookies to bring the patient. He stopped at the Lindt Chocolate outlet for a bag of truffles, then to the wicker furniture outlet to find the right basket to put treats in. The last stop was Starbucks for coffee.

Arial was staring out the window at the darkening sky. She looked up at with a forlorn expression, and her trouble communicated to him. Bill said a cheery "Hello!," and the greeting broke the mood.

—I was on my way to town, so I thought I'd stop by, since I was passing the hospital, anyway. I went shopping this afternoon, too. Thought you might like a couple of things you won't get here.

—Real coffee!

—Is it all right to have it?

—I don't give a shit if it's all right. They took my spleen; they won't take my coffee, too.

The mild profanity took him by surprise and he choked back a chuckle.

The nurse came into the room, and she said there was nothing Mrs. Trent couldn't eat—except the hospital food if she was willing to share that luscious chocolate.

The look on Ariel Trent's face as she opened the bag of truffles was pure pleasure. She offered the bag to Bill and the nurse, then unwrapped one for herself, taking tiny bites of it, closing her eyes as she savored the flavor. Then, she'd sip the coffee and he could hear her sigh. He couldn't remember ever feeling such pleasure just watching someone eat. He felt happy.

Bill took out the CD player and the selection of music. She scrutinized the CD selection, her face serious, and at first Bill thought she was thinking he hadn't made very interesting choices, and was surprised when she looked up and said, —How did you know this?

—Know?

—This music. The music you brought?

—Amy mentioned that you liked classical, so I picked a few from my collection for you to listen to until you get home.

—She didn't say anything about the Debussy? Or Ravel?

—She didn't know. She doesn't like classical music. Have I done something?

—No! Oh, God, I'm sorry. It's just—you couldn't have chosen better.

—Is there something else you'd like to hear?

—This is just lovely, just *fine*.

She asked if he would close the blinds. Bill did so, and when he turned back toward her she was wiping her eyes.

Had he inadvertently hit a nerve in her, causing all kinds of emotions to rise to the surface from deep within her? Was he doing too much, trying to please her, to be nice, to have her like him, to earn her forgiveness? Did she think he was only acting through guilt, when he was reaching out in friendship? One thing he felt certain of was that he was making her situation more difficult through his misguided efforts. He felt selfish and decided that whatever his true motivations were, he should not continue imposing his presence on her. He excused himself by saying he had to meet a friend for dinner, and then drove home to have dinner with the dog.

As he entered his dark house, a black shadow lunged at him, knocking him and the bag to the floor.

The dog pounced, noisily licking Bill's face and ears.

—Hello, Dog Breath!

The greeting only increased her fervor to nuzzle and playfully nip at him. It was nice to feel so welcome.

When she allowed Bill to stand he took the groceries to the kitchen, she was always at his heels, from counter to cabinet to refrigerator, the clicking of her toenails on the floor tiles oddly comforting.

He filled her food dish, popped a boxed dinner into the microwave, poured the remains of a bottle of burgundy into a glass, and then took Ariel Trent's necklace out of his pocket and put it on the dinette table.

He sat down and sipped the wine, looking at the seashell while the microwave oven hummed in the background and Little Eva ravenously devoured her food.

He was a little leery of opening the latch, for reasons that were uncertain just then. First he had to sort out his motivations, his real intentions toward Mrs. Trent. To open the locket, to read the letter, could reveal more about the woman than he had a right to know. Was he about to open a Pandora's Box that would help to sort out his feelings, or would the contents only serve to confuse him more? Even though she had said he could read the letter, he knew from the salutation he had read the first time he unfolded the paper, that it was personal and a remembrance of an important event in her life.

The microwave buzzed, he dished the pasta primavera onto a plate, and sat down to eat.

He didn't recall tasting the food, or finishing the wine, but after a while noticed the empty plate and wine glass.

Little Eva pawed at his leg to draw attention. Once she had, she left the room and ran to the front door. Bill took the necklace from off the table and slipped it into his pocket.

After the walk, they settled in the living-room: Man channel surfing in recliner; Dog, content to chew a soup bone.

He was awoken by the telephone ringing. *60 Minutes* was over and *Touched by an Angel* was on the screen. He reached for the phone and said, "Hello." A woman's voice responded in kind.

—Ariel?

—Who's Ariel? said Marge, surprised, and then an edge to her voice. —This is Margie. Were you expecting someone else?

Bill felt drugged, and was still tunneling out of the deep sleep he had drifted into.

—Are you there?

—Marge . . . Hi.

—Are you—are you alone?

—Yes! I'm alone, except for Little Eva.

—Eva? Little Eva?

—A dog. Long story.

—It's nine o'clock, and I thought we agreed you'd be over at eight.

—*Ohhh*. I fell asleep. I'm sorry, Marge.

—So, are you planning to come see me?

—Yes! I'll be over soon. I just need to wake up. I'll be over.

Bill got out of the chair, trying not to disturb the dog lying partially under the footrest, and went to the bathroom to splash cold water on his face. The exhaustion was reaction to the events of the weekend, he told himself while looking into the mirror and noting the dark circles under his eyes.

He brushed his teeth and combed his hair, and when he took one final look he saw that he was growing old, and the reality of that fact was daunting.

He moved closer to the mirror, to better scrutinize his reflection. Wasn't it only last week that he was young? The blond hair was infiltrated with paler strands. White.

Crow's feet and the laugh lines appeared to have gotten deeper, the jowls thicker and leathery.

I'm scaring myself, he thought. Aside from being tired, which made him look haggard, he hadn't aged so much in just a couple of days. It was all in his imagination. My eyes are still blue, the skin on my face still tight, and my body, aside from a lifelong struggle to avoid the family beer-gut, still muscular. I am considered an attractive if not a good-looking man, he reassured himself.

He decided not to shave, leaving thoughts of imminent deterioration and the bathroom, to drive to Marge's apartment six miles toward town.

Marge had created a romantic atmosphere for their reunion, and greeted Bill with a passionate kiss. She looked very beautiful in her red-silk kimono that stopped mid-thigh to reveal her lovely legs, thought Bill, as she opened the flaps of his coat, pushing her hands up into his sleeves at the shoulders, so that the coat fell off to the floor.

Her dark-brown hair smelled clean and felt silky against his face, and he thought, this is what I like best about her: The way she can be so soft and pliable under my embrace.

—I missed you, he said because he had missed the softness of her.

—Good! I missed you, Bumpy. Her hands squeezed his butt and there was a glint in her eyes. Bill read her thoughts.

But the look changed as she brought her hands around to his belt buckle.

—Whattcha got in your pocket, Big Boy?

—What? he laughed, thinking she was aiming at a sexual joke of the "Is that a pistol in your pocket, or are you just glad to see me?" variety. When she squeezed his right pants pocket he remembered the seashell.

—Oh, that, he said, suddenly wanting to keep the events of the past days to himself, especially the necklace. —Fix me a drink and I'll tell you all about it.

—It's not a growth of some sort, she giggled, —a tumor that's developed since I left town?

She was reaching into his pocket, and Bill grabbed her wrist. He brought her hand to his lips for a kiss in an attempt to soften the gesture.

—Fix me a drink and I'll tell you all about it.

—Why don't you show me what it is?

It was inevitable, he knew then. She had discovered it, and so he removed it from his pocket. When she raised her hand to take it, Bill tightened his palm around it.

—Is it for me? Disappointment in her tone.

She thought the piece cheap, and preferred jewelry set with precious stones. Bill knew her taste, and a seashell on a ribbon wasn't it.

—It belongs to someone, so I can't give it to you.

Cheap or not, she wanted it, if only because it belonged to some other woman.

They sat in the candle-lit living-room with Marge curled up next to him on the sofa. He recapped the events of the past few days quickly and devoid of feeling. Marge cooed, "poor baby" here, and "oh, Bumpy" there. He omitted a lot: the visit that afternoon bearing gifts of chocolate and fruit and music; the visit to Mrs. Trent's home, and the permission she gave to read what was in the locket.

Bill saw it coming a second before she said it.

—Well, aren't you going to open it, see what's inside?

—No. I'm going to keep it for her as she asked, along with her dog, until she gets released from the hospital.

—But, aren't you just a little curious?

—I suppose. But, it is not for me to see.

—Maybe she's got a stash of grass in it.

—I don't think she's the type.

—She lives in that old church, doesn't she? She was out walking alone in the snow at the stroke of midnight on New Year's Eve. Sounds Bohemian to me.

—Well, whatever she is, is her concern. As far as opening the locket, I'm not.

—Well, I will, then!

She reached over to take it, and Bill reacted with a push that was a little too hard.

—*Ouch!* she yelped. —What's the big deal that you have to be so rough?

She moved back to the far end of the sofa, and when Bill reached over, to make light of it, to pretend he was only playing, to tickle her, she got up and walked across the room.

Before there were words, Bill tried to change the subject.

—How is your mother doing? Is the therapy doing her any good?

It took a few more stilted replies to his rather forced questions before they were able to settle into a comfortable discussion about her trip. After another twenty minutes, Bill said he had to get back home. Marge's face set in a frown.

—I was hoping you could spend the night.

—Can't. I have a dog to walk, and a meeting with Tom Reynolds in the morning.

—Yeah, I understand, she mumbled, her eyes cast to the floor as she spoke. She didn't understand, couldn't understand what was going on inside him, but he spoke the required words, anyway.

—So, when can we get together this week?

—Not for a day or so. Want to try for Thursday night? If you like we can drive down to the Chateau and make up for tonight's missed dinner. Okay?

—Thursday? It sounds all right. I have to see what's happening at work. I'll call you if it's not good, all right?

They kissed briefly and said goodnight.

Bill watched the late news in an effort to unwind from the visit with Marge, and then went into the bedroom to throw off his clothing, and then himself into bed.

He placed the necklace on the night-table, propped the bed pillows, got under the covers, and sat up to read. He knew he wouldn't be able to concentrate on the book he was currently reading until he dealt with the contents of the seashell.

As Bill opened the catch, he was aware that he was opening a door. To where, he didn't know. But he told himself that whatever was written had nothing to do with him, and therefore should have no effect on him. I'm being silly, he thought, making too much of the whole thing.

He took out the photo and looked at the likeness of the man. It was the same blond fellow in the photo on the piano at the old Quaker Meeting House. He set the photo aside and unfolded the paper, a piece of lined looseleaf paper, and began reading.

1:30 pm
My Darling Gypsyheart!

I miss you! They're taking me downstairs in about ten minutes. One of us'll undoubtedly be

back before the other. In either case, let's not let
too many miles gather between us while we wait...
186,000 a second is far more than enough.

I love you.

W

He reread the letter several times, because he
didn't understand the reference to the distance between
them in terms of the 186,000 miles a second. Maybe
Ariel would explain it one day.

He looked closely at the photograph. The man was
indeed W, of the letter, and the initial stood for William.
Ariel was "Gypsyheart." Where William was being taken,
Bill could only guess. Could it be to a prison?

And then it hit Bill: On the night of the accident,
she had called him by name. But it wasn't himself that
she was calling out to! The signature initial W of this
letter stood for William! Another man named William.
Bill happened to have blond hair and blue eyes, just
like the man in the photograph. They both shared that
Northern European look. During those moments after the
trauma, Ariel Trent believed that Bill was her William.

Was William a long lost love? Was he Mr. Trent?
Was he alive or dead? If he was alive, where was he now
that she needed him?

He had no answers to the questions, but had a
peculiar sort of feeling, the kind you have when you've
missed out on something important and you can't get
it back.

After returning the photo and the letter back into
the shell and turning off the light, Bill wondered why

Ariel and William were apart. Maybe Amy knew the reason. It was too late to call her at that hour, though.

Little Eva slinked quietly into the room and then up on the bed, stretching out next to him, a lick on his chin, a pat in return to her head, and she went to sleep.

Bill laid awake thinking, his mind racing, searching for answers and finding none. Emotions he could not give a name to were scratching at his heart.

He'd had the feeling before, sometime, somewhere. William's frozen image in the photo played in his mind's eye. What did he have that Ariel should love him? She must have loved him or she wouldn't carry his likeness and his letter. He was pleasant looking, but not what anybody would call handsome. Not as good looking as me.

Not as good looking as me.

This is what jealousy feels like?!

Is it because I am lonely and wish I had a woman who would wear my photo close to her heart? That I could write a letter to someone with the kind of simple poetry that expressed my love? That I've missed knowing true love in my life?

He hated himself for the self-admission. Hadn't he been content that past year to be alone, to yearn for no one, to need no one, to want nothing but peace and a little pleasure, unencumbered by the demands of commitments? It was the first freedom he'd known since before he married Cassie.

Marge. What to do about Marge?

When they were together—Hell! When she would just call him on the phone, he'd feel cornered, put on the defensive, and he would have to edit his words and monitor his responses while trying to read the subtext of her words.

He didn't love Marge. Hell! He didn't even like her!

Bill had to admit, it was the sex, and it was easier to stay with her than to be alone.

But the truth was, even with Marge he was alone.

But it was unfair to Marge. Hell! It's unfair to me! Why was he trying to make it work with her? Why was he pretending? Marge was suffocating him. He had to get out. He had to end it before it became more difficult to get out.

That decided, Bill was able to settle down to sleep. A sleep troubled by visions of Marge and Ariel and William.

The accident was a front-page news item in the local section of the *Post*. It was all but waved at his face when he walked into the office.

Long faces met his, displaying concern, but beneath the knit brows and the pressed lips there was a glint of unadulterated curiosity for the details, and in the subtext of their carefully worded questions it was apparent: to find him at fault.

Bill closed the door to his office. He had a presentation that afternoon, and after calling around for estimates for the car's repairs and speaking with the insurance agent, he settled down to review the strategy for the firm's new client.

He hadn't got very far when Tom Reynolds walked in through the door.

—You all right, Bill? I heard—

—Fine! he said, surprised. Tom didn't usually come into Bill's office. Bill was usually summoned to his.

Tom was a big man of fifty-five years. Not so much fat as bulky. No matter what he wore he looked like an undertaker, with his thick, black hair and brows and square face. But when he wore a smile it was as if he'd just announced the happy news to the family that the corpse had revived and could return home at once. If it were not for his winning smile that transformed his face, no one would have done business with him, thought Bill, who admired his boss's intelligence. Tom's success was in knowing how to talk to just about anybody about anything, and whether he cared or didn't give a damn, he instinctively knew how to make a person believe he held their friendship sacred. In a crowded room, if he looked your way, you felt he was there only for your company. Bill worked for Tom for the last six years, and still Bill didn't know much about what Tom Reynolds really believed in, what he really thought about any issue, or anybody, for that matter. Tom revealed himself to nobody. At least, nobody Bill knew. Bill wondered if his wife, Irene, really knew him.

—I won't ask you how the weekend went. I'm sure you've seen too many long faces since you got here. But do you still want to meet with Waterston this afternoon?

—Why not? I'm all right, really.

—Bill . . .

The countenance of the undertaker returned, as he took a seat.

—If you need a couple of days, I don't see a problem. You have vacation time coming, and after this week, if Waterston likes the campaign, I can put Bob on it.

Bill wasn't about to hand his project over to Bob.

—That's very considerate of you, Tom. You know, I hadn't thought about asking. I had planned the vacation at the end of February—

—So take that, and take a couple of weeks, now, too. I've worked you hard, Bill. Don't think I haven't noticed what you do for our firm. I know you've been through a lot this past year, and now, what happened can't be helping.

Was he trying to get rid of me? The thought tripped over Bill's mind like a skipping stone on a stream, then quickly sank to the bottom.

—Let's do today and see what happens, if that's all right with you.

Tom's smile met Bill's as he rose from the chair and reached across to slug Bill's shoulder. As they walked to the door, Bill handed Tom a copy of the proposal and some accompanying reports for him to peruse before the two o'clock meeting.

There was no meeting that afternoon. Bill was told that Waterston canceled before noon. He did not reschedule, either. Tom didn't appear concerned, though Bill thought he should be. They didn't want to lose this client to a firm in Albany, Bill said, feeling the urgency to get to the reason for the cancellation. Tom said it was a family emergency, not to worry about it. Bill worried.

It was again suggested Bill take a couple of weeks off, and when Bill mentioned the project, Tom said he'd call when things were set up for a meeting.

It was early afternoon by the time Bill left the office. Hungry, he stopped at Sonny's Pantry for one of Sonny Molineri's overstuffed sandwiches. Sonny wasn't behind the counter, but his wife, Lilly, was, and she was busy taking a telephone order. Bill waved "Hello," and she flashed a smile. He waited, looking around the homey little cafe, brightly decorated with sky-blue gingham tablecloths and crisply starched gingham curtains. It had the clean, homey feeling of a seaside Cape Cod cottage on a summer's day: airy and welcoming. Their noontime rush was over, and for the first time in a long time, Bill wasn't eating lunch on the run. So instead of taking out his favorite, a roast pork with roasted red peppers between thick slices of Sonny's homemade bread, Bill took a table near the window.

He grabbed a copy of the *Post* left on a chair nearby. He hadn't looked at the paper that morning, hadn't wanted to, since he had been a little annoyed that everybody in the office knew what had happened over the New Year, and his reactions to their probing had been enough to deal with. As Bill started to read the article on the first page of the local section, he was glad he hadn't seen it while in the office. It would have put him on the defensive.

The details were damning. It said that Bill had left a New Year's Eve party and was on his way to another when he hit Mrs. Trent and her dog, and that the police had suspected he was driving under the influence. The reporter stated that Bill worked for the public relations firm of Harris & Reynolds, and when telephoned by the paper's reporter, Bill had replied with, "No comment."

But what checked his rising blood pressure was the final line, which read: "Ariel Trent suffered life-threatening injuries, but is expected to survive." It was the truth. Whatever may have been distorted earlier in the piece, when Bill read those words of truth put so succinctly, he no longer felt anger toward the reporter, but toward himself for feeling the insult to him predominated over Ariel Trent's injury.

Sonny suddenly appeared at the table.

—Billy! What's it to be today?

—I think I'll try something new. What have you got that's new?

—Everything on the menu is new to you. All you ever order is the pork and peppers!

Sonny was right, and Bill had to chuckle. In all the years Bill had been coming in or calling for takeout delivery, the only thing he ever ordered was the pork.

Bill's smile cued Sonny's, making the skin on café proprietor's bald head crease as his eyebrows lifted to slanted accents.

He had known Sonny a couple of years before he opened his café. He taught culinary arts at the community college, and when Bill was at the paper he was assigned to do a human-interest story on career options for college alternatives. Sonny Molineri's cooking class was featured.

Bill liked his pudgy, open face, the hearty laugh that would turn his sallow complexion red, and how he encouraged his students to find joy in the art of cooking. When he said, "If food is prepared with love, it will always come out delicious," everyone believed him. He talked about how his mother and grandmother cooked in Italy, and later, when they emigrated to the States, the joy of Sunday afternoons when the big meal was prepared after church. "A great chef is immortal! Even after you die, people will remember you for what you served at the table. When I cook stuffed leg of lamb, I can smell and taste Mama's presence in the room."

—Billy, do you want to try, maybe, the lobster salad, or maybe the ham with apple slices?

—The lobster salad sounds good. A chocolate shake, too.

—Lilly! Lobster salad and chocolate shake for Billy, he shouted across to the serving counter. Then, he turned back toward Bill with a more serious expression.

—I know you had a bad time. What you reading that piece of crap for? I thought you left the newspaper because it was a rag.

—Thanks for reminding me of the reason, Sonny. Bill sighed, ran fingers through his hair, and looked up at him. —They've got this all distorted, Sonny.

—I figured as much, he said with a shrug.

—To explain would only make me look, you know, like I *was* drunk.

—Okay, so you weren't. The police know that, right?

—Yes.

—So, that's that.

—She's such a lovely person, you know?

—Yeah, I know, he said with the weight of sadness.

—You know Ariel Trent?

—I've lived here for thirty-five years. When you live in a place that long you meet a lot of people. I know Ariel. Yes. I know her.

Bill motioned for him to sit in the chair opposite his, and he did so.

He asked if he could tell him anything about Ariel, but he seemed reluctant to speak, except to say that she was a good woman, and those who knew the real Ariel would say so, too. The way he stated it led Bill to believe that there were people who didn't think she was such a good person. Bill respected Sonny's reticence to speak about her. He was not a gossip and Bill liked him for protecting her privacy. Still, Bill needed to find out more about her. He decided to trust Sonny with the details covering the accident and the events of subsequent days.

—She has a quality about her, doesn't she?

—Yes, and I can't put it into words exactly. She's . . . compelling, I guess.

—She's either adored or hated. Wait, let me rephrase that. She is hated by those who fear her. Beautiful women hold a certain amount of power, you know, and that frightens some people.

—I don't understand. Why would anyone fear her?

—She called you William, *hmm?*

—Who was he?

—He was a lot of things. But mostly, he was the grand passion of her life.

—She thought I was him?

—And she looked at you as she might have looked upon him, right? With those big eyes of hers.

—Yes, I think so.

—And how did that make you feel?

—What do you mean? I thought she was hallucinating, I thought—

—No, Billy. When she looked at you thinking you were William, how did it make you feel?

—I don't . . . know. Confused, I guess.

He smiled knowingly, and Bill wondered if Sonny thought he was avoiding some underlying truth in his stuttered response. What was Sonny trying to pry out by asking how he felt? It would take time for his words to play back in his memory, time and events to follow that would help Bill to know what Sonny already knew about him.

—Who was William? Bill asked his most pressing question.

—William? Why William Trent was . . . *everything* to her. William was her second husband. When I first met Ariel she was married to John Rodgers. But William was the great love of her life. Dead.

Lilly brought the sandwich and shake, and the depth of conversation resurfaced to more shallow waters.

When Bill left the café a half-hour later, he was carrying a box containing a lobster sandwich, assorted Italian pastries, and a large container of dark-roast coffee to deliver to Ariel at the hospital, and carrying away no more real insight about the woman than when he entered. Lilly handed Bill an envelope with Ariel's name he was to give to her, too. It was a card.

The Molineris are like that: thoughtful. Bill knew that if he hadn't stopped by for lunch, they would have delivered something to her hospital room. And it had nothing to do with good business. If anybody was in need or distress, they'd show their concern. Bill remembered how they provided for a family whose house suffered a fire. The Molineris provided food for weeks, and in doing so shamed other merchants in the area into donating goods and services to help the single mother and her three kids recover from the loss.

It struck Bill as he walked to the car that he felt better for having stopped at the café, and he wished that he could be closer to the couple, able to know more about them and their lives, share their home on an occasional evening for dinner and the ease of their company.

Bill had no family left, just a cousin he rarely saw. In the past eight years since his parents died in the automobile crash while vacationing in France, he had missed the warmth of familial love. His parents weren't overtly affectionate; his mother more than his father, perhaps, whose show of affection was a handshake or a pat on the back. But they had been there, from conception and into his adult years, even if during the latter, only in the background scenery of his life. They had been there, they had existed, and it was enough to know they loved him. The Molineris made him remember and brought a painful longing up from the depths of his heart.

So, with the package on the passenger seat of the car, Bill had no choice but to pay a call on Ariel Trent.

After the visit of the day before, he had decided to simply call to inquire how she was doing, no more. When she was released from the hospital he might stop by her house to offer his services: walk Little Eva, run errands, take out the garbage, shovel her walk if it snowed again, those kind of neighborly things. The kind of things Amy might do. He'd send no more flowers, he'd not chose her books nor her music. He'd stop pressing for her forgiveness.

She was in the big upholstered chair by the window, free of the IV connections, dressed in her robe, her hair neatly brushed and curling down around her shoulders, and reading the alphabet mystery when Bill walked in. When she looked up and smiled, he was glad that he had come to see her. Eyeing the blue-checkered box with the words "Sonny's Pantry" scrawled on the outside, she put the book down on the bed. Her eyes were full of surprise and curiosity to know what treasure the package contained.

Bill handed her the envelope and watched as she gently opened the sealed flap to remove the card. Her long delicate hands held open the card as her eyes scanned the message inside. A smile parted her lips as she placed it on the windowsill alongside the big bouquet of tulips that sat loosely arranged in a large glass vase.

When her eyes settled on the bouquet, she reached a hand to touch the petals of a vibrantly colored pink one that bowed in an arch in her direction. Bill was glad he had sent them, that he hadn't canceled the order, for they were the only flowers in the room.

They talked as she indulged in half of the lobster sandwich, the other half to be saved for dinner, she asking questions, and Bill trying to find intelligent answers.

Bill liked her directness. From anyone else he would have thought such probing a discomforting intrusion into his private life. But from Ariel Trent there radiated a genuine interest. In only a couple of minutes she knew more of Bill's history than most people. When she asked about why he became a journalist, he answered with what he had never told anyone, let alone himself before.

—I can tell stories. I had nothing to say for myself, though I love to write, so as a journalist I can tell stories lived by other people.

—Why are you in public relations?

—Sometimes I ask myself that very question.

—And what do you do as a writer for the firm?

—I try to express other people's ideas. I try to write convincingly that the ideas of our clients make better sense than those who oppose them. I guess you might say I sell people's points of view.

—Do you agree with them, their projects, their plans, their ideas?

—Not always.

—But you enjoy your work?

—Not always.

—Would you like to one day write your own story?

—It would be nice, but as I said, I haven't found anything compelling to write about.

—Perhaps one day you will.

—To tell you the truth, I don't know that I'd be that good at it.

—When the time comes you'll write it, and if it is compelling to you, you'll have no choice but to tell your story, and if it springs forth from your heart, you will do it well.

—I don't know, but I'll keep a lookout for something compelling.

—One day I will write my story, if I live to do it.

—I'd like to hear that story.

—It's about the final five years of my life.

They were interrupted when a nurse's aide came into the room, half hidden by a bouquet that was so huge there wasn't room on any surface to place it.

Bill was curious about what Ariel had just said, more so about the way she had said it. But she was distracted now and he knew it would have to wait.

She asked the aide to put the arrangement down on the floor and to please hand her the accompanying card to read. She glanced at it and put it on the table next to her bed, her face expressionless, before looking up at Bill.

—I love tulips, she said, turning her attention on his bouquet. They remind me of spring. They're one of my favorite flowers, you know.

Was she deliberately ignoring the fabulous spray of blue and pink and white blooms, the names of which Bill had no idea, for his couple of dozen loose stems? Yes, the tulips were lovely and graceful, but they paled in comparison to the extravagant new arrival.

—Tulips bloom late and don't last more than a few days in our climate, but it's just that very tenderness of their nature that makes them so precious.

The nurse said it was time for Ariel to take a walk, suggesting two trips around the unit. Then, assuming

Bill was going to escort Ariel, she instructed him to take the patient's arm and stay close to the railing.

As they strolled around the unit, nurses and aides smiled or nodded approval and encouragement for Ariel's recovery. Bill felt massive beside her slim body; he was a little over six feet and a hundred and eighty pounds, and she five-and-a-half feet tall. Her hair had been washed; the clean fragrance rose as their shoulders met and he felt the warmth of summer. It shone amber and gold under the fluorescent lighting of the hallway. The wavy texture was an inviting depth of liquidity into which Bill wanted to dive his fingers. He diverted his attention elsewhere as his thoughts were leading him toward dangerous ground. He held her hand and saw that she wore two wedding bands on her ring finger. Simple gold matching bands.

What had been dormant in the primal center of his being, a yearning he had not known existed within him, had been awakened. He wanted to protect and defend her. He'd never felt this sense of responsibility toward a woman before. Women he encountered were self-sufficient and independent. Not to say that Ariel was not, but Bill saw a vulnerability in her that struck a powerful chord in his heart with its fragile beauty. Like the delicate preciousness of the tulip blooms she had spoken of. It moved him in all ways, and what he saw with his eyes closed startled him.

They circled the floor twice and returned to her room, where she thanked him as she got under the bed covers. She was pale, her energy spent, as if a candle flame had been extinguished and all that remained was a ghostly, spent wisp of smoke. Bill thought it was a good time to leave her to her nap.

He stopped at the nurses' station and asked the nurse to write down his telephone number should Ariel need anything or ask for him. It was one more step toward involving himself in her life, but why pretend that he already wasn't?

Bill was glad he had no obligations at work for the next couple of weeks. It gave him time to decide what to do. The downside was that there was too much time to think, to focus on Ariel. He hadn't indulged in fantasies since he was a teenager anxious to explore the possibilities of life. He had learned that dreams usually remain dreams and did not materialize into reality very often. Or, if the dream does materialize, its altered state is less than satisfying in the living. By thirty you learn that. And you learn to take one day at a time for what it's worth, expecting no more than what you've been given.

With the remainder of the afternoon Bill decided to deal with the car's bodywork. The insurance was paying for a rental until the work on the car was completed, so he made arrangements to drop it off at the shop and pick up the rental the next morning.

He then called the police station to inquire if there was anything he needed to know about any charges against him for the accident. The officer who answered must have thought he was nuts; his tone said as much when he hesitated and then asked, —Why? Is there something we should know about? Is this Mr. Davidson?

—Yes, I'm Bill Davidson. I just want to make sure before I write a letter to the *Post* concerning the article they ran this morning.

—Yeah, I gottcha.

—Will the department verify that I was not drunk?

—Listen, Mr. Davidson: Do what you have to do, but we don't verify anything.

—Well, will you tell the *Post* that I passed the sobriety test, if they call?

—Yeah, what's the big deal?

—My reputation in this town, that's what, and possibly my job.

Impatience was building in Bill's voice; if he'd been standing face-to-face talking with the policeman, he might have struck him a blow to the head, he was so frustrated. He felt indignant and he knew he had to change course.

—I'd really appreciate it if you could help by confirming that I passed the tests, Sergeant, should someone call, that is.

There was the raspy intake of air, which Bill hoped indicated concession. Then, —Sure, why not? Tell them to ask for Sergeant MacIntyre, and I'll confirm it.

Bill thanked him, feeling like a wuss for appealing to him when the truth was the truth and he needn't have begged for it, rather, he should have demanded it, but why fight City Hall? He got what he needed out of the man.

He sat down at the computer and ran off a letter to the editor of the *Post* detailing the errors in the article and stating that the Linden Falls Police Department would verify his statements. Bill's intention was to correct, make clear, *not* attack the *Post* for its article. He ended with his very real and heartfelt sadness and sorrow that Mrs. Trent had suffered injury at his hand, and that an accident of this nature has a profound effect on all people involved.

How true his final lines in the letter would strike anyone, he didn't know. How true it was, only Bill could know.

He faxed the letter to the paper. Little Eva was sitting by his side and he realized she hadn't been walked since early that morning.

Bill threw on a jacket and gloves, secured a ski-cap on his head, fetched her leash, and headed for the door. It was snowing again, delicate flakes that clung to the ground. There was an accumulation of a couple of inches, the snow having started while he was writing the letter. It was dusk now, and the light made everything look gray and washed out.

He let Little Eva off the leash for a good run when they reached the cornfield. The dog was in her glory, doing her maniac runs around him, flipping her body through the snow. She swam through the snow, her legs hidden from view in some places where the drifts formed higher banks, then, pointing her nose deep into the drifts, her head buried up to her ears, she sniffed hard for whatever it is that dogs sniff for. She'd raise her dark head and a mask of the white stuff would cling to her face, and she'd not even bother to shake it off before wading on through the next drift. Laughing, Bill once again felt happy watching this simple creature's wild and joyous nature.

There was something potent stirring within him, a volatile mixture of opposing elements, like the heady effects of a new drug, warming his blood with pleasure and at the same time rich with impending danger.

He hadn't known such elation for many years, not since falling in love with Henrietta Liebowitz when he was in the eighth grade, and later at college, when Jessica Damon fell in love with him for thirteen days.

He felt like a teenager, and as Bill ran along the road racing Little Eva back to the house, he found that he was actually breaking his sprint with the occasional skip, kicking up snow.

When they got through the door, he rolled around on the floor wrestling with her, until finally Bill became the submissive animal. She stood over his prone body and he let her lick his face raw.

He was in love with the beautiful Ariella Trent; what could be more wonderful than that?

Ahhh, the intoxication of love!

Eventually, she might come to love me, too, he thought. And that was where the danger was: *What if she doesn't?*

But, he would work to win her love. He wouldn't think about the possibility that she wouldn't.

A dialogue progressed in Bill's head:

If she did love me, would she allow a relationship to develop? How to approach her? He would certainly have to wait to tell her, at least until she was fully recovered, and then there should be a little time for us to be together in more natural conditions: a casual dinner at my place, or maybe I'd bring a video to her home she would enjoy. Then, when we had become friends, when she felt comfortable, without the conventional approach of going out on a date, well, then, there would come the time that I would tell her how I feel. And if I'm lucky, she will tell me she loves me.

But. . . .

What makes me think I possess any of the qualities that she would find lovable?

Bill's stomach suddenly and violently flipped and he could feel his pounding heart rushing blood into his head.

I'm crazy, he told himself. Insane! I'm a nice guy, decent looking, well groomed, educated, literate, but whatever could make me believe a woman like Ariel could love me? There's a generation between us. What could she possibly find in common with me? She is possessed of a gracious and gentle dignity. I'm just a guy, an ordinary everyday shlub. She's way up on the species list compared to me. I'm intelligent and bright and can, when I want to, be charming, yes, but I haven't the culture nor the refinement that she would find attractive.

Bill knew these qualities about her by the way she'd address him and the nurses at the hospital, and by the way Sonny looked when he spoke of her. Bill saw a reverence and sadness, too, flash across Sonny's face. And Bill had learned a little during the short time he moved around her home. Her home was a clear reflection of who she was. Bill had nothing to offer her. She was so individual, complete in herself, unapproachable for the average Joe without some impending emotional disaster in the wake. He would bore her. He would lose himself and gain her contempt. He could see it!

He was building a mystique around her, so he'd give up his foolish fantasy of Ariel returning his love. For Bill feared it would be unrequited. He would be doomed to chasing the unobtainable. She was the rare woman one might see standing still in a crowded room who had no need for the company of others, yet she'd be the one whom people would flock to. There was an aura of tranquility that was so very magnetic that he suspected the calm surface belied a magnetic current beneath.

She was the tall, imperious bloom in a vase filled with common daisies; she, the red that makes white pink!

And you, dear old Bill, are a dull brown.

The telephone rang, ending his hyperbolic soliloquy.

Thinking it a call from the hospital, he answered promptly rather than letting the answering machine take the call.

—You really are something! shouted a rough, masculine voice that Bill couldn't immediately identify. Bill thought it might be the *Post* reporter or somebody from the office.

—Who is this?

—I don't know if you know that I know what you're doing, but I know!

—Jesus! Is this a joke? Who is this! Identify yourself or I'm hanging—

—It's Roy.

—Carver?

—Now you listen to me: I don't know what you've been saying to that woman but—

—What the fuck are you talking about?

—You're *working* Ariel Trent, and I don't like it!

—What do you mean, "working"?

—She's in a very fragile state right now and you're taking advantage of her.

—Hey, buddy, fuck off!

—It's bad enough that she won't sue you.

—You get your rocks off suing people, don't you, you litigious little prick! Ambulance chaser!

—You calling me names ain't gonna get me off your case. What the hell did you say to her? Are you listening to me, Billy Boy? Don't mess with Ariel Trent, you got that? You hurt her and I come after you.

—You think I drove into her on purpose?

—I'm looking over her interests, don't forget that!

—Don't threaten me! Look, I hit her with my car; you think I take that lightly?

Carver's voice dropped down an octave to a menacing tone.

—You won't mention this call to her.

—I don't know if that's in her best interest—or mine for that matter.

—As her attorney it is in her best interest! As her friend, I'm looking after her. If you want to make things up to her—if you give a damn for that woman, you'll not mention this little talk.

Bill heard the disconnect and he replayed the conversation in his head.

Carver might have intended to behave in a businesslike manner, but something went wrong. There had been too much emotion in his voice, too much anger, and he had sounded more like an irate husband defending his injured wife than a public defender. He had an interest in Ariel's welfare, beyond a professional one: Carver was looking out for a friend, not just a client. The whole thing, Carver's attack, made Bill feel like a scoundrel. Made him feel like an outcast. The bad guy. Made him feel, well . . . jealous.

"The world in which we live lives in us. To look outward at the farthest star is to look inward into oneself."

Raintree County

SEVEN

Ariel and William

Ariel, John, and William had always agreed it would be terrific if they could find a space to lease that could accommodate an audience of a couple of hundred people as performance space for musical concerts and theatrical productions.

Over the couple of years that they worked together, they had looked at warehouses and old factories in and around Linden Falls, but nothing they had seen would work. Either the space was acoustically dead for concerts, or it had too many physical obstructions that could not be overcome to suit theatrical staging. The biggest problem was finding a place that did not need hundreds of thousands of dollars to convert to meet building code requirements.

Late one Sunday afternoon, during a snowstorm in January, William called and asked if he could drive over to see Ariel and John. She told him he was crazy, because no one should be out in the blizzard. William talked away her concerns and arrived an hour later.

John went to the door to let him in, along with a drift of snow that followed him. Ariel was entering the living room with a tray of hot cocoa and slices of the pound cake she had baked earlier in the day. She hesitated as she watched William stomping the snow from his boots on the foyer carpet before removing them. She was relieved he had made it through safely, and when she caught his eye she could see a spark of excitement.

She put the tray down as John took William's coat. When she looked up, William was removing his ski-cap.

Against the firelight the cascading snow created an aura of stardust around him. The moment stretched, suspended in slow motion, as she took in the wonder of it all: the angelic beauty of the sparkle of aquamarine eyes, even the static that had charged his soft blond hair, which shimmered in the glistening around him.

A voice whispered faintly in her ear. It was her own voice, an inner voice, speaking of wishes and longings and unveiled truths. She tried to ignore the voice, but her mind echoed with it.

She left the room for the kitchen on some pretext to regain her breath and wits.

Minutes passed as she stared out the window over the sink, her mind drifting along, following the world of white lineal patterns that molded the trees and rooftops. All was veiled in white, like the sheeted rooms of a long-shuttered house. She could not find out there what it was she was searching for. She turned to see William come bouncing in to call her back into the living-room to hear what he had come all the way from home to tell her.

She followed him in, and taking John's hand, sat next to him on the sofa.

They had finally found their space, said William, if Ariel and John agreed that it was acoustically wonderful for their concerts, and perfect for theatrical productions, too. The Old Quaker Meeting House on Route 67, three miles outside of town.

Ariel was ecstatic, knowing the old building, having once been in it when it was used as an auction house. John trusted Ariel's and William's enthusiasm. The price was pretty good, too, for a two-year lease with option to buy.

—All right, what do we do now? asked Ariel, poised for immediate action.

William was relieved that Ariel was as excited as he about the property. He laughed and said, —We form a nonprofit corporation, the three of us head the executive board, we pay two months on the lease, and start production!

—You make it sound so easy, said John, trying to catch their enthusiasm.

—Well, that's the easy part. The hard part is going to be putting on the concerts and shows. Ariel will be musical director, I'm artistic director, John can be the board's president.

Ariel's practical side kicked in.

—What has to be done to the physical plant to pass the codes and—

—Not too much, answered William, ready for such a question. —It's been used as a public building before. Handicap ramp, bathrooms; all we need to do is build flexible staging platforms. There's seating for a hundred and fifty. We need a sound system and theater lights; there's a back room perfect for dressing areas: You've got to see it.

—We can have a monthly concert series at last, and we can collaborate on some original musical plays. I can't believe this!

John rose from his chair and went over to the liquor cabinet. —Let's have a drink to celebrate. What'll you have William?

—I don't know, pour me anything you're having.

The three toasted to their partnership and discussed plans for the future.

—You know, said William, We need to pull together a group of really talented people who will want to take active roles in this company.

—You mean, like a repertory company? asked John.

When William nodded, Ariel offered, —There are so many talented people who have been pushed aside for years at the Community Players, like Bob Morris and Lillian Murphy and that terrific guy . . . Jim Marshall! They're perfectly capable of doing better work if given the chance.

John said, —True. They get shuffled aside because the Community Players don't often choose plays that suit their talents.

—Let's be honest, said William. —They get pushed aside because they are not with the organization's "in-crowd." They don't have money or social connections. I say we approach them and a few others and see if they want to do some real work on a regular basis. I mean, people like Howard Robinson should be acting and directing, not selling tickets or painting scenery.

—There's nothing wrong in asking people to help out in all stages of production, said John.

—Yes, agreed Ariel. —But not when they don't have the chance to do what they do best. Let's find people and help them to build their talents. There are plenty of folks who like to do the clerical duties, the ushering, the box-office sales. Let's help the creative artists to create.

—I agree with you one hundred percent, said William with a laugh. —We'll be accused of raiding their stable, you know.

—I don't see why, said Ariel. They can find plenty of volunteers who enjoy painting scenery and do it well.

—I'd like to do work that's a little different. We need to make critical choices in material we present.

John chimed in, jokingly: —I think this town can do without another production of *Hello Dolly!*

—Then we are all of the same mind. I think we might get an audience even if we present Tennessee Williams or Eugene O'Neill, whattcha think? Your concert series will have a permanent home instead of the high school auditorium.

—Hey, do you think the blizzard has let up enough for all of us to go look at the place? said Ariel.

—Oh, God, laughed John. —It's Judy Garland and Mickey Rooney gonna put on a show in the barn!

The men convinced Ariel that they would be more inclined to visit it the following day.

Three months after signing the lease they presented the first quartet concert at the Meeting House. Ariel was ecstatic the first time the musicians gathered for rehearsal. The sound of their instruments resonated and floated through the open space so beautifully that it was hard to believe there was any other room on earth where the heavenly tones could vibrate so sweetly, so effortlessly. All the major publications in a radius of two hundred miles sent reviewers who raved. The music subscription tickets were sold out, and William suggested that Ariel add two more concerts to the yearly series to accommodate audience demand. And they would produce four plays a year for the first year, two original works and two classic plays. After a production of the Stoppard comedy, they would present William's original play, followed by a Neil Simon classic, before ending the season with Ariel and William's collaboration of a musical based on an updated *Much Ado About Nothing*.

For the three months preparing the building for use as a theater, Ariel and William were in a mental high. The very progress of readying the space for their artistic presentations was, in itself, a fulfillment of dreams. Ariel could not wait each day until she could leave work and join John and William, who had been at the "theater" most of the day painting or building. As John was out of work, and William taught only three mornings a week at the university, they were able to put in the most hours for physical labor. Ariel spent every weekend there, pitching in with her talents at decorating and doing finishing work. In the evenings she would meet with William and Harry Winthrop, their new nonprofit corporation's public relations director, who was employed during the day as the Hartley Collection Museum's publicity manager, preparing the press releases, and designing the subscription forms, or planning fundraising events with Mariah Henderson, also on their board, known for her ten years of successful fundraising for the Adirondack Opera Company.

They had approached and attracted many talented and knowledgeable people to do what they did best in the administrative part of the company, and allowed them to take control of their various roles without the interference of rivaling board members. The same would be true for the artistic end: The artistic decisions would be left entirely to co-directors, William and Ariel. Each agreed to limit department spending according to a yearly budget voted on by all of the ten-member board. And the board was deliberately kept to a small number in order to avoid politicking among its directors. To sit on this board, you made decisions to benefit the company.

To assist the planners in implementing their projects were volunteers gathered by each: people they enjoyed working with and could depend on to get things done.

It was relatively easy for William to raid the local pool of dramatic talent in the area, people from several community theater groups who were frustrated with the social politics of the clubs. If there was not a role onstage for a particular show, they would direct, stage manage, or design the production. Everyone was required to help build, paint, or strike the show. It would be a true repertory company.

All in all, everyone involved in the new venture was energized and working at full speed to see to a successful first year.

There was nothing they believed they could not do that first year. Everything was right; it all fell into place. The people who joined the effort enjoyed the challenges set before them, and each grew more confident. It was as if William and Ariel had created a loving family where each member was respected for his or her contribution. If there were any jealousies, it was not evident.

John finally found full-time employment at a car dealership in Albany. He had to commute an hour each day, and when he arrived home from work, he'd be tired. If it was a rehearsal night, he would be more stressed than usual, finding it difficult to concentrate on the work at hand, sometimes to the restrained frustration of the cast members. By the time he and Ariel returned home at ten o'clock, he'd be irritable and go directly to the liquor cabinet for a great pouring of vodka. Ariel didn't mind occasional drinking; it helped one relax, and in moderation shouldn't be harmful. She would ask for a Cinzano on the rocks if John were pouring. But, her drinking was not to soothe frustrations, but, rather, to level her high, happy mood so she might rest her mind after a day of juggling demands.

And her days were demanding. She had to be available to the children, preparing breakfast each morning before she went off to work. Her job was demanding, although not unpleasant; she enjoyed working with the seniors at the residence, but some could be as difficult as children. She would drive the kids to and from sporting events and afterschool activities, and put dinner on the table, where they'd pick at each other until a fight erupted. When they had finally helped clear the dishes and scattered to their rooms to do homework, or started the battle for the use of the telephone, Ariel would dash off to rehearsal, praying there would be no bloodshed during her absence. Once at the theater, she would finally be able to find release from the stresses of her day through the creative exercise of her art.

People would constantly comment that she seemed to have unlimited energy. It was true when she was doing what she loved best. No one saw her when she first rose in the morning from a sleep so heavy she felt drugged and sluggish for hours. Her exhaustion was so profound and she masked it so well that even she didn't realize the toll it was taking on her psyche and body.

By the middle of year two, Peter and Jillian were becoming more rebellious in their behavior, constantly challenging her and John's decisions about what they could and could not do. Peter wanted to buy a new car with the college money his Aunt Maria had set aside in a fund when he was a baby. Jillian could not understand why, at fifteen, she could not go to Mexico with her boyfriend and his brother. They would work on Ariel and John, not taking "no" for an answer, finding arguments to plead their cases. Ariel and John would not vacillate from their decision, but the kids were persistent, and resentful toward their parents. They would find new battles to fight, challenging their mother and father almost to the point of concession. But, Ariel was stronger than John and would not allow herself to succumb to the pressure they exerted on her. She was as strong-willed as they were. Their tenacity was inherited from her. She secretly admired their talents at contriving a convincing argument to get what they wanted. Both were extremely bright and clever people, good students, and liked by everyone who knew them, but she was angered by their disregard and disrespect for her authority. It made everything in her life more difficult to handle, as she always played the villain preventing them from attaining their outrageous desires.

John was earning a decent wage at last, and for a while they were able to make ends meet without too much financial juggling. He had pulled back from responsibilities with the theatre company, however, feeling he could not give it the time and energy that was needed. Ariel believed he had lost confidence in himself as a performer. He was a trained singer, not a stage actor, and musical comedy demanded both skills. He had trouble learning his lines and could not keep up the pace of rehearsal. She was more sad for John than disappointed, for she had planned a concert for him to perform as soloist, and had collaborated with William to create a leading role for him in their original musical play. When Ariel pursued the real reasons for his seeming lack of interest in the company, he said it was too much to handle with work and the kids. Ariel wormed out the truth: He had a great voice, he admitted, but no real talent to back it. Ariel tried to convince him otherwise, but John knew he had less to give than Ariel or William, and held fast to that belief. Then, when John lost his job because car sales were down that autumn, he still did not want to be involved in the company.

Ariel was crushed, by the loss of the job and because of John's lack of interest in *anything*. He did some of the cooking, and a little cleaning, and helped run the kids around town to their various activities, but she saw something was missing that was once a part of John. His optimism and his dreams of success were gone. And he was drinking, even though she told him she'd found the stash of bottles, and he had promised to stop, insisting he was not an alcoholic, and didn't need help from the likes of AA

Ariel had always had an empathetic nature. Like a chameleon she would change shades of emotion by observing or interacting with those around her. She sensed another's pain, and because she really had an interest in people, she listened to their stories and could easily visualize what they described of their experiences. Now John's disappointments, and the children's struggle to pull away from her on their journey toward maturity, compounded with her failure at making everybody's life better. She felt redundant. She could no longer control, to any extent, their happiness by simply providing her love and care.

More and more, the kids were not home at dinnertime. They had plans with friends on Sunday afternoons. They were not interested in participating in the company or attending any of the premieres. They had no interest in their parents at all, and they were rarely available for conversation that was not stilted or monosyllabic. John withdrew into his alcoholic oblivion.

That winter, Peter announced he would be joining the Air Force when he completed high school in June.

And Jillian wanted to be emancipated when she turned sixteen.

Ariel had always encouraged her children to make their own decisions after weighing their options and her counseling, but there was no way that she would sit back and let Jillian leave school and home.

By March, Ariel was near emotional collapse. John needed help, she knew, help she couldn't give. He made no effort toward finding work. Jillian was becoming a young woman who viewed the world with cynicism. To Ariel, who had been the eternal optimist her entire life, had been dubbed "Alice in Wonderland" in high school because of her inherent naiveté, and grew to adulthood with a very rigid set of principles for determining right from wrong, Jillian's outlook troubled her. And Peter's decision to push aside plans to become a veterinarian was statement enough that he had won some foolish battle where his parents forfeited control of his future.

Then there was William. He was the only one she could talk with. The only person with whom she could speak of her innermost concerns, and yet she could not, she would not. He lingered in her mind in a way that she had chosen to consciously *not* think about. She knew that once she began to reveal her troubles and fears, she might risk saying more than she should. And, she was not of the nature to burden a friend with personal problems. It was out of character for her, being other people's problem solver.

During the downtime in production scheduling, Ariel took a week's vacation from work. There was no extra cash for a real vacation, so she spent the time at home with John, or driving in the car or window shopping, or going to see the new exhibition at the museum. She went to the library book sale one afternoon and picked up a couple of dozen books at a quarter apiece. One of the books she chanced upon was *Raintree County*. She added it to the pile, recalling William's comment that it was one of his favorite books and that he would reread parts of it each summer. She brought the bags of books home and piled them in neat stacks of five or six on the floor in front of the bookcases.

By the end of her week off, Ariel fell into a slump. She had lost quite a bit of weight during the winter months, when most people only gain it. She had dropped fifteen pounds, according to the bathroom scale, but it did not worry her. She needed to lose that extra poundage, and it was not unattractive. She was fitting in clothes she hadn't worn in years, and physically, she felt spry.

But, returning to work was difficult. One of her residents had gone off to live in a nursing home and another had been hospitalized from a debilitating stroke. The administrative assistant, who had become a friend, was leaving the area with her husband to move to California.

By the end of March, Ariel had lost another twenty pounds and had little appetite. She saw her doctor, who told her, after a series of tests, that she was experiencing a clinical depression.

She accepted the antidepressant reluctantly, hating the idea that she had to be medicated. She had never been depressed in her life, and had never used a drug stronger than aspirin, even during her labors.

And yet, there was no escape into the glorious spring days that had arrived when she still lingered in the gloom of winter's spiritual dormancy.

She took the medication and a leave of absence from her job.

Ariel would sit on the window seat in the living-room, not really seeing the robin bouncing between the crocus and daffodils that naturalized the back lawn, only fixated on the bird as a focal point while her mind bobbed aimlessly along a stream of consciousness. Hours would pass as she sat there. Then, as if some button had been pressed, she'd rise and go out the door for a very brisk walk, a walk she was not aware that she was taking; she might have been on a treadmill, for her disregard of her surroundings. Her mind would continue on the revolving belt of mental noise, as if searching for an answer to an unformed question. She felt caught in a maze, seeking a way out from the world of her brain's mindless chatter. She mourned the loss of her purpose in the lives of her children; memories of their tender infancy were fading now in the light of their adulthood. She was ineffectual to support her husband; the failings and addictions that plagued him through life could not be fixed by anyone other than himself. She could not understand his apathy and grew impatient with him because she could not face the truth that he had stopped bothering to try! Were there, and had there been, other women in his life? She suspected as much. Those nights when he said he was working late. Those months every so often when he would be short-tempered and irritable and resentful. At this point in their marriage she didn't really care. She just wanted him to pull his weight to help her keep the roof over their heads and the children fed and clothed.

In the early hours before dawn, she'd awaken restless and exhausted and stirred by some phantom *djin* that lurked in the darkness to taunt her. Sometimes, visions of her own physical decay and the dead would haunt her dreams, bringing her too close to the inevitability of her own mortality. In these nightmares, the stench of putrefaction would terrify her, and she would awaken and rise from the overheated bed where John snored, his eyes shuttered in blindness to the shadows that plagued her every vision. She'd drive out of the small town and into the black, winding roads of the countryside, as if by following the yellow lines of the divide she might be led to a place of solace.

She'd park along an open stretch of road, shut off the car's headlights, and step out. The silence was complete.

On moonless nights she would abandon herself under the indigo sky, eyes adjusting to the white, fiery light circling crazily above, until she could discern the patterns of the constellations. She'd stand in awe of the majesty and its ineffable beauty, at once aware of her insignificance in so great a plan.

She searched the sky, hoping to see beyond the limitations of human vision. A message, a clue, an answer that might help her, to guide her toward a safe place where she might take refuge from her demons.

Night after night, she'd look to the sky, toward what was familiar and constant, knowing with intelligence that life and the condition of the universe was always in a state of flux, that the changes within her own complex being were only a reflection of the changes in an ever-expanding universe. The shimmering light in the Big Dipper appeared to be a star, but in reality, the light was misguided and was only an illusion. What seemed a star was a black hole of a long-extinguished sun: What comfort could she find in the tricks of chaotic Nature? But, where else could she look? She had not succeeded by looking within herself, so she had to look outward for an answer. But, an answer to what question, she still didn't know. Still, the silence of the night was like a balm to her spirit.

She retained her sense of humor, however, remembering Gertrude Stein's deathbed words, "What was the question?" Through a lifetime of pleasant distractions, had the woman lost track of the original purpose of her intellectual pursuits, an answer to a question?

William surprised her when he stopped at her house one afternoon with the quartet's new publicity photos. She was wearing a white silk dressing gown, and her hair fell in fortunate disarray from the pins that held it in a knot on top of her head. She looked pale, he thought, when she opened the door, but soon a flush of pink colored her cheeks.

William was worried about her. She was not herself, lately. She stood there barefoot, waiting for him to speak his business, not at all offering her usual upbeat greeting, but displaying a vulnerability that she was unable to conceal. Her melancholy was obvious and disturbing to him. She had not returned his calls of the past couple of days, and when he had finally reached John, he had only said that she was "under the weather, a cold or something." When he called her at work after his class at the university, Ariel's assistant said that she was on medical leave for the month. That's when he grabbed the photographs and drove to her home. There was no urgency in choosing a photo; it was simply an excuse to see her.

—I didn't know you were taking a leave from work, he said, tentatively. —Sally told me when I called a little while ago.

—Yes. . . . I needed a vacation.

—And are you having a vacation, Ariel? Or have you been ill?

—Ill? she asked defensively. —Just needed a break is all.

He looked directly into her eyes as if searching gemstones for flaws. She averted hers, unwilling to be appraised with such scrutiny, and in doing so confirmed for William that something was indeed very wrong. She was avoiding him. But, why, he wondered?

—Ariel? he asked, lifting her chin with a finger so that she had to face him. —You need to tell me what's wrong.

—I need to? I don't know . . .

He was not about to give up. She was too important in his life to allow a distance to form between them. —*I* need you to tell me what's wrong.

—It's nothing.

—It's something, and I'm worried about you.

—The kids have got me down. . . .

—And . . . ? There was no cooperation, and he voiced a hidden fear.

—Have I done anything or said anything that might have upset you?

—No! she said, suddenly fiercely animated, She chastised with a laugh, —*Ach!* The conceit of actors! Don't be so self-centered, William; it's not about you,

A lie, of course. He had upset her, her world was upset, turned over, and she would never let him know that he was the cause of her turmoil.

—I'm going through a little clinical depression, as my doctor calls it.

—"Little"?

—Yes. Sounds funny, doesn't it? Like a meteorological term to say it's raining out, but only a drizzle, not a storm.

—So you're raining; but only a drizzle.

—I guess I am.

She was smiling but her eyes were moist, and William regretted his casual retort.

—Have we been working too hard?

—No. I suppose it's just a letdown from the end of the season. The concert series has ended and there are two months of downtime before the startup of the new season. It's nothing really. I'll be fine in a couple of days.

He accepted that explanation, as he often suffered the same sort of letdown at the close of a play.

—Don't worry, William, the quartet begins rehearsal on Monday for our May opening.

William talked about the casting for the play that would open in June. Soon, Ariel's spirits appeared to have lifted, and after half an hour she seemed herself. By the time John arrived home a couple of hours later, they were laughing over some silly joke William was telling over cheese and crackers and a bottle of burgundy.

At William's suggestion it was agreed they all go out to dinner. He called Susan to join them, but she was not inclined after her day's work at the library. So it was a threesome who went off to dinner at the Indian Palace.

The one important decision she made after their dinner together was that she had to dig out of the hole she was in. She began walking, morning and early evening, at a brisk pace, her legs stretching in an easy gate, her posture straight. She consciously adjusted her posture throughout the day, lifting the weight of her torso from the slump that mimicked her depression, upward and aligned with her hips. And she held her chin up, so her eyes would not be directed so much to the floor. It produced an air of confidence at first, if not the expression of her real feelings of the moment.

She forced herself to eat small meals at regular intervals during the day, even though she was not hungry. She had become slim and fit, her muscles had firmed, but she feared losing any more weight and appearing gaunt. For years since the birth of her children she had maintained a comfortable plumpness. Now, when she looked in the mirror, she saw a woman who looked years younger than her biological years, as if she had shed a thick skin added for protection. Protection from what, she didn't know. But, she would no longer allow herself to be afraid of the transformation. She couldn't fight it, and she really didn't want to.

She had never really understood people who got depressed when it appeared they had everything to be happy about.

But her life was lived by the rules. She prided herself in being the best at whatever she chose to do. She had stopped performing so that she could become a mother. It wasn't fair to the children that she would have to travel the circuits for weeks, even months at a time. It had been a conscious decision, and one she was happy to make. There was only one way to raise her children, only one way to be a good, supportive wife. She loved passionately those who filled her life. They could do no wrong as long as she was there to love and guide them through their trials. Ariel was everybody's rescuer. But now she was lost and needed rescuing. She would have to use her wits and inherent strength to find her own way out of this rut.

She had been overwhelmed by the changes occurring around her. The children were growing up suddenly. Peter was quickly scoffing at her daily protection, and Jillian refused it completely. John had tried so hard to shower her with kindness over the past couple of months, even though he was sinking into the musk of his alcoholism. His attentiveness was not in character, but she could offer no help to unburden him from concern about her except to fix what was wrong with herself, by herself.

But, it was evident after their dinner that, although William may have been a factor in her depression, his friendship might provide a way out. She had only to convince herself that it was friendship, nothing more that she needed from him. And she would concentrate on maintaining that one constant in her life, while allowing her husband and children the freedom of being who they chose to be without her censure. She would release them from the burden of trying to live up to her expectations.

When she stubbed her toe on a pile of books she bought at the library sale, one volume landed on her ankle. She picked up and fanned through the one-thousand-sixty pages of *Raintree County*. This was the novel William liked so much. Wasn't it about a veterinarian in the highlands of Scotland? No, that was a different book.

She began to read, not really intending to conquer the doorstopper, just seeking the author's sense of style to determine if it was something she would want to invest the time in reading. She looked up from the book two hours later, when Jillian dropped her backpack in the foyer with a great thud.

—Hi! You're home!

—Good to know I chose the right house. Anybody call?

—On the phone? No. Not yet. How was school?

—I didn't want to leave. Is there anything to eat?

—There might be a crumb on the counter, better lick it up before your brother gets home.

—Very funny, Mom.

—I aim to make you smile. There're oranges in a bowl on the table. They're orange in color, so you can't miss them.

Jillian pulled a face, rolled her eyes, and huffed off to the kitchen.

The phone rang on cue for the first time that day. Ariel knew it wasn't for her and was just the first in a long series of calls between Jillian and her friends that would continue into the evening.

Raintree County consumed her attention over the next few days.

At first she found Ross Lockridge, Jr.'s prose difficult to deal with because of its classical style. One reviewer had written that it was the American *Ulysses*, the great American novel—with a dash of hokum. But, there was great and beautiful poetry that sprang from the page, a cadence that was musical and lyrically sung, and what fiction did not, to a degree, include some amount of hokum? Ariel found herself reading the words out loud while musical compositions played in her mind's ear.

As she became more and more absorbed by the magic of the book, the author's words and images seemed to delve deep into the tender parts of her, a subtle, sensual probing, and as she followed the prose she found herself drifting through the dreamland Lockridge had created, a place between yearning and morality, a world of water and shore where human existence held no superiority over the other creatures of the earth, a land aglow with an exquisite green luminescence.

When Johnny, wandering along the banks of the Shawmucky River on his search for the legendary Raintree, is awestruck at the sight of Nell Gaither rising up from her swim, he sees that her nakedness is free of shame because she is at one with all living things. Modesty had been peeled off and left along with her garments on the riverbank, to be reclaimed when she departs this fragrant green paradise for the city of men.

Later, when Johnny whispers the words, "You are beautiful, Nell," you know it is not all he wants to say, not all that is in his heart, for those longings must be tamped down and remain unspoken for they are about forbidden desires that will cause him damnation for sure. The music composed of the rustling of leaves, the whispering wind, and the buzz of winged creatures ceases, not only in reverence of Johnny's stuttered declaration, but as if in hopeful anticipation of words he fears to utter.

These inspired passages awakened something inside Ariel, and she saw in them the universality of love and desire. From beneath the sun-touched surface of the river, winding its path through Raintree County, down in the murky depths of mud and silt and algae sprang all life. The river fed, gave sustenance, and offered no morality.

Obscenity was a human concept that sullied a perfect plan. Guilt did not exist in nature, only in the minds of men, Ariel realized as Johnny would come to understand, because the confluence of all living things is, at the same time, both sacred and profane.

Never before had she consciously considered this simple and obvious truth. It had always presented itself, if only she had before looked out over the landscape!

The materialization of God and His love were not in the church but everywhere in the natural environment that He had created. And Ariel saw that all was good in His world and that evil could not thrive and wage war to distort that perfection if it were not nurtured in the hearts of men. This magical book was both startling and liberating for Ariel.

She wanted to discuss the book with William, to share her discoveries. That was an integral part of their friendship and it was what had been missing in their relationship over the past months. She wanted to reinstate their mental jogging, and, like jogging, it was more fun with a friend. But, William was off with Susan and the kids visiting his parents in New Mexico during the spring break. She decided to put her thoughts to paper so that when he returned they might discuss a few things.

Why not write him a letter, send it to his house. After all, he had sent or hand-delivered scores of lengthy observations to her over the years. Her responses were briefly scribbled notes or a verbal comment at best. Why a letter? It was a step in getting back on track.

She kept reading, slowly savoring the novel, and it had a strange restorative effect. Writing down her observations of the life of Johnny Shawnessy, who lived and learned and absorbed life on the banks of the Shawmucky River, which wound its way through the landscape of Indiana's Raintree County, seemed to expand her mind. Johnny would spend a lifetime searching for the magical Raintree hidden amid the tangles of swamp vines and marshes that fed, and were fed of, the river. What signified the Sphinx Recumbent, lying naked and languorous on the stone slab at the post office? Why could he not see the pornography squirreled within the drawings of the ancient atlas, as legend had promised? Was the makeup of human beings the dual personalities of the uppercase *John* and lowercase *john*? The novel was wrought with marvelous symbolism to be interpreted by an open imagination. And soon she discovered that the story was more about the women in Johnny's life than about his own aborted dreams and his search for the raintree that when discovered would reveal the meaning of Life.

After several days, and some fifteen pages on the legal pad, she mailed off her letter. Within a day of William's return, he stopped by her house with a sheaf of papers bearing his own thoughts on the book.

They had begun the first of a lengthy correspondence that changed the course of their lives.

As easy as it had always been to express their thoughts to each other from across a table or during a congenial visit in either's living-room, they now, unwittingly through their letters, began to reveal more personal aspects of their lives, their attitudes and feelings, likes and dislikes, neuroses and fears.

Neither realized the intimate nature of the room they had entered until they began innocently discussing their marriages in relation to the novel. Soon, they began to layer their discussions with their own experiences with love. Each admitted that they had never strayed from their marriage beds. Each loved their spouses. Ariel admitted that she had never slept with a man she didn't love. There had only been two men in her life before John, and one she had loved and had never had sex with. His name was Michael, and the experience taught her that you could not *make* someone love you, and that sometimes, you just had to let go.

William wrote of his promiscuous life in the Seventies, how he had actually fallen in love with a girl when he was fifteen. The relationship remained chaste for the eight months they were together. She was an officer's daughter, whom he left behind when his family was transferred to another base. He wrote about fathering a child at age twelve and the rape by a young airman the same year. "By the tender age of fifteen I'd had sex with two people I didn't love and had never had the love of the one person I really wanted. What lesson do you think Little Willy learned from that period in his life? Sex and love are *not* interrelated, and can exist in isolation, one from the other.

The brief sojourn during his youth into homosexuality was never a secret. He didn't advertise it, but he never denied it when asked. It was simply an incidental fact that he had once had a short relationship with a boy in college. But he was trusting of Ariel as he had never been of anyone before, and he told her about the rape and its consequences when he wrote, "This is something I have never told *anybody*: By the time I was in college, I *knew* that I was not attractive to the opposite sex, as much as I was attracted to, and wanted, the love of women. I found, however, I was quite attractive to my own sex. I had carried no shame from what happened to me by Randy, and being wanted by someone, *anyone*, even another man was enough for me at the time. Sex was sex; I had no homophobia. And very important: I had to prove what my mother said was wrong, when she talked about the rape as 'ruining my life.' Had I been more settled in my heterosexuality, back then, I suppose I might not have seen that love was possible on both sides of the fence. But, the paradox resulting was that I could not *feel* loved unless I was wanted sexually. So sex became an emotional substitute. Then, Susan came into my life. She was not beautiful; she is plain and simple, but I knew that my life would be poorer without the shining example of her goodness. She accepted me, and I found comfort in that acceptance."

Ariel cried after reading the letter, and loved him more than she ever thought imaginable. She was often saddened, sometimes surprised, but never shocked at what he shared in his letters. But, she feared that she might have, through the intimacy of their letters, laid the groundwork for a perilous journey into the future. William was lowering his guard, perhaps for the first time in his life. His seriousness was clue enough. He was not masking his words behind his usual double entendres or puns. Oh, he threw in a humorous comment now and then, but on the whole he was tapping into feelings that had been protected deep inside himself. She feared for her own future, not knowing where all of it would lead.

It was necessary to make a deliberate attempt on her part to shift the tone of their correspondence. She always acknowledged the important revelations, the personal accounts, and the concerns he expressed when she replied, but she'd quickly change to another subject. Her letters became shorter, and she'd let more time lapse before replying. It was extremely difficult for Ariel to edit herself in this way and she hoped he wouldn't notice the restrained construct of her writing.

But, he did. William was too intelligent and tuned into Ariel not to notice a change in style. He decided to ask her directly. He had started several letters that he ripped up because they skirted his fear. He had to know if he had said too much, if she resented his intimacy.

"I hope I haven't written anything to offend you, my dear. Our friendship has meant so much to me. I would never intentionally hurt you, I think you know that, so please do not fear being honest with me."

Ariel replied with her great sorrow if he had that impression. She, too, valued their friendship, she wrote.

It was not as if they did not see each other on a regular basis. They were together three, four, sometimes six days a week during production. Their letters were not discussed when they'd meet, only exchanged. Not only were they too busy rehearsing, or seeing to set building, or meeting with other members of the company to sit and converse face to face, but the letters became an expected addition, deserving their own private time and place in which to be read and replied to. They no longer used the mails; they would hand each other an envelope in the evenings upon greeting. The letters were like interior voices, where all that was spoken was silent to the ear while singing to the spirit.

Ariel wondered if they would ever sit down face to face and discuss things stated in their correspondence. She became more and more frightened of just that possibility.

It was commonplace for William to sit in occasionally at a quartet rehearsal, though in the past he'd only rest a few minutes watching from the back row between tackling other chores around the building. Lately, he was sitting through all of their rehearsals for the opening concert of the season. He'd arrive not long into rehearsal with some mission: paperwork to do in the office, a leaking faucet in the ladies' room that needed repair, finding the hornet's nest under the eaves of the roof.

Ariel would see him watching her from the back row, motionless, contemplative, as she and the musicians played. He had started to brew coffee in the dressing room for their break time. It was habit, now, that he would hand her a cup, prepared with cream and sugar the way she liked it, as she came down from the stage for a break outdoors.

She would not, *could not* deliberately avoid him. She did not want to avoid him. During these days she felt like a grain of sand being swept away in the chaos of a desert storm. Where she might settle she had no idea. She was helpless, caught in that wind, and could do nothing to fight a force so much greater than her resolve. She remained true to her commitment: She would endure her private conflict, alone.

That he was enamored of her, she was now certain. She had provided through their innocent letters the means by which William was learning more about himself, and through these small breakthroughs, he was freeing himself from his inhibitions. Through her admiration of his finer qualities, he was seeing a more attractive face in the mirror each day. That in itself was a powerful aphrodisiac for the depressed libido. That he loved her long before the onset of her letters was never a suspicion in Ariel. From the start Ariel had found the complexity of his mind fascinating. She looked upon William as possessing a mind that challenged the best in her. His attention over the last few years was something that she prized. He made her feel connected, her ideas valid, and confirmed through his avid approval that she was not strange or eccentric or an artistic snob, but a person who reached far beyond others to catch a star when others wouldn't dare to even try.

More than anything, William was taken by her courage. She never courted defeat; although she admitted to many failures in life, it had never stopped her from trying again. It was an attractive and admirable quality and he was in awe of that vibrant core that fed her creativity. It was contagious, and he always felt it emanating from her and flowing into him when they brainstormed or just sat around discussing trivialities. Something would pop up and inspire their creative juices to flow. William wanted to learn from her, and was always eager share his own knowledge.

He couldn't take his eyes off of her. It made him smile when she stood there, listening intently to someone's concerns, the tiny frown that appeared along her brows, the slight pout that set about her lips. There was a youthful innocence about her when she was fully engaged. And when he saw the dimple on her left cheek when she smiled, the curl escaping its clip at the nape of her long neck, the sweet, graceful lines of her shoulders curving voluptuously toward slim arms and long fingers, he found himself sinking into a drowning of desire.

It was becoming unbearable for Ariel during those times when they were alone. She'd feel his slow, deliberate approach, catch the direct appeal in his face when he walked over to say hello. Once, he lifted a petal, fallen from the weeping cherry tree, from off her breast with a touch more gentle than a whispered breath against her skin. Ariel wanted to weep like the tree.

And William was becoming more circumspect, so careful in his advance for fear of stumbling out of favor. He could barely speak to her without stammering humility.

It had to stop, Arial thought, and so, too, did William.

"Had the woman of his dreams, whose face had been teasingly familiar, known the answer to this riddle?"

Raintree County

EIGHT

Bill

Bill decided not to visit Ariel at the hospital the next day. It took all of his will power not to go and see her, wondering if he could get through the day without a glimpse of her face.

The snow had not let up and by morning fourteen inches had accumulated. The snow plow had topped another couple of feet from the road to further block access to the street, so Bill spent a good part of the morning shoveling out to free his rental car. When he had just about finished, the county plow truck roared passed to block him in again.

Little Eva, tied to a fencepost while he worked, appeared upset by Bill's storming around, if not by his colorful language. *The Powers That Be* must have heard the despair in his protestations, because not a minute had passed before Harris Haley suddenly appeared at his drive. Bill noticed the plow attached to his truck and was about to beg a plowing when Harris offered to do it.

Haley zipped the truck back and forth a dozen times. When he was finished, Bill wondered if he should offer the man money, or accept the deed as the kindness of a neighbor. They had not met before, other than a wave or a nod when their cars passed on the road.

Bill thought it was a good time to make a more formal introduction, so he walked up to the driver's window, which Harris Haley rolled down, and introduced himself. Haley returned the greeting. Bill thought the best way to offer him payment for his services would be to ask if he, or anyone he knew, would clear Ariel Trent's driveway.

—I would, of course, pay for the plowing.

Haley was suited up as any sensible farmer would be in winter, from his cap down to the heavy mud boots. But he had the face of a movie star; handsome, ruggedly so, with heavy-lashed blue eyes, and even from his perch up in the truck Bill could see he was tall and solidly built. Here was Gary Cooper and Cary Grant melded together to form the image of Harris Haley.

—Done, he stated with a wry smile.

—Oh, great, Bill said, a little confused.

—Did it half an hour ago. Get to it again when the snow stops.

—I didn't know she contracted you. I was going to call around, and do some of it myself.

—No contract. I do it because I like to.

His manner unsettled Bill. The smile was gone, and he kept his eyes riveted on Bill's. His intense scrutiny made Bill uncomfortable. He was thankful that Haley had plowed him out, but Bill had the distinct impression he did it for the opportunity to look him over, size him up, as he was doing now.

—I suppose you and Mrs. Trent have been neighbors for a long time. I'm glad to know she has such friends.

Haley responded by looking at him blankly. Bill didn't like feeling intimidated, so he came right out with, —What do I owe you for the plowing?

—Nothing. You needed help and I was around. That's how it works.

—Well, thank you. Thank you very much, Mr. Haley.

—Name's Harris.

—Harris, then. . . . Thanks.

He nodded, rolled up his window, and drove away.

Bill was left with a strange paranoia. There was something menacing about the guy. It wasn't what he said, but how he said it. A message had been sent and Bill took it as a warning. It had to do with Ariel, and his was more than just neighborly concern.

Bill brought Little Eva into the house, and then drove to the body shop, trying to reason away the uneasiness that was building in him. If Haley and Ariel were indeed friends, then of course he'd want to check out the man who had put her in the hospital. Bill was relieved that the accident wasn't mentioned, because talking about it put him on the defensive. He wouldn't have known how to respond without a flow of apology that would just as well accuse himself of guilt through carelessness. Perhaps it was guilt, after all, that had suggested the idea that Harris Haley had been examining him.

Bill wondered why everyone was acting so mysteriously. Sonny, Amy, Roy. Roy's call the evening before still played on Bill's mind—and now, Harris Haley. I have to let it rest, he told himself.

The errands were done by one o'clock. As Bill hadn't eaten breakfast his stomach was making gurgling sounds. He was in the village, after bringing the chain for repair at the jeweler's, so he stopped at the newsstand for a paper and walked over to the Pantry for lunch.

It was a madhouse when Bill walked in: Sonny and Lilly were racing about trying to fill lunch orders. A line had formed for seating and the counter was packed for takeout. He waved "Hello," but Sonny didn't see Bill as he was too busy behind the counter. It would have been nice to talk again with Sonny. Maybe he had stopped by for Sonny's advice, maybe not, he wasn't sure exactly which, but he needed the security of Sonny's friendship at the moment and he was not about to get it during the noon rush. He drove over to Taco Bell to grab a burrito.

The newspaper had printed the corrections. Bill had hoped they would have printed his letter to the editor, too. But, the corrections were all they were required to do. Few people looked at the correction column, and the impression would remain in the minds of many that he was DWI. As he ate the burritos, the thought ate at him. That, too, he would have to let go, but it wouldn't be easy.

He rented a couple of newly released videos, stopped by the Full Moon Restaurant for Chinese takeout to reheat later in the evening for dinner, and then started for home to spend the evening alone.

He had to pass the hospital to get to the highway, and the urge to stop was so strong that he pulled into the hospital parking lot. Bill's body was functioning on its own as he grabbed the shopping bag of food and walked to the hospital entrance. An interior voice screamed, "Go home!," but his legs continued onto the elevator, his finger pushed the floor button, and his eyes anxiously sought Ariel's as he entered her room. She wasn't there. At the nurse's station, he was told Ariel had been taken to X-ray. An hour, maybe less to wait for her return. He went back to her room to wait.

He couldn't concentrate on any of the magazines. He walked over to the window and looked out over the parking lot and the white geometrics of rooftops and to the Hudson River beyond. It had stopped snowing; the sun had broken through mid-afternoon and was now fading fast in the west, gilding the river with shards of silver filings.

The tulips needed fresh water. In the bathroom sink he refilled the vase. A few petals fell as he set the tulips back in place; yellow, wine purple, pink. Then several more fell to the floor as he returned to the window, leaving only a petal and stamen on one stem, the rest threatening imminent and total collapse if not careful.

The massive bouquet that had arrived the day before was still moist, and he recalled Ariel's expressionless face upon reading the note card that came with the flowers.

He went to the bed table and found the card. She was using it as a bookmark in the novel she was reading. He opened the book, and read the card. There was only a signature: "Harris."

Instantly, Bill understood Harris Haley's behavior earlier that day. He was in love with Ariel. No doubt. Some truths don't need to be expressed in words. Some truths are revealed in a flicker of movement, evident through a gesture that belies what words may deny.

"Harris." Not "Get well soon, affectionately, Harris"; not "Speedy recovery," or "Best wishes," or "From the Haleys." Just "Harris."

Why not from Harris and his wife? Bill thought the woman he'd seen at their mailbox, or driving the Land Rover, was Mrs. Haley. That had been his impression, anyway.

I'm creating scenarios in my mind, he told himself, because he wanted to believe that the man loved Ariel. More important to his own interests was the question, How did she feel about Harris Haley?

Bill was becoming irrational, and desperately needed a shot of Jack to calm his nerves.

He decided not to wait for Ariel's return. He would go home as originally intended. If he didn't, he would make a fool of himself. Hell, he thought, I am a fool, insinuating myself on the woman! When he shut the front door of the bungalow, Bill felt tremendous relief to be entrapped within its walls, safe from carrying out his urges if not safe from this new and sudden torment.

The following afternoon, Ariel was released from the hospital. Amy had called to tell Bill that he could bring Little Eva to Ariel's that evening. He resented Amy; he should have been told Ariel was being released that day so that he could be the one to bring her home, to settle her in, to see to her needs. Totally irrational, he later thought. He agreed to walk the dog over.

Bill began to formulate plans, the ways and means that would give him daily access to Ariel's home. The most practical solution was to keep the dog for a while and walk her down to visit her mistress a couple of times a day. It wasn't an imposition, he assured Ariel, upon arriving at her home that evening. He was on vacation from work and he found that having the dog with him was quite nice.

Ariel reluctantly agreed. It would be a good idea, as Amy had her hands full with children and carpooling to have to walk the dog, too.

Little Eva was ecstatic to see her. It was all Amy and Bill could do to keep the leaping sixty pounds of dog-flesh off her mistress's lap. Ariel was beside herself with laughter, and it filled him with joy and his eyes with tears to see the display of love between them. Ariel cooed as she ruffled the dog's ears, which egged the creature on into performing her "crazy runs" around the expanse of the large sanctuary. The dog sprinted in circles around the plants, leaves waving in the wake of her speed; she'd make the corner around a sofa, over an ottoman, hugging the legs of the grand piano, then leap up and crash herself against the pillow backs of the loveseat, before starting the next round. Ariel laughed until it hurt. But her spirits were raised, as was a wonderful pink in her cheeks, and the moisture in her eyes made them glow emerald.

It was Amy who said Ariel had had enough fun for one day, to which she replied, —You can never have too much fun, Amy!

Amy began fixing the area she referred to as the "reading nook" into a bed. It was a large, thick-foam-cushioned lounging area set against a corner of the room, with huge pillows surrounding the two walled sides, and lit with wall reading lamps. On the platform were books, photos, candles, and assorted writing papers and pens surrounding a Moroccan leather–tooled book chest secured with an ornate brass lock. A couple of shelves mounted on the wall held a few pieces of decorative art glass, two rather worn copies of the modern classic, *Raintree County*, by Ross Lockridge, Jr., and a series of leather-bound journals, the years stamped in gold dating from 1993 through 1998. After tucking a sheet over the wide cushion seat, Amy went up the spiral staircase to get bed pillows from the bedroom.

Little Eva settled at Ariel's feet for a snooze. Bill was at a loss for words as he looked around the room, trying to relax into Arial's world for a few minutes before it was time to leave.

—Why do you do this? asked Ariel, taking Bill by surprise. Her voice was soft, just above a whisper, and when he turned his attention toward her there was the ephemeral smile that held not a hint of censure, only an honest curiosity.

—What do you mean? he asked. —Do what?

—Is it from guilt, Bill? You don't owe me anything. I don't want you to feel you have to do anything.

—No! I do it out of love! Because—I—out of love, all right?

There! He had said it and he couldn't believe he had. So what was the point in making light of the fact?

—Thank you, Bill. I appreciate your kindness, that you care, that you like me, but it is not necessary.

In one reckless moment Bill had aborted his original plan to give Ariel time before telling her how he felt. He had said what was in his heart and there was no turning back, no insipid corrections or revisions that might save him, so he threw himself head-on into the declaration.

—I didn't say "like," I said, "love"—because—

—Wait, Bill—

—Because I do. I love you.

He waited for the ceiling to crash down on him. He wanted to hide, but was so shocked at himself that he became paralyzed with fear and expectation instead.

—I like you, Bill. You are a good person.

—I guess I'll have to be satisfied with that.

She extended her hand, and Bill realized that he was no longer sitting on the sofa, but standing and pacing.

What has driven me to spew out the words? I have no control over what I say.

He felt out-of-body, watching while some other entity spoke through his physical being. No control to edit his words, pure emotion driving him on, and that realization brought him to his senses. After a few seconds while his sanity was restored, Bill took her offered hand and smiled in response to her troubled expression.

—I am flattered. I am grateful for your affection. I am glad for your friendship, Bill.

Amy appeared on the stairs, and he turned to face her when he felt her presence. She hugged the pillows violently. Bill stood his ground while wondering how much she had heard.

Amy helped Ariel out of the room to prepare for bed, leaving Bill alone in the room and giving him a chance to look around. A red-leather-bound journal lay on the platform, untouched, and the year was stamped in gold, *2000*. There couldn't be any entries yet. He hadn't noticed it in the hospital. He opened it. The pages were blank.

He returned the journal to where he had found it, and then saw a similar book, one he hadn't noticed because it was hidden by a framed photo of Ariel and a teenage boy. The book was dated *1999*.

About to open the cover of the journal, he changed his mind about peeking in. He placed it beside the current one.

He spotted an eight-by-ten frame displaying a piece of paper covered with familiar handwriting. Bill leaned to reach for it and saw that it was the same handwriting as contained in the letter secreted in Ariel's seashell. He carried it to the lamp to better see.

Some time ago on this date—July 23, 1995, to be exact—I sat across a picnic table from you, staring at you as you sat haloed by the light of a westering sun. With all the courage I could muster, I opened my mouth to speak. I achieved a hoarse whisper, nothing more. It was a whisper I could barely hear myself for the blood pounding in my ears. But, you seemed to hear it loud and clear.

"I love you," I said.

You whispered back that you loved me.

Oh, my, how lucky I am!

Returning the frame from where he'd taken it, the scene playing vividly in his mind's eye, he envied William Trent. The man was dead, yet Bill envied him.

If Bill hadn't then looked up on the shelves above the platform, or if the women had returned, he might not have entertained the idea that popped into his head. He reached up and pulled the journal for the year 1995, the year described in the letter, and then moved the remaining journals to fit snugly together. He took his coat off the chair and slipped the journal into one of its deep pockets. If Bill had second thoughts, he had no time to put the book back, because the women reentered just as he closed the pocket flap.

He put on the coat, fetched Little Eva's leash, and made ready to leave.

Amy said "Good night," and left, while Bill made several attempts to wake the sleeping dog.

—Would you like a drink, William?

Bill considered the sudden reprieve from banishment.

—That would be nice, he said.

Ariel pointed to the liquor cabinet in the corner behind the ornamental tree. —Nothing for me, she said.

Bill poured Black Label into a tumbler. When he turned he saw that Ariel had risen from her chair and was standing expectantly by the piano, playing with the fringe of its scarf, and then touching one of the picture frames. The room was dark, lit by only one table lamp, its light swallowed up into the shadows at the corners of the room.

Ariel looked up from the photograph and studied the man who lingered at the far end of the room, a glass in his hand, blond, tall and lean. And then she sat down at the keyboard, lifted its cover, and poised her fingers over the keys.

Bill walked to her side and watched her play and spoke vaguely of things his mind could not process for the fascination of watching her command over the instrument. She seemed to be lifted from this world to another by the very sound of the music she was producing, and it was as if he weren't even in the room with her. The offer of the drink had obviously been a polite gesture on Ariel's part to extend a hand in friendship even after his ridiculous pronouncements of love. He finished his drink, leashed the dog, and walked out into the night.

He had gone too far, he knew. But, hadn't the past few days changed the rules? Suddenly, it seemed that there were no longer any rules. He had never felt this way toward any woman. If bothered by conscience, he did not heed the niggling voice inside his head. He had stolen the journal and now he began to rationalize his thievery: It was all-important to know more about the woman he loved. Here was the opportunity to read her thoughts, and the chance to do so had presented itself.

He would return the journal tomorrow, he thought, as he hurried Little Eva along the road toward the bungalow.

The night sky had turned to opaque white, the color of stone, and as they walked along the quiet road toward his house, they advanced in solemn procession, man with dog at heel, as snowflakes tumbled down like feathers released from heavenly pillows. He looked up at the gentle cascade, flakes cooling his burning eyes like worthless blessings.

As he walked on toward the bungalow Bill came to believe that Ariel had not rejected him and had handled things brilliantly. He had blindsided her with his amorous proclamation and she had tried to save his pride by saying that he did indeed have value in her life. Although she later spoke of her husband, William, much of it as if he were still alive, Bill brushed those sentiments aside, believing that she had not rejected him. There was hope for him.

Home now, and with a rock glass filled with Jack Daniels, and a little drunk, Bill walked into the den and settled in the old red-leather chair, bought at a tag sale for twenty dollars fifteen years ago to furnish his first apartment. Almost everything in the room was the "junk" Cassie had referred to when they married and had relegated to the basement of the house. All was comfortably shabby, from the ancient Persian carpet rescued from someone's rummage day on the side of the road, to the floor lamp/magazine rack that needed a new shade, the worktable made from a walnut door picked up from a townhouse renovation in the city and covered with half completed short stories and reference books. Unlike the crisp, contemporary textures and lines of the living-room and bedroom furnishings he was granted with the divorce, Bill fit more restfully in the red chair; his identity was stamped upon each object in the room, and to be cocooned within his better past, his more hopeful past before his days with Carrie, put him at peace. He lit the tinder under the logs in the grate and quickly the room was warmed by firelight.

Little Eva made her bed for the night on his coat after he retrieved the journal from its pocket. He was nervous. He sipped at his drink. Like a ten-year-old kid hiding with his dad's *Playboy*, he feared discovery, for there existed an erotic anticipation of adventure into uncharted territory. He held the book, unopened, anxious to begin reading, yet hesitant.

Another gulp of Jack to calm him. He broke out in a sweat.

Bill wanted to go directly to the day of July 23, but knew that all that had transpired up to that day would give a clearer picture of the way things really were.

Bill leaned back in the chair, took a deep breath, and opened the cover.

There were no entries for January or February.

March 16 had a short note in the middle of the page:

This is supposed to help, I don't know why, but I'll do what he says. What's the point? Why record any of this? To what end? I want to get out of this mire, not wallow in it. How am I to convince myself that I don't feel this way when I do? What is wrong with me? Don't I have a good life, as trying as it gets sometimes?

March 20:   I walk miles each day. I put on music and dance freestyle, embarrassing the children when they come in with their friends to catch Mom prancing around the living-room looking silly. Is it the winter that has pressed so hard against my spirit? Is it that the last performance shattered me? I wonder if I focused too much, gave too much of myself to the music— or the man who is my friend.

March 23: Picked up Raintree County after I stubbed my toe on a stack of books I picked up at the library sale. It's one of William's favorite novels. Over a thousand pages: daunting. What else do I have to do all day?

April 2: I love this book! I've been drawn into it. I never understood it when William would say he reread parts of Raintree County every summer. I read a novel once and then shelve it. But, I understand why he rereads this one. There is a life force; it's strong and renewing as it is expressed by the poetry that is so much a part of Lockridge's brilliant prose.

April 4: Walking and reading. John is kind to me. I am sorry to do this to him. His wife is ill, and he doesn't know why, even if she suddenly does.

April 10: Food is of no importance in my life any more. I know I have to eat, but I can't seem to get much food down. John plays Drdla's Souvenir for me on the stereo, as it is one of my favorite violin romances. I have not been able to play the piano. I cry. The music that comforted me now stabs me with sharp melancholy. Oh, what has happened to me! Don't I know? What to do?

April 1: He has been writing to me about this or that for years, so I decided to write him about the book.

April 13: John, are you reading this? I sense that you are, if only to help me out of this depression. But, please stop. I cannot be free to express myself truthfully if I fear hurting you. You have been a good husband and I love you. Something has happened to me, and I need to get through this alone, without fear of disappointing you through something I might write that is careless and not meant to be read. I love you.

The rest of the journal was blank, except for the circling of various dates. July 23 was circled with a sun. August 2 had an exclamation mark through the middle of the page. That was it.

After a nightcap, Bill went to bed wondering what had caused Arial's condition. Tomorrow he would get a copy of *Raintree County*, and perhaps after reading the book he would understand why she and William loved the book. He would also have to find a way of replacing the journal to its rightful place and secreting out another.

Bill woke the following morning at 6:00 A.M. with work on his mind, more specifically, Bob Dunning. Bob Dunning, upstart ass-kisser and all-around smarm. Bob Dunning, who had successfully ingratiated himself into the firm under the tutelage of Roger Harris.

He never could understand why Roger had taken such a liking to him, unless he saw something of himself in Bob and knew how to tap those qualities for use in the company. That was probably it! Bill never liked Roger, either. Bob was cut from the same cloth, from a pattern that was money grubbing and unprincipled. If Tom Reynolds wasn't Roger's partner, Bill never would have lasted at the firm past the first year.

Tom had said he'd put Bob on the project if Waterston wanted to meet before Bill returned to work. Bill couldn't let that happen. Tom would retire within the next couple of years and someone would take his place. It would likely be Bill, if Tom had anything to say about it, but Roger would prefer Dunning. So, Bill decided he would drop by the office to show his face and interest in the project.

Although it was too early in the morning to go in, he was revved-up for action. Bill arrived at the firm before eight and went directly to his office to check for messages and memos. Nothing. At his secretary, Marsha's desk, Bill looked in the appointment book. There was an appointment scheduled with Waterston that afternoon at two. Next to Waterston's name were Tom's and Bob's. He had to make that meeting.

Tom arrived at 8:20 with Dunning at his heels. Tom looked surprised to see Bill, even though he didn't say so, but Bill sensed he had consciously checked himself because the funeral director's face dropped into place.

Dunning, humble, tentative, approached with a frowning, head-shaking look of simulated concern. His tone was sympathetic while bewailing Bill's misfortune over the holidays; there was most definitely an underlying attribution of blame. *Oily bastard.*

Tom, at Marsha's desk, picked up the appointment book.

Tom started for his office. Bill thanked Dunning for his concern, and immediately followed Tom in, asking if he might have a private word with him. As if he had expected the request, Tom replied— Of course.

Bill closed the door on Dunning, who was approaching fast, pretending he didn't see him coming. The gesture was satisfying.

Tom walked around to his desk with a measured step that was out of character. He was waiting for Bill to speak. How well Bill knew this little dance: Tom's mind was working behind the blank exterior; he'd seen him do this with reluctant potential clients, the waiting for cues, the mental spinning to evaluate how best to secure a contract. But Tom had never behaved like that with him before. Bill watched as his boss fiddled with file folders on the desk. He feigned distraction and avoided eye contact, and that alone made Bill uneasy.

—What can I do for you, Bill? he finally said.

Bill jumped right in.

—Well, I am doing fine, actually. I've got everything squared away with the car and insurance, and I'm ready to come back to work. I don't need to take any more time off, Tom. We've got work to do.

Back turned toward the window, Tom said, — There's no hurry, Bill.

—But I want to, Tom. I enjoy my work. I'm not ill, and Mrs. Trent—

—What?

—The woman, the accident.

—Yes, Ariel Trent.

So, he knew her on a first-name basis!

—She's home and doing well.

—That's good. Glad to hear it.

—Yes. We've become friends, you know.

Tom looked at Bill for the first time and his jaw literally dropped.

—I'd been visiting her in the hospital, and now, at home. I've been taking care of her dog, too.

Jaw lifted and firmly set, he made no reply, just the blank funeral director look.

—Anyway, everything is good, so I want to come back and work on the project, today.

—Well, Tom said, eyes flitting to the appointment book on his desk. —There's nothing to do until we can set up a date to meet with Waterston.

Now I know, thought Bill; *Now I know . . .*

If he allowed Tom to dig that proverbial hole, the deeper he got, the higher the man's defenses would rise. Bill had to decide quickly. Either come right out and tell him he knew there was an appointment with the client that afternoon, or pretend ignorance, thereby allowing Tom to give some lame excuse for why he wasn't needed yet.

—I can make the two o'clock meeting. Actually, I'm glad it's today, because yesterday I had another idea. I've got an approach he might like if he doesn't buy the first proposal, but I want to run it by you first, Tom.

Tom pulled back the desk chair, and then with a world-weary look, sat down with a great exhalation. His hands were big and with a gesture he motioned Bill to sit. Bill was ready to make an impromptu pitch. But Tom cut him off at the first few words.

—Bill, I'm taking you off this project.

Bill tried to act confused, a little perturbed, but not on the defensive. *Never be on the defensive. Just present your case rationally with the facts to support you.*

—I thought you liked the presentation, Tom. I have an alternative plan that you might like better—

—It was fine. I have no problems with it just as it is.

—All right. Then perhaps you might be able to tell me why?

—Right now I want you to take the rest of the time off.

—Yes, but the meeting?

—And then we'll put you on something else.

—Tom, I've worked on this for—

Watch your tone!

—Why take me off?

So much for applying that well-learned theory, thought Bill, when he realized he was no longer sitting, but pacing in front of the desk. *I've got to stop looking so agitated. Stop running fingers through your hair, keep your hands out of your pockets and unclench your fists, stop shifting your weight from one foot to the other.*

—People can be stupid, Bill. Waterston picked up on the accident, the article in the paper, and he doesn't want you representing him.

—But he doesn't know me. He's only met with you and Roger. You put me on this and you're replacing me with Bob? Bob's busy with the mayoral campaign. Are you saying you think I'm a detriment to the firm?

—Certainly not!

—Roger! This was Roger's idea!

It was a statement, not a question, and it was accusatory in tone. Bill didn't care any longer if it sounded indignant. He was indignant! As Tom made no effort to refute the accusation, Bill knew he had hit upon the truth. Should he insist that the accident was simply that: an accident? That he wasn't drunk, wasn't irresponsible, that he was driving below the speed limit because the road was icy, that he made every effort not to hit Ariel, and that he was not charged with reckless endangerment? Why not add icing to the cake of excuses and proclaim he was in love with Ariel Trent, that he would give his life for hers! No words would serve to dispel the impressions that existed, short of Bill having been critically injured in the accident. And, yet, had he been, would that have served his reputation? He doubted it.

He was burning bridges, now, all sensible strategy thrown out the window.

—I'm going home, Tom, as you suggested. If you want me to return to work after next week, give me a call. If I don't hear from you, I'd appreciate a letter of reference, my medical insurance paid up for the year, and a decent severance. I think that's only fair.

Tom came around the desk. His voice lacked conviction when he said, —Bill, I don't want you to leave, that's ridiculous!

—I don't want to leave, Tom. I like working with you, but I suppose you've guessed, I don't like Roger. I've never said it, but it's the truth. That's my problem, though, not yours. I don't like the aspersions to my character that can't, or won't, be dispelled by my employers. If I am now bad PR, so be it.

Tom looked down at his well-shined shoes, and then his gaze followed the pattern of the carved rug. With lips pressed, he nodded.

Bill walked out of the office, leaving the door open.

The restrained anger Bill felt in Tom's office exploded as he went out through the front doors and walked briskly across the lot to his rented car. The biting cold air energized him and served more to fuel the fire than to cool it down.

By the time he had turned the ignition he was in a fury. Tires screeched as he backed out of the parking space. He stopped, took a deep lung-burning breath, and told himself, if I don't want to be seen as reckless, I should not drive off with such hopped-up fury.

He took a long moment, and then drove carefully out of the lot for home.

Bill's behavior in Tom's office was not as it would have been a couple of years ago. But, a couple of years ago he was married to Cassie. Life back then was entangled with financial obligations that no longer existed today. The pressures of living up to Cassie's expectations, and to be fair, his own, would have forced him to have taken a more cautious path to save his job. He would never have put his livelihood at jeopardy by giving his boss an ultimatum.

I might have groveled, he thought, I don't know. . . .

It didn't matter much, suddenly, if he continued to work for Harris & Reynolds or not. The job is not who I am, it was only what I do. And now, perhaps, he told himself, I will do something else.

What that something else was, Bill had no idea at the moment, nor did he particularly care. There were all sorts of possibilities to explore. He was far from broke, not rich, but he'd not be out on the street for a while. I don't have to live up to anyone's expectations of me, only my own, he reassured himself.

Within a couple of minutes on the drive home, a sense of freedom and adventure sprung up to displace the anger. It was as if a rotten tooth had been pulled, and he felt relief in the moment. Any trepidation he may have harbored upon entering Tom's office had completely dissipated after his haughty display. Bill had to laugh at himself, at how the whole thing backfired into an eruption of puffed-up bravado. He respected Tom Reynolds, but for the first time, Bill thought that Tom may have come to truly respect him, not just for the work he did, and certainly not because of his outburst, but because Bill had not taken the blow with humble acceptance. So, by the time Bill arrived at the bungalow, he had simmered down.

Little Eva greeted him with great enthusiasm and then followed Bill to the kitchen, where he heated the remains of the morning coffee. He gave her a chewy, and then took the coffee to the study, where he perused the worktable of neatly stacked folders containing manuscripts of first-draft short stories, a half-finished novel started after the divorce to fill in the hours after work, and articles intended for submission to *The New Yorker* and the *Atlantic Monthly.*

There was hope for the future, and yet none of the work on the table held any interest as he looked through the heaps of manuscripts, handwritten legal pads, and spiral notebooks filled with the seeds of ideas. He would have to spend a little time reevaluating his future before he could find something that would inspire the writer within to start afresh.

In the meantime there were other distractions, welcome distractions.

With the dog as his entry, he could easily visit Ariel every day. He would make himself available to do her bidding: run errands, prepare a meal, do a little housecleaning, and, as required of all men, to the unabashed delight of all women, throw out the garbage.

It was too early to walk Little Eva to Ariel's, so he sat down in the old leather chair and reread the journal.

There were no new insights that he hadn't already discovered at first reading. He intended to return the journal and take no others. Borrowing the first one had been on sudden unchecked impulse. But "borrowing" was simply a euphemism for stealing. However Bill preferred to view his thievery, he felt ashamed of himself and wondered if the curse of Eros was only to test the moral fiber of his victims.

It was not as easy to return the journal as it had been to take it, however.

"Bare feet of lovers, thudding on the roof of mounds, press lightly on these crumbled hearts."

Raintree County

NINE

Ariel and William

It had to stop, thought Ariel, and so, too, did William. And it eventually did on an evening in early June, during a rehearsal for the play that was scheduled to open on the twelfth.

William was not feeling well when he arrived at the theater. He was directing the comedy that was sailing along with few problems. The casting was perfect, the set completed days before schedule, and miraculously, everyone knew their lines. He almost called off rehearsal to give the cast a much-needed day off, but he wanted to see Ariel, knowing she would be there that evening for an interview with a reporter from one of the Albany newspapers.

Midway through the run-through, William eased quietly out of the front doors to sit on one of the benches in the front garden. Ariel happened to look out of the office window, where she was being interviewed, and saw William fall forward off the bench and onto the ground. Leaving the stunned reporter in mid sentence, she ran down the stairs and out to the garden to find William clutching his stomach and writhing in the lavender, unable to reply to her frantic pleas.

She looked up and saw the reporter leaning out the open window and shouted to him to call the emergency squad.

Kneeling beside him she lifted William into her arms, his head cradled on her lap. People were rushing out from rehearsal, and Ariel shouted that someone should get a glass of water, and to get Susan on the phone.

Checking his pulse she found it very weak. Color had drained from his face and his jaw was slack. She shook him gently for a response.

He looked up questioningly. Someone handed the phone to her, and she told Susan, with extreme care, the situation. She answered with assurance that he was conscious, and rather than drive him home, she was getting him to the emergency room at the hospital. She should meet them there. Ariel ended the call just as the squad's sirens could be heard in the distance.

—Don't leave me, Ariel. . . .

—Of course I won't. The paramedics are here, Will.

—You'll stay with me?

—I won't leave you, I won't. I promise.

—I need—

Ariel was told to stand aside. Within minutes William was being wheeled by stretcher into the ambulance. Ariel directed the cast members to close up the theater, make calls to John and for someone to drive her car and park it in the hospital lot on their way home.

The paramedics wouldn't let Ariel ride in the ambulance. William voiced his distress.

—I'm going with him, do you understand? she ordered, giving no room for dissent.

She was told to stay seated in the corner.

Susan arrived in time to follow the stretcher into a curtained cubicle. Ariel took a seat in the waiting room, anxiously awaiting word. Two hours later, when she was at the point of despair, a nurse came out and called her name.

—Mr. Trent is asking for you, she said.

—Me?

—Are you Ariel?

—Yes, but his—

—Come with me, he's in number fourteen, down this way.

—Is he . . . ?

The nurse anticipated her question.

—He's doing well. The doctor is admitting him for observation and a couple of tests.

Ariel was nearing room 14, when Susan came out. She glanced sideways at Ariel from the downward tilt of her head as she walked passed. She looked stressed, as if she'd been given bad news. When she stopped to speak to Susan, she saw a face set in stone. Susan continued to walk determinedly down the hall and out the doors, as if deaf to her surroundings and Ariel's plaintive summons.

Should she go to William or run after Susan? An ominous sense of foreboding swept through her and settled into the pit of her stomach.

William was pale and still, and the doctor saw the panic in Ariel's face. He smiled and said, —He's just asleep, we sedated him. It's a bleeding ulcer. He'll be fine.

—Oh, thank God! she said, color returning to her cheeks, the tension in her stomach and spine ebbing.

—You're Ariella? He's been calling for you. He may sleep through the night from what we've given him.

—I'll stay with him.

—You can do that. We're getting a room ready for him on the third floor, Mrs. Trent.

—Oh, but, no! I'm not Mrs. Trent. I'm a . . . close friend.

The doctor didn't seem to hear her denial, as he left the room.

She spent the night in a chair next to William's bed, watching over him as he dozed. He awoke once, when a nurse came in to check his vital signs. When he saw Ariel, and felt her hand on his, he gave her fingers a little squeeze; contentment washed over his face before he drifted off to sleep again.

—Well, I'm glad somebody got some sleep last night!

Ariel, her head down on the edge of the bed, woke at the harsh announcement. Sunlight was shining through the window, onto William's butter-colored hair. She followed his glance across the room to where Susan stood in the doorway, with an expression as frozen as her stance. It took Ariel a moment to get her bearings. William was awake, a smile on his face, and he was holding her hand. She eased hers free. Offering a smile and greeting, she was met by Susan's icy glare.

—Susan . . . I'm glad you're back. I was waiting for you, but I didn't want to leave him until you returned.

—Well, I'm back.

—Good. Great. William, you look better this morning.

—I feel—

—Yes, much better, said Susan.

—I'll be going, then. John and the kids must be— said Ariel, rising from the chair to gather her sweater and purse as quickly as she could.

—Good idea, said Susan, flashing a bright sardonic smile as she walked over to kiss her husband on the lips before claiming the chair.

—Thank you, Ariel, said William, his voice subdued and his eyes darkening.

—Yes, thank you, Ariel, echoed Susan, trying to match the tone of his sincerity, but missing by a longshot. She left the room with no further words to meet John coming out of the elevator.

June 5th

Dear William,
I am relieved that you are feeling better. I hope you will forgive this coward for delivering this letter via a nurse to your room., but there are things I must say that I feel are better said in writing. The truth is, I don't know how I could speak the words, perhaps because so much is at stake, and I would probably fumble things up voicing them out loud.

Over the past few months we've enjoyed very intimate conversations through our letters. Writing to you and receiving your letters has helped me out of the depression I fell into. I am as grateful to you for indulging me with your thoughts as I am of your friendship. Little did I know, however, that as I was being helped out of one melancholy, I was diving into one of a different sort.

Never once in the twenty years of my marriage to John have I ever glanced at another man. It was easy for me to turn off any man's active interest with the words, "I love John." That is still, and always will be true for me.

"Raintree County" became a lifeline to me; a lifeline to the only real friend I've ever had since we moved here six years ago. But, it also served to spark questions within me about things I had never dared think about before. Who I had become was not necessarily the person who lived inside me. Not to say I'm a sociopath in hiding or anything, but I had conformed in so many ways to become the image of what other people needed me to be. I think most people do that to some degree.

I won't deny that I have cared deeply for you for a long time. Perhaps I wanted to recognize you in the character of John Shawnessy in "Raintree County" when I read an apt description of him, for it describes you as I have come to see you: "He was Raintree County's one true aesthete and somehow managed to erect all things beautiful and ugly into an ideal existence." I think that's one of the qualities I most admire in you, William, your ease and determination to make even the worst experiences a positive force for growth in your life. I'm trying to apply that same spirit, to always make things better, to my own life. But, I fear I may make a muck of things and negatively affect the people in our lives if I'm not careful right now.

I am aware how you feel about me. Susan's face confirmed this morning what I've known for a long time now. Need I say, I feel the same way about you?

A quote from Herodotus I recently pondered: "Circumstances rule men; men do not rule circumstances."

I think there are too many variables to take that to heart, don't you? I think men and women sometimes create circumstances because of the need to fulfill their desires. The danger is that men may fall victim to the circumstances they themselves helped to create.

I do not wish to create a situation that compromises us and those we love. Some might say this letter is doing just that. It is not my intent. We care too much for each other not to be honest.

I have been in conflict for many months about my feelings for you in relation to my feelings toward John. I am no longer confused.

I do love you, as I heard you whisper to me as you stroked my hair while I dozed beside your bed. I thought at first I was dreaming.

I feel no guilt in the love I feel for you, although I know John would be very shaken should he ever become aware of it. I suppose Susan only intuits our feelings. That in itself may be creating circumstances that will rule our lives.

So . . . I think you'll agree with me that we should cease our correspondence and try to return to a friendship that keeps us on safer ground.

Please know that I've come to understand that my love for you is something quite wonderful, not a feeling that need conflict me. Your presence in my life is a joyful thing, not a thing to be frightened of or sad about. It's what makes it possible for me to write this letter.

John and I will stop in this evening to see you. Don't worry about the opening! You've got a terrific show and a competent stage manager!

Yours,
Ariel.

P.S. Please destroy my letters. Innocent as they are, they compromise us and may be hurtful to Susan should she read them.

When Ariel and John came by to visit early in the evening before going to the theater, William handed Arial an envelope, asking her to deliver the enclosed notes to his stage manager.

Ariel knew there was a letter for her in the envelope, too. When she'd have an opportunity to read it, she didn't know for sure. John was going with her, to help where he could, in light of William's absence. He was being released in the morning, William said. The visit was short. She squeezed his hand and said she would see him in the morning, and then they left.

Later, upon arrival at the Meeting House, while John was distracted by greetings of members of the cast he had not seen for some time, Ariel went to the ladies' room and tore open the envelope.

As she expected, along with two sheets of notes for the stage manager was a letter for her in a separate envelope. She was nervous as she tried to read, skipping words and having to start the sentence again to glean meaning. Finally, she settled down and read:

From my hospital bed, June 5th
My dearest Ariella—
I don't have my glasses with me, so God only knows what I will write!
It isn't you who is the coward, It is I!
It has taken me long enough to discover how I really felt for you. Let me go back a while:
I cannot remember a time in my life when I believed I would NOT be alone.
What does that mean?
Surrounding me are almost impenetrable walls. I don't peek over them often—I haven't needed to for many years, as I've had Susan and the children. I don't encourage others to look in. If you don't get too close, you won't get hurt. So, I live happily alone.
All I was aware of (walls being what they are) was that I thrived on your company. Your smile, your laugh, your literary intelligence. I felt rather than knew I could be unguarded around you to an extent I'm not with others.
I also began to let my guard down around myself. Growing up in the Air Force you move constantly, as did those around me. I had my mother when I was small and, upon her third marriage and the resulting children, I felt I had

only myself as a constant in my life. It didn't take me too long to "learn" that if I fell in love one of us would move away.

But, you came into my life, and you made me rethink it. I wanted to discover the truth, whatever it might have turned out to be. But, I feared that, if I rushed it, flinging myself at it like a football defensive tackle, I'd find only what I WANTED to find and not what was actually there. In short, I'd contaminate it with what would have pleased me to think was true. My fear was that if I made it (whatever "it" may be) too important, I'd never achieve "it."

So what is "it"?

Was "it" coming to grips with the reality of an unrequited love, or an awkward romance? Was I, AM I afraid that, underneath all the fun and gushy romance we might simply have fallen in love with falling in love? Was "it" the opportunity to be young and vulnerable again? Was the "it" that we were nudging closer to, letter by letter, paragraph by paragraph, to what neither of us ever contemplated having before: an affair like big people have?

Was the "it" the fulfillment of desires at a time in our lives when the only real beneficiaries could be only our egos and genitals?

Are we really only an aging Romeo and Juliet? DON'T, whatever you do, DON'T drink the poison!

Was I afraid, since I, not you, have never felt there has to be a connection between love and nookie, that all I wanted was sex?

Am I afraid that I don't really know what L-O-V-E is, and so I cavorted through a lovely maze in the hope that at "ITS" center I'd find out? THAT is a daunting fear, my love, daunting. For it is a form of using someone - you - very unfairly for what is, in essence, an intellectual pursuit.

And, was I afraid that you were simply flirting with the company's socially inept hermit?

I can honestly say yes, to all those questions, but that I love you as deeply as I love life itself.

YES! I LOVE YOU! WILLIAM LOVES ARIELLA! Find me a tree to carve it into!

And, yes, William is also afraid, for our innocent families, that he's in love with being in love, that he's simply hoping for the opportunity to have an affair, that he's simply horny for something forbidden by society, that he's rushing into something that he truly cannot see without his glasses, and he really doesn't want to age like that; That he's using a wonderful, vulnerable and extraordinary human being for the wrong ends—purely selfish ends—and even that he's the butt of some cruel joke by the company flirt.

So you see, I figured out that I adore you, and decided not to tell you. It was unfair for me to whisper as you slept. I guess I secretly wanted you to hear what I could not bring myself to say with those green eyes leveled on mine. I am the coward, here.

I will not destroy your letters. They are dear to me because they are expressions of your thoughts and feelings and spiritual beauty, just as I could never destroy a photograph of you, because it is a reflection of your physical beauty.

I love you. I whispered the words as you slept; I've written then in this letter. One day, perhaps, if I'm very lucky—and brave!—I will look into your eyes and tell you, again.

—William

She stayed up writing after John had gone to bed. She was fearless now, with no concern, no thought of the future other than that they shared a love, and that William be content and his ulcer healed. Had his turmoil over loving her contributed to his illness? Her love for him should not be a troublesome thing but should bring him peace and happiness.

My very dear William!

Thank you for your honest and loving letter. It brought me great happiness to know that you feel for me as I do you.

We are quite a pair, are we not? We've chattered for months about everything. We've talked ourselves to death without uttering a word of our most pressing thoughts! I don't know what our futures will bring, but our feelings should not be a burden, but rather an emotional uplifting.

I'm no longer in conflict about whom to love or not. My love for John is a given. I finally accept both loves as miracles—precious gifts bestowed upon me. One love does not negate the other. There are no scales to weigh each love's worth. They simply ARE!

How wonderful is love's power! It is not singular and exclusive, but large and expanding, like the universe. I don't feel perverse in feeling love for both you and John. I accept the love I feel, and that which is given by each of you, fully aware that yours may never be experienced in a physical way. And, that's all right, too. I am happy to just love.

Sometimes realizing love is a long process. Perhaps that's why what I feel for you is so valuable to me. I honestly didn't know what was happening to me. It began about a year ago, one winter night when you entered from a snowstorm.

So you see, it matters not if we ever speak of our feelings because the love exists. We need never kiss, because our spirits have touched. I've no right to ask for more.

Rehearsal went well tonight, no problems.

It is very late, and I should be asleep, but I'm too restless. I will drive to a place where I can see the stars. Did you know that the constellation Cassiopeia is a "W" flipped to stand on point? I will look at your initial that God so cleverly penned on the heavens! I will look for it tonight!

With love, Ariel

My Dearest Love!

I've not much time to write, so I'll address some pertinent parts of your letter:

Will we ever "speak"? When the time is right for us to. We'll know.

Will we ever "kiss"? Against my better judgment, and despite what my head tells me, my heart and hormones tell me YES!

Will we ever make love? My question, and yours implied. I HOPE so. And I'm not discussing simple sex or lying together spent and entwined, but joining physically what seems to have joined in every other way. Lying together without need for hurry or talk or anything but simply lying together.

—Your loving W

On the evening of June 8th, William insisted on attending rehearsal despite doctor's orders that he stay at home and rest. Susan acquiesced: He was worse off at home, worrying about the state of the show. Ariel agreed that, if he did not extend himself too much, she would pick him up at his home and drive him to the Meeting House.

More than concern for the season's premier, William was desperate to see Ariel. The twenty-minute drive to and from rehearsal was all he wanted in life that day. He only needed to look at her, and then, perhaps, he could relax and let the medicine do the rest.

When he got into her car and they drove down the steep drive from the farmhouse, they didn't speak;

each only stared at the road ahead. The rolling green landscape of timothy-covered meadows and newly rising cornrows was fragrant with the scent of blooming lilac. The world was bursting with the vibrancy of color and warmth and hopeful new life springing up all around them. A young calf, shaky in its footing, leaned against its mother's shank for support. The calf reminded her of William, still weak from the days in the hospital. She turned to look at him, and he smiled, touchingly.

They spoke only about the production and the plans for the opening-night after-show celebration. They spoke as they had become accustomed to conversing over the years, with an easy flowing camaraderie, except that now there was subtext to their words that each repressed, as if their declarations of love would be reserved for the secret world of their letters. Neither knew how to sound out those feelings. When the Meeting House came into view, each regretted the lost opportunity.

The cast and crew were overjoyed to see William, and he perked up with returned delight. After speaking with the stage manager and tech crew he went backstage to approve several costumes that had been made from designs he had only seen on paper.

Ariel was not working on this show, and William was looking and behaving as his usual self, so she took a magazine from the dressing room, grabbed her big picture-frame gardening hat, and went out into the backyard. She sat at the picnic table, enjoying the sunny rays of the late spring evening and the sounds of people rushing about doing what needed doing before the start of the run-through rehearsal. The chirping of nesting birds and the happy voices wafting through the open windows of the dressing room was harmonious music to her ears. Peals of laughter and chatter lulled her as she closed her eyes against the setting sun. The birds, the people—that divine meeting of community working toward a single purpose—was a beautiful thing to hear. . . . And, William was well and happy in his element.

Something was blocking the sun through her shuttered lids. When she opened them, William was standing before her, silhouetted by the sun.

She squinted and William moved aside to sit across from her at the picnic table. Ariel pulled the ribbon to release the bow that tied the hat on her head and placed it upon William's.

—You look rather pretty in that hat, you know.

—So did you.

—Is everything looking well?

—Oh, yes.

—I meant about the show. . . . Keep the hat on. You're fair, and will burn.

—I am burning.

—The sun is still hot.

She was being silly, but what else could she be? She was never so shy in her life as this moment under his gaze. He watched her so intensely, with that dreamy little smile. His eyes were the color of cornflowers. It hurt to look at him, but every time she tried to look away she was drawn back.

Soon there was no looking away, just a steady hypnotic wave that drew them into each other, and the chatter of humans and wildlife faded as they basked in the warm sun and adoration.

He spoke, and then, so did she, before the company smokers came out for a last puff before rehearsal.

William would write of those moments with a mortal's endeavor to record each detail, to capture the art and poetry of its rapture, and in an effort to return—if only in his mind, when all else was lost—to the profane and sacred beauty of a place they had lingered in for a time, both brief and eternal.

The next evening was "dark" on the production schedule so that the cast and crew could have a well-deserved rest. Ariel would not see William that day, as it was Peter's graduation from high school.

She would have liked to have been with William for just a little while, for she was feeling the effects of melancholy, remembering Peter's first day of kindergarten, when he went off in the school bus proudly sporting the swollen eye from a bee-sting. The other little boys at the bus stop asked him if he had been in a fistfight. Peter replied, "Kinda."

His dark hair had once been as golden as her wedding ring, and his toenails so tiny she had been afraid to clip them herself. Now, at six-foot-three, standing in his size-twelve loafers, she could only find a hint of that baby peeking out through his eyes. It was inevitable that he would arrive at the brink of manhood, just as surely as time advanced. It was all over. She had brought him this far and now she had to watch him go on his way toward a life of his own making, where she existed only in the periphery of his world for occasional visits, holiday dinners, and Mother's Day cards.

They had planned a graduation party at their home after the ceremony. The house was packed with friends and relatives when William and Susan arrived. Ariel was surprised they had come, and was concerned that William was overtaxing himself. She was in the kitchen replenishing several serving dishes when William came up behind her and touched her shoulders.

They had no time for discussion that afternoon, which was just as well where Ariel was concerned. He was too much a distraction and there were too many observant people.

He wrote his impressions:

> *You reached over me twice—quite innocently and innocuously in the kitchen tonight. We were alone. I may have been teasing about locking everyone else outside, but the physical reaction was no joke. I had butterflies in my stomach. My eyes literally crossed! I nearly dropped the salad bowl I was holding. I am not one for irresistible urges, but I came within a sigh of pulling you into my arms and kissing you as (I hope for my sake) you have never been kissed before. Had you reached over a third time . . . ?*
>
> *I won't see you until tomorrow's dress rehearsal. That is in 24 hours. You who profess to like science fiction realize that electronic communication travels only at the speed of light. Thus, the farther away you get, the greater the time lag between communicants must be.*
>
> *Now, then, ponder this: I read tonight thoughts you wrote 24 hours ago. That's the equivalent of being 16 billion, 70 million, 400 thousand miles away from you while we try to speak coherently to one another. I did the math: 24 hours X 186,000 miles per second = 16,070,400,000! It's very hard to hold hands across such a distance, No?*

How do we fix that?

Yours in need of a good eye doctor, with love unbounded that has you name on it—W

The opening was well received, but the play was not William's and Ariel's focus.

It was just one more in a series of opening nights for William. But a first of many experiences that charmed him and touched him with a poignancy that he would draw on in memory until the last.

My dear, sweet Love!

Somehow, I don't know how, we managed to get through the last 16 billion miles. How many more before I hear your voice? How many more before I can hear you say you love me? Strange, I cannot hear you say it often enough to suit my current greedy state of mind!

To see you again grows more important to me all the time.

To touch you, however "innocently," becomes my goal.

Why, at this age, after all the blessings of my life, why, now, has one touch, one kiss, one whispered phrase become so vital to me?

I am both tortured and charmed by you. When I arrived to bring you to the theater this evening, you, in the best tradition of coquettes since time out of memory, kept me waiting. Then you flounced down the stairs in short-shorts and my imagination went berserk!

You didn't come all the way down the stairs, but beckoned me to meet you where, both of us precariously balanced, we lose our emotional equilibrium in an embrace Anthony and Cleopatra could never even dream of, much less experience!

Your face, as I approached the stairs, should have been the main feature of a Tintorello! Joyful, suffused with an inner glow that was—is—will always be to me ineffably radiant: soft, warm, and inviting, yet so flattering to me, as though I were some sort of fantasy suddenly made real, instead of the clod you must perforce share a stage with.

Your skin was soft, cool and dry in spite of the heat of the day, yet the muscles underneath moved to my touch. I felt ham-handed and clumsy holding you there.

Then you rushed off to the hall closet to fetch your gown. I followed, so I might bury myself in your hair, surround you with me, if nothing else. I am not one to be possessive of people, mainly because I don't like being possessed, but for those too-brief moments, I felt as though you WERE MINE! And that can be very heady stuff! Not in terms of power and control, but pride and a screwy sense of accomplishment: Look, Trent, at what you can achieve: the love, affection, and joy of a woman like this! All I wanted to do was to please you.

You nearly touched a "no-no," but pulled away. You needn't have.

I tried to see your eyes. You hid them. I held you by your jaw, amazed by its delicacy. I wanted to rip away your blouse and brassiere—not from lasciviousness or misplaced macho, but to see you without barriers and covers—to revel in the cool, soft, dry skin of your whole body and to feel it move to my touch.

When, at last, you pulled away and moved about, I enjoyed watching you move, without calculation, with no other thought than living the moment. I couldn't tell if you were lithe or graceful, or tight as a spring about to snap. You were natural to the moment. And that, too, increased the vigor of my passion: It turned me on even more than I already was.

We laughed occasionally, about something or other. You were trying so hard to pack up for the theater, by the time you sat down to recover, you worried about looking disheveled. And for the life of me, all I could see was the most angelic sort of beauty I've ever set eyes on. No hair out of place. Your face still belonging on the profane Renaissance canvas, its inner light still alive—now in eyes that I could look into. I wouldn't have left the house for all the spaghetti in the world! What, and share that beauty with any jerk who happened to pass by? Not on your tampon, my love! Not in this life!

I had nothing intelligent to say to you. Like a dope—some rube from the sticks—all I could think *was: I love you! Not original enough for you, not what you deserve!*

How could I luck into the tender strength of your arms, the hunger of your hands, the gentleness of your lips, or the shy way, in our embraces, you would not look into my eyes—then, seated, the audacious gleam of them when you DID look into mine, like a beautiful happy child just for happiness' sake!

Later, at the picnic table, I could not keep my eyes off you. The public, even the private Ariel had vanished. In their place: The secret Ariella: a sexy, sensual enchantress who, with me, can be a little girl more beatific than Munier's children. It was there at the table that I made a discovery. Your love is a very powerful thing, kind, gentle, and unselfish. It softens you in all the right ways. I felt something I couldn't explain then, but, now...? You were vulnerable without fear. You'd opened everything but your legs to me. And the omission of the legs grew unimportant, not worth considering.

Whenever "IT" happens, I want light. I want to see you the whole time. I don't believe in kissing or making love with my eyes closed. Not with you. I want to look at you, memorize you, paint your portrait in my mind and in my heart—the you that I know is there when we are alone together.

I have only one regret about last night: I was unable to kiss you goodnight. That left me with a small hollowness.

I started out meaning only to describe you last night, kind of as a way of proving Robert Burns right or wrong. "... would that God the giftie gi'e us to see ourselves as ithers see us." I wanted you to see you as I do. As always, the portrait says more about the painter than it does about his subject.

I love you, unseasonably and unreasonably, with a sureness that makes it incredible to me that I have not known and loved you all my life.

Come to me soon, my beautiful Venus, and smile your secret Ariella smile for me, please.

Your W

It was shameless, and yet she felt no shame. Sitting side-by-side on the picnic table bench outside the Meeting House; others were there, too, squeezed in, a mini-board-meeting before a performance where they were discussing advertising sales for the concert programs. She, bare-armed; he in a short-sleeved polo shirt. Their arms barely touching, gliding over the fine downy hairs of her arms, an inconspicuous rub of his forearm—as the others were talking, talking, and she weakened with longing, and when she heard a low, throaty moan escaping his lips, a sharp, bolting ache shot through from down her navel like a shockwave. William cleared his throat, and then replied foolishly to a question posed to him. . . .

Sleep only came with complete exhaustion, hours after Ariel slipped in under the sheets. But something, a dream, some interior alarm, would awaken her and she'd lie there in the dark room, restless, thinking of

William; was he sleeping, too, or had he awakened her telepathically? She would try not to move, looking at John, restating her love for him. She'd try to remain still so as not to awaken him, even though she knew he had imbibed enough to keep him in a deep sleep until the alarm went off at seven. Restlessness would win and she'd get out of the bed and pace through the house, aimlessly, like a cat on the prowl. The beetles would rattle their wings against the window screens as if calling her out to play.

If the night was clear, Ariel would throw on an old cotton sundress and leave the house, inhaling the moist cool air of the late-spring night, potent with the fragrance of breathing grasses reaching through the humus of autumns past. Being outdoors in the darkness, where all but the crickets slept, gave her the silence and the sense of consolation she had begun to thrive on. It was as if her attention could be directed away and outside of herself and from the people who consumed her energy. Where her eyes deigned to travel was not in response to anyone's wishes but her own. And the sound of the night bugs in the distant field and woods had become the music of preference to the snoring of her drunken husband. His snoring had never bothered her before now; rather it had once been a reassurance of his presence in her life. But, it had become a cacophony that bore through her and wracked the delicate parts of her brain. She would not move out of their bedroom, for fear of hurting John. She loved him still, but she found herself shrinking from him. She would not allow herself to see what he had become: She would only focus on the good in him, with the hope and the faith she had always had in the past. Wasn't it her own fault that he had become like a child to her? Why had she always accepted his irresponsible behavior? Hadn't she indulged him, perhaps too much, by defending him? When they were at the beginning of their relationship, it was she who set the tone that would exist between them. She treated John as she wished to be treated, and that was important in all relationships, to give and to share respect. She'd been through an abusive affair when in Europe studying, before her mother had become ill and she returned home. The only way she had been able to extricate herself from the man was to leave the country. She had decided, then, that no one would ever treat her so carelessly again. And John was good and kind and willing to be the man who fell into the pattern of behavior she needed. Was he the way he was because she had never had expectations of him beyond gentle communication? Had she set unreasonable standards for herself and for John and the children to live up to? Perhaps her expectations for herself had been set beyond the possibility of human reach. Was John suffering at her hands, his behavior a negative response to unspoken expectations she had imposed on him?

Those thoughts ran through her mind, but only on occasion. The truth that she loved John was not a question. The truth that she loved William was all-important. She used to see things, hear things during the day and think, "William would like that." She'd search for ideas that would please him, a book that he might enjoy reading, a composition she thought he'd like that she'd include in the next concert.

Alone under the stars, she could let down her guard, her mind could wander to thoughts of William, she could dream of William, hear his mellow voice, enjoy the fantasy of his kisses, and know the comfort of his embrace without fearing John's or anyone else's constant scrutiny. Here, under the presence of the ancient gods that circled the heavens, she could shed the cloak of disappointment that she wore like the soiled and shredded burial cloths of the corpses that plagued her dreams with forebodings of death and decay. Here, free, in this clean and open space where hope invariably rose up each spring like shoots of grain, she breathed unburdened for a time.

Two days after the season opening, on a moonless, star-studded hour past midnight, Ariel drove along the meadow farm road three miles out of town. She parked at the usual rise, set high on a winding hill and overlooking acres of pasture and cornfields. The silence was interrupted only by the distant lowing of a cow and the chittering of the night critters silenced at the tread of her footsteps.

Crossing over the wooden planks that served as a short bridge across a stream flowing parallel to the road, she walked a few yards into the alfalfa grass, threw down a woolen blanket, and sat legs crossed, head thrown back, facing the sky like a sunbather basking in the sunshine.

Some people were afraid of the dark, she thought, but there was such beauty in the night. The stars circling in the sky above now, where during the daytime they couldn't be seen for the sun. There was that "discussion" she and William argued: He held to the belief that any "truth" was determined by an individual's perception; Ariel countered with her belief that whether or not one can perceive *anything* is moot to the fact that there is an underlying truth to everything, *perceived or not*. Like the stars, she argued. Now you see them, now you don't. But they are always there.

Headlights coming down the road at that hour of the night always gave Ariel pause. Someone might be stopping to see if anyone was in the car and if it had broken down, left stranded. The State Patrol that cruised the area had stopped once, and she explained that she was stargazing. She'd had her telescope with her that night, and the officer was very excited at the peek of Jupiter and one of its moons orbiting the planet.

Now a car was slowing, passing around her car, before coming to a stop.

For the headlights, she could only discern the silhouette of a man walking from the car to look into her driver's-side window. She decided to call out, saying she was fine, the car not broken down, when he called out.

—Ariel? Ariel, John? Where are you?

—William? I'm down here. Across the footbridge.

—What are you doing?

—Stargazing.

The car lights shut off and she watched his approach.

—I saw your car and thought it broke down. It's two o'clock in the morning.

—And what are you doing up at this hour, may I ask?

He didn't reply.

As they stood in suspended silence, she gradually became aware that the meadow was alive as the crickets resumed their chirping, peepers in the distant brook sang their urgent call, fireflies flashed a haphazard lightshow, a brazen challenge to the power of the stars. The land was teeming with life and the shameless procreation of all things living, the natural coming together of all God's creatures. The tall grasses waved approval and a random breeze swept up to rustle the leaves of the distant birches. Her senses peaked, her vision keener as if the world around her was suddenly swathed in a revealing luminescence.

—I've been here ten minutes and I've seen three shooting stars. Did you know there may be as many as 200 million meteors cruising by each day that can be seen from earth?

—And it's been 38 billion years since I last saw you.

—I'm glad we didn't have to wait any longer.

—It's been ages.

He took her into his arms, as if he had done so a thousand times before and traced his finger down along her cheek to her lips, following the soft outline of her mouth. His hand retreated to her hair and gently he brushed his lips on hers. She could feel him tremble as he pulled her closer and the kiss deepened. Ariel responded with a shudder.

—I prayed I'd find you. I didn't think I'd last another hour away from you, he sighed into her ear before returning to her lips.

—I've missed you.

—Ariella! We're alone, you know. . . .

—No. They're watching.

—The gods? I know they're jealous of me.

He would not let her speak, for he placed a finger on her lips, and whispered, —Hush.

He looked into her eyes, a glimmer of light reflecting like pinpricks on her irises.

—It's all right. *We're* so right, Ariella. I've never known a time when it was so right. . . .

Through her silence, she acquiesced, and as he gently glided his lips along her neck to linger at the hollow of her shoulder, she breathed in the warm, clean, masculine scent that rose with his heat. Hair, so soft and feathery at her cheek, the scent of newly cut hay; the smooth firmness beneath his shirt. To the touch, to her fingers, he was unfamiliar, as there had been no other man but John all these years, and yet she knew William as intimately as if they had shared a womb. She rejoiced in the music of his breath, the rhythm of his heartbeat.

There was no doubt that they had been made for each other, and, as was destined, had come together in this moment after a lifetime of longing.

He is right, she thought; *we're so right!*

He touched her with the care of handling a precious treasure, with wonder, and then with the fierce, heady pride of possession, he removed first one, and then the other sandal, kneading the arch of her foot as he fought to contain the hurried desire within him.

Ariel remained motionless with expectation, inhaling the soft night air. His whisper, a low throaty rush at her ear.

—I just want to look at you for a moment you are so beautiful I can't take all of you in fast enough.

A great wave coursed through her, and she feared that her soul would snap free of an invisible cord to leave her body.

His touch was light, and he nestled the softly rounded hill of her belly, reveling in the luscious silky feel of her skin, finding it more difficult with every discovery not to rush on to the next.

She reached for him, to guide him to that part of her that ached for his touch. They sighed as one, and then lay motionless for a long moment, trembling with the rapture of their first union.

She had never really understood when people said "time stood still" until now. Gone was the sense of time, of space outside the meadow with its star-spangled ceiling; nothing else existed as she drifted off into that new and brilliant dimension. Lost in William, and yet, at the same time, she wasn't lost at all, but safe within the warmth of his embrace: loved and cherished in a way she had never known before. There was only William and William was she!

—*I'm home, at last, I'm home,* he whispered.

Ariel took in the stars as they spun with ever-increasing celerity. That she should be his *home* made her tender to his need.

She held him in her arms for a long time, unable to let him go, stroking his damp hair and weeping quietly with the joy that filled her. He was reluctant to be let go of, reluctant to be released from the closeness he had given himself up to. And he heard a voice inside him appeal:

Don't give of yourself, give up yourself.

For isn't that what he had done, for the first time in his life? He had given himself up, totally, to this woman, this gift to his life. He had allowed himself to feel a love that made him vulnerable without fear. She could do with him as she chose, and he would gladly give his life for hers. How had it come to pass that now, after nearly half a century of living, after cultivating a self-contained life for himself, after loving Susan as he admittedly did, with admiration and affection and respect, could one little woman manage to sneak into his heart and proceed to tear down all his defenses?

So all the silly stuff of poets and romantics was true! There were no defenses against Ariella. She touched him in places that he never knew existed. Something miraculous had happened: She had rescued him from the desolate landscape where he had resided for most of his life, that bleak, dark place where he had hidden for all the years of his forsaken existence, and he savored the newfound paradise at his fingertips.

This phenomenon of finally belonging, of a connection to all living things, he could acknowledge, but not explain. That raw, hidden hurt within him had been eased. *He had made a connection.* In a profound way the barren soil of his center bloomed with hope and happiness. Suddenly, he was struck with clarity where before he saw only an enigma in the book that drew him back to reread year after year. Ross Lockridge, Jr. had described love as "A tall, imperious bloom."

As their breathing fell in sync, a thousand thoughts would flicker and extinguish with the breath of their convictions. They would remain together, no matter what, each knew, because the value of their love was greater than anything else life could offer them. They would give up themselves to each other, but never give each other up at any price.

That June night, in the early hours of a summer morning, their lovemaking was a celebration of their commitment, an affirmation that they had finally found their true homeplace.

It came to pass that over the next week, although they saw one another each day, they were unable to meet alone. So they spoke through their letters, exchanged at each evening's performance.

It was 12:03 P.M. and there was no car in sight.

William stood looking out the parlor window of the farmhouse at the S-curved road leading from Linden Falls, six miles to the south. He'd walked anxiously from the south window to the north window in the kitchen, looking for Ariel's car. It was now five minutes past noon. Where was she? Five minutes lost, they might have spent together.

The luncheon basket and blanket were ready on the steps of the back porch. Had he forgotten anything? If she didn't arrive soon, he'd die, on the spot, from anticipation. Where was she?

The day was perfection: blue sky with not a wisp of clouds, the sun high, but not oppressively hot. It was a day made in heaven, and if she'd only arrive, they'd find heaven again.

Why did she excite him so? With just a glance he was rendered powerless. All he could think of was the desire to remain locked within her, to remain there in the searing condition when they joined together, moments that were sweeter than any ultimate release. Her flesh, so cool and clean and smooth, and the warmth that rose up to warm him, cajoled him into welcomed submission. This *thing*, his body, was quite apart from his mind. It betrayed him at every flicker of her eyelashes, every parting of her lips, every quiver that played along the long muscle of her thigh. Why, when he fell into her with more grace and ease of motion, was it so natural a leap?

Oh, Ariella, my love, how do you do it? Is it true when you say you love me?

She drew him to her without artifice, and when he was across a room from her, he could not stop himself from watching every move she made. He could not help himself, and if it drove him nuts, it was made worse by the fact that John seemed always to be watching him watching Ariel.

A car appeared at the rise in the road. William sprang out the squealing screen door of the farmhouse to meet it as it wiggled up the bumpy dirt drive.

Ariel got out of the car to find a very distressed-looking William standing at the foot of the porch steps. She walked slowly toward him, and then he smiled.

—You don't seem happy to see me. Are Susan and the kids—

—No, they're gone to her sister's for the day. I was afraid you weren't coming, and then, you were suddenly here. Never mind me. I thought you changed your mind.

—Silly man! I would have been here ten minutes ago, but I was following a slow truck. I'm here now.

William took her hand and started to lead her up the wooded hill toward the east meadow of the old farm. When he remembered the picnic on the porch, he left her to run back down to fetch the basket and blanket. She laughed at his endearing confusion, and any nervousness she may have felt being at his home evaporated with the humor of the moment.

As soon as they were safely hidden from view by any passersby on the road, William dropped the basket and embraced Ariel.

A cow mooed a couple yards away, startling Ariel so that she jumped, her head hitting his nose. They laughed until the giggles faded as their playful kisses became more intense.

—Where are you taking me? Down the garden path?

—Up the garden path. To a place that I've dreamed of showing you.

—I'm intrigued, she said, allowing William to guide her along the sun-mottled path and then through the tall grass at the edge of an idyllic meadow.

—Oh, it is so beautiful here! said Ariel, as she took in the pastoral scene.

—It's mine.

—What do you mean, yours?

—I bought these twelve-point-four acres from my father-in-law a couple of years ago, not long after we moved here to take care of Susan's mother. I don't own the house or any of the farm, but this meadow is mine. I come here a lot. It's the one place I've ever found where I can . . .

—What?

—Sounds too corny.

—Since when have you been afraid of sounding corny?

He turned with a smile and pulled her to him. Laughing, Ariel pulled away and pranced through the tall grass. William dropped the basket and caught her by the hand. Leading her around a knoll surrounded by saplings they fell to the ground and rolled down through an egress of a smaller clearing enclosed by woods. They made love in the tall grass under the midday sun to the chorus of chittering cicadas.

Later, as Ariel lay in William's arms, luxuriating in her nakedness under a temperate sun that warmed and soothed, the cushion of the future hay crop gentle on her back, she broke the silence of their meditation.

—I've never been outdoors and naked; it feels wonderful.

—It's as it should be. You, unlike me, have a body that should not be obscured by clothing. There is no garment as wondrous as this lovely flesh. He suckled her nipple and then pretended to suckle her nose.

She giggled like a girl and blushed, turning onto her stomach to stretch and reach the palms of her hands along the feathery seeding lawn. How many blades of grass could she touch and memorize in this moment? How faithful is memory in recording the minute details of the paradise God had lent her for a time? There was a prescience of loss forthcoming. Mortals are not entitled to remain in such altered states for very long. To be afforded a glimpse of Eden is prerequisite of the fall. She would not think about the future, not now, not today. She would drink it all to replay for the rest of her life.

They ate the lunch of cheddar slices and crackers and peaches washed down with a dry white wine, speaking only when Ariel would note a point of interest: A small flock of turkeys in the distance, the neon-blue of dragonflies mating on a blade of chicory.

—Is there such a thing as one man possessing a woman's soul and another her body?

William looked at Ariel considering the question.

—In *Raintree County*, Johnny asks the "Perfessor" that question. About Nell.

—Yes, I remember.

—Just a thought . . . Johnny possessed Nell's soul, but she married Garwood and he had claim on her body. Johnny married Suzanna, and he could only ever claim her body, never her troubled soul. . . .

—Are you asking in reference to yourself?

—To us. Are we lying to ourselves, Will? That we love each other *and* our spouses?

—I don't know how to qualify love. I love you and I love Susan. Each is different and unique, not to be compared.

—Why not compare? Are we afraid of what we'll see? I wonder if we should make choices based on intellect or the heart.

He chuckled and kissed her thigh.

—Well, you can't be sane; you're out of your mind to love me, so it must be your heart.

—I can't separate my soul from my body.

—Then it's moot.

—No.

—Why?

—Why? Because I've never felt like this before: *Blissful* when I'm with you. *Myself* when I'm with you . . . and *free* when I'm with you. In an altered state when I'm with you! So it makes me wonder if I really do love John at all, and if I ever loved him? And, also, if I only say that I love him because it is correct and logical and expected. You see?

—Correct? Logical? Expected. . . . You love other people. Your children! You love friends, don't you? You love them for their individual qualities. You don't sit and ponder why you care about them, you just do. I remember that line in *Raintree*: "The secret of human love and desire was to discover something that was at once universal and particular—beauty and a person." Isn't that enough?

—It's not that simple. I know the order in which those other people stand in my life. I know who has my affection. I'm talking about the love between a man and women. Can true love exist between a man and a woman without the mutual possession of both the body and the spirit? Shouldn't only one person possess both aspects of another?

He waited, a frown of bewilderment creasing his brow. And then, looking into himself, he voiced what he'd found there.

—First of all, what is love? It's like trying to describe Heaven. Perhaps love is just the ineffably intoxicating emotion that moves us beyond the mundane, stirs us to dream. Maybe it's the glue that connects all living things. It is an enigma. It's something I feel, something that drives me beyond what is rational, but it is something I cannot possibly explain. Poets have tried, and most have failed. What I do know is that love is impure if it is all about possession. Love is not the possessing of anybody. You don't belong *to* anybody, you belong *with* someone. Philosophically, I believe in free love; in practice, I am a one-woman man, I admit. And, I want you, and yes, I want to possess you, goddamn it, and that's against all that is safe and sane, I know. I am obsessed with you, have been for a long time, if you demand confession. I relent. You possess me, my body and my soul. I am yours. Completely. So maybe what we have is as ineffable as Heaven.

Had he succumbed to the allure of being wanted? How long could this fire rage within him without consuming him, both of them? A month? Six? A year before they settled into a contained burn and then the inevitable cool-down?

He thought as he looked at her with tender gratefulness. *Of all the thousands of orgasms for orgasms' sake I sought during my youth, they all seem meaningless. Why, oh, why, couldn't they have been with you?*

Haltingly, with vulnerability, he laid it all out before her.

—Should Susan die tomorrow, I would mourn her passing. Should you die, I strongly doubt I would ever recover from the loss. Forgive me, God! but, you are the air I breathe, the food that sustains me. For the first time in my life, making love is a way of becoming a part of you, an extension of you. I've not known that particular joy *ever* before . . . body and soul.

He watched her expression turn grim, and his grip on her arm increased.

—Does that answer it for you?

—It frightens me, what you just said.

—I suppose it is daunting, what I just said.

—It means that your wellbeing is my responsibility.

—Forgive me.

—Why? You have to carry the burden of mine as well. Such a powerful attraction as the one that exists between us threatens to sweep aside everything and everybody else in our paths. That is what frightens me. You see, you own my soul, and if our bodies never touched again after today, you are still in possession of it.

A breeze rustled the trees and resounded through the undulating meadow grass. The bucolic beauty of the scene before her brought to mind a phrase from *Raintree County*: "What difference now does it make that love was a tall, imperious bloom beside the river? What difference if face touched face beside the river? There was no guilt. . . . There was only love that is the desire for beauty. We were like flowers that seduce each other without memory and without guilt."

Alarmed by her sudden emotional withdrawal, he pulled her around to face him, a finger lifting her chin. He kissed her violently, as if to reaffirm his commitment, and they were soon enclosed in a world free of troubling thoughts, one radiant with enchantment.

My delicious Gypsyheart!

I do not joke when I call you "Gypsy." I am utterly and unredeemably serious: Your skin, your shape, the way your hair frames your face, the color of your hair, the color of your heart—You are a Gypsy!

I am home today with the children, as I begin my summer holiday, so I have to feed them lunch, and take the mongrel dog, Bobo, to the vet for his annual shots. Back home to start folding the week's worth of laundry , and then throw the chicken in the oven for dinner, before rushing out to the theater and you! I get through my days doing anything that will distract me, keep me sane until I can see you again, you wanton gypsyhearted wench! You've cast your spell on me, haven't you?

Later, while we kids sit waiting at the vet's office—

You Blackhearted Wanton!

I surrender! I can do nothing else but concentrate on you!

Is this what Cleopatra did to Anthony? Delilah to Samson? Eve to Adam? Ariella to Willie-Boy?

We are as strong as ever—you (Cleo, Delilah, Eve, and YOU) do not sap our strength. You do not "unman" us. You do not merely tempt us. Any of us could resist mere temptation. You simply distract us. None of us works 9–5 at an office, our lives are essentially unstructured, the only order being imposed by our own sense of self-discipline. You distract us. Our discipline crumbles, for we lose the power to concentrate. And we are lost! Adam had the apple, Sampson, his appointment at the hairdresser's, Anthony had Actium. I have lines to learn for our summer play!

The other black widows may've been more famous, but in NO WAY more effective than you! You, gypsyhearted woman, cast spells no Salem witch could ever equal! You don't play fair. You weave your webs of distraction that would bewitch a spider! And the victim never knows he's in a trap until it's been sprung upon him, by which time he's absolutely delighted to have been snared!

Is that goofy shit, or what?

It's as ridiculous as my inability to concentrate!

I knew what I was getting into. I simply goofed in not being able to predict the strength of what would happen to us . . . to me!

And it's not your fault, my sweet love. It's no one's fault. You can be at fault for things you can reasonably control. I think either of us—beforehand—would have fled like rabid hyenas from the prospect of having an affair. And now look at us!

I can hardly remember my name, much less my lines. You and I cannot spend eight hours a day writing to each other.

You must have a gypsy heart as black as midnight.* But, God, how I do love it!

Would you please put your clothes on and GET OUT OF WHAT'S LEFT OF MY MIND!!!

Your defenseless victim, who loves you DESPITE your wicked designs,

W

*Do you really understand how you've disarranged my mind, for me to write something as trite and as clichéd as that?

The windshield wipers were not much help in dividing the torrents of water slashing down from the sky. The windows kept fogging over, making the sheet of gray opaque. She resorted to the occasional wiping with an old woolen glove, found in the glove compartment and long forgotten in the search for its twin. How appropriate, she thought, to actually find a "glove" there. The irony was not lost on her as she trudged the car along the main route to the theater. June had been so balmy and temperate until that evening, almost erasing any memory of the past cruel winter.

When she finally pulled up to the theater, William was at her door almost immediately, a brightly colored golf umbrella shielding her way to the building's entrance.

—This may not be of much help, he said, assisting her out of the car.

Her sandaled feet landed in the lake that had formed in the drive, and when she glimpsed William's totally soaked condition and wearing the tropical-fish-patterned bathing trunks worn by an actor in the current show, she laughed and asked, —What are you doing in Henry's pants?

—I couldn't get into yours, so—

With a gentle push on his arm, she moved the umbrella away so that it fell pointing to the ground.

The rain was warm and yet refreshing after the ninety-plus-degree temperature of that muggy afternoon. She closed her eyes and aimed her face upward to receive the wet blessing. When she turned to look at William, his lips met hers in a kiss.

—I canceled tonight's performance, he said. —No one's here, and no one will see us, he said, bending over for a kiss.

—Those shorts are like a beacon in the night, she said, breaking free.

She stepped out of her sandals and, dangling the straps on her fingers, raced after the umbrella that bobbed down the side lawn like a tumbleweed. Leaping through the gigantic puddles with open arms she twirled in an impromptu dance about the yard, recalling the summer rain-showers of her childhood and the sense of abandon of yielding to Nature's whims.

In no time, William was alongside her, stomping and jumping like a kid, each leap an effort trying to make each splash rise higher than the last. She did a cartwheel, and then another. On the third attempt, her palm hit a pebble and the pain threw her momentum off, landing her on the cushiony grass beneath several inches of water.

The mishap startled her; she was not hurt, only muddied, and when she looked up to see William kneeling beside her, a look of concern replacing his smile, she pulled him down to her and rolled over on him.

—You did that pratfall on purpose, you strumpet wannabe! he said, as he locked her between his legs.

—Not really, but I know how to take advantage of the moment.

He tickled her and she let out a howl, unable to free herself from his stronghold. When he rolled her over so that she was once again on her back, a bolt of lightning zigzagged across his line of vision and the thunderclap shook the ground under them. The smell of ozone rapidly spread through the air.

William brought her to her feet and then pulled her along the lawn and in through the backdoor of the building.

When they were stripped of their wet clothing and toweled dry, Ariel slipped into her sky-blue Chinese kimono from the wardrobe. As she sat down at a dressing table combing the tangles out of her hair, the lights went off.

It was barely seven o'clock, but the room was dark. William lit an old oil lamp, a prop from the Stoppard comedy, *The Real Inspector Hound*, and Ariel reminded him that after a concert performance last year, when they lost electricity, she had purchased several lanterns and enough candles to light the stage, as the emergency lights only served to light the exits from the building.

She tried calling home, as the phone lines were still in service, but the line was busy. She tried again a few minutes later, and still the busy signal.

By the time Ariel entered into the main hall, the stage was brightened by the gentle, flickering flames. The stage set was a living-room, so they sat together on the sofa, encircled by a dozen candles.

—Don't you think you should put some clothes on?

—Why? Don't you like what I'm wearing? he said, looking over his naked body.

—The emperor's new clothes, *hmm?* Somebody might walk in.

—I locked the door. Why are you wearing *that*?

—As I said, somebody might walk in. And anyway, I didn't want to catch a chill.

—Won't let you catch a chill, he said taking her in his arms and pushing open the robe.

But, Ariel was distracted. Something felt not quite right. There was a nervous little flutter, a kneading in the pit of her stomach.

—Where's the radio? I know we have a battery-powered radio somewhere around.

—You want music?

—That's a good idea, too. Actually, I wanted to listen to the news. Peter went rafting this morning, and I thought—well, I'm a little concerned if he's all right, you know?

William took a lamp and went into the storage area below the tech loft. A couple of minutes later, he returned with the radio to see that Ariel was once again on the telephone. She disconnected with a frustrated look on her brow.

—Jillian's not answering, or the lines are down in town.

He placed the radio on the table and proceeded to turn the dial in search of a news report. When he found one, he sat beside Ariel.

The storm was worsening. Power lines were down all over the place, as were tree limbs and branches scattered along the roadways. There was a weather alert until nine o'clock that evening, when hopefully, the brunt of the storm would have passed. There were reports of several traffic-related accidents, a tree slicing through the roof of a house in town, and a shop sign falling to crash onto the sidewalk, narrowly missing a pedestrian walking along Main Street. "Don't go out unless you have to," was the message.

William found an easy-listening station on the radio while Ariel remembered that Peter had a cell phone. She dialed his number on the unlikely chance that he had taken it with him that afternoon. He picked up on the third ring.

She relaxed a bit when he told her he was fine and at home. Jillian was not on the phone, he told her, because the lines were out of service. She was about to hang up after telling Peter she would remain at the theater until the worst of the storm had passed, when Peter added, —Dad's not home yet.

Ariel hesitated before asking, —Have you heard from him?

—No.

—If he gets home before I do, or calls you, tell him I'm at the theater, okay? And that I'll get home, weather permitting, as soon as it's safe to drive home.

—Mom, you sound like Dr. Templeton, when she "addresses" the school assembly. "Weather permitting, we'll conduct our annual field day." Peter was an excellent mimic, and Ariel had to chuckle at the precise tones and inflections he invoked to produce Dr. Templeton's voice.

—Goodbye, smart-ass, she said, ending the call.

She turned to William and sighed relief.

—Better now?

She thought about her answer, and finally said, —I guess I should be, but there's something eating at me.

—That's me nibbling at your ear.

—It's not that, she replied, brushing off his little joke. —Maybe I'd better try to get home.

—Are you mad, with what's going on out there?

As if helping to make his point, a great flash of lightning illuminated the room with an eerie white light. The hit, close by, was startling, and then thunder rolled to quake the building around them.

—All right. You have a point. Maybe it's just—
She didn't finish.

—Just what?

—Nothing. It's nothing. Just . . . a feeling.

—I've had it all day, too.

—Don't make fun of me, William.

—I'm not!

—I'm a little afraid, William.

And then, from out of the blue, —Do you think Susan—

—I don't know what she may think. I think we're all right. I mean, I don't have any real indications that she knows about us.

—You said "real." Do you have any suspicions?

—She told me she was happy that I had such a friend as you. Someone who would stay overnight with me in the hospital, and with whom I could talk about books and music and stuff.

—She knows.

—You think so?

—What are we going to do?

—She doesn't know because she hasn't said, and until she says something about it to me, I won't worry about it. Now, where was I about ten minutes ago? Oh, yes, he said, rising from the sofa to stand facing her. —I was trying to remove that robe.

Moonglow, from the movie soundtrack of William Inge's play, *Picnic*, played over the radio, as Ariel's robe dropped to the floor.

—I remember this, said Arial. —William Holden and Kim Novak danced their way into love. I thought it very romantic when I was a little girl and saw it with my mother at the movie theater.

They fell into a slow dance of shifting feet and swaying hips, barely moving from their spot on the stage. And Arial thought that dancing had never been such an intimate pastime before as it was in those three minutes, their bodies held so tenderly in one another's arms, bodies moving together as one: breathing, feeling, *living* as one. Wasn't that the essence of love: that easy intimacy?

They both froze to the sound of a metallic click.

That was it, just the faint click breaking through the riot of the storm outside.

Ariel fetched her robe and William went to the back room where his jeans were hanging to dry.

The sound of the door unlocking was faint but unmistakable. She ran to the entrance door, finding it unlocked. Sticking her head out into the storm she could make out the taillights of a car racing down the road.

No one need tell her who their unexpected visitor was, although it might have been any one of three people besides herself and William who had keys. But, she knew it was John; she had no doubt it was he.

—I've got to get home, she said, trying to fight back the hysteria that was rising inside her.

William took her by the shoulders. —Ariel? Will you be all right or do you want me to come with you? I will if you think I should. I'm not afraid of loving you. I'm not afraid of John.

—Funny, she said, realizing that he, too, knew instinctively that it was John at the door.

—What's funny?

—Nothing. I've got to find my shoes and get home.

—I love you, Ariel. Know that I love you with every fiber of my being. I'll accept whatever it is you decide to do, my love, whatever you need to do, I won't love you less.

For a second she was taken aback, and she turned to him.

—You mean, you'd give me up?

—I'll do whatever you say.

—A hollow sentiment, William, because you know I'd never leave you.

She couldn't cry, she couldn't even think. Terrified with facing the full weight of consequences, she drove through the deluge.

He was sitting in his chair in the living-room when she arrived. Ariel sat down in the wingchair opposite John and looked around the room, her body very still, mimicking his stillness. His lips were tightly set, his jaw working rigidly as if he were grinding his teeth. The glass of scotch in his hand. His eyes said everything in the heavy silence of the room.

Her voice shook; her legs felt too weak to hold the weight of her.

—Are the children—?

—They're next door. How long has this been going on, Ariel?

He rarely called her Ariel, and the way he spoke her name was rife with disgust.

—For a time.

—So now it's over, right? When the husband discovers, it's over, right?

When she didn't answer, he said:

—It's over, right?

Her eyes were wide and unblinking as they traced the pie-crust carving of her mother's tiered tea-table.

—*Am I right?* he hissed.

Still no reply, and John now became more animated.

—Don't tell me you love him?

—I do, she said, meeting his astonished gaze.

—You can't mean that!

He was on the edge of the chair, waiting, waiting . . .

Ariel's eyes filled with tears, but she didn't cry when she said:

—I love William.

Quietly, very quietly, more in shock than he had been an hour before when he peeked in on them, watched their intimate dance, he said:

—So, where does that leave me, us?

—I love you, too, John.

—Don't tell me that! How can you say that and expect me to believe it!

—It's the truth. I love you! And I love him, too.

John looked at her with contempt as he rose from the chair and went to the liquor cabinet to refill his glass. When he had poured a sufficient amount of scotch, he turned to face her.

—What are your plans?

—I have no plans.

—You going off somewhere together?

—No, John. I don't want to leave you, she said. *How to make him understand her dilemma?* How to make him realize that she loved two men? That just because you are with one, doesn't mean you can't love another.

—Then stop doing this. Stop seeing him. Stop—

He pressed his lips tightly shut, and then spat it out.

—*Stop fucking him!*

His words were meant to shame her, but oddly, she was not ashamed. She was only hurt, hurt for John. She wanted to reassure him that he was precious to her, but anything she thought to say sounded trite or condescending, so she kept silent.

Her silence maddened him, and he smashed the glass into the fireplace before demanding:

—You *will* stop having sex with him!

Ariel considered.

—Do you think that will make me not love him anymore?

He raised his hand, and for the first time in twenty years, she feared he would strike her.

But, he didn't. Instead, he set his jaw and said, —We'll move away.

—No, John, that won't make a difference.

—Then, I'll leave you!

—No, John, you mustn't leave. This is our home, yours and mine; neither of us should leave! We have children!

John was losing the control he had so desperately tried to maintain since Ariel had walked into the house. He paced, ran nervous fingers through his dark hair, rubbed his thumbs and index fingers together, over and over again. His face was red, the veins in his forehead and neck protruding, his eyes darting around the room, not daring to look at Ariel, now, for fear that the truth be read in her eyes.

She rose from the chair, and he turned on her, grabbing her arm.

—Where do you think you're going! he said, his mouth twisted with anger and frustration.

—Nowhere, just over to you, she replied, hesitating, and a little fearful of him for the first time in their marriage.

—I'm sorry I've hurt you. I love you. I don't want to hurt you!

John pushed her away.

—How can you say that? You can't mean that! You say you love me, but you say you love him? Were you so dissatisfied with me that you had to look elsewhere?

—It was never that, John. I never looked, really I didn't. It has little to do with sex. I've always been there for you, and I love you.

—I don't understand you!

—I didn't understand myself at first! Whether or not I'm with you or William—Oh, how can I make you understand what I am going through?!

—Try me!

Ariel fell back down into the chair and tried to verbalize her conundrum. She wanted to be truthful, but not hurtful. She could lie to John, but at whose expense? She could not express anything in terms that John could understand without disbelief. So, she asked him a question.

—John, do you believe that if I never see William again, or if I make the promises that you want me to make, that a promise will tear him out of my heart? He knows I love you. Do you think I could deny my love for you to William?

—You'll have to decide who you want to be with.

—I won't decide. There is nothing to decide.

—You are mad!

—Maybe I am, I don't know! I don't know how I can work this out without someone getting hurt!

—Does Susan know?

—I . . . I don't think so.

His face changed suddenly, as if he'd actually found a weapon with which to smash William's world.

—John! You wouldn't! You wouldn't do that. You might be getting back at William, but think about Susan.

—You should have thought about Susan before you slept with her husband! I'm not going to tell her. I won't have to. She'll find out soon enough.

—What do you mean!

—Exactly what I said! Now, get out of here. And don't worry, I'm not going to bother you. I'm not stepping foot into your bed again.

The rain had stopped and a cold damp breeze wafted in through the windows where the beetles were scratching at the screens. An icy shiver ran down her spine. She left John to his drinking.

She did not see John that following morning, and she tried to get through the day as if all was fine and good with the world. When she arrived home from work at four o'clock, Jillian handed her the phone, reminding her mother that she had her own important calls to make, so not to stay on too long.

—Very funny, said Ariel with a smack on her daughter's bottom, before speaking into the receiver.

William was on the other end of the line.

—John?

—Not on the phone, William.

There was something odd about his tone that made her shiver.

—What's going on? Are you all right?

—I'm not. You're not here. I'm not all right if you're not here.

—You aren't, are you?

There was a great sigh from William's end of the line. She heard something else there, an almost desperate, if restrained, cry of distress.

—Where are you calling from?

—I don't know. I'm at a phone booth.

—Yes, but where is the phone booth?

—Main Street and Maple?

—You're near Sonny's?

—Yes.

—Go there and wait for me. I'll be right over.

She didn't wait for his reply. Grabbing her purse and car keys, Ariel left the house after instructing Jillian to take the roast out of the oven in half an hour, and if she weren't home by six, to serve it with salad and potatoes when her father arrived home from work.

William was sitting in a back booth. Ariel sat across from him and waited for the words to come. Words she had dreaded hearing: Susan knew.

—William, talk to me.

The cream in the coffee cup had settled into a grayish ring, and he absently stirred the spoon trying to release the milk scum that clung stubbornly. After a long moment, he removed the spoon and looked up at her.

—I went to the doctor this afternoon, for my checkup about the ulcer. The ulcer was just a symptom. He says I have cancer.

The revelation tumbled about in her brain, assaulting her piercingly, painfully.

—*What!* What do you mean?

—I have—cancer.

Stunned and growing feverish, she knew she had to pull herself together quickly, if only to rescue William from the quagmire of despair he was sinking into.

She took his hands away from the cup he was gripping and gently massaged each in her own.

—No! No, William! There has to be some mis—

He looked at her, and saw the smile that attempted to mask her sorrow, the moist green eyes and quivering mouth betraying her all the while.

—We'll get through this! We'll get the best doctors!

—We have a great cancer center here, Ariel.

—I have a friend, a radiologist friend I went to school with, at the Mayo Clinic. I'm calling him!

William threw off the optimism with a flick of an eyebrow and a wistful smile of irony as he glanced for distractions around the room.

She repeated, this time with more conviction, — *We will get through this!* We have to!

When his eyes settled back on hers, there was stupefaction, a desire to believe her words, and then, finally, a look of gratitude.

—All right, then. So what else did the doctor say? What do they propose to do? Who are they consulting?

It was easier, now, to speak. Ariel was there with him and he was suddenly safe in the warmth of her love.

—It's a tumor, near the pancreas. They don't want to do surgery. They think they can get it with chemotherapy.

—Has it metastasized?

—No. It's in the early stages. The ulcer was a result of the tumor's pressure on the duodenum.

—The connection from the stomach to the intestines?

—Yes. It may have been growing for years, and I would not have been symptomatic of the disease for years more, but for the ulcer.

—Thank God they discovered it. Okay, when will they begin? She asked, trying to keep the manic tone out of her voice, but failing.

—A needle biopsy to confirm the type of cancer cell we're be dealing with, and then, a chemo schedule right away.

—All right, all right.

She felt the panic rising within her. She couldn't just leave things to the doctors; she had to act, to do something or she would explode.

—What can I do?

Astonished at such a question, he just looked at her eager face and reflected on it.

—Don't stop loving me. . . .

The child-like whisper wrenched her heart and the rising of emotion choked at her throat as she spoke with trembling voice.

—I will never stop loving you, don't you know? We will fight this thing! I won't let anything take you from me. Do you hear me? Oh, God! I just want to hold you forever, and I can't do it here.

His lips trembled but he made an effort not to let the tears of relief welling in his eyes fall.

—My sweet love, you are. You are holding me.

They left the café, promising to meet later that night.

"I was expecting you, Johnny, the woman said in the husky voice. Where have you been?"

Raintree County

TEN

Bill

Bill walked Little Eva down the road to Ariel's a little before noon. It wasn't until he was nearing the arbor that he realized he hadn't her house key; that she'd have to get out of bed and come to the door.

Bill considered stopping at Amy's to get the key, but thought better of the idea. If anybody thought him an interloper, it was Amy. Even though she was polite, there was a prickly edge about her. She wouldn't give the key to the house. He would just have to ring the doorbell.

Harris Haley greeted him with a laconic, —Yes?

Harris, whose arms were extended from door to doorjamb like a sentinel at the gate, was no barrier for Little Eva, who ran in through the space between his leg and the doorframe, tugging Bill along and forcing Harris to get out of the way or risk being knocked to the ground.

Ariel, sitting in the overstuffed chair, was dressed in a floor-length robe of shimmering pink velvet that flowed along the contours of her shoulders and breasts. There was something very nineteen-thirties movie star in the cut and fabric, and the ridiculous contrast of thick red woolen socks instead of sexy, high-heeled slippers gave an unpretentious childlike finish to the ensemble. A pink silk embroidered fringed piano shawl had fallen from her shoulders to drape the thick arms of the chair. The polished seashell hung from her neck and rested on her bosom. She wore no makeup, but the diffused sunlight in the room brought out the luminescence of her skin. Bill felt light-headed, stricken by the gentle radiance of the woman: a translucent petal of the palest pink rose. Little Eva tried to leap up on Ariel's lap, but he stopped her. It proved a welcomed distraction for Bill.

A tea service and a plate of assorted scones and buns from Sonny's Pantry sat on the ottoman. Little Eva's wagging tail threatened to swipe the tray and its contents to the floor. Harris intervened, removing the tray to a table, and then sat down on the sofa adjacent to Ariel. As the dog happily licked her mistress's face and hands, Harris refilled her teacup. Ariel fawned over her pet for a few minutes, asking, "How'd you get so pretty? Who's the best doggie in the world?"

Then, she turned to Bill and offered tea and a scone. Ariel looked over at Harris with a silent plea. He got up and left the room.

While Harris was gone and Ariel turned her attention again on her pet, Bill glanced over at the shelves above the reading nook. It was as he had left it the evening before. It didn't appear he'd have the opportunity to slip the volume into its proper place on this visit. But, the longer it was before he replaced it, the greater the chance that Ariel would discover it missing.

Harris returned with a cup and saucer.

Ariel beamed him a smile of thanks as she reached for the cup and saucer, but Harris did not give her opportunity to take them. He filled it from the pot, and when Bill settled in a chair, handed him the cup.

—I'm a coffee drinker, you know, said Ariel. —But, scones go best with tea, don't you think? Or hot cocoa?

Please, have one, she offered, handing Bill a plate. He took a scone and placed it on the table beside the teacup.

—This is rather nice, having my neighbors visit, she said, nestling into the thick cushions of the chair. She threw her head back and stretched her long neck, her languid eyelids half descending as she rubbed her head from side to side against the back of the chair. A kittenish, self-satisfied smile of the proverbial cat who got the cream washed over her lips and remained there as she spoke with Harris about a mutual friend who was recovering from emergency bypass heart surgery.

Bill listened, Ariel including him in the conversation with a glance here and there, even though he didn't know the friend of whom they spoke.

It was hard not to look at her, he thought. There was nothing affected about her movements or speech, no artifice. Her complete and riveted attention was so without distraction as to draw in and unwittingly mesmerize anyone she focused on. When she was listening to you it felt like you had possession of her for a time. But, it was really the other way around. She had possession of *you*. What you said had importance, and no one else was more interesting or exciting for her to be with. It was a powerful seduction, that aura she created within which you were safe, and made you aware that the little things in life—the comfort of an overstuffed chair, the company of friends, the playful devotion of a pet, the taste and aroma of food—should be deliberately and fully experienced and revered.

When the discussion about the sick friend ended, there was a long moment of silence as they sipped their tea.

And then Harris broached a subject that seemed to rile Ariel:

—When you go out at night in the dark, Ariel, you need to wear light-colored clothing and carry a flashlight so that you can be seen.

—Yes, yes, I know all about it.

—We talked about it before—

—We did, and I heard your concern, Harris. I was just out walking my dog and looking at the stars, is all.

—We almost lost you, Ariel, said Amy.

Tension was growing between Harris and Ariel. Her eyes flashed at Bill, a message of chastisement at Harris. After all, the man who had run her down with his car was sitting right there in the room with them.

Bill told Ariel that Harris had been kind enough to plow his drive the day he was snowed in.

In reply, Harris changed the subject, talking about the storm that was predicted to hit on Saturday.

—I haven't gotten to know too many of my neighbors, Harris. Who is the gentleman at the very end of the road? What is his name?

Ariel jumped in. —Mr. Wood? In the big old Victorian?

—Yes, the big house at the very end. He appears quite old, and I wondered if he lives alone?

—He does. He is ninety-six and quite young in mind and spirit. You know, he called me every day I was in the hospital, the old dear.

—I should think he would, said Harris, with the first real expression Bill had heard in his voice.

—Stop, Harris. He's my friend.

Bill decided not to pursue the disagreement between them. He had other questions.

—The blonde lady I've seen driving your Ranger? Is she your wife, Harris?

He hit a nerve, as intended.

—That's Cathy, said Harris, refilling his teacup.
—Ariel, did you read the paper this morning?

—Amy brought it in, but I haven't looked at it yet. Why?

—There was an article I thought you might find funny.

And the conversation was once again directed to exclude Bill.

Bill had often been called tenacious, so he looked around the room, searching for a point of interest to use to bring him back into the running. He didn't bother waiting for an opening; he interrupted Harris by addressing Ariel.

—You have a beautiful grand piano, Ariel! You play so well.

—Yes. It was my first instrument.

—You play others?

—I play the violin.

—When and if she chooses to, said Harris.

Bill wondered if he was making a statement of fact, or warning him not to make a request for Ariel to play.

Bill's confusion was evident.

—I was trained and have performed as a concert pianist. I later studied the violin. I do not play either any longer.

—I see. . . . But last night—

Harris kept his eyes glued on Ariel as she spoke. Bill wanted to ask why she no longer played the instruments, but saw impatience in Harris's demeanor, the nervous shifting of his jaw, the flaring of nostrils when Bill spoke, which led Bill to believe it was a sore topic with Ariel.

Bill suddenly despised the man, his possessiveness of Ariel, his controlling of the conversation, the vainglorious expression of contempt that transformed his smile into a smirk that boasted of intimacy with Ariel. He disliked the posturing he himself was engaging in, so like two roosters circling in for a cockfight.

What disturbed Bill was that Harris was married, had a wife, Cathy, but he was obviously in love with Ariel. Bill didn't fault him for that. But, the way he skirted the question of his having a wife seemed a dishonest effort to minimize the fact.

Bill wondered if Ariel was aware that Harris was in love with her, and if he ever told her. Did she look upon their relationship as that of friends and neighbors, or was there more between them than friendship?

Bill thought Haley would never leave, but knew that Haley was waiting for Bill to leave first.

It was Amy who forced both to go. She intended to assist Ariel for a bath. She said she wouldn't be able to return until later that evening because she'd forgotten she had to drive her kids to the Mountain for their ski lessons after school.

Bill offered to see to Ariel's dinner, but Ariel said a friend had called and was bringing dinner, so it wasn't necessary for anyone to worry. She'd be fine, she insisted.

—I'll humor you today, Amy, my dear, but I am perfectly capable of bathing without assistance. I shan't get my stitches wet, I promise you.

Bill hadn't heard the word *shan't* spoken for a long time. Most people couldn't get away with it without inspiring peals of laughter, but it did not ring false when Ariel said it. It was charming and perfectly natural.

The men rose to leave. Bill clipped the leash on Little Eva.

Ariel asked, —If you don't find her to be too much of a handful, I would appreciate it if you would keep Little Eva with you for a few more days.

—Oh, no, as I told you before, she's a terrific companion and I enjoy having her with me!

—You're too kind. Her green eyes swept the room and then lighted on Bill's.

—I'm nervous about walking her just yet, Bill. These stitches. If I fall, they might pull away.

—You let me know when you want her home with you. I'll return her, but I have to say, I'll return her reluctantly.

Haley was caught in a discussion with Amy, glancing at Ariel and Bill as they conversed.

—I'll stop in tonight so you and Little Eva can visit.

—Thank you, Bill.

Amy was picking up the tea-tray. Bill was about to offer help, but Harris took the tray from her hands. Bill took the cue to leave. It didn't matter that Haley remained, that he had lasted the longest. Bill would return that evening with good reason, and he was smug in his macho victory. Bill found the humor of the ages-old competition and relished it.

Later that evening he walked Little Eva past the Meeting House, but an old Toyota wagon was parked outside. An hour later, fearing Amy would spot him loitering out on the road, he walked just far enough toward the house to see if the car was still there.

On the third outing, it was getting late, and Bill wanted to see Ariel, even if he could not be alone with her.

Ariel came to the door, dressed in a royal-blue turtleneck and stretchy pants, the seashell around her neck. Little Eva greeted her like a long-lost friend, and once off the leash, bounded into the big room to sit at the feet of a woman of forty-something years, who was introduced as Susan.

It took a while for Bill to discover the relationship between the two.

At first, Bill thought they were just old friends, perhaps neighbors or fellow employees. They did indeed have a common interest, but it was not of the sort he had imagined. It was only after Susan had left, soon after Bill's arrival, that the relationship became clear.

What confused Bill was that there was a relationship at all, considering the differences in the two: Susan, frumpy and staid, was barely animate as she rested against the back of the sofa. Perhaps Bill's "Nice to meet you," was spoken with too much bravado, for she wrinkled her eyes together, as if assaulted, and his gesture to shake her hand was responded to with limp and sluggish reluctance.

Ariel was open and attentive to Susan, where Susan appeared guarded. The conversation sounded stilted and forced. From the little Bill had seen of Ariel and her ease of connecting with others, Bill thought it odd that she and Susan could have shared anything in common. An image popped into his head: Where Ariel was sunlight, Susan was an overcast sky. Nothing mysterious about her, just a gloomy countenance.

When Susan was about to take her leave, Ariel insisted on seeing her to the door. They embraced in the foyer and then Ariel reentered the room.

—Well, that was a pleasant visit, she said, with a little smile that made Bill wonder if she was being facetious.

—That was nice of Susan to bring dinner, Bill offered ineffectually.

—Yes . . .

—You've been friends for a long time?

—No, not friends, and not for a long time.

Bill's expression prompted Ariel to laugh quietly as if enjoying a private joke.

—Susan was my husband, William's, first wife. He left her to be with me. Excuse me, Bill, I have to take a pill. Have a seat, I'll be right back.

Little Eva rose from the sofa and cantered after Ariel as he wondered why a woman, rejected by her husband for another, would bring the interloper dinner and share a loving embrace at departure?

Then Bill remembered one of the purposes of his visit: To return the journal. He walked over to the reading nook and removed the book from his jacket pocket. He could hear Ariel talking to her pet as he nervously shifted the tightly packed books apart. He replaced 1995 between the others just as he heard Ariel approaching.

But the force of his hand caused one of the journals to push away from the others, and when Bill tried to force it back into its place, another pushed forward and began its tumble off the shelf. He caught it before it hit the platform and moved quickly away from the wall as Ariel walked back into the room. As Little Eva circled in playful prances around her, Bill slipped the journal into his jacket pocket.

He glanced over toward the shelves. The journals were not perfectly aligned; one jutted out slightly. With luck, Ariel would not notice anything had been displaced.

The telephone rang, and when she answered it her face lit up as she spoke.

—Oh, my darling! How wonderful to hear your voice! Oh, sweetheart, it's so good to speak with you!

Bill was getting nervous because of the "hot" merchandise in his pocket and worried irrationally that if he stayed much longer, she would know from the guilty look on his face that he was a thief.

Ariel cupped the receiver, and looked up with wide questioning eyes, as Bill clipped the leash on Little Eva's collar.

—Are you leaving? she asked.

Bill thought he heard an element of disappointment in her voice.

—I'll see you later.

—It's long distance, my daughter calling from Australia.

—I'll let myself out. Enjoy your talk.

As man and dog walked briskly along the road toward the bungalow, Bill realized how much he didn't know about Ariel's life. She had a daughter. That was a fact he might have acquired through simple conversation. Why hadn't he asked her? Perhaps, he thought, he wanted her exclusively, for he didn't want to share her with anyone, and there were too many others in her past with whom she had acquired shared memories, others she had loved. And, truth be told, he resented them all.

> *"Love is the all-important discovery*
> *that one is not alone in the world."*
> Raintree County

ELEVEN

William and Ariel

The day of the discovery of William's cancer came within twenty-four hours of John's discovery of his wife's affair. When John confronted her that evening, telling her she had to decide to stay or go, she told him about the cancer diagnosis. John was torn, stopped in his tracks at the signposts of danger in losing his wife forever should he make his demands immediate that she have nothing more to do with William.

—I will always love William, John, just as I will always love you, Ariel said, trying to keep back tears of despair. —Just as I would never let you go through such an illness alone, I cannot abandon William. If there is anything my presence in his life can even hope to do to effect his cure, I will not hesitate to do it. Can't you understand that I am committed in my heart and soul to both of you?

—He has a wife to be there for him, said John, his anger growing. But, when she continued, he aborted any further argument.

—Yes, he has a wife, and I will be there, too.

So John tried very hard to be nonconfrontational with William through the months of his chemotherapy. At night, however, he would get to the point in his intoxication that braved him to begin his systematic destruction of his wife. He would awaken her to sit and listen to his ravings, and then, when he'd had enough, he'd force himself on her before passing out.

When she told John that she wouldn't choose between them she didn't realize that she expected John to make the choice for her. Finally, she begged John to wait if he couldn't accept her feelings, wait if he wanted a divorce, until Jillian was graduated from school. She could endure his nightly drunken abuse if it would protect her kids. This was the punishment she allowed herself to endure to pay for her transgressions.

At two o'clock one morning he yanked her out of bed, threw a packed suitcase out the door, and then, as if to make a literal statement, kicked her out of the house. Once she rose from her fall into the hedge, Ariel considered where to go. She stayed in her car that night, in her nightgown, with a thin blanket from the trunk as cover from the autumn chill. In the morning she sneaked back into the house. Breakfast and lunches had to be prepared and Jillian sent off to school. John behaved as if he had no recollection of his actions the night before.

She was not blind to John's pain, but the heart connection she had with William ruled her; it was something she had never known with John, and it became obvious that John's passion had increased in relation to her stubborn refusal to discard William from her life. John's love became an ugly distortion from which she recoiled, when she saw he was not driven by love, but by the need to retain possession of her body. Although she felt responsible for the transformation, she also understood that John had it in his power to make choices, too. How he reacted to the knowledge of her love for William was self-determined. He could behave with dignity and self-respect in the light of his situation, or indulge in cruelty and futile self-pity. It would be a long time before she would realize that John's need to seek revenge was a far greater force than his proclaimed love for her.

When the good news arrived that William was cancer-free, Ariel told John and watched his reaction.

John's hatred was evident through the strange little smile that flashed in his eyes as he said, — That's wonderful. Ariel saw menace behind it.

She had to get out before he did her physical harm. It was as difficult to leave Jillian and her home as it would have been to bid farewell to William forever. But, she had no choice. She didn't fear being alone, she feared continuing to hurt her husband, even if her love and respect for him had diminished. Things might be better for him, for everyone, if she wasn't there.

Jillian knew nothing more than a deep caring relationship existing between her mother and their family friend, William. Jillian liked William; he was cool. He didn't condescend to her and he had always seemed to be really interested in what she had to say. Ariel asked John not to tell Jillian the real reason for their separation, even though John's self-righteousness required his wife's humiliation. He felt Jillian should know the truth about why Ariel was leaving, but Ariel convinced him that the knowledge would only serve to hurt their daughter, not her. John left the den while Ariel broke the news to their daughter with many tears and assurances of Ariel's love. All Jillian was told was that her parents were not happy together.

—But, you never fight; I never hear you argue or disagree on anything!

—I know, Jillian. It seems like everything is fine, but, Dad and I have grown apart and we do have disagreements, only you don't hear us argue.

—But, you were always . . .

—What were we always . . . ?

—Close. Like you loved each other more than anything in the world, more than me and Peter.

It dawned on Ariel that perhaps the reason behind Jillian's rebelliousness might have stemmed from insecurity of her parents' love for her.

—Jillian, you have to understand something: My love for you is different from the love I have for your father. Even if we should go our separate ways, we are always there to love you unconditionally. Do you understand?

—Yeah, that's what they all say.

—Who?

—My friends' parents when they split.

The teenager left and the little girl came in.

—Why aren't you happy? Don't you love Dad, anymore?

—I do care for your father. I don't want to leave, but I have to.

—I want to come with you.

—It's best if you stay here. I'll see you every day, that's for certain!

—Why can't I go with you?

—Because I'll be staying at the Meeting House. There's no shower, no hot water, no place to sleep except an old couch in the dressing room. I don't even have a refrigerator. And Dad needs you here.

—But, Mom—you shouldn't be there!

—I have nowhere else to go.

—Then, why can't you and Dad just get along! Lots of people don't get along and they stay together!

Ariel wished that John could see the logic in Jillian's words.

—We are only separating. We are not getting divorced, Jilly.

Ariel would not say that John had pushed her toward the move. But it was she who had been the one to set the changes in motion in the first place by falling in love with William, so she would accept total responsibility. She would protect John as best she could and protect her children. At the tender age of sixteen, when all was viewed in black or white, right or wrong, Ariel doubted Jillian could handle the whole truth. She would see it as a betrayal of her father by her mother. Wasn't that how everybody would see it?

—It's his drinking, isn't it, and because he's always out of work, right? I hate him!

—No, Jilly, it's not that. Don't hate your father. He loves you and he needs you more than ever!

—Is he making you leave? What have you done, Mom?

—Nothing I'm ashamed of, and he's not making me leave. It's a mutual decision, and it's for the best. Remember, I love you! That will *never* change, Jilly, never. I'll pick you up after school tomorrow and we can have a sundae at Friendly's.

—I'm not a kid! I don't need to have a sundae at Friendly's.

—I'd like to have a sundae, Jilly, and I know you're not a kid. I just want to see you.

—I have stuff to do tomorrow.

—Then, let's have dinner.

—Maybe another time. I have plans tomorrow night.

—I'll call you. And, if you want, drive out to see you.

—Yeah.

Jillian was helpless to effect any change in her parents' decision. When her mother kissed and hugged her, she melted into her arms, for the first time since she was a child, and nestled there, sobbing quietly. Ariel moved her gently away to look into her daughter's eyes and felt a moment of deep regret and a weakening of her convictions. She looked into the face of a love that was more constant and nurturing and unconditional than any love she had ever felt for *any* man, powerful enough to reverse her decision, to ban William from her life, if not her heart, by its very force, even if it meant giving up the half of herself that *was* William. Would she not offer her own life if it meant her children might live? If she had to give up William, wasn't her children's happiness more important than her own?

She was about to say she would work everything out and would patch things up with John. The words were forming, slowly, hesitantly. She started to speak, about to say she would stay, that she would fix things with John, that it was all a mistake, she wasn't going anywhere. But when she raised her eyes from the embrace of her daughter, John appeared at the doorway. In one crucial moment, as she caught his expression, she knew there was no way to return, to make things right. Things had gone too far. She had gone too far. In that moment she understood that there was no such thing as unconditional love between a man and a woman.

Her words died a sudden death. Ariel left the room.

Peter would be told when he came home from boot camp.

It was not easy living at the theater, but Ariel was adept at making a home wherever she called home. She fashioned a bed for herself behind several folding screens in a corner of the dressing room. She had a water heater installed to provide for a shower and tub she purchased on sale at the local plumbing supply house. They were installed for her by a volunteer at the theater who owned a plumbing and heating firm in Linden Falls. She bought a refrigerator at a lawn sale for twenty-five dollars. Fortunately, the old church kitchen housed a ten-burner Garland stove, which she scoured. She'd manage until the winter months, when productions ended. The furnaces that heated the sanctuary were not sufficient to heat the back dressing-room. She saved as much as she could from her paycheck after paying the mortgage on the house in Linden Falls to purchase a gas heater for the winter months. She was seventy-two dollars shy of her goal when Jillian called her after school one day to say the utilities at the house were going to be cut off if the company didn't have eight hundred dollars by the end of the business day. John had not paid the bills for two months, so Ariel took all the money she had saved scrimping on food and other necessaries to keep the power on at the house.

John found a part-time job, but a fifth of vodka a day and a couple of packs of cigarettes were expensive habits for a man making little more than minimum wage.

Harris Haley lived just down the road from the Meeting House, and would often help fill her larder with fresh milk and butter, vegetables, and fruit from his orchard of pear, peach, and apple trees.

At the start of winter, after the first snowfall and after he'd plowed and shoveled the entrance to the building, Harris found her huddled in the cold, the ten burners of the cooking stove barely warming the drafty nineteenth-century structure. That afternoon, he brought over a kerosene heater. The next day, Harris had installed a gas furnace, insisting it was a gift to the theater. He knew Ariel would not have accepted such an expensive gift otherwise.

The house in Linden Falls had been on the market for six months and there were no buyers, even though the asking price had been reduced. Foreclosure was imminent as Ariel could not make the payments without John's help. John sat there waiting for the house to be taken, ignoring the pileup of bills while Ariel tried to arrange things with the bank to give them time to sell. The property was mortgaged up to the asking price and no one was bidding.

William's hair was growing back and his gaunt and exhausted countenance filling out with a glow of radiant health. He asked her once, when he was pale and haggard and trying to maintain some strength, insisting he would keep a normal schedule of teaching and living, why, when she could have walked away, she had bothered to waste her life on so pathetic a man?

—I'll waste my life on whomever I choose, she said, laughing, and then biting his nose.

—You must be mad! Look at me! I'm certainly not something any woman in her right mind would chase howling into the woods to catch! Maybe it's because you're blind! Yes, that's it! Boy, am I a lucky man!

They would be together as often as they could. And their time together grew precious as the winter wore on, for with no productions in the winter months, William had little excuse to see Ariel.

And Ariel was growing more concerned that Susan would find out about them if she did not already know. Susan must not find out about them.

William would reassure Ariel that Susan showed no signs of knowing anything, but she was not so sure.

—If she did find out, what would she do?

—Susan endures. She is an endurer. She would wait it out. Wait until it was over between us, believing I would never leave her.

—And would she be right in believing that?

—We have children. She'd endure because of them and because she loves me.

—Yes, but, that's not what I mean. Would she be correct in believing that we would end?

—No.

—And would you allow her to believe that lie?

—If it has to be. If that's what she needs to believe. If that's what it takes to see that the kids don't suffer. The truth is, I do love her and I don't want to leave her or the children. Susan is the sort of woman who would rather live with what she has than seek new pastures. She believes that what she doesn't know won't hurt her.

What William said about Susan's denial made sense, although Ariel did not think the woman an idiot. William and Susan had not had sexual relations together for years, if William was to be believed. There had not been anyone else until Ariel, no casual encounters, even, only a self-imposed celibacy, relieved, as William shyly and blushingly admitted, by necessary long showers.

—You can say, I was saving myself for you, he joked. —A little "self-abuse" saw me through.

No, Susan was not an idiot, she was a fool, thought Ariel, but did not ask why they had not slept together for so many years. Contempt for Susan grew in her and she began to hate the woman for having been so careless in her marriage to William.

But, Susan was not blind; she could read with her glasses on, and early on found a letter that William was writing to Ariel. After a thorough search of his desk and files she found the hundreds of pages of love letters from Ariel that William had assured Ariel were safely tucked away.

If what William wrote was not enough, Susan tortured herself by reading Ariel's letters, and finally, by the following spring, confronted William, demanding he stop seeing her.

The argument that ensued went on for hours, broken only by the arrival of the children from school. It continued after dinner when the children were sent off to stay the night with Susan's sister, who lived in town and who came to pick them up at Susan's request.

—My real work is at the Meeting House. That's where I do theatre! I won't stop working with Ariel.

—You will give her up! You will not have sex with her!

—But why? You and I haven't slept together in years! Why should it suddenly make a difference to you if I've found someone who wants me?

—Because you said you love her!

—Would you like it better if I didn't love her?

—Yes.

—So, I'm supposed to find loveless relief outside this house, but come home to you for real affection? I hate to be hurtful, Susan, but it had less to do with sex, me and Ariel, and more to do with connection and sharing and communication and love, before it ever had to do with sex.

—But, still you wound up fucking her!

—I've never "fucked" Ariel, never! I may have lain with her, and I most certainly have made love with her, but I've *never* fucked her! But if lust is a part of it, so much the better!

—How can you say you love me in the same breath as you say you love her!

—Because it is the truth! I love you, *and* I love Ariel!

—You don't love me! You're just stuck with me!

—That's not true!

—I'm fat and dull, and she's got it all. I don't blame you!

—What are you saying?

—Do you want to leave me?

—No! Of course not!

Then, as if it had just dawned on him, William asked with an expectation that charged through him like an electric surge:

—Why? Do you want me to leave?

Susan read the hopeful look and replied, —Not yet.

William was correct in his belief that Susan would endure it all. But he was not to mention Ariel's name to her again, and she would never be allowed to set foot in *her* house again.

It was agreed.

Ariel was greatly relieved that William had fared so well, considering what she was going through with John. His nightly drunken phone calls began with the pleasant inquiry to see how she was doing. Then, John would become vicious, demanding and frightening as he hissed his mean words into her ear.

He would arrive at the Meeting House, banging on the door until she threatened to call the police. One time he told her that Jillian had been trying to call her but couldn't get through. Another time, he said his car broke down and he'd walked the mile to call from her place, but when Ariel looked outside the window, his car was parked on the lawn. She told him to go home, and he banged on the door, threatening to kill her. Ariel called the police, but John was gone when they arrived. They suggested a restraining order and promised to keep an eye out for his car in the future.

When he called one night, crying and saying that he was ill, Ariel rushed to the house in Linden Falls.

Jillian was at the door to meet her and told her that John had been throwing up. She was afraid her father was very sick.

But, if he was sick, Ariel knew it was probably a virus, or the result of too much scotch.

She and Jillian tried to get him into bed, but he tossed and cried in his misery, fighting all the while. When it appeared he had settled down, Ariel went to the kitchen to prepare some herbal tea for him to sip, and as she was about to carry it up to the bedroom, she heard Jillian's distressed voice at the top of the stairs. John was descending from the landing. Jillian, above at the hall railing, had a panicky look on her face.

—*Mom!* she shrieked in appeal, as John stumbled and then tumbled down the thirteen steps to crash head on into the marble-topped corner table, which cracked into three parts at impact.

He lay unconscious, bleeding from the top of his head where the marble had gashed the flesh.

Ariel tried to ebb the tide of hysteria that rose within her when she glimpsed Jillian's. As she had often done at work after an elderly resident had fallen, she quickly assessed for broken bones. John's eyes fluttered open.

—Bring the car around, Jilly. I don't think anything's broken, but we need to get him to the emergency room.

—Jillian, she added, in an attempt to calm the child, —I think he's all right, honey, but he'll need a stitch on his head.

And he was all right. The doctor told her that babies, sleeping people in car wrecks, and *drunks* weather accidents better than others because there is no resistance at impact. After a series of X-rays and five stitches to the crown of his head, John was sent home to sleep it off. Ariel remained the night on the living-room sofa and left in the morning after waking Jillian.

Over the next few days, Ariel and Jillian discussed John's alcoholism. He had refused to seek help over the past years through AA, when Ariel had gingerly approached the problem, usually ending with John's self-righteous anger at the very suggestion that he had a problem. Now it was decided that Jillian would broach the subject in an appeal from a loving daughter concerned for her father's welfare. Ariel cautioned Jillian not to demand anything of John, and that she should accompany John to the AA meeting that was scheduled the next day. The idea was not well received by John, after Jillian approached him with tears in her eyes.

—What is this, your mother's idea?

—No, not just Mom's, but mine. You scared me the other night, Dad. I thought for a minute that you were going to die. And you weren't sick with the flu; you'd had too much to drink.

—I had a couple of drinks to kill off the bug!

—The doctor said you were—

—What!?

—I want you to go to the meeting. I'll come with you, Dad. I love you, Daddy. I don't want to see you like that again.

They did not go to the meeting. John said he had to work late, but Jillian knew he wasn't at work. John continued his stalking and terrorizing of Ariel.

One evening after a rehearsal, William and Ariel joined several others in the cast to have a late snack at a diner in town. When the others had departed and just Ariel and William remained, John walked in, and sat at the counter to glare at them. The diner was packed with people, many coming off the night shift at the paper mill. John did not always have an outward appearance of being intoxicated, but Ariel could always tell by the dull, veiled look in his eyes when he'd had too much to drink.

William and Ariel decided not to leave. They were simply talking over their cups of coffee, William making notes on a legal pad to work out a new idea he and Ariel had for a new show. But, John's constant scrutiny was upsetting Ariel, though she tried not to let it show. If they left, would John follow them out? She sensed a danger in being in a dark parking lot with John in the state he was in.

She sat there, facing the counter, William across from her, his back to John at the counter, waiting, watching, hoping that John would leave. When John rose to amble along the aisle a table row away, Ariel thought he would continue toward the doors. But he did not. He circled around toward their booth, leaned on the table with both hands and studied their faces for a minute, before hissing, "How ya doin'?"

John hadn't expected a reply, and he smiled his little smile. In the next moment he stood up straight, turned his back to them to face the other diners, and threw his arms out and up into the air. Ariel thought he was about turn and strike her. She looked at William; he appeared mentally crouched for the spring, ready to strike should John prove violent.

But John did not strike with any physical blow; rather, he called out for everyone's attention.

—Hey, everybody! I want you all to see something!

The dozens of diners lent their attention to the jovial-looking man, expecting an announcement of marriage or the birth of a child.

—This woman here, he pointed at Ariel with a great flourishing dramatic gesture.

—is my wife!

Then, with his other hand, he repeated the movement toward William.

—And this, people, is her lover!

He now turned back to lean both palms on the table and announced, —I want that you remember their names! She's Ariel Rodgers my wife! And he is her lover, William Trent! She's the fuckin' cunt, and he's the fuckin' prick!

With a swing of his body he threw a punch at William's head, which William blocked with his forearm.

The waitress at the counter caught Ariel's eye and indicated that she was calling the police. The manager and the cook came out through the swinging kitchen door, waiting for the right moment to move in and take the man by force out of the restaurant. John turned to the motionless mass of faces, some paralyzed in fear that he should produce a gun, some enjoying the floorshow, but all riveted by the drama unfolding before them.

A couple of men rose to grab John, who shook them off before staggering down the aisle.

Ariel felt that the danger had passed; William was not hurt. She watched John with a helpless frustration, and then she stood, intending to follow him out of the restaurant, to convince him to get in her car so she could drive him home and into bed.

Before William could stop her, Ariel grabbed John's sleeve.

John was ready, if not anxious for a physical confrontation, and he was about to lash out when he saw William standing behind him and several men moving in quickly.

He hissed at Ariel.

—Don't you touch me! You're spoiled goods, you fucking bitch!

He rushed the glass doors; the manager locking the door after him. The police arrived within a minute of John's departure. William settled the bill as the police officer escorted Ariel to the parking lot. When William joined them, they were asked to sit in the back of the patrol car while a report was filled out about the incident. The officer suggested a complaint be made and an order of protection requested for both of them the following day at family court.

William decided he did not want an order for himself. He could defend himself against John. He believed that John's threats were all bluster and felt sure John would not attempt to come to William's home.

A week had passed since the incident at the diner when Ariel called Jillian, as she did each day, to see how she was and to ask her if she wanted to go out for dinner. Jillian said that her father had left town for a week because he had to go to Boston to see a specialist. He had lung cancer.

Ariel began to fall apart on the phone as she questioned her daughter, who was not in the best of states to deal with providing answers. She said he had driven off that morning for the hospital in Boston, leaving only a note for Jillian to read upon waking. He left no address or phone number of where he would be staying and didn't say which hospital he was going to.

Ariel went to the house and searched for some indication of where he may have gone, but found nothing. She called their family doctor, who refused to tell her anything about John, on John's order that he not speak to her about his medical concerns. She tried to explain that he had gone off leaving his teenage daughter alone to fend for herself, claiming in a note that he had lung cancer. Jillian was very frightened, as was she. Was that true? Did John have cancer?

When he refused to answer, Ariel appealed.

—Look, Jack, if he's ill, I have to know. We have kids and a house that will be foreclosed on if we can't sell it. I have to know what I have to do to help him through this! Try to understand, Jack, I want to help him, not hurt him!

She had known Dr. Jack Connelly for all the years they had lived in Linden Falls. He had seen her through her depression, Peter and Jillian through all their illnesses, and now, he wouldn't level with her. She hung up the telephone, fearing the worst for John and determined that he would not go through such a terrible illness without her support.

For a week she was tortured with the fear of John's death, and had begun to make plans for her return to the house in Linden Falls.

But, it turned out to all be a lie. John had not gone to Boston, he went to Manhattan, where he saw several Broadway shows, and had dinner at the Russian Tea Room, Ariel found out when the evidence of his trip lay one morning on the dining room table when she arrived with bagsful of groceries: *Playbills* and matches from the restaurant. She suspected he stayed with his old friend, Charlie, while in the city, doing the town. Ariel told Jillian her father was fine, he did not have cancer, and left it at that.

She was not as furious as she was relieved. But his mean-spirited lie had threatened to turn Jillian's world on end as well as her own.

During one of his late-night phone calls, John threatened to tell the kids the truth. He would tell them that Ariel and William were lovers.

—If I don't do what?

—Give him up.

—You're blackmailing me?

—I think they need to know the truth.

—To what end? Why do they need to know anything? To shame me? To lay the failure of our marriage all on me? Our marriage is private, private from everyone, including the children. I have never spoken badly about you to Peter or Jillian. I have never pointed to your failures or your lies and transgressions. I've never spoken a disparaging word against you! Why do you want to make them think badly of me? Would that make you feel better, John? Hurting them is for their own good, is that it?

—You hurt them, not me, when you went off to be with your precious William!

—No, John, you hurt the children by the way you conduct yourself. It's always been about you getting your way, and I've had enough of your narcissistic self-pitying threats.

—They should know.

—Then I will tell her myself, John. I won't be blackmailed for something I'm not ashamed of.

She slammed down the receiver, got out of bed, and began to fix a cup of tea when the phone rang.

She picked up, expecting John's raging obscenities on the other end, but it was Jillian, her voice soft and frightened.

—Mom . . . .

—I need to talk with you, honey.

—I heard Dad yelling, and when I got up, I heard him on the phone. I didn't like what I heard, Mom. He was talking to you, wasn't he?

—Where are you?

—I'm in bed, calling from my room.

—I'm going to tell you something I don't think you'll like to hear, but I have to be the one who tells you.

—You're scaring me, Mom. Does Dad have cancer after all?

—No, honey. He's not sick. It's not that.

The silence on Jillian's end was broken by an intake of air, and then, as if the girl was holding her breath, she said:

—Try me, Mom. I'm not a baby, you know. I can handle it.

—I hope you can, honey, I hope you can.

—Does it have to do with William, Mom?

—Yes.

—Do you love him?

—Yes, I do.

—What about Dad?

—The problem has been that I love William, too, and that just can't work in a marriage.

—Are you sleeping with him?

—Listen to me, Jilly—

—Oh, Mom. . . . How could you do that to Dad?

—I'm sorry, honey—

—You go out and have an affair—

—It's not like that, Jillian. I love William and he loves me. We love each other, can you understand? I had to leave, because it was unacceptable to your father.

—I would think so! said Jillian, anger in her tone. —What did you expect? That Dad would say it was okay?

—I didn't—

—And what about William? Did he tell you to leave Dad?

—No!

—Does Susan know about you two?

—Yes.

—Is she divorcing him?

—Jillian!

—Well, is she? Or did she find the whole thing "acceptable"?

—What should I have done, Jilly?

—You should have told William you'd never see him again.

—But, I couldn't.

—Shit, Mom, what does it matter if you do or not. You belong to Dad.

—I don't belong *to any one!* I belong *with,* but not *to,* anyone!

—Then you belong with Dad!

—No, honey, I've come to see that I do not belong with him. I thought I did once, but I no longer belong with Dad. I may have started all this, but I am not responsible for your father's behavior. There is a lot you don't know that's happened between your father and me that I won't tell you, but it makes a life with him in the future impossible.

—I know he's awful! But, can't you forgive him?

—I have, at each turn, because I do care for him. I've made excuses for him and blamed myself for the way he's acted. But, it's gone beyond fixing. And, if you want the whole truth: I don't want to be with Dad anymore. . . . Jillian? Are you there?

—I'm here.

—Go to sleep, if you can, Sweetheart. I'll pick you up after school tomorrow. I want to see you.

—I can't. I have track.

—All right, then, soon, though. I love you, Jilly. I love you and Peter and that's something that will never change.

—Yeah, said Jillian, hanging up the phone.

Ariel sat with her cold cup of tea until dawn lit the windows.

When Peter came home on leave, Ariel met him at the train station, determined to tell her son before John made a hash of it. In the car ride to the house, she told him of the separation.

It seemed to Ariel that he was not shocked by the news. He had known for a long time that his parents weren't happy, he told her. Sometimes people are better apart than together, he said as if he'd heard the line in some trite movie. And he said he knew about William.

He was angry at her, but he was angrier at his father, and his growing contempt for John had reached its peak. His onetime boyhood hero, his childhood protector who could do no wrong, had become a pathetic drunk. John disgusted him. Ariel cried at Peter's disillusionment and the loss of his faith in womankind.

> *"Words were more naked than flesh,*
> *and he could never get them back."*
> Raintree County

TWELVE

Ariel and William

On the heels of his cancer's remission, and his separation from Susan, William began moving his things to Ariel's. It was then that William received a telephone call from his stepsister. Their mother, Violet, was in the final stages of ovarian cancer. He flew out to New Mexico, where he spent two weeks watching her die.

Before he left for New Mexico, Ariel, seeing William's distress over the turmoil in his life, tried to tell him that he needn't leave Susan; that she could live alone, at least until his children were grown. But he had objected, saying that would mean too many years apart. He longed to walk down the streets of Linden Falls, arm-in-arm with her, without worry of hurting Susan or John with their display of affection. Living together was a beginning toward that end, he insisted. When his divorce was final, they would marry.

As she had aged, Violet had become increasingly difficult to live with. With her strident tone, she was critical of her husband and their relationship was strained. She'd pit her daughters against each other. William, having long ago acknowledged the strain of impatience he'd inherited from her, had been determined from adolescence to tamp down that trait in himself. Over the years he came to care more for his half-sisters, as they lived near their mother and received the brunt of her daily frustrations. A day after his arrival, she was hospitalized. For the first time in his life he heard her speak the words to him, "I love you," and the power of that proclamation shook him to his core. The words filled his heart with regret, and as he held her wizened hand in his own, all resentment of their past had been displaced by the innocent forgiveness of a child.

William arranged everything for the funeral. His stepfather hardly spoke to him, as had become his habit, a way of escaping the braying demands of his wife over the years. Too many failures, too many lies, too many secrets between William and the old man. The rift was great and beyond repair. His sisters fought constantly. Each believed that their mother was partial to the other, and they looked at William as the big brother who had successfully escaped their mother's daily scrutiny and their father's alcoholic detachment. He was forced into the role of mediator, and for William, who had always avoided emotional conflict, the time there proved trying.

While he was away, Ariel became increasingly concerned about the toll it would take on his kids to have their father gone only a few days after losing a much-loved grandparent.

Ariel wrote a letter, the most difficult one she had ever written to William. In it, she asked him to stay with Susan, because the kids needed him at home, and knowing that Susan would never give William custody. She loved him enough to live without him if she had to. Love wouldn't end because they were apart. She was confident Susan would take him back, if he approached her carefully. It was to Susan's advantage. She would be seen as the wife who had won her man back from the grips of the wicked adulteress who had cast a spell on her husband; she could save face, and Ariel didn't care about anything but William's happiness.

But, when William arrived to see her the evening of his return from the funeral, his depression was evident and his exhaustion profound. He'd just stopped in to tell her he loved her, and by tomorrow night, they would be together. She pushed the letter deeper into the pocket of her skirt.

When William moved in, they spent most of the first night reveling in the manifestation of their dream to one day say "goodnight" in one another's arms and to waken with the sun to kiss "good morning." Their slumber was fitful, their wonder at spending their first night together, their bodies touching all the while, were fleeting hours not to be missed. If one's hand slipped from the other's waist, they'd awaken to secure their hold. They had never been so close, nor so vulnerable as they were that first night, clinging to each other, as if frantic not to let go for fear they might be torn apart.

The days and weeks that followed was a period of adjustment that didn't seem to settle them into a routine as a couple. Ariel had lived alone for over a year, and the home she made was decorated in her taste, furnishings arranged as she thought best. William's books now doubled the collection to be shelved. Although he brought a horrid old recliner and a couple of tables that had seen better days that Ariel would rather have seen discarded, she made an effort to work them into the decor of the house.

But William did not seem interested in hanging any of the many pictures or the few paintings he had brought with him. He seemed to have no interest in the household at all. Whatever Ariel tried to do to make him feel at home was received apathetically. They got to the point where they were, as Ariel put it, "pussyfooting around" each other, or "walking on eggshells" trying not to disturb each other.

After a day of teaching, William would then pick up his children from their school to return them to Susan's house, where he would help them with their homework or watch them as they played outside until Susan arrived home from work. Often, he would fix things around the house, do the laundry, pick up the messy rooms, trim the ivy vine taking over the chimney, rake the lawn in the autumn, or salt the drive in the winter. He'd return to Ariel around six o'clock, where they'd have a quiet dinner and spend the rest of the evening reading or watching TV.

One evening Ariel noticed that when William closed the cover on a novel he had finished, he got out of his chair and took the next book from the "to be read" stack.

She knew that something had gone dreadfully wrong.

—William? He sat back down and opened the book without looking up at her.

—*Hmmmm?* he mumbled.

—William, would you look at me for a moment? He looked over to her questioningly.

—Yes, what is it?

—I just wanted to look into your beautiful blue eyes.

A smile swept fleetingly across his face, as he said, —That's sweet, and the smile disappeared as he turned the pages to the first chapter his book.

At times, whether he would be across a table, preparing lessons, or lying awake next to her, she suspected his mind was elsewhere, as if he was pacing endlessly through some labyrinth of thought where there was no visible gateway for escape or rescue. The silence became a palpable, smothering thing floating between them.

They began to argue, about little things at first, as they dealt with the debris of everyday living. Frustration suffused into the bigger things. They began to challenge and belittle each other's differing opinions. They could not discuss what was happening in the world of politics any more than they could agree on what to have for dinner at night. Each had always been aware of the other's differences of political philosophy, but now William laced into Ariel because she supported President Clinton, whatever his sexual peccadilloes, and she was angry that William thought America should not send troops to Bosnia, in spite of the Serbian genocide. Where they used to spar happily, enjoying the mental gymnastics of contrary opinions, William became frustrated in not being able to convert Ariel to his way of thinking and he was vocal in his contempt for her points of view. Ariel felt like she was put on the defensive in a way that was no longer a fun-filled excursion into a game of wits, but a sad, destructive battle with no apparent victor.

When Elizabeth and Timothy would visit, Ariel insisted that she and William sleep separately. Ariel behaved like any good roommate would. She would not impose on William's time with his kids; instead she would just drift off into a corner to read, or leave the house on the pretense of a shopping trip.

The children had only been told that their parents were not happy together, and they had decided to separate and that William was going to live with his friend Ariel. He had wanted to tell them the truth, but Susan and Ariel had each insisted that for a while, the children need not know the truth. This in itself was against William's nature, for he had built a trust with his children and believed they would have understood that he loved Ariel and that Susan was not happy with that fact.

William was spending so much time at Susan's that Ariel realized that he was living two lives. She was watching their relationship perish before her eyes long before William ever did, and she opened the door to the possibility that he might return to Susan. She became paralyzed with fear as she envisioned her already shaky life collapsing before her.

But the mood was maudlin, the oppressive silence of a tomb, Ariel thought.

But of course that was what it was, she realized: They'd turned their new home together into a tomb for the dead.

The dead.

And she and William were the mourners.

There came a day in February, after a solemn St. Valentine's Day dinner, when Ariel could actually read his thoughts. The candlelight dinner and flowers and generic card could not disguise the truth: She had lost him. William's divorce had become final three weeks before, and yet he still wore his wedding ring.

Harris had mentioned it to her the week before, when he asked when their divorces were to become final. When Ariel told him that William was in fact divorced, Harris said, "Oh . . . he's still wearing his wedding band." Ariel made the excuse that William had given her, that his fingers had grown fatter since putting it on seventeen years ago and he might have to have the doctor cut it off when he went for his quarterly scans. She couldn't face the possibility that William had not tried to remove the ring.

The next day, William stated that he wanted to spend Susan's birthday with her, because the kids were out of town staying with one of Susan's sisters during the winter break. Ariel, feeling the red-hot surge of jealousy, blurted out:

—So, you've got a date with your ex-wife?

—It's not a date. It's her birthday. She shouldn't have to spend it alone.

—Send her a fucking card!

—Ariel! Coming from her lips the profanity was a surprise.

—What kind of crazy shit are you talking, Will? "She shouldn't have to spend it alone," she mimicked.

He stood for a moment dumbfounded.

—You're telling me you're going on a date with your ex-wife! And you're still wearing that goddamn wedding band. Why?

—I don't know. It just doesn't feel right taking it off just yet.

—What do you mean, it doesn't feel right! *What?* What crap are you feeding me? Why doesn't it?

—It's not time. I'm not ready.

—You do know what you're saying to me, don't you? *Don't you? Are you out of your mind?* You've made a date with her. You love Susan.

—I'll always care for Susan. Just as you care for John.

—But I took my ring off long ago, when I knew my marriage was over, even before the divorce. What this says to me is that you didn't want to end your marriage to Susan.

—I didn't. But I couldn't stay at home *and be with you.*

She reeled as his statement hit her square in her midsection, as painful as if he had sent a fist into her. But, of course, it was what they had both wanted, wasn't it, back when it all began? They hadn't wanted to abandon their spouses, their families. They simply wanted inclusion in each other's lives. But, Ariel had come to understand the folly of their ways long ago when she realized that John wouldn't let her remain in the marriage until the kids were out on their own. He would not make the children a consideration. And her decision to stay with him had only brought torture into both their lives, forcing her to make the final break from him. Susan was no less insidious, but she was smarter and more calculating than John. She had held her ground, waiting, enduring, *expecting* that William would get over his fascination with Ariel. And hadn't William given her the upper hand, telling Susan that she must decide when he had to leave? They had finally parted when William could no longer stand her smug control any longer. His children were told, and together Susan and William tried to make it an easy transition for them.

—No, Susan wouldn't let you keep me. *Your new toy.*

His response was silence.

She had learned, oh, God, how she had learned over the years, the hard lesson. She felt as if she was about to explode. But she knew the power of words, the force of emotions that could drive words out of her mouth that she could not take back, the lasting consequences of what people say to each other, the devastation wrought by words.

She wanted to blast him, eviscerate him, as he had her, to return threefold the agony he had inflicted with his casual, careless admissions. In the past she knew the wisdom of never asking a question that you can't live with the answer to, because the truth can be as devastating as the lie.

With all she'd been through with this man, how could she go on living a lie? What would become of her if she didn't have the courage and dignity and self-respect to face up to a terrible truth? Was the truth that he never really loved her, that he had never really given himself up to her, that his had been nothing more than a sex-driven journey through his midlife crisis, that she had been no more to him than the lustful fulfillment of his fantasies?

But after the blind eye she had turned where John was concerned, accepting his excuses, his destructive habits and his narcissistic disregard for the welfare of his family, Ariel could never again live with lies.

"Truth is truth 'til the day of reckoning. . . ."

She felt a nauseating disgust, suddenly, of John, of William, and of herself for the fool she had been, and she didn't care to contain her feelings any longer. She wanted to blow to smithereens all memory of what had happened between them in the past; she wanted to go back in time and recover what she could of her life before William had ever entered it. Her disappointment with John and the turmoil of their home was better than this heated torture. She blurted out:

—Are you planning on sleeping with her, too? A little birthday cake, blow out the candles, a hop in the sack for old time's sake?

When the accusation received no response, unbridled fury took over and had she a weapon at hand, she might have used it against him. Instead, she doubled-down and spurted:

—*A little birthday fuck?* Is that what you have in mind?

—Ariel, no! I love you! And then with strained and whispered desperation, he called her name:

—*Ariella . . .*

—Yeah, sure! You love me. *Why else are you trying to kill me?*

He couldn't look at her, his hands tried to massage away the conflict in his head.

—Do you think she'll take you back?

He looked at her with incredulity, and then she could see his fear.

—I don't know. That's not why I want—

—You just made the mistake of saying "I don't know,' which tells me you've been thinking about it! Well, you better hope she does! She's a stupid cow, so you might be able to convince her with—

—Ariel!

He leaped toward her, grabbing her arm.

—Well, what the hell do you think, I'm gonna let you come back here after your little birthday bang?

She viciously pulled away.

Ariel's eyes scanned the room, looking at the evidence of her attempt to build a new life with William—the books, the furnishings, the photographs. And she remembered too, the halfhearted attempts on William's part to make the place a home while she had invested so much of herself. What was the point, anymore, of trudging on? Her anger was abating and overriding it was disappointment and despair.

—Assure her that you will never see me again. And it will be the truth, William. It will have to be the truth. We *end.* That's the one thing that *might* get you home. But, you've never considered this place your home, have you? If she rejects the idea, I won't throw you out into the street. You can have the sofa for a short time until you find a place to go. *But you will not hurt me again.* I won't be the consolation prize.

William, weeping quietly, looked up at her with such desperation that she thought he had changed his mind and would never leave her side. He rushed to take her in his arms, and for a moment that felt like redemption, as if all the harsh words had never been spoken, her resolve dissipated a little as he whispered:

—We've had three wonderful years together, Ariel! Three years! I will never forget that. The memory will always live in me. I've never known your kind of love, but I have the memories. I will live on our memories.

The memories!

The hopeful moment passed, the ache returning threefold.

The memories. . . . Is that what we were all about, making memories? Memories fade as they grow tired and worn, like old celluloid film, with the passing of time and the very replaying. Was the devastation their love had wrought worth only the accumulation of memories?

Fuck the memories! she wanted to yell through her pain as she pushed him away. She, nothing more than a ghost now; nothing more than a sad vestige of the woman she had once been, now consigned to live with the ravages she had wrought on herself and on those she professed to love!

She pushed him away—and he let her, oh, much too easily, without much resistance, without a fight—she started to walk away. He called her name and she turned. He reached out a hand in a gesture of—what was it? Gratitude? She glimpsed the wedding band on his finger and the reality of it hit home in her heart.

—Memories. . . she whispered, —They're nice things to recall when you're making new ones . . . but they are not enough to live on, to sustain a person.

—My love!

His voice broke and he moved in, grasping for her. She released herself with deliberation, prying each finger with firm resolve, and she felt an odd power in the doing. She looked at him with a hardness he had never seen before and then, suddenly, her cold stare vanished, washed away with tears.

—You said—you said—*you told me*, William, remember? You said that we were magic together. We were the music of the heavens! Was that just corny malarkey I fell for? Are those the words I should remember? Are those the memories I should keep? Meaningless babble? Three years? I want to forget these years!

—Ariella! Memories are all we collect in life; it's what we have left when all else is gone—

—Memories of us, memories formed from mist; they hold no truth. They dry up in the sun. *Memories?* Should I keep them in a box with your love letters?

Determined to obliterate him and his treachery from her life, she ran up the stairs to the choir loft, where they had made their bedroom. She fetched the box that she had guarded lovingly on her side of the bed, the box that contained the more than three hundred letters he had written to her, letters chronicling their three years together. Standing triumphantly at the rail overlooking the sanctuary, she tore off the lid. With a wild, ruthless abandon she grabbed handfuls of the loose papers and threw them down at him like an autumn rain of leaves. The task completed, the insult returned, she walked regally down the steps and appraised the scene before her.

—Clean up this goddamn mess, she ordered. —You made it!

She grabbed her coat from off the hook beside the door, quit the building, got into her car and drove toward town. She began to shake as the aftermath of the ordeal began settling in. She pulled off to the side of the dark road because she couldn't see through her tears. She got out of the car. Her eyes, stinging from the salt of tears, found cooling relief in the chilled night air. She looked searchingly over the snow-covered meadow. When she saw where she had unwittingly arrived by some cruel trick of fate, to the meadow where it all began, the meadow where on a summer night she lay stargazing and William had first made love to her, memories assaulted her.

It had started with the book. The book that seduced her, awakening a dormant part of her nature. Now, in despair, she saw a darker truth: Yes! God *had* created a sublime world, all right, but then He abandoned it to unworthy caretakers, practitioners of Free Will! What she perceived was once heavenly perfection had fast become a living hell. There was no Free Will. What a joke! Free Will was nothing more than a kneejerk reaction to what Fate threw at you. She was living in Hell and there was nothing she could do about it.

When he returned from spending the evening with Susan on her birthday, William was downtrodden. He rambled aimlessly around the big room, trying to find a way to end it all. The night before, after Ariel had walked out, he had spent the hours before her early morning return retrieving the letters, reading them through before returning them to the leather-tooled box where Ariel had until now so pridefully kept them. He had succeeded in making everybody's lives miserable, including his own, and he was better off dead.

Ariel came down from bed, and asked him how things had gone with Susan.

—Nothing.

—She won't take you back?

—I didn't ask. I don't want to go back.

—I'm going up to bed. You can, if you like, sleep in my bed tonight.

—It's up to you.

—It's not an invitation for you to touch me. I am going *to sleep*, William. You look a wreck. Just stay on your side of the bed.

He followed her up the spiral staircase. Without a word, she got in under the covers and turned her back to him. As she tried to quiet her roiling thoughts so that she might fall into some phase of sleep that would temporarily release her from the world, William watched her.

The moon washed the room in pearly pale-gray light and he recalled how much he had longed to see her in the moonlight for the first time. It had become just one of many obsessions: to see her naked body whitened to alabaster in the soft, cool glow of a full moon. He recalled with renewed astonishment the first time she fell asleep in his arms, and more amazingly, the first time in his adult life he had ever fallen asleep while being held in an embrace.

He lay there beside her, haunted by the memories he had so brazenly offered this woman as consolation at their parting the night before. How very brutal he had been! More than ever he wanted to end his life, if only to release this tender soul of the woman he had professed to love from any more of his cruelty.

This woman, this miracle lying beside him, this manifestation of his secret prayer brought out in him a passion he had never known he was capable of feeling. A passion that short-circuited any intellectual reasoning by which he had conducted his life before they came together, undermined all the defenses he had built around his heart, and bored through his psyche with ruthless abandon. His condition was a state beyond addiction. The physical connection to her was unbreakable, a welcome prison, the rejection of that pragmatic part of him that had heretofore ruled his life, and the hold she had on him could never be broken by any promise he might make to Susan.

For he did not love Susan.

He began to wonder if he had ever had more than grateful affection for her. To rip himself away from Ariel would surely kill him, he knew that. His conflict was a fight with himself over honor, of duty, but at the same time he knew, too, his actions could further devastate the precious woman who had pledged her love to him and who had paid a high price in doing so. He was being driven to return to Susan for some other reason, and he thought he would go mad if he couldn't name it, look it in the eye, and confront the answer.

I am not worthy of Ariel's love, he said to himself; to leave her was to throw away the chance of what little happiness he might know before he died. For he felt his imminent mortality more keenly of late, sensed that the final smothering darkness ahead was hurtling toward him at an accelerated speed. Cured of the cancer for two years, Death was still lurking in the dark, soon to reveal itself. He could not shake the feeling.

He rose from the bed and dressed. Ariel, lingering in a dreamscape between lucid and unconscious nightmare, opened her eyes to see him standing over her at the foot of the bed. She was frightened at what she saw. A face drained of color. Then she realized it was the effect of the moonlight through the window casting shadows on the planes of his face.

—What is it?

—I don't know! I don't know anything!

—Will, I can't go through any—

—I think I am going insane, Ariel!

—What are you trying to do to me!

—Please! Please help me!

—I told you what you must do to go back to Susan, Will. I can do no more!

—I thought— he stammered, trying to find the words. —I *believed* in what Johnny Shawnessy discovered about a man's life at the end of *Raintree County*: "Periodically, each man has to build his world again." I thought that was what we were doing! I think I'm going crazy! I don't know what's happening to me, Ariel.

She began to reprimand him, to tell him to go back and build a fucking new world with Susan, but she had hardly spoken a word before he interrupted.

—You must understand. It's not to be with Susan! I have to figure out my life, what the hell it is I'm doing, what I must do! I can't seem to find where I belong!

Compassion aborted her escalating rage. And when he bolted from the room she followed him down the staircase, and watched him pace the floor, always just a step behind him. She was hurt and angry; she was at the end of her rope; she was suffering grief so profound, so like the death of a loved one. And it was a death, really, wasn't it? Still she would be forced to witness the last breath.

—I need to walk. Come out with me for a walk, please. I need to walk, but I need you to be with me, please, Ariel, stay with me while I try to sort out what's happening to me. I'm on the brink of something important, and I'll tell you, I'm scared.

An odd feeling swept through Ariel at his words. Whatever he had done to her, she couldn't ignore the danger she sensed would befall him. She threw a coat over her nightgown, and slipped into her mud-caked garden boots.

How quickly the weather had turned, but then, there had been rain in the forecast. The moonlight of just a few minutes before suddenly became obscured with clouds, and as they walked in silence for a time, a soft drizzle began misting the streets to a black sheen. William set a fast pace, and Ariel kept up with him, waiting for him to say what was on his mind. Waiting for more of last night's blatant announcements that would no doubt stab at her heart.

—It's the whole package, you know? It's not Susan, it's what's familiar, it's the kids. Oh, God, I miss the kids. Before you, the children's were the only real and lasting love I'd ever known. I miss the natural way of living that I'd grown used to.

He stopped suddenly and turned to grab her by the shoulders.

—I know I can't leave you, say goodbye and mean it. I'd only return, begging you to have me back, and cause you pain, or I'd sit out there on the side of the road in the dark, in the car, watching for you at the end of the day, just to catch a glimpse of you. I don't love

Susan, I know that, now. It's a lie to think—a lie I told myself that I loved her *and* you, but I understand that I don't love her in the same way or with the same intensity or quality of love that I love you. I just didn't want to *abandon* her. Like I've been abandoned by people all my life. I just didn't want to be the kind of jerk who would abandon his wife for another woman. I had too much affection for her to be cruel, and yet I was cruel! Cruel to think I could have it all! I wanted to be a better man than that! And I've failed! I've failed to love you the way you deserve to be loved.

Ariel touched his arm and spoke quietly through her tears.

—It took me some time to realize that about John. I loved two men. I came to understand that although I refused to qualify those loves, the truth was, is, that it was always you I belonged with.

—Who were we trying to fool?

—Ourselves, I suppose, in hoping that John and Susan would not see the truth we refused to see, all because we didn't want to behave like *bad people*. The truth is that we had made commitments to them, which you and I tried to keep. And so we have great affection for them, but certainly not the kind of love you and I have shared.

—And yet, I try to convince myself that I can give you up in order to have the past back again. A past that was lacking, a past that was starving me. . . . What's wrong with me?

It struck her like a revelation.

—Guilt.

—I never felt guilty for loving you.

—Then what else can it be?

— Yes . . . guilt, I suppose. Guilt for causing pain. I caused pain to relieve my own agony, my own loneliness. But never guilt for loving you, Ariella.

—You used to say that with me you could be vulnerable without fear. But something has made you fearful. Now you are fearful. Why?

—How did it come to this?

—William, she sighed heavily, trying to pull the words from out the sky, and when they weren't to be found among the raindrops, she looked inside herself.

—When you went away to be with your mother, I was having a difficult time of things. I thought it was a mistake for you to leave Susan. I felt guilt, I suppose. With you gone I was in Limbo, and I missed John—the John of long ago, the man—well, the man I once thought he was . . . and my kids, and the life I once lived; as miserable as I was back then, when I couldn't admit I was miserable. It was doable, livable, better than the tearing apart I was going through being away from not only you, but my children, and yes, John, even. I thought I might return to John, if he'd have me back. It's funny, you know? You only remember the good times, the best of days, when you look back with love in your heart. And I couldn't help but to look back with love because I loved all the people concerned, in that past I once knew so well.

—On the night you flew back from the funeral, I was going to give you a letter I had written, but when I saw you, I realized that there was a reason I had traveled so far with you, a reason I had changed my life. I had never doubted we were meant to be together. I couldn't give you that letter sending you away.

—Why?

—You were vulnerable just then, and I just couldn't be the martyr, letting you walk out of my life. It was selfish of me. I knew my life would be miserable without you, and I suddenly remembered how much richer my life had become in spite of all the ordeals we'd gone through to be together, and all the lovely memories of my life with John suddenly faded to the background while the times that were so awful shifted to the forefront. I didn't want you to go back, all right? *I was selfish.* I dared to be *selfish*! I didn't want to sacrifice you for some distorted belief that the lives of all concerned would be better for our parting. It was too late and I had made my choice, I told myself, and then, selfishness aside, I understood: There was never any choice to make in the first place. I belonged with *you.* That was why we came together, why our paths led us to this town at this particular time in our lives.

　　—If you believe that, then why didn't you try to stop me from even considering returning to Susan?

　　—Hold you against your will? Like Susan tried to do? No. . . . That's not love.

　　Ariel touched his arm with gentle appeal.

　　—After thinking hard about it today, and now putting all the clues together, I know it was not really Susan you wanted to return to. You needed to sort out the real reason, and it was about something I—any woman should never challenge, because in the end you lose and are left alone and miserable—it was all about the children.

　　—I miss them. Yes, I see them at Susan's, in the house I left, and it's there I say good-bye to them when I leave to come home to you. And I feel like an outsider, a stranger at the gate, peeking in through the windows, watching the lives that they are carrying on without me. . . .

Like when I was a little boy at the gate, watching the happy little family, a mother, a father, and two little girls framed in the bow window, complete without me.

—I thought it better they stay with their mother and for me to go there every day, but they need to be *here*, at their new "other home," too, don't they? Oh, Ariella, we've shut ourselves away here, afraid to be seen together, careful not to flaunt our love at the expense of our spouses, when we always wanted to be free to walk down the street hand-in-hand like other respectable couples. I've been trying to protect the kids, and all I'm doing is living two separate lives, and you shouldn't protect children from reality. . . . Is it guilt that's got us at last, Ariella? Is it shame? Because we dared to love one another? Is this what guilt feels like?

She smiled wistfully.

—It's what it looks like, anyway. Only you can say what you feel.

—Why would you let me go so easily? Why didn't you fight for me! Were you just tired of me, of my miserable self?

A time in the distant past flashed before her when she had been faced with her unrequited love for a young man.

—I once loved a young man, deeply, while I was at Julliard. He was troubled and I wanted to help him. I did in a way, and he never failed to express his gratitude. I fell in love with him. I sensed that he loved me, even though we never spoke of love. But his emotional conflicts at the time needed sorting out. One afternoon, after I spent the day visiting him in his East Village apartment, as he was walking me to the subway station, he told me about this very pretty woman he had met at the bookstore where he worked. He spared me no detail of how he had fallen head over heels in love with her. I was crying inside with a smile plastered on my face as he asked me to wish him luck. He was going to ask her for a date. I remember it was early Autumn and the sun was setting fast and the light made his brown eyes shimmer as he spoke about her. I wished him luck, gave him a hug, and said I'd see him real soon. It was one of the hardest things I ever had to do, William. I had to walk away. I had to let him free. That's when I realized that you can't make someone love you. No matter what you try to do, if he doesn't love you, well, you can't force him to. And one shouldn't mistake gratitude for love, which is what I did, you see. If you really love someone, you let them go. John never understood that. His wasn't a fight for my love, but a war against my love for you. Possession, not love. . . . So, I guess you might say I was letting you walk away this time. Not back to Susan. I've never really feared Susan. She was a symbol of what you lost—the kids. I was letting you go home to your kids.

A remarkable change transformed him.

—Who are we trying to protect, anymore? Why do I feel like we still have to hide the truth from everyone?

—You didn't want to throw "Us" in Susan's face. You didn't want to embarrass her publicly. You were trying to protect her and the kids. But I could see that whenever the children leave our home, you sink into an awful funk. It's all about the kids.

—I was afraid she'd take the children from me and try to end shared custody. We're not going to hide anymore, my love! Susan can't take the children away from me; I won't let her do that, ever! But I won't give you up, ever! He pulled her in his arms as the drizzle turned to a driving rain.

He laughed heartily as he held her close to him. And then his mouth covered hers in a deep, blissful kiss of thankful salvation.

—Where's the olive oil? he said when it ended.

—What? Olive oil? Are you planning on cooking me dinner? It's two o'clock in the morning!

—I want this ring off now! Oh, my God, what I've put you through! You're shivering

—That's because I'm freezing.

The next three days were a long weekend, and they spent most of the time in bed planning their wedding in June, the third anniversary of the day that William sat across a picnic table from Ariel; the day she had placed her hat on his head to shield him from the rays of a westering sunset, when it took all his courage to fulfill the first necessary hurdle in their relationship: "Will we ever speak?"

"*. . . with all the courage he could muster, he opened his mouth to speak. Out came a hoarse whisper. . . . He could barely hear it himself for the blood pounding in his ears. But she heard him loud and clear!*

'*I love you, Ariella,*' *he said.*"

"Everything was still on the wide fields and sleepy stream of summer.
Raintree County

THIRTEEN

Ariel and William

The cancer came back.

A month before the wedding, William had his scheduled quarterly scans. For two years he had been clean. Ariel always went with William to the hospital's cancer center for his follow-up visit with his oncologist. The day of the appointment they brought with them the wedding invitation to hand-deliver to Dr. Montero. Rudolfo Montero was not only William's doctor, but had become a friend, attending all the concerts and plays performed at the Meeting House with his wife, Edna. Their teenage son, Rudy, star-struck, had apprenticed under William's tutelage and had been given his first stage role performing a small part in one of the summer productions.

When Rudolfo entered the small examination room with a big smile on his face, William was about to hand him the invitation. He didn't get to do more than stand up from the chair when the doctor began to tell the news.

The tumor had returned in the same location, the size about seven centimeters, just as it measured the first time it had been discovered.

Ariel and William could not look at each other, for fear of betraying their feelings. They kept their eyes riveted on the doctor, who kept on talking about the next course of therapy while the dialogues within each of their minds muffled much of what he said.

Intensive chemotherapy, scans after three courses to see how much the cancer had reduced. The drugs had worked quickly before, so they should again.

William refused to show anything less than an optimistic attitude, but he did say solemnly —It always comes back, doesn't it?

—A great percentage do, and then some never do. But we've found it early, before it's metastasized.

—So, we may just be buying time?

—We're all buying time, William. But I know what you're asking.

Dr. Montero pulled his chair closer to the couple and leaned in to rest his elbow on his crossed leg, cupping his chin with his hand.

—Sometimes, when this kind of cancer returns for a second visit, it can be resistant to the drugs that originally destroyed it. CT scans can't show us remaining clusters of a few remaining cancer cells. That's why, last time around, we gave you an extra course of therapy to destroy those undetectable cells.

—Yes, said William, nodding rigidly. —And if these drugs don't work?

—We try another cocktail.

—And after that?

—Surgery. Surgery is the best way to get it all out, but first we try the chemo because it's less invasive. There are too many veins and an artery that may be involved there.

—So, first the chemo, and then if necessary, surgery.

—Or, there are new drugs coming out all the time that may get rid of it once and for all.

Both Ariel and William understood from the doctor's last statement that surgery would be last on his list to effect a cure. Dr. Montero obviously had reservations about the surgery, as he implied its complications.

—All right, then, said William, —When do we start?

—Right away. Next week? I say we go with four five-day courses every three weeks. Then we do the scans to see where we're going. I've consulted with a colleague at the Mayo Clinic and another fellow at Johns Hopkins who specializes in rare cancers, and they both agree to the cocktail. So, Monday, okay?

—Great, said William, the tone of his voice sounding like he'd just cut a business deal. As he rose from the chair, he saw that he was clutching the wedding invitation. He was about to slip it into his pocket when Ariel touched his hand. He looked at her, a frown of amazement on his face.

—Are you sure? he asked.

She didn't reply with words, just flashed the secret smile, before turning to Dr. Montero and handing him the envelope.

—We hope that you and Edna and Rudy can attend.

—Oh, my God! Oh, that's wonderful! said the good doctor, laughter and affection genuine.

—I'll have to get you a special wedding present!

—The best thing you can do for us, the only present we could ever want, is a cure for my William, said Ariel, planting a kiss on the cheek of her future husband.

—We'll cure this. It can be dealt with.

And so began a year of debilitating treatments. The original cocktail failed to reduce the tumor and only made William more ill from the side-effects than he had been the first time around. The next combination of drugs was not as harsh, until they failed to prove effective, and when the dosage was increased, William had to be hospitalized because of the side-effects. William had to be closely monitored; his immune system was affected, he was prone to dehydration, his hair fell out, and once again, he did not like the drawn, gaunt, sallow face he saw in the mirror.

Ariel saw the physical changes, but the changes were just that—physical—and that didn't change the devotion she felt for him. She saw only the beautiful man she fell in love with and she loved him more than ever.

He amazed her at times: He never allowed himself a break from work or household duties. It worried her that he was doing too much, and she'd beg him to take things easier. He'd refuse, but instead of arguing, she found other ways to reduce the strains on him.

She hired a garden service to deal with the garden and lawn, and hired a neighbor's son to take care of any heavy outdoor work she and William would have dealt with. She hired a cleaning woman who came in twice a week to do the laundry and the heavy cleaning. She learned to give William his nightly injections that were part of his chemo courses. It was the hardest thing she had to learn to do, and at first she became physically ill with having to stick the needle into alternating arms each evening. She tried not to show her distress and William tried not to wince. Since childhood, the worst part of going to a doctor, or being transferred to a foreign country with his family, were the shots he had to endure.

But, nothing worked. The tumor increased in size.

After much consultation with specialists and surgeons, a day was scheduled to perform the surgery.

They were looking forward to the day he would be rid of the evil thing that could potentially take his life. It would be a good thing to actually hear the surgeon say, "We've got it all!" which he did say, after thirteen hours of surgery at the big New York City hospital. William fell asleep again after hearing Ariel repeat the words the doctor had said to her, with the confidence that the nightmare was finally over. They had been married for almost a year and a half and had yet to live without the overshadowing of the disease.

After a week of recovery William was anxious to return home. He missed the children and the puppy that they had adopted from the shelter eight months earlier. They named her Little Eva, after the heroine of Uncle Tom's Cabin, as the pup was a sleek, black creature with happy brown eyes and an energetic disposition, and because of The King and I story told in Siamese music and stylized dance. Ariel had purchased a velvety soft black stuffed dog on his second day in ICU and laid it next to William as he slept. He laughed when he saw it, and treated it like a puppet as he'd talk and play and bark for Ariel's amusement.

Ariel, who spent her nights sleeping on a cot beside his bed after days of doing William's bidding when the nursing staff was stretched to the limit, was anxious and ready to see to his recuperation at home, where he could be around the people and things he loved. Perhaps, now, Ariel thought, they might return to Cape Ann, where they had spent five days honeymooning. Ariel loved the ocean, and William loved the sun and the smell of the sea and watching Ariel plunge into the waves to swim along the beaches.

They had found an old Victorian bed-and-breakfast overlooking the ocean and lighthouses off Rockport.

There, they ate lobster and clams and chowders in the little village of Rockport and shopped at the quaint shops along the point. William had bought her a beautiful polished seashell purse, and nestled inside was a pearl ring. Ariel bought William a Mont Blanc fountain pen.

They'd drive around in the car, find a secluded dune near the shore, and make love to the pounding of the waves. Some nights they'd sit hand-in-hand on the inn's porch swing, reveling in the smell of the sea as it wafted on the breeze, the full moon, its beams tickling the expanse of water, the lighthouses chasing the moonbeams with their own manmade streams of light, and the joy of being together.

It was the first time that they had ever had to relax without timetables and schedules of daily living to interfere with their pleasure in each other's company. It was the only time they ever knew a sense of peace and tranquility in their mutual love. It was too good to be true, they each thought, but dared not voice to each other. There was the specter of imminent loss should the chemotherapy fail to cure William, but for five days that first summer of their marriage they acknowledged that all they had been through to arrive at this time together had been worth the struggle.

Yes, thought Ariel. We will go back next summer to Cape Ann. We will go back every summer. It will be our own vacation place. We will get the same room at the inn, and each year we will write about what we did each day that we were there. Thirty years from now we will read each week's account and relive how our love took bloom by the sea. . . .

"The act of love's a burial whose afterfruit is sadness."

Raintree County

FOURTEEN

Bill

What exactly was it that shocked him to consciousness? A memory? Or was it a voice? Yes! It was not a familiar voice, not one he had ever heard before, but he knew to whom it belonged. The voice shouted *at* him with the intent to awaken Bill.

He was bathed in a puddle of sweat, the covers thrown over Little Eva, who lay beside him, having stolen into the bed during the night.

A thought had awakened him; *a voice had awoken him.*

As he couldn't shake off the sense of foreboding, he decided to challenge it, yet he was not sure how. What he feared had something to do with Ariel. He threw on clothes, grabbed his coat and car keys and drove to her house.

He didn't care if she thought him crazy for knocking on her door in the middle of the night. He was driven by a forceful compulsion, a premonition and a sense of purpose in what he was doing that would not be shaken by reason or common sense.

A faint light glowed in the house. It was after three o'clock in the morning. Bill would knock on the front door and ring the doorbell, and if she didn't respond, find a way in through a window or the cellar door.

He remembered Amy's scolding remark that Ariel never locked her doors at night, that Ariel lived in danger by not securing her home. At the moment, though, Bill feared no intruders doing her harm, only Ariel causing harm to herself. He turned the doorknob and found that the lock was not engaged.

The conversation earlier in the day when he visited Ariel with Harris and Amy present kept replaying in Bill's head as he walked quietly toward the platform where Ariel rested peacefully asleep.

I am an alarmist, he said to himself, sighing a great breath of relief as he looked over her peaceful expression, her hair dark from the distant light of the lamp across the room, flowing in waves on the pillow. He did not want to awaken her or frighten her, but he found himself compelled to move in for a closer look at her resting figure. This ethereal nymph lying across the bed, the folds of her pink-silk nightgown caressing her sensuous curves, a Bouguereau masterpiece come to life before him.

How lovely she is in repose, he thought, moving still nearer to her bed. He could stay and watch over her for the rest of the night; watch the pillows of her breasts rise and fall and listen to the hushed whisper as she breathed in restful recovery.

He moved closer still.

As her breasts rise and fall, rise and fall . . . rise and fall . . . and listen to the hushed whisper . . . hushed . . . whisper, whisper . . . as she breathed . . . as she breathed . . .as she breathed . . . Breathe . . . Breathe . . . BREATHE!

After his efforts, he stared down at her, spent, miserable in his failure to revive her. He had tried to breathe life into her over and over again as he pressed his palms against her chest, at the place between the ribs, above the hollow of her stomach, of her stomach where the incision was marked with stitches. He had caused this, he knew. He had caused her injury and now he could do nothing to save her!

He fell to his knees before her lifeless body, threw back his head and howled her name like an animal in the last throes of agony. Lifting her to cradle in his arms, he rocked her, burying his tear-ravaged face into the sweet silk of her hair. He felt the softness of her cheek against his own, and his fingers traced the line of her brow, his lips lingered on hers. And yet, she would not respond to him.

Grief prolonged brings madness. But was it madness or a nightmare he was dreaming?

Soon, he fell into a swoon beside her limp body. And after a time, when he opened his eyes and saw her rounded shoulder at his cheek he lingered in a sublime fantasy of his own making.

Gently, he pushed further down the strap of the gown that had fallen from her shoulder during his ordeal to save her. Slowly, carefully, he pushed the garment away to reveal the gentle slope of her breasts. Respectfully, he regarded the curved sweep of her thigh, the ample mound between her limbs, where he nestled for a time, in reverence of her beauty. Her flesh was warm to his touch; her scent was a potent mixture of summer breezes and exotic places.

He must know the full meaning of this glorious wonder lying here, so still, so composed, in his arms. She would come to love him in time. He would wait for her to open her eyes and smile at him. He longed to plunge into that delicious, pliant flesh.

A sharp pain jolted up through his arm and ripped through his shoulder. When he opened his eyes, Bill's met Harris Haley's looking down at him with hatred.

Harris's eyes were wet and agony-stricken, narrowed against the horror he had witnessed. And, with his pain came fury. His face was fixed in the fierce expression of a man who is about to kill.

Then, as if giving Bill no further thought, he retreated toward the bed to kneel beside Ariel.

As Bill rose to sit on the floor, the pain tearing at his shoulder was dimmed by a more demanding agony: Ariel was dead.

Bill watched the scene moving closer and closer until he found himself standing a few feet away: Harris, emitting great gulping sobs, rocked Ariel's rigor-ridden body to his chest, as if the kneading and warming of her flesh would make her soft and pliable and animate and yielding life.

That Bill stood there naked made little impact on him, and had it not been for Harris, who turned and snarled: —You disgust me. Put your clothes on! Bill would have remained an observer rather than a participant in the scene before him.

When it came crashing back to him, he yearned for his own death, to be with Ariel, to lay down beside her in an eternal bed, to know the warmth of her spirit if not the warmth of her body that he had held through the night, growing colder against the fire of his love, to bring her back, to know her love. He felt no shame, only failure and the complete annihilating torture of loss.

Bill dressed.

Harris, pulling the nightgown over Ariel's head, wept quietly as he struggled with the garment. Bill became angry that he would try to obscure her beautiful form, as if the sight of her nakedness brought shame rather than reverence. Even in death she possessed the cool translucence of the polished pink seashell.

Shaken out from the hiding place deep inside him where his subconscious mind shut him in safely, Bill sprang at Harris to pull him away from her, and the disfiguring gown from around her neck. Harris did not resist.

—I found her naked, and that's how she will remain!

Harris spoke in a soft, oddly compassionate tone,
—You don't want them to see her like this, Bill.

Them? Who where *them*?

Bill considered Harris's comment. Ah, yes . . . there would be people. They would see her only as a naked corpse, not as one of Nature's more perfect creations. He drew the sheet and comforter to lay in a neat rectangle over Ariel, folding the top of the sheet over the comforter's edge and then smoothing it to cover her shoulders.

Gently, Bill placed the pillow under her head, arranging her honey-colored hair in a fan to frame her face. He became transfixed remembering how, only a few hours before, he had come to her in the small hours of the morning. Her hair shined so dark and lustrous against the white of the bedding. . . . And he had thrown himself, willingly, achingly, to swim within that drowning pool of fragrant fantasy.

He was once again aware of Harris's presence in the room, watching him from a distance, waiting for something now, as he came out of a chimera of sensuous memory.

Bill looked up at him, and saw only confusion in the man's face to match his own. Harris remained silent, tears falling quietly like snow on a windless night. Bill rose to his feet.

Bill picked up the telephone receiver and dialed nine-one-one. He was reporting a death, he said, and all that he would remember from that night was that in stuttering the word, "death," the finality of its meaning in his life became a reality.

Harris said nothing as they waited for the police to arrive. He offered nothing to the police other than he had seen Bill's rental car parked outside Ariel's house as he was driving past at six A.M. As it was dark out and he could see lights on in the house, he was concerned that something was wrong. The front door was unlocked and he entered to find Bill there and Ariel dead on the bed. He did not mention Bill's nakedness, or finding him holding her.

He is not lying to protect me, thought Bill, but to protect Ariel from any further violation, and by so doing Bill saw that Harris's love for her was powerful.

Bill told the police that he was at home in bed when he was awakened by a dream. He did not say, "premonition," and he did not say that he was shaken awake by the shout of a voice calling him to action. When asked how waking up in the night had caused him to come to Ariel's, Bill said that something in his unconscious mind had surfaced, something that had been mentioned earlier in the day that he had not reflected on at the time. He was asked to elaborate.

—Harris—Mr. Haley—had made a comment to Ar—Mrs. Trent—that when she walked her dog at night she should wear reflectors so that she would be seen by cars as she walked along the side of the road. Well, the accident was the reason for his, Mr. Haley's, concern. She . . . in a way, how do I say it, fluffed it off? And he,

Mr. Haley, was—and I can't blame him—was, I think, a little annoyed at her response to his concern, and he asked her what she had been doing walking her dog at midnight, something like that, and she said, it was to look at Orion.

Bill was more confusing than enlightening. He was asked to reiterate.

—Last night I was walking the dog, and the stars were bright, and I looked at the constellations. I went home to bed, and I woke to remember that Ariel—Mrs. Trent—had said she was out looking at the stars on New Year's Eve.

They all looked at Bill, waiting for him to make sense. He thought they understood, but they didn't.

—Don't you see? It was snowing at midnight of New Year's. The sky was white.

He remembered the quiet moments he had enjoyed after escaping the party that night, when he had stepped out of his car to watch the pattern of snow cascading from the heavens.

—You couldn't see stars for the snow!

Harris knew what Bill was getting at, as did Amy, who had arrived a minute after seeing the police cars parked out front. They looked at one another, and in their unspoken communication, decided not to offer the detective any help in interpreting Bill's statements. They had a reason, Bill was sure, and when they offered no assistance in helping him get his point across to the detective, he began to understand that their silence was another way of defending the woman they both loved. Picking up the silent cue, Bill pretended to be speaking off the top of his head, from shock and grief at finding his friend dead.

—I couldn't go back to sleep, so I decided to take a drive. I saw the lights still on here, and it seemed unnatural that Mrs. Trent would be up and around at that hour, so I parked the car, and found that the door was unlocked, so I came in to check on her.

—And at what time was that? asked the detective.

—Three, three-thirty. I'm not sure.

Bill was coherent enough to expect the follow-up question: Why had it taken three hours to report the death? The question was coming, so he jumped ahead of the detective.

—At first I thought she was asleep, and then, on closer inspection, I saw that her chest was not moving as it would had she been asleep. I shook her, but there was nothing, no response. I felt for a pulse. Nothing. Her body was warm, so I had hopes, still, that I might revive her. I tried CPR, but it was useless.

—Why three hours?

—I don't know, Bill answered. —I guess I just sat there watching her for a while, I don't know. I was . . . so . . . distraught. I never thought to call anyone. There was no longer any emergency. I guess I fell asleep. Harris came in, and—

Bill buried his face in his hands, and as hard as he tried to keep his emotions in check, he lost control of them. He gushed like a pathetic drunk, and the sound of his sobs prompted Amy's loss of composure. He fell into her arms and she into his.

There were no other questions, said the detective. There might be questions later, but no more for now.

Bill didn't remember very much of the next few days. Only that it was very cold and there was a storm during one night, the day before the memorial service for Ariel.

He spent most of the time in his bungalow, sitting in his chair in the den, Little Eva at his feet, sensing as dogs often do when the people they live with are troubled. He only went outside to walk her, and when they would get to the end of the drive, she'd pull toward the right, toward her mistress's home, and then turn to look at Bill with her big brown eyes and an ear cocked as if to say he was headed in the wrong direction. Bill would give a little tug on the lead and she'd reluctantly turn to follow him. On one occasion, she stood her ground, and from exhaustion compounded with grief, Bill became impatient and tugged so hard she flipped to the ground as he yelled, —No! You can't go there! I can't go there! She's not there, anymore, don't you understand, you stupid thing?

The dog cowered when he shouted and dropped her leash to walk away from her, bracing himself against the stinging January gale, great sobs choking him, tears icing on his cheeks.

She gingerly walked to him and then kept step at his side as they proceeded back to the house.

Bill wouldn't answer the telephone. He let the answering machine screen the calls and didn't bother returning any. There were calls from Margie: In the first, there was a strident tone of annoyance to her voice as she stated that he hadn't called her about dinner on Thursday. The second expressed concern; was he ill? Another message, very officious in tone, said he should call her immediately. On the last, she called Bill "a shit-faced cocksucker."

There were hours passed in complete silence, Bill not noticing the progressive decline of the sun into evening. Little Eva would lay her head on his knee, pleading for attention, a game of living-room catch, a walk, or some food in her bowl. He'd turn on lights all over the small house and then wander aimlessly from room to room. He'd have a long night to get through, one of many when he would try to remember the exact color of Ariel's eyes, the contours of her profile. Wasn't there a tiny mole on her left cheek? Or was it her right? He didn't have a photo of her, and he was frustrated at being left behind with only impressions. Hers was a face he would never forget, but when he tried to conjure her image in his mind's eye, he would fail.

There were times when he couldn't stand the silence, and yet he couldn't go out because he feared meeting people. No one knew what Ariel had come to mean to him. He would get no consolation from anyone for his loss.

On the contrary, a lot of people might suspect that he killed her. Bill had nobody to go to, to talk with who would understand that he grieved, not only because he may have killed Ariel, but because for the first time in his life, over a period of little more than a week, he had found, loved, and then destroyed the woman he had waited for a lifetime. Little more than a week of his life falling in desperate love, with the rest of his life to mourn her loss.

There were moments, albeit seldom, when he hated and resented that she ever came into his life to turn his world upside down, and to leave him stranded in the cold, dead, stark plane of this existence. Then, in a turnabout, he'd remember the smile she would grace upon him and he would rise up in gratitude that she came into his life at all.

He would put on music: Billy Joel, Sinatra, at full volume to fill the air and deafen his thoughts. But it didn't help. *She's Always a Woman to Me*, and *It Never Entered My Mind*, and *A Cottage for Sale* caused more pain than comfort.

There was pounding on the door one afternoon, and when Bill peeked through the drapes he saw Harris Haley with a stack of mail in his arms. He didn't go away, just kept on banging the door. Bill finally relented.

—Your mail. You haven't collected it from the box.

—Thanks.

Little Eva was all over Harris, relieved to see a human being again.

—You're not answering your phone.

—I didn't know there was a law that said I had to.

—May I come in?

—Sure. Want a drink? The other guests should arrive momentarily, and then we can dine.

Bill didn't care for the look of concern, or pity, or whatever it was that was on the man's face. He hadn't shaved or bothered to shower in those three or four or five days, and Bill suspected that he looked like death warmed over. But he hadn't asked Harris to play the Merry Mailman. He couldn't read the man, and at that moment couldn't be bothered to.

Bill poured himself a drink, and one for Harris, too, whether he wanted it or not. If he didn't want the drink, I know who'll drink it, thought Bill.

Harris stood in the middle of the dark living-room, looking around, as Bill poured. He took the offered glass.

—Where are my manners? Won't you have a seat? said Bill, with hospitable sarcasm, as he plunked down on the sofa. Harris circled a couple of times before resting on the arm of a chair.

　　—You could turn on a light.

　　—I like the gloom just the way it is, thanks.

　　—I came by to tell you a few things. First of all, the autopsy showed that Ariel died of pulmonary embolus.

　　—The accident? The surgery? What does pulmonary—?

　　—Embolus.

　　—Yeah, what's that mean?

　　—Blood clots traveled to her lungs.

　　—Clots?

　　—Well, I was told it sometimes happens after surgery. Clots form in the legs; they called it a vein thrombosis. The person who is anesthetized and is then immobile for a while can develop them. Sometimes, the clots break free and travel to the lungs. It causes . . . suffocation.

　　—I killed her.

　　—She died of complications from the surgery.

　　—I killed her.

　　—If you're talking about the accident—

　　—I was afraid she was trying to commit—

　　—We don't know that either, Bill. She just didn't see your car.

　　—She couldn't see any stars, either. . . .

　　—It was an accident! said Harris with firm insistence. —Nothing more, do you hear me?

　　—So she didn't . . . ?

　　—No.

　　—Blood clots.

　　—Yes.

Sitting there, Bill's eyes burned, his nose dripped, and his throat closed up as he sank back into the cushions of the sofa and gasped for breath like a wounded animal. He opened his eyes to see Harris solemnly staring down from his perch on the arm of the chair, his jaw working vigorously, his nostrils in a flare against the rising tide of tears he was determined to keep dammed up. Bill remembered that Harris loved Ariel, too, and although Bill had once seen him as a rival for her affections, he was no longer an enemy. And he envied his stoicism. Bill was too low and drunk to pretend himself strong.

—She's gone, he blustered, stating the fact more for his own acceptance than anything else. Harris remained silent.

—I only knew her for a week, he said, and after a long time asked, —How long did you know Ariel?

—Oh, we met when she formed the trio. I was cellist.

Bill came out of his reverie of grief.

—You? I thought—

—You thought I was a country bumpkin farmer. I am. But, I also majored in music. I play several stringed instruments. My father left me the farm, and I like the farming.

—You were in love with her.

—Don't be ridiculous! We were friends.

—C'mon!

—I'm married. My wife, Cathy and I, we—

—Look, Harris, some things a man can't hide so well.

—I've noticed.

Bill laughed and shook his head. —But you deny it?

There was a very long pause as the men held each other's gaze. Harris turned away first and changed the subject.

—Ariel's daughter is arriving in the morning on an early flight. The memorial service is at eleven at the Unitarian Hall. I thought you might like to be there.

—Yes. I'll be there, Bill said weakly.

They just sat, lost in a wake of their own thoughts. Then, Harris rose to his feet, and looked inclined to start for the door.

—You despise me, don't you? Bill said accusatorily.

But, as soon as he said it, he regretted it.

He had lost the ability to edit his thoughts before speaking them, and he had no control over his emotions, he realized, as he looked into the pained expression of the man standing there before him. He was certainly giving Harris reason enough to despise him for his pitiable lack of control. He was venting his hostilities on the man, and it was vicious. They were no longer competitors; they were the survivors, the victims left behind, and yet, Bill was still ready to duel for her love. He sobered up in that moment, realizing he was forcing a confrontation that neither could win. To make things worse, the sound of his own whining voice disgusted him.

—I don't despise you.

—I'm sorry, Harris. I don't know why I said that.

—Sure you do. I've given you reason. All right, the truth is I did, but now I don't.

—You don't have to say any more; I was out of line.

—It's just—it's just that you look so much like him.

—What?

Harris searched his ragged face, and wondered if Bill was blind or just plain stupid.

—Nothing. You look like a man who loved her, is all.

—Yeah. I suppose we both did.

As Harris was about to walk out the door, he turned.

—Oh, yeah, Roy Carver's been trying to reach you. He'd like you to be at the reading of the will tomorrow, after the service.

—Me? Why?

—Look through the mail I brought in. He sent you a letter. And Bill?

—Yeah?

—Take a shower, he said as he let himself out.

Bill fell asleep on the sofa.

Bill arrived at the Hall at 10:45 A.M. the next morning, clean-shaven and in his best navy-blue suit and topcoat. He was not stoned at the steps of the hall by Ariel's friends and family, all of whom appeared to know he was the man who ran her down with his car. He expected that his presence would provoke angry comments. In an odd, masochistic, grieving way he had hoped they would have done it, if only to put an end to his misery. He walked without hesitation, avoiding eye contact with anyone, but braced for angry whispers and violent confrontations.

The Hall was filled with a couple hundred people. He found Amy and asked if he could sit with her, and she agreed.

—I had no idea she knew so many people, had so many friends, he said, for something to say.

—You said it only half right. Ariel knew many people.

It took a second to understand what Amy meant. Bill looked around at the filled seats and caught the eyes of many looking in his direction. Tom Reynolds was there, and so were Sonny and Lilly Molineri among the couple of dozen he knew. The president of the Linden Falls National Bank was sitting about five rows behind him, as was the director of the arts council, and the representative to the state house and his wife, alongside United States Congressman Montgomery Albright. Harris sat next to the woman Bill had seen driving his Ranger, his wife, Cathy. An elderly man hobbled down the aisle supported by a cane as thin and bent as the man himself. As he passed Bill's row of pews he recognized his neighbor, Mr. Wood, who lived at the end of the road. He'd only seen him from a distance and had never had opportunity to speak with him. Bill recalled Ariel's affection for the gentleman, and Harris's dubitable remark.

—You mean, they aren't all friends? he asked Amy.

—No. Call me bitter, but a lot of them are here out of a macabre curiosity. Some of them snubbed her privately, if not publicly, trashed her with gossip, and a few who owed her a lot deliberately forgot what she had done for them. Out of all these people here I can count a dozen or so who really cared about her.

Roy Carver and his wife were sitting in the first row next to an attractive woman in her late twenties who bore a striking resemblance to Ariel.

—Is that Ariel's daughter?

—Yes. That's Jillian.

—I don't know what I can say to her, Bill said aloud to himself.

—She won't bite.

—I'm not afraid if she does. She has every right to blame me. I killed—

—You'd better pull yourself together. You didn't kill Ariel. The accident was not your fault.

Bill couldn't believe Amy was acknowledging his innocence. He was about to challenge her when the service began. She slipped her arm through his in a show of support, or contrition for her past coldness, or from mutual grief, he wasn't certain. The gesture unnerved him with its implied concern, this unexpected friendly affection, and he wanted nothing more than to unburden himself, his guilt, to throw himself into her embrace so that someone could hold and console him and let him cry for a time. He gave her hand a squeeze instead, and stiffened his jaw so as not to emit the howl forming at the back of his throat.

Harris rose from his seat and walked to the stage where he took up the cello and sat before a music stand. He was joined by a young woman at the piano, and a man who bore a striking resemblance to a famous violinist and conductor.

The service was to begin with a program of music played in her honor, which included Ravel's *Modene*, Drdla's *Souvenir*, *En Bateau* by Debussy, and the second movement of Alban Berg's violin concerto. A jazz arrangement of *I'll Be Seeing You*, sung by Mary Whitney, was followed by the ending music, Debussy's *Reverie* with lyrics by William Trent. When Mary Whitney sang the lyrics written by Ariel's husband to the haunting melody, Bill began to vividly relive his last moments with Ariel before she died, when she sat down to play for the last time, and it was the first germ of his understanding of the powerful emotional bond that held her to William, even in death. William's lyrics expressed what he may have feared the most: the ineffable loss of Ariel from his life. Some very personal feelings are not always personal and unique. They are universal.

> *Sunlight*
>
> *On the folds of an old memory*
>
> *Calls you back to me,*
>
> *Again. . . .*

The music and the words took Bill back to that night, to the pain of rejection, and to the understanding that he could never have had the place in Ariel's life that he had hoped for.

> *Moonlight*
>
> *Like a dream half-remembered*
>
> *Of the leaves of September,*
>
> *Draws you into my arms*
>
> *Where you smile*
>
> *And you linger. . . .*

Those who filled the hall may have been weeping for the loss of Ariel Trent from their lives, but Bill mourned the lost possibility.

> *Starlight*
>
> *Sends me back to that lost reverie,*
>
> *To a fantasy*

Of reality

As it should be

No, not is, but

Should be

So, I start to cry, and

I start to cry and

I feel. . . .

And then, like a current through his brain, the bridge of the song lent a startling clarity to his recollection of events after finding Ariel dead.

Lips on my own

That do not exist!

Lips I have known

That are sadly missed!

You descend to my dreams,

You transcend all my dreams

With a kiss I shall not

Feel again. . . .

My, God! thought Bill. *The man knew he was going to die. William said as much through the lyrics he wrote to* Reverie *for Ariel to play and sing.*

I don't belong here, he thought.

He no longer knew what had been real from what may have been simply a dream of his own making. He felt guilt, but he wasn't sure if his guilt lay in fact or fantasy. He had no God from which to beg forgiveness for a deed or a dream, he wasn't sure *which*, and could never know atonement. Out of shock or panic or despair or plain madness, Bill could not be sure what he had *done*.

As soon as it was possible to do so, he left the service.

—It doesn't make sense, Roy!

—That's what I said to Ariel, when she insisted.

Roy Carver sat at Bill's kitchen table with a stack of documents spread out before him. As Bill had not gone to Roy's office for the reading of the will after the memorial service, Roy came by the following afternoon.

—When did she do this?

—When she was in the hospital.

It took Bill a couple of seconds to make sense of it.

—That phone call? The time you shouted your way into my home? Is that what you were upset about?

—Yeah, but you have to understand, though. First, she insists that, should she die as a result of the accident, you are not to be charged. Then, she tells me she wants to leave you her house, and when I ask her why she wanted to leave so much to a man who nearly killed her with his car, a man she really didn't know and had never before met until the accident, she tells me that you are a writer and that you will need the house. So, Bill, does that sound rational to you?

Roy took a sip from a cup of the first fresh pot of coffee Bill had brewed in the past five days.

—I didn't know what was going on. I thought—
well, I don't know you that well, Bill. I mean, our
dealings have been on opposite sides of an issue. I
thought maybe she was being influenced. She decided
all this after a very profound trauma. I insisted we wait
a while before I drew up the new will.

—Why didn't you?

—She said she'd call somebody who would do it
if I wouldn't. That wasn't unlike the Ariel I knew, so I
caved in and prepared it for her to sign.

Bill was as incredulous as he was confused. He
didn't understand why Ariel had left him her home, the
Quaker Meeting House, along with all its contents, with
the exception of the Steinway, family photos, five oil
paintings, several pieces of furniture, and her jewelry;
these would go to her son and daughter with the bulk
of her estate, which included a hefty portfolio of stocks
and bonds. Ariel left her violin and her father's cello to
Harris, fifty thousand dollars and her car to Amy, along
with trust funds for Amy's two children. There were
numerous monetary gifts to individuals Bill didn't know,
the Linden Falls Library, a yearly music scholarship in
her name and William's at three high schools.

—She left me her home. . . .

—That's right, said Roy, again, for the fifth time.

—Little Eva?

—Oh, the dog. Let her daughter take care of that.

—I want her.

—I don't think anyone would object. Oh, yeah,
I have a small trunk in my car. It's really weird, you
know, but Ariel called me the afternoon of the day she
died and asked me to pick up a box from her home to be
kept in my safe until her death. I was to add a codicil
to the will stating that you were to have the box and

its contents at the time of her death and that no one be allowed to open it except you. I saw the box. It wasn't a box, it was a trunk! I said to her, "Ariel, my safe isn't the size of the one at Linden Falls National." I took it, anyway. I'll get it for you before I go.

—Roy? Why do you really think she left me her house?

—I've been trying to figure that one out since she called me to draw up a new will. I don't know. I guess maybe she felt equally responsible for the accident. Maybe she thought it might hurt you in the long run and she wanted to make some compensation to you. She was a very generous woman. She was good to a lot of people.

Roy's expression softened and his voice took on a warm and personal tone.

—I know firsthand how generous she could be. She didn't always have so much money, you know. For a few years she had nothing. And, when she had nothing, there was always something she could find to give, even if it was her time or care. Ariel took in my mother and me and my two sisters when my father burned down our house one night in an attempt to—well, he died in the fire. Ariel nursed my mom, who was sick at the time, all the while making arrangements to set us up in our own household again. You know how she did it? She wrote a letter to the editor of the *Post* mentioning the failure of the community to respond to the needs of families that had suffered the ravages of an abusive parent. Nearly sixty people called the paper to respond, and they banded behind Ariel to find us housing and clothing and furniture. A dealership even gave us a new car! It didn't stop there, either. A safe house for abused women and children popped up downtown, funded by grants from three banks and two corporations. The churches were shamed into participating in doing what they preached, and together created an emergency fund for the needy in the community. It goes on and on. But, Ariel was the instrumental one. She was the angel.

—How did she come into money? Was it William's?

—John was dirt poor, and then, so was William, like I told you. No, she inherited it, after William died. She used to work in one of those adult homes. One of the old geezers kicked off and left her his money, quite a fortune. She invested it very well. But, you know the "Anonymous" you see on charity donation lists? That was Ariel.

Bill signed some papers, and then Roy got up from the table, returning folders to his attaché case. He stopped what he was doing, reached into his overcoat pocket, and removed a ring of keys.

—Do you think you'd want to live there, at the house?

It dawned on Bill that her house was now his. There had been nothing more that he had wanted than to live in that warm and elegant womb that was Ariel's home. But it was because she dwelled within its walls, lending vivid color and light to chase the shadows from the corners of its rooms, breathing warmth to fill a space that made it a haven in an otherwise cold and barren world. She was absent from it now, and like Bill, the house was rendered hollow like a shell.

He wondered, though, if some essence of her still lingered within the house, just as within him would always live her memory.

—Yes, he said, now certain that he would go there, if only in pursuit to capture and hold fast some of her illusory magic.

Roy handed him the keys.

—The house keys? I thought it would be months before—

—Yes, usually. It will be a while before the deed is transferred, but it's at the discretion of the executor when you take possession. No one is living there; her daughter left this morning. Oh, and Jillian asked if the piano and the artwork could remain there for a while until she decides what to do with them. Move in whenever you like.

Bill nodded. He had no words, he was so overwhelmed.

While they walked to Roy's car, Roy commented that Bill looked like he'd lost weight, and asked what project he was working on at the firm.

When Bill told him he wasn't planning to return to Harris & Reynolds, Roy was surprised.

—I'm going to write full time.

—Oh? Freelance?

—I suppose. I'm not sure, yet.

Roy lifted the small trunk out from his Mercedes. When he placed the weighty chest into Bill's arms, there was no longer any question of what he would write about. Later, upon unlocking it and peering into its contents, at the journals that lay within and the hundreds of pages of love letters, Bill understood that Ariel was asking him to write her story. He did not realize, however, until the tale had taken root inside of him, bewitching him from night into day to set it down on paper, that the specter of William would reach out from his grave to poke an ectoplasmic finger at his heart that Bill should not fail to recount his life without prejudice, but with compassion and respect; or that Ariel, his constant enchantress, would weave a spell that would provoke Bill to question his moral philosophy and his perceptions of the nature of love.

Soon Bill would discover a clue in one of William's letters that would explain why Ariel would have bequeathed him so much of value, why she had recognized William Trent in the eyes of Winston William Davidson that night of the accident. For Bill was to recognize much of himself in a black-and-white scalloped-edged photograph of William taken in 1954 on the beach at Honolulu. And more startling was the discovery of William's high school yearbook photo. He had always felt in his bones that his beginnings were not so unlike the Viking tale of his childhood. With emotions in conflict, Bill, a wandering, searching soul, sat down each day at the computer to write, never certain that he would make sense of or even survive the unrelenting struggle of his mind over his passions.

"He had tried his best to reason her out of the delusion, but he had soon found that the chance to talk about it only confirmed her in it."

Raintree County

FIFTEEN

Bill

Bill was alone all day, every day, except for Little Eva's companionship. There was no stimulating conversation, and he began to enjoy his solitude. There was work to do, a story to tell, and he set a regimen: Walk the dog first thing in the morning, while the coffee brewed, watched a half-hour of the *Today Show*, as he prepared and ate breakfast. By nine o'clock he was at the computer, writing his impressions, even if only to organize the day's goals. He'd break for lunch around noon, walk the dog, spend a couple of hours outdoors working on the garden, which was inundated with weeds, mowing the lawn, painting the wooden-plank front steps, replacing a rotted clapboard, filling the birdfeeder, playing catch with Little Eva. Spring had finally arrived after a cold and rainy April, when the sun had only appeared for six days that month. By May, the weather turned as warm as June's final days.

By three o'clock, Bill was back on the computer, until restlessness set in, so then he would take a Jack Daniels break, watch the news, eat something or drive out for a burger with the dog in the backseat; home again, write some more, and then try to forget how much he missed Ariel with the distraction of television, a rented movie, or a fiction novel.

By May, Harris & Reynolds seemed a thing of the distant past, as was Margie, and the couple of friends he went to Ice Hockey games with or met on Sunday afternoons to watch broadcasts of seasonal sports.

He hadn't set foot in his old watering hole, *Richie's*, since before the Christmas holidays, and that was fine, too. There wasn't much to say to people these days, and the old camaraderie that Bill once found there among the regulars seemed as stale as a drunk's breath. Nothing in common with anyone who hung out there, except the common desire to imbibe enough to get through the night. He knew few people intimately, because at a bar one wants to forget their troubles, not talk about them, and those who do talk you avoid, because they remind you of your own troubles. Anyway, he didn't want them knowing any more about him.

When Bill moved into the old Quaker Meeting House he also moved away from the life he had known. Ariel had come into his life briefly and yet in a timespan of only a week had changed the purpose of his existence. He felt compelled to write, but not articles for publication or short stories. No, he had to write about Ariel, and that meant he had to write about William, and John and Susan, and all the players in the drama.

The first time Ariel appeared to him was in a lucid dream. He told himself that he didn't believe in ghosts, and yet there she stood, restored, beautiful and palpable.

The second time he saw her was as he raised his head from a book he was reading. She stood near the bookcases, touching one of the volumes. When Bill walked over to catch the illusive vapor that vanished before his eyes, he became frightened.

She was watching him.

That's ridiculous, he said to himself. *If anything, she is watching over me.* Yet, he found it difficult to shake off the sharp sense of menace that permeated him.

He began to talk to Ariel, believing that, if she were in fact watching, she might hear his thoughts. But, she did not respond again through an ectoplasmic appearance. Bill only sensed a presence, but discarded the idea, as any rational man would, as imagination.

He began to drink more and with greater regularity. He needed a drink in order to settle down and write at the computer. And, always he was frightened that what he was writing was not quite the truth. Worse was the knowledge that he could only serve as a tool in the recording of past events, aware that he had had little impact on Ariel's life and yet played a great role in her death. His part in her death plagued him. They said the accident was just that, an accident, her death a complication of surgery. He was punishing himself, they said, for something that was not really his fault. *He was at the wrong place at the wrong time.*

But, he knew better.

So he set about his writing, his penance for the harm he had caused, all the while feeling a presence observing quietly from behind the shadows in the room, watching his progress.

Amy paid Bill a visit on the day he moved in, at the beginning of March. She handed him the spare key that she'd been given by Arial. Amy had been watering the plants, and Bill told her to keep the key. Isn't that what neighbors do?

She showed him around the place, telling him all the usual things a new homeowner needs to know, like where the water main was, and the breaker box, and giving the phone numbers of Ariel's plumber and electrician, and Little Eva's vet and kennel, how often to water some of the plants, and others how often not to.

Bill asked if there was something she'd like to have that was Ariel's, and she surprised him with,

—She's left me so much, but I don't have a photo of her. May I have one? I know where some are.

She walked to a blue metal file cabinet in the office off the foyer and took out one of the files. Inside were twenty or so black-and-white glossies, Ariel's professional poses, one in which she held her violin. It was the same photo hanging next to one of William over the desk. Bill told her to take one, and she thanked him with a sad little smile.

—Is there anyone else who you think might want a photo? he asked.

—Harris. I don't know if he has any photos like these.

Reluctantly he said, —Why don't you take a few and give them to people who loved her.

Amy appeared to have filed off those prickly edges of protection since Ariel's death, and it softened her dramatically. It would have been good not to be thought of as the villain any longer, just a nice guy who loved her friend, but at first the change in attitude only worked to unsettle Bill all the more.

Amy would stop in a few times a week with a pie or a great slice of her "famous" chocolate cake or vegetables from her garden. Out of politeness he'd stop whatever he was doing to brew a pot of tea, as she wasn't a coffee drinker, and they'd chat for a while about her kids or her job at the hospital. She asked him over for dinner one evening in May, and he expected to see her daughters there, but they were both off on a school trip.

A couple of times she came by in the evening with a video and freshly popped popcorn, and that was nice for Bill, because they didn't have to talk much while the film was on, only comment here and there about the actors or the plot or the score. He'd settle in his armchair, Little Eva nestled next to Amy on the sofa, and it was pleasant. She appeared curious about his past, about what he was writing about, and he offered a few details about his life and his family, but nothing about the book he was writing. He was glad for her neighborly attention, but oddly relieved when she left.

Occasionally, he'd see Harris Haley drive by and wave while he was walking Little Eva. A couple of times he'd pulled up and asked Bill how he was faring. When Harris would roll down the window and lean out to speak, Bill wasn't sure if the look on his face was one of concern or of watchful waiting. It unnerved him that since Ariel's death Harris addressed him more kindly and appeared relaxed in his presence, and yet Bill tensed from the suspicion that there was shrewd calculation behind the friendly demeanor.

That first week of May, when the grass suddenly popped up half a foot on the lawn, Bill found the lawnmower in the back shed and set about the first mowing of the spring.

Harris pulled up in his Ranger as Bill finished the first row in the series along the side yard. Harris got out of the truck and walked over to speak over the roar. Bill let the motor die.

—I wouldn't mow along there if I were you. Down there, near the maples. That's going to be covered with forget-me-nots in a couple of weeks.

—Okay, thanks.

—And there're grape hyacinth all along that stone wall at the back.

—Right. . . . Anything else?

—Those shoots are Rose of Sharon. Big, busy flowering plants. They were cut back down to the ground end of last summer.

—So, I shouldn't mow?

—Sure, mow, but if you want the flowers, stay within twenty feet of the building.

—Did Ariel plant them?

—The bushes, yes, but the ones bordering the lawn, no; they naturalized over from the woods. She loved them. The lilacs are blooming, I see.

—I thought I'd cut some and take them into the house.

Harris smiled. —She would have.

Bill stood there waiting for Harris to say more, or leave, but he did neither, just stood, looking around the big yard dappled with sunlight peeking through the tender pale-green foliage.

—Want a beer, Harris? Bill asked, suddenly feeling generous, or, if not truly generous, taking the opportunity at hand. Maybe he could tell him things, fill in some of the blanks, give a firsthand observer's view of what Ariel's and William's relationship was really like. He might answer some of Bill's most pressing questions, so that he might better understand the dynamics of their relationship. Harris might tell far more about William and John than he had gleaned through Ariel's journals and William's letters. Anyway, it was time to break the ice with Harris.

—Sure. I could use a beer. And I'd like to talk to you about something, Bill.

They sat with cold beers on an old park bench under a flowering cherry tree.

—You know that money she left to set up the foundation?

—Yeah, the grants to community organizations?

—And to individuals with entrepreneurial projects who have a difficult time getting grant money.

—So, is it set up and everything?

—I need to form a board of directors. There's me and Roy Carver, who's doing all the paperwork to set it up, and Mae Stewart of the quintet, and Sonny Molineri—

—I know Sonny.

—And Ariel's daughter, Jillian, who will vote by proxy. I was hoping you would take a seat on the board.

Bill was surprised and doubtful that he could offer anything or even wanted any distractions from his writing. It showed on his face because Harris went into an explanation of the ease of duties on the board.

—Don't make your decision now, just think about it.

—I'll think about it.

—Good.

They each took swigs from their Heineken bottles and sat silent for a minute looking over the yard. Bill said:

—You knew John, Ariel's first husband? What was he like?

This time it was Harris who looked surprised.

—I once thought he was a nice man.

His reticence showed, and Bill could almost see, if not hear, the dialogue that was going on inside his head.

—He gave Ariel a hard time. I know all about it, well, maybe not all; that's why I'm asking.

In answer to his frowning look of query, Bill elaborated:

—Look, Ariel left me all her papers, all her journals, and letters written between her and William. She wanted me to write about what happened. That's why she left me this place.

—Yeah, I know. And are you? asked Harris, tentatively.

—Yes, in fictional novel form, of course; names changed to protect, etcetera, etcetera.

—Is that really why you think she left you this place? he said with incredulity.

—I don't get what you mean. Why else? She knew I wanted to write.

—I see, said Harris, vaguely, and Bill was left wondering if there might have been another reason for the bequest. He put that suggestion aside for more pressing questions.

—Yes. But there are things I need to know, to be fair to everybody involved.

—Fair?

—To everyone involved. I want to depict them fairly, truthfully.

—Fairly . . . truthfully, yes. That was the problem, you see: Trying to be fair.

—Me?

—No, Ariel.

It took a long moment of thought and a swig of beer before he could continue. When he met Bill's gaze, he smiled.

—I always thought it was excessive empathy, too much compassion: She never seemed to learn that not everyone merited her care and concern. I thought it was misplaced compassion toward those in her life who ultimately—but now that you say it, I think she was always giving people the benefit of the doubt, even in the light of boldfaced lies, trying to be *fair*. Even at the cost of her own happiness. But life doesn't make it easy to do what you believe is right. Life always challenges you to prove your convictions. Isn't that what living is all about, a series of challenges you have to try to live up to?

—So Ariel's flaw was a desire to be fair? Isn't that a virtue?

—Yes, it is. But life isn't fair, you see, and all the people in our lives have their own very specific agendas that may or may not be to another person's benefit, if you know what I mean?

—I'm not sure I do.

—You see, Ariel was a conflicted woman. She was raised a Catholic, assuring her a thousand conflicts, if you know what I mean. She wasn't practicing as an adult, but the seeds had been sowed early on. She didn't want to betray John; she loved him, so she said— well, she had married him, anyway. But she couldn't abandon William, whom she adored. She was . . . can I say, *tortured*, without sounding melodramatic? Well, she was. She was standing in the middle of this—this maelstrom. She wanted to be a good person; she didn't want anyone hurt; so she refused to make a decision that would cast either man out of her life. And because of that refusal to decide, everyone suffered, especially Ariel.

—You say she brought it all on herself?

—She was a highly moral person, Bill; that was her trouble. No, Ariel felt . . . remorse, and grief, and a need to protect everybody she loved. I'm not sure John ever really understood that. He was dealing with his own pain, wallowing in it too much to ever really see Ariel's dilemma, or anyone else's for that matter.

—So, John wasn't a really bad person—

—John Rodgers was a narcissistic son-of-a-bitch, if you want the truth! A narcissist who made bad decisions, spoiled everything he touched, and needed someone to blame. Although Ariel accepted the blame in regard to her love for William, it was not enough for John. He wanted retribution. He used their kids as pawns; he used the sympathy of anyone who would agree that Ariel had done him wrong. She did nothing publicly to embarrass him. It was he who caused all the damage, playing the cuckolded husband who was driven over the edge by an unfaithful wife and her lover. All true, of course. But, John was for years an alcoholic, couldn't hold a job, had this overblown sense of entitlement, and could never take the blame for any of his actions. He enjoyed playing the victim, if you want to know. He was full of his own prideful hubris.

—Well, it's clear you didn't like the man. Love can turn otherwise-sane people into lunatics.

—Yeah, but people move on. People with love in their hearts *accept*, even if they can't understand. John wallowed in self-pity and relished his revenge.

Bill tried to pose his next question carefully, because he wasn't quite certain of Harris's feeling about William.

—Of all I've read in the old journals, I've wondered about William's character: He appears at first a brilliant, highly educated man who settled for a professorship at a university. A weak man.

—Weak? I don't think so. John's loud blustering threats only made William stronger, more determined. William wasn't weak. He was brave in the face of his cancer, his convictions, his love of Ariel and his children. . . . Needy, maybe. Just because he wouldn't hurt a fly didn't make him weak. No, William had dignity and great integrity. William was like Ariel, wanting the people he loved to understand and accept him and his love for Ariel for what he called "a miracle in his life." He was plagued with guilt.

—I'll bet Susan didn't like hearing that!

—I'm sure William would never have said such a cruel thing to her. He was deeply committed to Susan and the children. No, Susan was insidious while John was violent.

—I watched one night as John came up behind William and punched him in the nose. William bit his hand, and kneed John in the groin. I was walking to my car after a rehearsal, and when John saw me, he made a run for his car and sped off. I have to give William credit. He never backed away. He stood his ground, waiting for the next attack, acting only to defend. I asked him if he wanted to call the police, and he said, "It would cause John more grief." William's lip was cut and his eye was blackened, and he said he'd be all right "because physical pain goes away, where emotional pain lingers on, and John would be hurting long after my wounds heal."

—It got crazy. William asked me my opinion about some quote he had read in a book, I don't remember what book it was from. He asked: "Is there such a thing as one man possessing a woman's soul and another her body?" I am still unsure what that was all about, to tell you the truth. He had Ariel body and soul, after all. Anyway, Ariel didn't know I knew what was going on, and I didn't want to offend her by trying to give her advice, but I was worried that Ariel would get hurt by both of these men.

—Yeah, William had her love, on terms that he could live with.

—Yes, he did, but that didn't stop him from making her life even more difficult. The guy pressed her. I saw him do it. He was relentless. If she could not see him when he wanted to see her, he would call her house, infuriating John. Or he would arrive at her door when the household had just gone off to bed, begging to just get one look at her for a few minutes. When she said no, he'd become petulant and depressed, and later repentant, acknowledging he was so greedy for her love that he went temporarily insane. When he went through the chemotherapy for the cancer, he would appear strong to the outside world. But, once I saw her holding him, and I could see who was the strong one. It was Ariel. It was like she was taking all the weight of his fears onto herself.

—But, he never deliberately harmed her?

—What do they say? "You always hurt the one you love"? Maybe she hurt him, too, but I never saw evidence to that effect. Love is one big brawl, ain't it?

Harris chuckled at his last remark and then the serious face reappeared as he continued.

—I did see some of the things William did, and before everybody knew about their affair, Ariel had confided in me. I guess she knew I could be trusted, and she had no one else to talk with about her problems. I was glad I could be her sounding board.

—She had really gotten herself into a mess: She was alone here at the theater, John was stalking her, her children were barely civil to her, most of the women she knew, many of whom she'd known for years, shunned her, probably for fear that she would be after their husbands. She received a couple of letters from anonymous "friends" sending her pieces of their little minds. And there were a couple of guys who preyed on her, hoping for their turn with the town slut. It was not very nice, and she pretended it wasn't happening. And, then, there was William.

Harris leaned back on the bench in a stretch.

—We had a rehearsal of the quintet one evening, and I had arrived first. Ariel was a wreck: shaking, her eyes wild with fear. I followed her out the back door from the dressing room. She started crying. All her defenses and pretenses fell away like a shell, and all that was left was this vulnerable creature. She said she had thrown William out, earlier, told him she never wanted to see him again. When I asked why she had broken with him, she said, "After what he told me last night, I just flipped out!"

—You mean they had a lovers' quarrel?

—William and Ariel could fight like wildcats! This was nothing new. But their arguments were generally of the philosophical kind, if you know what I mean. This time it was personal.

—Susan knew for nearly a year about their affair, but never said a word, and the evening before I found her in such a state, William told Ariel that he'd again asked Susan "how she was doing," and if she wanted him to leave. He told Ariel that Susan said, "Not yet."

—The fight that ensued was because William was always saying that as soon as Susan released him, he would be free to be with Ariel all the time. "Would I leave Susan for you? In a minute! But we have children and that changes everything," he'd said to her. And Ariel said, "And Susan knows that! She will keep you imprisoned by your very love for the children. 'Not yet,' means I'll keep you with me. I won't let you free, because I won't let any other woman have you if I can't."

—Ariel told him, "Stay with Susan, for whatever good it does her to have a man who doesn't want to be with her in the first place!"

—So, Ariel is falling apart before my eyes, when suddenly William arrives looking worse off than she: pale and anxious and ready to spring. I started to leave the room, and when I glanced back they were locked in a passionate embrace. We rehearsed for an hour and then I made excuses to leave. If no one else noticed, I did, because Ariel was not at all into rehearsing her music. She and William were eye-locked across the room, and the transformation in both of them was astonishing. They went from Hell to Heaven in one embrace, and we weren't getting anywhere being in their way, so we left.

—A short time later, he left Susan. The timing seemed perfect, because Ariel had been left a great deal of money from the estate of one elderly gentleman she knew. It helped to solve the two family household financial obligations they each had to carry. I don't think money would have kept them apart, though. I don't think anything or anybody could have driven them apart for very long. They belonged together. I've never seen anything like it.

—Was it difficult for you?

—What do you mean?

Bill could have kicked himself for putting Harris on the defensive by bringing the man's personal feelings for Ariel to the forefront.

—You mean, did I envy William?

Bill nodded and stated, —I do, Harris, and the man is dead.

—Shit, yes, I envied him. But, when you know you haven't a chance in the world, you find perspective. I won't deny I loved her, but she didn't love me. That is a great leveler.

—And you had Cathy.

—No. Not then. I met Cathy a couple of years ago and we were married last year. And I do love my wife.

Bill had to get off Harris's personal life. He could see that the man was sensitive about his feelings for Ariel and that he had said all he would on the subject. And Bill didn't want to accidentally imply that he married Cathy when there was no hope of having the woman he really loved, if only because of the timing of William's death and later his own marriage. Bill realized, however, that he had underestimated Harris when the man admitted what Bill had been privy to through Ariel's journal of her year spent alone at the Meeting House. So Bill was surprised when Harris continued.

—Ariel had been here about six months, through a miserably nasty winter. I would come by occasionally to see her on some pretext or other. I was worried about her. She had the look of someone on the edge of sanity. You know, the funny thing was, where all the stress and grief sometimes makes a person haggard and drawn, Ariel appeared to have this inner glow that made you think she might spontaneously combust. She always seemed glad to see me, so I started to drop by a couple of times a week in the evenings. We'd sit and talk. Sometimes I'd bring my cello and she'd sit at the piano and we'd play for a while. At first I thought she needed the distraction; Ariel's friends had pretty much abandoned her. Actually, some were indulging in the gossip, and I and a woman she worked with were pretty much the only ones left in her life who cared.

—I had never told her how I felt about her. As I said, she was in love with someone else, and even if I told her, it would have been pointless. It would have only made her shrink away from me, our friendship. I was glad that I could be in her life even if only as a friend.

—One night I asked how things were going with William and she kind of tossed the question off. I asked her what was wrong, and she said she was aware of the hold Susan had on him, and voiced a comment William had made: "Why can't they leave us alone. Why can't they find other people to love, and leave us alone!"

—Ariel doubted William would ever break the ties, and she wasn't sure she wanted him to. She didn't want to cause any more pain. Her children, on the brink of adulthood, had suffered, and she was being punished by seeing their confusion and unhappiness. She didn't want that for Elizabeth or Timothy. She planned to tell William—*insist* was the word she used—that they stop considering a future together. "I'll always love him, but this can't go on! I need to move on with my life. I can't remain like this, in Limbo, forever waiting, forever hoping against the odds that we can live together a normal life."

—That's when I threw caution to the wind and gave her a way out. I asked Ariel to marry me when her divorce came through. I told her I loved her, and it was all right if she didn't feel the same way about me, but that I would take care of her, always, and we were close friends, and we did make beautiful music together (it was a joke, of course), and wasn't that enough to build a future on?

—She started to cry, and I held her. Then she looked up at me with that sweet little smile that lifted the left corner of her mouth, and told me in the most gentle way, "I'm so grateful to have you in my life, Harris. So grateful that I would never do anything to hurt you."

—I asked her to think about my proposal, and left it at that. Anyway, it seems that William finally told Susan he wanted out.

Harris looked at Bill, waiting for a response.

Bill was putting the pieces of the story together and in sequence with the facts in Ariel's journals. So, Harris was the man she had not named, but alluded to, in her papers! He was the rich, good-looking widower who wanted to rescue her by a proposal of marriage! She had told William about him, in a request that he release her. William thought at first it was an attempt to make him jealous, and for the first time in his life, William felt that green demon with a force so powerful he became enraged with her. When she told William they should stop thinking about being a couple in the future, that she believed he should remain with Susan, he couldn't live with that. She was trying to save William from future grief, because she loved him, but he didn't see it like that.

Here, the man who felt no guilt in loving Ariel was wrestling with the probability of losing his children to a woman who hadn't wanted them in the first place, a woman who had her tubes tied without consulting him, after the birth of their son. He could not admit, even to himself, that he had married a woman who had accepted him at a time when he could not accept himself as worthy of anyone's love; he had married this woman because he had wanted children more than anything in the world when he was thirty, a woman who had pushed his needs aside over the years in a selfish attempt to rise above the truth that her husband had married her for all the wrong reasons. William told Ariel that, no, he would not release her, that he would always love her and she had to live with that knowledge whether she chose to walk away or not.

—So, William moved in with Ariel.

—Yes. She bought this building that she'd been renting from the old man down the street. The house in Linden Falls had been taken by the bank when John filed bankruptcy. She had a ton of bills to pay in order to settle with creditors. John got away, owing nothing. But, she did what Ariel always did: She gave John money because he needed it to start over again.

—And then things appeared to have settled down . . . until that night in early June, the night they packed up the car for a trip to Cape Ann. . . .

—They had been there the year before, a short honeymoon trip in between William's courses of chemotherapy. It was night, the street pitch-black, and William was walking the dog when the car hit him.

—*What?*

—What do you mean, *what*? said Harris in a frontal attack.

The two men locked eyes. Harris incredulous; Bill, searching.

—He killed William, ran him down with his car, for God's sake! said Harris.

—Are you telling me—John killed William?

—Yes, the bastard!

—But, I thought it was the cancer that finally killed William. There is nothing in her journals that says that John killed William.

—She would never talk about it, so I suspect she wouldn't have written about it. Probably because she felt responsible for both men's fates. John struck William and left him to die, said Harris, —then smashed up his car a few miles away, The drunken son-of-a-bitch wrapped his car around a tree half a mile down the road and pretty much got away with just a broken arm.

—That's when she had a breakdown. William dead, and the father of her children in a hospital across town. What's she going to do? Send John to jail?

—You mean he killed William and he got away with it? Tell me you're not—

—Jillian turned him in.

The weight of this new revelation was heavy on Bill's mind.

—It was the beginning of Ariel's mental decline. You know the rest.

—There's so much I don't know, don't understand!

—When you came into her life, she thought she had been given another chance. And yet deep inside she knew you were not William returned to her.

—What do you mean—that she thought I was—*what?* I don't see how she—

Harris stared at Bill with a disbelieving smile on his face.

—Look in the mirror, and then look at the picture of William that used to be on the piano. You've hidden it away, haven't you? Blond, blue-eyed, tall, same coloring, same build, too. . . . You're about the same age William was when he first met Ariel. And what year were you born? 1963? Do you understand, Bill?

Bill was struck silent. Swiftly, he pieced together all the facts, all of the clues, coincidences, and inferences from all of the letters and the journals he'd read, and he wondered if it was possible. *Was it possible?* He couldn't move, couldn't respond, only kept his eyes fixed on the ground.

Harris rose from the bench, thanked Bill for the beer, and asked if he could call in a few days for a decision to be on the board of directors of the foundation.

Bill nodded numbly and mumbled "yes," and remained frozen on the bench. He didn't notice the long shadows cast by the setting sun, or feel the sudden cool down that marked the arrival of dusk or the breeze that shook the blossoms from the cherry tree, or hear the distant whistle of the train as it chugged past the crossing a mile off in the distance. After a time, Little Eva rose up from her repose, from the wedge of shade created by the open door of the shed. She crossed the now-darkening lawn to her new master and nosed the hand. He looked at the dog without really seeing her, for he was so deeply entangled in his thoughts. Finally, after a more forceful nudge, he rose to his feet, looked around, eyed the abandoned lawnmower and opened the screen door. Little Eva followed him into the house.

He had to make sure. He had to find one letter from William to Ariel in particular.

Suzanna. . . .

My sister *Suzanna*, service brats, blond and blue-eyed child, Winston *William* Davidson, Air Force base, my birthday. . . .

"God knows, unless we drew a little blood now and then, there wouldn't be room on the globe for us all."

Raintree County

SIXTEEN

Ariel and William

A stream of light lit the path to the driveway as William emerged from the front of the house. He popped open the car's hatch and threw in the suitcases. He repeated the process of loading up the car in preparation for their trip to Cape Ann. He shut the hatch, locked the car doors, and then fetched Little Eva for a walk before bed. Man and dog walked briskly along the edge of the country road. The drowsy chirping of crickets was abruptly silenced by the revving of a car engine somewhere in the neighborhood. There was the screech of tires, and William figured teenagers were out for a joy ride on one of the side streets. But then he was caught in headlights that flooded the road ahead. A vehicle traveling behind them was approaching fast. He felt a shiver raising the hairs along the back of his neck. The instinct to get off the road caused him to tug the dog onto the shoulder. As he turned, expecting to see the car pass, he was blinded by the light. At the last moment, he let go of the leash.

Within a minute, Ariel was aware of shuffling and clicking heels on the linoleum corridor as the team of doctors rushed in and made her leave the room. Ariel stood gaping with horror from the door. How could she leave his side now?

He will be all right, she told herself; *he'll be all right! Dear God! Make him all right!*

She looked from one white coat to another, waiting for someone to tell her something, anything about why it was all happening, and what they would do to fix it.

Oh, dear God! Fix it! I'll do anything you want, dear Lord, but fix this!

She caught the eye of one of the doctors as she bolted back into the room, only to be met with restraining arms. He spoke with practiced assurance.

—The injuries—his heart is still strong. We have to get him into surgery now, Mrs. Trent.

—I want to see him, speak with him—

—You can go in, of course, but we've sedated him. And we'll be taking him down for surgery in a few minutes.

Ariel peeked into the room where William lay unconscious. As soon as she approached the bed in the crowded room, a stretcher arrived to take him away. She followed the team as they went down the elevator and her heart stopped for a moment as the big steel doors closed behind her husband.

After many hours of surgery, William was taken from the recovery room and into ICU.

Ariel heard a disembodied voice break through her stupor:

—I think it would be a good idea if you called the family. Anyone who needs to be called.

She looked up, following the white coat to the face of the surgeon.

—Are you saying—

—I'm saying . . .

A great sigh from the exhausted and frustrated doctor.

—It can go either way. Call the rest of the family and keep on praying.

Like an automaton, Ariel rose from her chair in the waiting room and walked to the telephone at the desk. With trembling hands she telephoned Susan.

With a task at hand, she called Harris and asked him to drive Susan and the children to the hospital. And then she called Jillian. When there was no reply, she tried her daughter's cell phone.

—Where have you been, Mom?

—You must come to the hospital, Jillian.

—I'm at the hospital. I've been trying to reach you. Why aren't you here?

—Please, Jillian! Please come. I'm at the hospital. I need you! William is—oh, God! He's—

—Mom. You're acting crazy. I'm at Wellesley General with Dad. He totaled his car. He's going to be fine, all right? Drunks and babies, remember? Mom? What's wrong? Answer me? What's wrong with you?

—*William.* . . . whispered Ariel as she hung up the receiver, as the knowledge of what had occurred on that dark road plummeted her into dark despair.

For the next ten hours, Ariel wandered in and out of the hospital, going into the ICU cubicle to talk to William, who lay there surrounded by the monitors, his veins and mouth and nose intruded with tubes and needles and bag after bag of blood and fluids and drugs. When his blood pressure would begin to decline, his nurse would enter to give him a shot with a hypodermic needle directly into the port they had inserted into his carotid artery. Ariel saw the blood being pumped out of his stomach and knew that he was bleeding to death, and there was nothing she could do but watch the monitors' constant vacillation in blood pressure and pulse; always slipping, always on the rise when the needle was injected.

She would stand beside his bed and touch his hand, as she cooed in his ear, loving words, fighting words to bring him over the crisis point so that he would come back to her, so she could take him home, so he could lay in her arms in their bed as he slept, words that told of her passion for him, her need for him, and once again the fighting words that he had to hear, to reach some distant, dormant part of him and to shake him to life again. And then, when she could do no more, when she thought she might scream, she would bolt from the room to wander the hospital hallways, or walk in the cold drizzle of the night, until she could no longer bear being away from him and she would once again race to his side and repeat the prayers and the yearning, pain-filled song of her love for William.

They were keeping him alive through a respirator, accelerating his heart and pressure when they were failing.

My William is dying.

It was like being caught in some absurd abstract painting, a cubist's dimensional nightmare, a Dali time-warp, she didn't know which, because she was entrapped and could never quite see where, exactly, she was. She was caught in a quagmire of desperation; she wouldn't let William go. No! She couldn't be parted from him!

A nurse pulled her out from the room to the lounge, where a man placed a cup of coffee in her hand.

A calm, soft-spoken voice. He told her to pray. His name was Sam, he said, with a deep and ever-so-tender voice, and she must pray for her William.

She could no longer listen to Sam's words; she was fighting a deep faint, one she had only experienced once before in her lifetime, during her long labor to give birth to Peter. Try as she might to stay conscious, the veil would shut out the light. She must go back and take the last few moments allotted her with William, but she could not overcome the drugged feeling, and again her mind would shut down, her eyelids closed, and prostrate she would go off into oblivion. Sam helped her down on the stiff vinyl sofa and covered her with a blanket.

And, as she dozed she traveled to a place of darkness and calm where William came to her; sweet and gentle visions of his smiling face, the exquisite reflection of love, a face so filled with compassion of a kind she had never known before engulfed her.

William's smile.

As he came into focus, flying into her vision through a dark dreamscape, his ineffably beautiful face, his blue Sargasso Sea eyes gleaming health and expressing his love and the joy she had given him, it warmed her. A moment of sublime, uplifting ecstasy engulfed her and she felt cherished and protected.

She was in a world of feelings and wordless communication that was like a balm on her aching center, soothing her, comforting her in its profoundly healing way.

When she opened her eyes, refreshed and oddly calm, it took a moment to get her bearings. And then the frantic surge of emotion overtook her again at the realization that William might have died alone while she lay in a selfish sleep. She had to get to him; he must not die alone. He must know that she was there, that he was never abandoned, that she was always guarding. Susan arrived without the children. Where were the children?

—There isn't much time, Susan! The children must be here! William needs them.

She delivered her lines with slow, practiced deliberation.

—I don't want them to see him die. What do you think? They should watch him die?

Die, Susan had said, and the very speaking of the word was so filled with portent inevitability that Ariel cringed. Susan waited for Ariel's response, and when Ariel finally looked up and met her eyes, she saw the undisguised hatred behind the insolent stare of Susan's prideful victory.

This, thought Ariel, is her moment of triumph: If I can't have him, she's thinking, nobody else can!

It had come full circle. A hospital room three years ago. Only this time, I won't walk out of here with this woman's husband. Susan jumped at this opportunity at payback. A misguided victory, but still a victory of sorts. Ariel turned her back on the woman and asked Harris, who had watched silently, to take Susan home. Ariel turned to reenter the curtained cubicle, on the tail of Harris's scolding.

—That was beneath you, Susan! he said.

Die. . . . That's what he was going to do. He was dying. He beat the cancer, and yet death was taking him, ripping William away from her. Ahead lay a landscape of barren loneliness.

She had done this to him! She was responsible for this! And she was responsible for leading John down a path of violence. She had, by her actions, destroyed the two men she professed to love. Now she was to suffer the ultimate punishment: to live the rest of her wretched life alone with the knowledge of her treachery. And isn't this what she deserved? Payment for her hubris for daring to love this man?

Susan burst through the curtained enclosure and grabbed Ariel's arm.

—I'm sorry! I'm sorry! Susan cried, all pretense gone. —That wasn't right. It was never right. None of it was right. Forgive me, Ariel. Forgive me, William!

Susan fell to her knees when she saw the man she had once loved, now unresponsive in pale relief upon the bed. Ariel turned away as Harris led Susan out of the room. There was only William now, only William.

Ariel resumed her mantra: "Fight, work harder, my love, my most precious Heartbeat!" And she'd brush his brow with her fingers and whisper into his ear that he was loved, so very much loved, and that he was the love and life of her life, the reason she was born, the meaning of her life, the center of her soul, the spirit that gave her breath.

And when she saw the numbers begin to descend on a monitor from 125 down to 115, down to 106, down, suddenly and sharply to 85, she screamed a silent scream from the very bottom of her being, a sound that would not come out, no matter how hard she tried.

72, 68, 51—

He was at the brink, and the moment had arrived; she *knew* it was the end. There was no stopping it, and suddenly, she knew only that she had to release him.

—Go! Go! Go on, my darling love, my Heartbeat. Go, my love! My precious! Your mother is waiting, she is waiting, all who have loved you are waiting. I release you! I release you . . . I release . . . you.

She watched as he released a last breath. She watched as he became still. She felt his sudden absence from the cold, silent space.

They came, another team, when the alarms sounded, a shrill, painful cacophony that tore through that silent void and stabbed at her heart, and her mother's death thirty-five years ago flashed before her.

William was gone. She knew the essence of him was no longer present.

She walked from the curtained room as the team of doctors pounded his chest in an effort to revive him. They were brutal in their attempt, and she turned and screamed.

—*Don't touch him. Don't do what you know in your hearts will not bring him back. He's gone. He's gone! Let's not pretend anymore.*

She collapsed in Harris's arms.

—His ring. The wedding band I put on his finger.

She grabbed the arm of the nurse. —Please don't forget the ring. It's all I'll have left of him.

Then Harris helped her to walk out through the steel doors one final time.

Harris made the arrangements for William's cremation, as William had instructed in his will, and then drove Ariel home in her car while Susan drove home in his.

Jillian was at the house when Ariel arrived. Jillian, who had been away at her first year at college, had gotten the call about her father's accident. Peter flew in on emergency leave when Harris had called him, explaining the rather complicated events of the early morning hours.

There was silence as they kissed and embraced. A time of quiet weeping as the three came together, holding each other in the darkened living-room, trying to process the tragedy that had occurred. It was a time not for recriminations, but familial solidarity and comfort. Like survivors of a catastrophe they could not look at the devastation without being swallowed into an unspeakable, perhaps inescapable, abyss. So instead they turned toward each other in their moment of pain.

In the quiet of the Meeting House Ariel felt truly alone. There was comfort in her home and she had desperately wanted to be within the familiar surroundings and the objects that spoke to her of William. That William would not return had not quite struck her as real. That all she had left of him were the objects that marked evidence of a life lived lent a comfort of sorts.

She was numb in her disbelief, and for hours would sit in William's recliner, very still, listening for the sound of his car on the graveled drive, waiting for him to come in through the front door. She would walk through the room looking at every photograph that captured his image. The memories flooded back, and because the loss was so fresh and tender, she kept envisioning the final days of his life and the horror of his death.

Why had she not seen it coming? Why did she ever believe they were safe, from the disease and from John? *She* had killed him. *She had killed them both!* And how was she to go on?

At day's end Ariel would climb the staircase to the loft and exhausted from grief slide under the thick down comforter, clutching William's pillow. It had been a week since they had lain here together. Could it be so unfamiliar without William? The covers seemed to flutter slightly at her back. Was it William's absence beside her that felt so strange, or was it his spirit presence beside her that felt like the wings of birds beating gently against her spine?

She would drift off into a deep, dreamless, coma-like sleep.

One dawn she was awoken by the wind chimes. When she looked down across from the loft's railing, she could feel a cold draft and knew that the kitchen door had blown open. The chimes hung on the door as a makeshift burglar alarm, a remnant from John's stalking days.

Ariel threw on a robe and went down into the kitchen to close the door against the frigid morning air. The door had been locked, she thought, but she was unsure now. Perhaps one of the kids had opened it and forgot to set the lock.

It was barely five in the morning, but she could not go back to bed. Nor did she want to. For she knew that she would begin to play that tape of memories in her head of her times with William. Once, not so long ago, they had both spoken with bittersweet longing of a day when they might be together and say "goodnight" and wake up in the morning in one another's arms. That dream was realized, but would never again be known.

She turned on the television, suddenly needing the sound of human voices. Nothing but infomercials, cartoons, local programming. . . .

She flipped stations, and there on the screen was a favorite old film she had not seen since childhood, when it was played repeatedly: Jennifer Jones and Joseph Cotten in *Portrait of Jennie.* An artist who falls in love with the wandering spirit of a young woman who had died thirty years earlier. The idea had intrigued her when she was ten years old, and when she found a copy of the novel from which the movie was made, it had the same haunting and sentimental beauty of the film.

But, it was not just the romance of the film that struck her. It was its score. And she had no recollection from her childhood of the music that was now playing and so familiar and close to her heart.

Her music. Debussy's *La fille aux cheveux de lin* was Jennie's theme, with the rest of the film's score an arrangement of other Debussy compositions.

Her music! as William used to say, and he called it "Ariella's Music," for when he would hear it he'd close his eyes and see the secret smile that was singularly hers.

She watched the remainder of the film and was genuinely content through her tears for a while. A fantasy about love existing through the time and space of separate lifetimes.

Ariel picked up Little Eva from the boarding kennel. She cried when she saw the enthusiasm of the pup's greeting. When they got home the puppy looked for her master, and when she saw that Ariel sat in William's chair, she paced confusedly around the living room. The dog spent the remainder of the day poised at the door awaiting William's return.

The next morning Ariel was again awakened by the wind chimes and the cold draft through the house, this time accompanied by Little Eva's whining cry. She *had* checked the locks the evening before, she was certain, and when she got to the door to close it there was resistance. She opened the door again to see if something, some stick or twig, was stuck in the hinge, but there was nothing. No obstruction, no wind at all moving the tree limbs in the yard.

Again she tried to close the door, this time with more force, but suddenly the door offered no resistance and banged shut, trembling in its frame. She slid the bolt into place and walked away. Little Eva, ever at her heels, sat thumping her tail on the linoleum and remained transfixed on the fluttering café curtain on the door's window.

She would never forget his face. Some people would try to recall the features of their loved one and see a blank pallet. But Ariel could close her eyes and see William as clearly as if he were standing there before her.

But when she'd look into the picture frame, as she came to do often during her day, she would see an inanimate William entrapped behind glass. At night, before switching off the lamp, she would lift the picture frame and kiss the image of his lips. One time she caught her own reflection in the frame's glass, saw her own eyes over his, like a double-exposed negative.

My eyes on your eyes. . . . I can see my eyes on your eyes, and I feel safe.

Anything could make her cry: Sunbeams through the windows at three o'clock one afternoon brought a flood of memories and tears, as the quality of the room was identical to days when William had returned home from the university. The expectation of his imminent arrival was brief, and the letdown sent a pall through the house that remained until darkness fell and was relieved by the lighting of lamps.

She languished in memories both bittersweet and filled with longing. Often, after they'd made love and William lay over her, he would rise up onto his elbows and smile down a blessing of humble gratitude at her and whisper, "Thank you, my love." With gentle fingers he would comb her damp hair, marveling at its dark richness in the moonlight, or its shimmering golden weave in the sun, as he wove the tresses into a starburst around her, his eyes gleaming, always watching her, looking for some secret hidden deep within her that he had yet to discover, and she would smile as she drowned in the vast blue Sargasso Sea of his eyes: a place of such ineffable joy where she could see the bountiful goodness of their world. With reverence he would stroke her face and kiss the corners of her mouth and brush his nose along her delicate chin and then nuzzle into the soft contours of her neck and her breast, breathing in time with the rhythm of her breaths, heartbeat to heartbeat, fingers intent on the smoothness of her pliant flesh, while inhaling the sweet, clean, exotic fragrance, so singularly female and so uniquely Ariella's—he always called her Ariella—and he would smile once more and say with such force, with such wonder, in a voice she would never forget, "Why is it I can never get enough of you?"

And in the mornings, awaking alone on her side of the bed she would reach out, remembering how they would awaken with the sunlight streaming like spun gold over their bed, her hand in his, held to his chest. Wasn't it just the other day? She knew those hands so well. She had studied his masculine, compact fingers. And hadn't she always studied the hands of those she loved, those musician's fingers of her mother, her father, John's, the children's. Hands marked the individual character of the person, she always thought. Her mother's lovely hands remained alive in her memory: the tapered fingers, the full-bodied palms, the smooth unveined backs. . . . Ariel had studied William's hands at the end, as she had her mother's before she died. She had tried and failed to knead life into their palms at the end, instilling her own determination and will to live so that they would not abandon this world and her.

William's hands expressed his love, his tender approach; they served to express his thoughts, his intelligence as a writer. They were the hands of a lover, a laborer, a disciplining parent, a nurturing father, and once, long ago, were clutched to his mother's breast for sustenance. Ariel had held his hands precious from the moment she loved him, and near the end held them to memory, every detail her brain could record. For she was never to hold them again and memory had to be enough.

Do they die when you know their hands, she wondered?

They had been mailed to her home, mistakenly, but Ariel was not at home to receive the package. There was a delivery slip in the door stating she could claim the package later in the afternoon. What was it, she wondered?

She busied herself, looking through papers, trying to decide what to keep of William's, what to give to the children, what to throw away. At three o'clock she drove to the post office and gave the clerk the notice slip. The woman returned with a package, and a receipt to sign.

Ariel's eyes read the package's label, and her hands shook as she struggled with her signature. This "package" was supposed to be picked up from the mortuary, not sent through the mails, she thought, angrily. She avoided making eye contact with the postal clerk, for fear any sympathetic expression would make her cry. They had both seen the typewritten address label with the words in bold type:

THE REMAINS OF WILLIAM ARNOLD TRENT.

Hurriedly, she took the package to the car and drove home with it on the passenger seat, her hand atop the brown paper wrapped box, hoping not to burst out in tears until she entered the house.

I'm taking you home, William. You don't have to kick in the door anymore, my Heartbeat. You'll be home, like you wanted, my darling. I just wish it wasn't like this.

Five pounds, it seemed to weigh, five pounds, like a bag of sugar.

Into the house, and she moved purposefully to the dining table, cutting into the wrapper with a steak knife, almost slicing a finger in the process.

Within the cardboard box was a black plastic container. On the lid was stamped,

TEMPORARY CONTAINER.

The remains of her beloved were contained in black vinyl plastic.

She opened it, cutting through the packing tape that encircled the fitted lid. Was she superstitious of disturbing the remains of the dead? Or was it simply the fear of seeing what had become of the body she had so cherished? The flesh and blood and smile and glow that was William, unique and alive a few days ago, now rendered to five pounds of indistinguishable ash?

There was no morbid curiosity in her as she slashed through the tape. There had been no wake, no service, no last goodbye at the church, no roses thrown onto a grave.

As he would have wanted.

Inside was a clear plastic bag, tied at the top in a knot. The everyday lowliness of the knotted plastic bag pained her as she freed the opening.

She looked into the sack of gray ash.

With a thumb and index finger, she reached in to touch and feel its texture.

So this is what has become of my love, my Heartbeat, my most precious reason for living—a gritty, granular ash of bones, ground cartilage, and papery flesh? Reduced to this . . . sand? This dirt? Ashes to ashes, dust to dust?

Where is the man?

With reverence she lifted her hand from the container and brought the clinging dust to her lips. Solemnly, she kissed her fingers and tasted the acidic ash with the tip of her tongue. The salt of her tears combined, for she could not taste the William she knew.

Could this be the William she knew?

She crossed her forehead as a priest would do on Ash Wednesday, and then, opening a button of her blouse, she touched William to her heart.

After the cold winter months gave way to the warm burst of spring, Ariel left her dark sanctuary in favor of things green and teeming. There were times when she'd be driving along the route to the meeting house early on a summer evening, as she had done in the past on the way to the theater on a performance night. The slant of the sun and the lush rolling landscape resurrected memories of speeding along the road with the pulse-raising expectation of seeing William again. Caught in a timeless dimension, she would abandon the present for the past, as a keen, throbbing ache spread through her heart. She could relive the anticipation of days gone by as if she had traveled back in time, and would see him standing there as she pulled up to the drive, that smile and light in his eyes that shone whenever she appeared. She'd shake off the fantasy, wrenched back to reality, but in a moment be drawn back with a force stronger than her own willpower and again indulge in that long-lost splendor. But at times the exquisite pain wrought by the stimuli of the verdant earth played havoc with her mind and she'd long for escape to the cold and colorless winter again.

More and more, little things would bring her back to her days with William: the elaborate song of the wood thrush that made its home in the oak behind the meeting house; the clean, woody scents of the earth at dawn; the hum of winged insects zipping through the still afternoon air; the smell of streams and ponds, and the springy moss beneath her feet as she wandered through familiar rural landscapes, places in which she found herself more and more as the summer passed. She'd imagine William waiting for her just beyond the glen, just beyond the wood, over the hillock to the next clearing, and she was there, again, racing to his embrace. From expectancy she'd plunge into despair when William failed to appear, but always, with increasing fervor, she would return to those moments of hopeful anticipation more and more often. Soon, she didn't bother to leave the past in the past.

"The saddest moment of our life is the moment of betrayal. To love someone is to betray someone."

Raintree County

SEVENTEEN

Bill

Bill's work was at a standstill. The novel was almost complete, except for one final chapter.

He would sit down to write, fingers at the keyboard, but there were no thoughts to direct them. He simply drew a blank. Ariel died, and in the retelling of the events leading up to the discovery of her death, Bill could only discern through the fog that had settled into his brain the distant strains of music.

He could not go beyond the music.

It wasn't that he didn't try. Some of the details were there, and easily recalled. Others came back to him while resting, or mindlessly tracing the patterned cutouts decorating Ariel's writing desk. Once, while walking Little Eva, he suddenly remembered something Ariel had said to him while he visited her on the last evening of her life. The comment, now remembered, served to confuse him further, because it didn't seem to fit into the reconstruction of their final conversation. And yet she had spoken those words, and he remembered, too, his reaction to them.

Ariel's words lingered in his ear, floating disembodied in the mist of his fragmented memory. The sound of her voice rang clearly, and if Bill was caught unaware when the sound would rise up suddenly, he would find no defense from them. They marked his emotions with indefinable and elusive feelings that he could not capture, nor escape.

Away from the computer, with pencil and paper, Bill would attempt to fit each individual, detached memory of that last evening in a logical order. And yet, there was always a blank, always something missing, and he felt—he *knew*—from the empty spaces within him that there was more there than he dared to remember.

Think! Write, write, write! What happened? What happened? What happened that night?

Ariel said . . . she said . . .

I feel . . . I am hollowed . . . aching. . . . She said . . . Ariel said to me . . .

And, one morning, just upon waking, Bill remembered just where her words fit in.

It was on the last night of her life, that's when she said it.

She walked across the room toward the piano, around toward the keyboard, tracing her fingers along the expanse of its satiny ebony finish, brushing the fringe of the shawl and then gingerly flitting along the edge of the golden frame that housed William's photograph. She could not have been aware that that tiny gesture teased Bill's heart, for it betrayed her innermost thoughts, causing dread to rise up and flood over him.

She stood at the keyboard, staring at likenesses from her past. Then, she moved the bench to sit.

She studied her long fingers as she stretched them out before her as if to determine their worth or ability for the task ahead. Then lifting them to form the steeple of prayer against her lips, she looked down at the keyboard. Closing her eyes, Ariel's fingers lighted upon the keys.

And there was music, ethereal and timeless that flowed from her body and sprang through the resonance of the instrument, filling the room.

She played Debussy. Reverie. So simple, so popular and recognizable, and yet, a haunting melodic expression of bittersweet anamnesis. And to Bill, from Ariel, a message so profound and a statement so final.

She played the piano. She played *Reverie*, and then I left. . . .

No. Not yet, I didn't leave . . . . I said . . . I said something. I called her name. Yes. I spoke out, "Ariella." And then she said those words.

—*You'll have to leave now. He'll be arriving shortly.*

—*Ariel*, Bill said, *as he rose to his feet and walked toward her*, —*Who is coming?*

She didn't break a note of music as she replied, —*William, of course. My husband.*

—*Ariel?*

—It really is time that you go.

Bill stood at the piano observing the smile that formed as she continued to play. She was transfixed, far away in some other, more-gentle world of her own making, and the radiance illuminating her features sprang from her vision into that private place. She was irrevocably removed from Bill, and he felt punished and rejected and angry in his isolation. He wanted to shake her out of it, bring her back, force her to see him.

—Where are you, Ariel?

—Why, I'm right here.

But, she wasn't there. Her voice traveled a far distance.

—William is dead, Ariel.

Her hands lifted from and did not return to the keys.

—He has passed over, yes, I know, she replied, turning to look up at him where he stood beside her at the piano. She shivered when he rested his hand on her shoulder.

—I am here now, Ariel.

—Yes, she said in a long drawl. —But I won't be fooled. You are not my William. And you must go away now.

With her last remark, Bill released his hand from her arm, understanding that he could not break her trance. It was not the time for reason or confrontation, as there was something fragile about her that handling would break.

He walked to where Little Eva lay asleep on the reading nook. He secured the leash to her collar. She yawned and stretched and finally appeared resigned to leaving the comfort of her mistress's bed. Bill took the journal from his pocket and placed it on the platform where Ariel would be sure to see it.

There was a great sense of relief at the recollection of that last evening with Ariel, and a satisfaction that he finally fit that piece of the puzzle into place. Why, he wondered, had he blocked it out?

There was a chill in the morning air, and as Bill lay down on the bed pillow he inhaled the earthy scents wafting in through the bedroom window. After the hot spell in late July, the cool-down of recent days was a relief. He could smell the approach of Autumn during these last weeks of August. The maples were turning, the foliage of the elms and oaks had darkened, the meadow grasses were tipped a lavender-pink. Bill knew he could finally return to his writing and the completion of his novel. The haze of lost memory had finally lifted.

As he wrote the depiction of that final visit with Ariel, and the discovery of her body in the early hours of the morning, questions began to form in his mind about details he had not previously considered.

When he went to replace one of Ariel's journals, he saw that all the others were gone. Had she discovered his thievery?

Harris had found him with Ariel; had pulled him from the bed, where he had lain beside her. The memory of the discovery of her lifeless form beneath the covers was a sight indelibly marked in his mind's eye. He remembered shaking her, slapping her wrists, her cheeks, in an effort to revive her; He tried breathing his life into her until he understood that it was too late to bring her back, for she was gone . . . .

And at that realization, he held her to him, desperately, aware that soon she would be taken from his arms, and that he might never know the touch of her flesh.

He winced at the recollection, ashamed and yet glad that he had taken the only chance he would ever have to feel her close to him. And he remembered removing his clothing and then getting under the covers to hold her to him, to glide along her contours as he cried out in grief and loss. His despair overshadowed his guilt and shame.

What he had done might be viewed as sacrilegious, necromancy, he knew, but at the time it was only worship.

Harris.

Harris *knew*. Harris had shielded him.

Why?

Harris's discovery of Bill, naked and asleep, holding her body in his arms. . . . Why had Harris *not* spoken of it to anyone? Not the police, and not, again, to Bill?

Perhaps Harris pretended nothing was out of the ordinary in finding Bill beside Ariel. Did he not say anything to the police in order to avoid scandal? For Ariel's sake? For her children's? For whom?

An hour later, after rising for the day, Bill was contemplating all the possibilities as he walked Little Eva along the road in the crisp morning.

The dog jerked at her leash, breaking his concentration, and he followed along in tow toward Amy, who was unloading groceries from her car. She stopped what she was doing to pet the anxious dog, who greeted her with wagging tail and lopping tongue.

—Such a good puppy! Amy cooed, enjoying the canine show of affection.

—Sometimes, said Bill, thinking about Little Eva's new passion: his socks.

—I haven't seen you for a while, Amy said.

—Guess not.

—What ya been up to, lately?

—Same old, same old. . . .

Vague, pointless smalltalk, she thought: Nothing said; nothing worth saying. Amy began gathering the bags once again, a little annoyed by Bill's self-involvement. For months she had tried to be neighborly, bringing over an extra pie she had baked, inviting him over for a barbecue, showing him how to trim the roses over the arbor so that it would flower all summer, and once inviting Bill to a gathering of friends at her home. She knew he had been distraught after Ariel's death, so she would walk over when she saw him in the yard to inquire how he was faring. He was closed-mouthed, and would simply nod, and reply, "Fine," never bothering to ask her how *she* was dealing with her best friend's death. He was difficult to talk to as his remarks were always clipped and dry.

So she was surprised when Bill suddenly and uncharacteristically asked if he might help by taking in some of the grocery bags.

She smiled, and led the way into the house.

When the bags were placed on the counter, Bill started to leave through the kitchen door.

—Bill? Want a cup of coffee? I was just going to make a pot.

Bill hesitated. She turned back and pulled the cans and bottles from out of the bags, determined to not bother with him anymore, when again to her surprise, he said:

—Yes, that would be nice, Amy.

It was the first time she could recall that he had actually addressed her by her given name, and the first time his voice contained a soft tone in response to her, as if his defensiveness had dismantled.

—Where are the children? Bill asked.

—School started yesterday. The quiet is mindboggling. Unleash Little Eva. She knows her way around the house.

—Any socks lying around?

—Socks? Probably. Oh, missing socks?

—Missing socks are like ghosts.

There was a healthy, outdoorsy quality about Amy, tan from summer activity with her children, a few strands of her blonde hair frosted naturally from the sun and making her eyes very blue in the light of the sun-washed room. She was a tall woman, five-ten, with a muscular firmness in her arms and legs. In her white short-shorts and sleeveless top she reminded him of a tennis champ. He admired that clean, wholesome quality about her.

—Ghosts?

—I'm told the Meeting House is haunted. But, I haven't seen any, he laughed. —And yet, I hate to blame the dog for missing socks.

A frown angled her brows as she stopped and stared at him with a look that made him feel foolish for asking.

Then, studying the objects on the counter before her, she ran fingers through her hair and let out a sigh, followed by a hollow, forced chuckle:

—Spirits of long-dead Quakers, that sort of thing?

It was pointless being cagey, thought Bill. He would be direct with his question, saving them both the maneuvers and ambiguity with which they each wrestled.

—Did Ariel ever say—tell you—that she had seen William's ghost?

—Yes, she did, replied Amy, throwing her head back and leveling a steady gaze at Bill, waiting for a comment, an expression, or a movement that might belie his disapproval. —She told me she saw William's spirit.

—How often did she see his . . . *uhh* . . . apparition?

It was easier, suddenly, for Amy detected no sign of censure from Bill at her admission.

—Quite often.

—Regularly, you mean? Like, every day or week or—

—I don't know, Bill. Sometimes she'd just say that William was with her the night before, very casually, you know, as friends do talking to each other about having seen a mutual friend at the supermarket? Nothing out of the ordinary, just a thought in passing.

—And what would you say when she'd tell you that?

—Say? Well, something like, "How nice he's with you," or, "You must have been happy to see him," that sort of thing. She was delusional, you understand.

—And did she give you any details about these meetings between them?

The lost expression on Amy's face prompted Bill to press on.

—Did she say what she and this "ghost" talked about, or did, or—

—Well, yes, a couple of times, actually. You see, I was afraid that if she felt I didn't believe that she actually was in contact with William, if she thought I was patronizing her, playing along in some fantasy, she'd close up on me. She had been through an awful time after he died, and I was worried about her, you know? I was afraid she'd break and crumble to pieces. She needed to be believed, and you know what? I do believe she actually saw William, even though it is against everything I believe possible: Ariel did see him.

—Often?

—Yes, often.

—Did he ever make an appearance when you were in the room?

—No. Of course not! She said he only came to her at night.

—While she slept?

—I'm not sure. She never mentioned dreaming about him, so I don't know. Wait!

Amy's lips were poised to speak, and then, as if thinking better of it, she stopped, clamping her lips together. Silently, she continued preparing the coffee.

—You were going to say something, but you've changed your mind.

—It has no direct bearing on what we were talking about.

—Well, tell me anyway.

—You know how sometimes she'd leave her front door unlocked? That was so that William could get into the house without a key if he should arrive late at night.

—A ghost is supposed to be able to walk through locked doors. She believed him still flesh and blood, not just a spirit? I'm sorry, it's just that—I'm just trying to understand, is all. Ariel never appeared delusional.

—That's the paradox, really. She was with William, but to her he was not a ghost in any way, shape, or form. He was flesh-and-blood real. He would have needed a key had the door been locked, you see. He was, to Ariel, a physical reality. One night, very late, not long after she told me about William's visits, and about the unlocked door, I was throwing out the garbage. That's when I thought I saw something, a shadow; maybe it was a cat running across her lawn.

—As I started through the yard toward my back door, I turned and looked across the road again. I saw what appeared to me a shadowy figure entering through her door. It was just an impression, of course. I thought I saw the door close behind the coattails of some person. Whether it was a man or woman, or Ariel herself, I don't know; I thought it was a man.

—I walked across the street and up the path to her door, and when I tried pulling it open it didn't budge. I felt a little foolish and was afraid of waking and frightening her—all the lights were off in her house and it was after midnight—so I started back down the path and across the road. I reasoned it out, of course: Ariel had told me only recently about William's visits. So, I guess I was susceptible to the suggestion.

Amy took two mugs from off hooks beneath the kitchen cabinet and filled them with coffee as Bill sat quietly envisioning her story.

As Amy fetched milk from the refrigerator, Bill followed her progress, and then asked:

—Weren't you curious to know if maybe—

—If maybe it really was a person entering the house? Yes, of course. I asked her the next morning if she'd has a visitor late in the night, and she said that William had come to visit. It made me feel a little strange. Maybe I, too, had glimpsed William's ghost!

—Did you tell her what you saw?

—No! I didn't want to feed into the fantasy!

—Did you discuss the ghost, what Ariel told you, or what you saw, with anyone?

—I don't know what you're getting at. Why is any of this important, now? The ghost thing was simply a process of her grief over William's death. It shouldn't and doesn't reflect on the wonderful woman Ariel was.

—I didn't say it would, Amy! Just humor me a minute, okay? Did you tell anyone else about the ghost and what you thought you saw that night?

—I don't remember! Why are we still talking about Ariel?

She brought the coffee cups over to the kitchen table. Bill followed to join her as she sat down to stir sugar and milk in her mug.

—I'm sorry I snapped at you. I mentioned the ghost to Harris, all right? But only because Ariel was giving us reason to worry about her.

—She attempted suicide.

—Yes. I thought the ghost thing was one of the reasons why she tried to kill herself. She wanted to be with William in his world.

—But, you told me a minute ago that she didn't perceive him as a ghost, but as a flesh-and-blood human being.

—Yes, I said that, but—I don't know what she thought! All I could see was that she was not happy in this world; ghostly or human visitations were not enough to replace the life she had had with William.

Ghostly or human visitations were not enough.

She paused to sip from her mug.

Bill's mind was flooded with questions, questions that needed form to express. Something nagged at him; something Amy had said.

—When you talked to Harris about William's visits, how did he react?

—Surprised, I guess. Concerned, for sure. Why?

—Did he suggest a psychiatrist?

—No. I did, however. Funny you should bring that up. Harris thought that suggesting Ariel see a shrink was the last thing to do. He said she would balk at the idea.

—And what did you think?

—I gave the matter no further thought until this morning when you brought it up.

—You just let it go?

—Well, yes, Amy replied, a little on the defensive, wondering why Ariel's ghost fantasy was now of concern to Bill.

—After all, what was the point? Harris was going to have a talk with her, and she never talked about seeing William's ghost after that, so I thought she'd been freed of her haunting. And yet, when she talked about William's visitations she seemed contented. If you want my opinion, the ghost was actually good for her. But now, looking back on it, after she stopped talking about William's ghost, that's around the time she sunk into a rather depressed state. I suppose Harris chased the ghost away, or something, I don't know for sure, but she was never the same after that.

Bill abruptly stood up from his chair, knocking against the table, causing his mug to rock and spill a pool of black liquid around its base.

—I'm sorry, Amy! I've got to leave.

—Bill? called Amy, rising, too, as he bolted out of the backdoor.

She followed behind, but stopped to watch as Bill ran along the road in the direction of the Meeting House.

I don't know why I tolerate that rude man, she asked herself. I wish I didn't like him. I wish somebody nice would come into my life, somebody I could like as much, she thought, as she fetched a dishcloth to wipe up the spilled coffee. "I'll take care of Little Eva, Bill, old boy; don't give a second thought about the dog," she said aloud with both sarcasm and resignation.

As she walked to the sink with the sodden towel, she stopped. She had said something that sent him flying out. About the ghost, about William, about Harris chasing the ghost away. . . .

—Fend for yourself, little puppy-dog, she said, throwing the rag into the sink and then running out the kitchen door.

Ghostly or human visitations were not enough, Amy had said. The words had jogged something in him and suddenly he *knew* what had happened on the last night of Ariel's life.

Bill ran across the road and leaped over the split rail fencing that bordered Haley's Farm. Harris's truck and sedan were parked in the circular drive of the Georgian farmhouse. Bill made a beeline toward it, but stopped when he glimpsed the tractor moving along the south meadow beyond the barn and outbuildings. He changed course for the meadow.

Harris was bundling the hay, the last cut of the summer, and when he turned to see Bill running in his direction he cut the engine and climbed down to meet Bill, whose expression was troubled and solemn as they neared one another.

With every step closer to his target, Bill was more determined and certain. And that determination gave birth to a vengeance that superseded reason or civilized conduct. Something primal had risen within him and he was in its control.

The smile on Harris's face died, as did his greeting, when Bill arrived within a couple of yards from him, and the murderous glaze of his eyes alerted Harris's defenses.

Bill lunged at him.

It was too late for Harris to block the strike; Bill attacked frontally and with such unflinching aggression that Harris didn't have time to move defensively. He was pinned to the ground and although he was the bigger man, the fall had knocked the wind out of him. Before he could take a breath, Bill punched his fist into his face.

Bill raised his fist to strike again, but Harris had recovered enough to block the impact on his jaw, and then grabbed the flying return at the wrist. He twisted Bill's arm, and as his attacker's body lifted to follow suit,

Harris rammed his knee into Bill's groin, sending him toppling over to the ground.

Rising, Harris placed his booted foot on Bill's back.

—Have you had enough?

After a few seconds of pressure, Bill's nod was assurance enough for Harris to let up on him.

But set free, Bill grabbed Harris's ankle, sending him sprawling face-down onto the grass.

Bill pounced on his adversary with his full weight.

—You'll be dead before I've had enough!

Harris didn't doubt Bill's intention and knew he was fighting for his life as Bill pummeled blow after blow at the back of his head. When he felt his neck being twisted, he nearly lost consciousness, but his instincts fed him a burst of power, enough to shift his weight and send Bill over onto his back and Harris atop him.

With blood dripping from his nose and his cheek, Harris pinned Bill's arms down to the ground.

—I'm not going to let you kill me, you pathetic bastard.

Bill's energy was spent; his body shook. Every part of him burned from the impact of his attack on Harris and he lay there helpless under the man's weight. He tried to build up the energy to escape the stronghold, to finish what he had set out to do, but the pain in his right shoulder was hot and stabbing.

Harris rose to his feet and quickly moved away, waiting defensively for Bill's next advance.

—Get up! growled Harris through the throbbing in his head.

Bill remained flattened on the tall grass, and when he tried to rise he fell back with an agonizing groan.

—Get up, get to your feet! shouted Harris, smearing blood from his forehead out of his eyes.

—I . . . can't, moaned Bill. —My shoulder. It's broken.

Harris warily scrutinized Bill and the validity of his claim of injury. When he approached with caution, he could see that there was indeed a strange set to Bill's arm.

—You punch me again or try anything funny, you'll be the dead man, do you hear?

Bill closed his eyes against the pain, as Harris lifted him to his feet and steadied his weight.

—Can you make it to the barn?

Bill couldn't answer with more than a nod that sent a sharp stab into his shoulder. A wave of nausea wracked him.

Harris supported him as they slowly made their way toward the barn. Once there, He seated Bill on a bench.

—You've dislocated your shoulder.

—You dislocated—shit!

—You want some more pain?

—Keep your fucking hand—

—I'm going to pop it back in place. Trust me?

—Fuck you!

—Suit yourself, said Harris, turning to leave the barn.

—Wait! came a strangled cry. He felt like a helpless, beaten dog.

—It's here right away, or in a couple of hours at the hospital. Which is it to be?

—Do it! Fucking do it!

—Grab that bar next to you. That's right, said Harris, positioning himself for the pull. —Now, when I yank on your arm, try not to resist, relax it as much as you can. It's going to hurt, I'm not going to say it won't, but then, when it's back in the socket the pain will stop, you understand?

—Here we go, said Harris, pulling and separating in a snap of movement that made Bill scream out.

When Bill caught his breath, and the pain subsided, he looked over at the swollen, bloody face staring down at him.

—Where'd you learn to do that?

—Air Force. Now you want to tell me why you want to kill me?

—You were the ghost.

—What are you talking about? What ghost?

—You were the ghost. You pretended to be William Trent's ghost.

—Where did you ever come up with such—?

—Ariel was visited by William's ghost.

—I never heard of anything so crazy!

—You're denying Ariel talked about William's ghost?

—You're out of your mind!

—I don't think so. Amy told me.

—Amy? And you—? Oh, that's rich! That's really over the top, Bill.

—Amy said she discussed with you that Ariel was seeing a ghost.

—So you think I was pretending to be—shit, Bill, you shouldn't be listening to Amy. Yes, all right, Ariel was dreaming about a ghost.

—And Amy said: "Ghostly or human visitations were not enough for Ariel." As there are no such things as ghostly visitations, that leaves only one possibility: Human visitations, Harris! You played William's ghost!

—Shut up!

—Even Amy started to believe in the ghost. A ghost who needed an unlocked door to enter a house.

—You don't know what you're saying.

—Don't I? You fed into her grief by posing as William! And she wanted to believe it was he who came back to her at night!

—It wasn't like that—

—It explains everything: Why you said nothing to the police about finding me naked and in bed with her.

—You're not making sense!

—It makes perfect sense to me!

—I was trying to protect you!

—Cut the crap, man! You weren't protecting anybody but yourself, you son of a bitch! You despised me, Harris. I was in the way, in *your* way, wasn't I?

—You were never a threat to me! But, to Ariel, to Ariel you were dangerous.

—I asked myself, why, why didn't you give me over to the police if you thought, suspected even, that I killed Ariel? I see, now, that you knew I hadn't killed her. You wanted the police to believe I was the last person to be with her before she died, if later it was determined by the coroner that she had not died of natural causes. If it was murder, then you would turn me in, isn't that right, Harris?

—You think I murdered Ariel and that I used you as some sort of insurance?

—Isn't that what you did?

—And how could I have planned such a thing? I didn't know in advance that you would be there when I arrived that morning. How could I know that you'd be there?

—You didn't know. You just took the opportunity: a lovesick man, found naked in bed with the body of the woman he obsessed over. Who would ever suspect you?

—She died of pulmonary embolus, Harris shouted.

Harris turned his face away from his accuser. He bent over, hands on knees, trying to regain self-control, but his breath caught and he whimpered. Then, wiping his face with the sleeve of his shirt, he stood straight and said in an unsteady voice:

—I loved her. I would never have harmed her.

—If that's true, you knew I hadn't killed her, either, Harris.

—I knew you hadn't killed her.

Harris began to scour his face with both hands, to wipe the drips of sweat and blood from his eyes, but the skin was tender and he winced. Then he looked over to meet Bill's stare.

—What I tell you, Bill, is something that will remain between us. Each of us can point the finger of guilt toward the other at any time, but it will always be one's word against the other, do you understand?

Bill nodded.

—Yes, I was her ghost. I thought at first that she was reaching out to me. But, it wasn't me she embraced, it was William.

—One night, when the village lost electric power to a freak lightning storm, I stopped by to check on Ariel. The place was dark, and the door unlocked, and I went inside. I called her name, and suddenly she was at my side. And she whispered, "William?"

—But before I could reply, she dropped her kimono and said, "Remember the movie, William? Remember *Moonglow* and how they danced into love? Dance with me, darling," she said, as she moved into my arms, naked. . . . By day, she saw me as Harris Haley. At night, in a darkened room, I became William. And you know what? I didn't care. After all those years of wanting her, I didn't care who she believed was holding her, making love to her. It was enough for me that *I loved her*, don't you see? And for a time, she was content in her delusion.

—"Is it possible for one man to possess a woman's body and another man her soul?" said Bill, aloud.

The expression on Harris's face was one of astonishment, and to Bill he looked about ready to break down.

—She asked me that. Like she knew I wasn't really William, but wanted to believe I was. I suppose she was telling me that I had her body, but only William had her soul. That last night, the night she died, when I entered through the unlocked door, I found her at the piano. She'd not played since William's death. We embraced, and then she looked at me in such a strange way, I can't describe it. I can only say that it was as if she suddenly realized I was not William, and that she would no longer lie to herself about it. She accused me and you, Bill, of trying to replace William. She shrank away from me, and then ordered me to leave, saying William was coming to get her.

—I didn't know what to do! I couldn't just leave her in the state she was in. I feared she was hallucinating, had gone over the edge. When I made the mistake of saying that William was dead, and that she had to go on with her life, that made her hysterical and she cursed me for saying she had to go on with her life; it was her life, and she didn't want to go on without William. I tried to calm her down, and when I touched her, her body was feverish. She pulled away from me and went to the bed, crying, thrashing about, screaming, "Why won't you let me die?"

—I went over to the bed, to take her in my arms, trying to be a comfort, a presence of strength holding her together. Myself. Harris, not the ghost of a dead man. But she pushed me away. The way she looked at me! There was disgust in her face, at the sight of me. . . . She tried to strike me with her fist. I grabbed her wrist and laid her down onto the bed, trying to stop her thrashing. I was worried she'd rip through the stitches.

Harris could barely continue for the tears that choked him, and when he did, when he looked up again to level his eyes on Bill's, he whispered, —And, then, she just passed out. I covered her with the blankets and left.

—When I found you with her a few hours later, it was because I couldn't sleep and had to make sure she was all right! And when I saw she was dead, I thought perhaps I had killed her while I tried to restrain her. I thought I might have struck her, twisted her neck in the struggle and not remembered, blocked it out. When I left her, she was breathing, and I had covered her with the blankets. . . . She was alive, I swear, it! She was alive!

The vision of Harris discovering Ariel's body on the bed at dawn came back to Bill. He relived the moments conjured by that vision of Harris rocking Ariel in his arms, and he could hear the man's grief.

—She died of a pulmonary embolus, Bill. Perhaps our struggle aggravated the condition, broke loose the blood clot. I don't know. I've agonized over it. Anything could have caused a clot to break loose, sending it to her lungs. It was a complication of her surgery, Bill. I didn't kill her, and neither did you.

—Ariel tried to commit suicide the night you hit her with your car. She went out to see the stars, she said. Remember, I told her she had to be more careful walking in the dark at night? What stars? It was overcast and snowing hard when she flung herself in front of your path!

It was Bill's turn to come to grips with his conscience. Months of fear and guilt at the possibility that he might have caused Ariel's death, months of repressed doubts, forgotten words, hidden guilt, and blank spaces that haunted his days and nights.

Nobody had killed Ariel. Nobody had struck a fatal blow.

And yet, hadn't they all? All those who professed to love her? John, William, Harris, and himself? Hadn't their love for Ariel struck her with blow after blow after blow until their accumulated strikes had finally killed her? Hadn't these men who professed to adore her entrapped her instead to the point of madness, from which she could only escape through death?

And yet, thought Bill, look at the condition of all of us men after having known and loved the woman. Hadn't her influence, her very existence determined our fates and complicated our lives?

When Amy found them she saw a scene that she dared not enter. It was dangerous enough to be caught listening and watching through the crack of the hinges on the open barn door, let alone risk being drawn into the confessional within.

Quietly, after listening for a few minutes, she backed away and retraced her steps across the dirt drive and into the woods. It was over now, she sighed. All settled.

But, she suddenly didn't care. Harris had made it clear a long time ago that he didn't have feelings for her. He was a gentleman, of course, and would never mention to Bill how she had behaved that night a year ago when she had asked Harris to come to her house.

As for Bill? What was the point? He's a lily-livered, self-involved, badly mannered bore. Not worth bothering with. Ariel would never have given him a second glance if he hadn't reminded her so much of her precious William. My God, didn't the idiot realize how much he looked like him? Ariel only humored Bill's interest because she had it in her head that Bill was the son William had confessed to fathering by another army brat when he was only twelve years old!

Why did that bitch have to have it all? Amy thought. Why did some women attract all the really good ones?

—They weren't worth it. They just weren't worth it! Amy said aloud, looking up toward the cloudless blue sky, and then taking in the reds and yellows of the trees that lined the meadow beyond.

At her approach, a murder of crows feasting on dogwood berries rose up from the treetops with an audacious flapping of wings and a racket of *caws*.

—*They just weren't worth the bother.*

About the Author

Agata Stanford is the author of the humorous Dorothy Parker Mystery series. She lives with her family in New York.

DorothyParkerMysteries.com
Visit 'Dorothy Parker Mysteries' on Facebook

www.ingramcontent.com/pod-product-compliance
Lightning Source LLC
Chambersburg PA
CBHW031032030726
47497CB00004B/1102